SHADOW SUN

SURVIVAL

By

Dave Willmarth

Chapter One

Devastation

The earth trembled as Allistor ran through the rubble of his hometown. He stumbled when the ground shifted beneath him just as he placed his forward foot on a broken concrete slab. Using his momentum to control his fall, he rolled forward and came back to his feet, barely slowing.

The thing behind him was gaining ground. It wasn't pursuing him in particular, but rather herding the small number of survivors of which Allistor was one. Out of the corner of his eye, he saw a child stumble and fall, tripping her mother in the process. The two went down in a tangle maybe a hundred yards from him, the girl sobbing hysterically from fear. Her mother looked up at the monstrosity bearing down on them and chose to try and hide. She picked up her child and scurried under the remnant of a half-collapsed stone wall.

Allistor shouted at her even as he changed direction toward them. "No! Don't stop! Keep moving!" but there was no way she heard him above the pounding of the monster's footsteps and the sound of crashing debris. He pushed his tired legs as fast as they would go, angling toward their position. A glance up at their approaching doom told him he wasn't going to make it. Still, he pushed himself.

He let out a scream of frustrated rage as he lost his race. The monster's right foot came down directly on top of the hiding spot the mother had chosen. Allistor imagined he heard a brief scream, abruptly cut off as the two innocents died. Looking up, he directed his rage at their killer. The thing that had single-handedly destroyed his home and killed nearly everyone he knew. Out of frustration he grabbed a broken chunk of concrete from the ground and flung it upward at the monster's head with all the strength he could muster.

> *Void Titan*
> *Level 10*
> *Health 7,810/8,000*

The rock bounced off the thick skin of its face, doing a single point of damage, and not even attracting its attention. The monster was three times his level, and he hadn't really expected to do any damage. It continued on its path, disregarding him completely as it pursued a group of townsfolk that were firing ineffective weapons at it as they retreated toward the river.

How the hell are we supposed to beat something like that? Allistor thought as he collapsed atop a rubble pile, exhausted. *It has been almost a week since the apocalypse, and I'm only level three. Dad killed more of these new creatures than anyone, and he was only level five when they got him.*

He paused, wiping his eyes with the back of one hand as he thought of his family. When it all happened on that first day, the day everyone was now calling *Apocalypse Day,* they had all been together at the house. He'd come home from college to visit his parents and little sister for the break. They were all still asleep in the pre-dawn hours when the sky seemed to catch fire, and the ear-shattering blast of what sounded like a giant foghorn ripped through the early morning silence. The house had vibrated, windows rattling and cracking under the assault. Allistor had covered his ears in an attempt to muffle the noise before his brain burst.

A moment after the tremendous sound ceased, Allistor and everyone else on the planet received a notice. It came to him as both a voice in his head and a strange text that appeared in front of his face like a hologram. Initially, the text looked like nothing more than scribbled lines of electric blue. But as the voice in his head continued to speak, the scribbles resolved themselves into characters that he somehow understood.

>>>*Attention all inhabitants of the planet known as Earth*<<<

Your world and everything on it has just been claimed by the Universal Collective as compensation for protecting you from your sun's supernova.

Earth, now designated UCP 382, has been removed from its orbit and placed in a stable system closer to the Galactic Nexus. You will have three of your solar days to prepare yourselves. Detailed information can be found in the 'DETAILS' subsection of your status interface.

It has been determined that UCP 382 is currently overpopulated. The dominant species, known as humans, have polluted the lands and seas to an unacceptable level. Measures will be taken to reduce the human population and stabilize the environment before citizens of other Collective worlds will be allowed to immigrate. Initial estimate of human population reduction level is ninety percent.

And that was it. No further explanation. Allistor had initially assumed it was a nightmare inspired by way too many hours of gaming, and he tried to go back to sleep. But his sister, Leah, began pounding on his door, then burst in with wide eyes. "Did you hear that?"

Allistor was about to chase her out of his room when his parents appeared behind her. His father's face was grim, and his mother immediately gathered Leah into a tight hug.

"You… you guys all heard that too? Saw the weird holo-thing with the words?" Allistor had sat back on his bed, legs unsteady. His family all nodded at him.

"This can't be. I mean, it can't be real. Some kind of mass hallucination or something, right?" His mother looked at his father, hope and fear in her eyes.

Allistor's father, George, was a former mayor, town councilman and retired soldier. He'd fought in three different wars over the fifty years he'd served. Nearly half of his body, including parts of both legs, one arm, and his right eye, were cyberbiotic replacements for bits he'd lost in combat. Just over halfway through the 21st century, the human race had gotten almost as good at putting the body back together as they were at tearing it apart.

George shook his head slowly, putting an arm around his wife and daughter as he looked at Allistor. "This sounds almost like one of your damned games, boy. Could somebody be playing some kind of prank?"

Allistor didn't have a clue. He tried to reason it out aloud. "They said the sun went nova. I remember the sky being on fire." He looked out the window. Everything outside had a bluish tint to it. "Look!"

His bedroom had a single French door leading out to the back deck that overlooked their pool. George opened the door and stepped out, looking up at the sky. He cursed quietly to himself as he stepped to the side and made room for the others to join him. Allistor and the others looked up.

6

There were two suns in the heavens above them. One a pale, almost white ball of fire just cresting above the horizon. The other was a much smaller dark blue, almost purple sphere higher up in the morning sky. Allistor searched the rapidly lightening space above them, looking for any of the familiar constellations. He blinked at the sheer number of stars visible.

George had a similar reaction. "It's... the sky is so full. Even out in the desert during the war, the sky was never this full of stars. I mean, they were always out there, but not close enough for us to see like this. I... think maybe they really did move Earth. Or, move us and make us *think* they moved Earth. But wherever we are, I think we're much closer to the center of a galaxy than we were before. The density of stars..." his voice drifted off as he took in the implications of their new situation.

Leah had stopped crying and was staring at the suns. "So, like, these people moved our whole planet a bazillion light years in seconds? And where's the moon?"

Her mother rubbed her back gently and answered. "They can't be 'people' like us if they want to kill ninety percent of us! And Leah's right? Where's the moon? Without it there should be earthquakes and tidal waves, right?" Tears were running down her face now, and she hugged Leah tightly. "Is this the end of everything?"

Allistor's brain ached. He wasn't sure if it was from the foghorn assault or the flood of incredible information. As he wondered whether he was suffering some kind of brain damage, another holographic screen popped up in his field of vision. As a lifelong gamer, he recognized it as a character status. Looking at his family, he asked "Can you guys see this? My screen, I mean?"

7

They all shook their heads no, and Leah asked, "What screen?"

Allistor poked a finger at his own hologram, saying, "Try thinking 'status' and see what happens. He watched as all three of them began to stare into space. If he wasn't so scared, he might have laughed at his family looking like game avatars with the thousand-yard stare as they checked their UIs.

He went back to examining his own screen as the brighter sun continued to rise. In the back of his mind, he noted that his skin was warming quickly under the brighter light.

His stat sheet was pretty straightforward, and his numbers were pathetic.

Designation: Human 1,512,241,003	Level: 0	Experience: 0/100
Planet of Origin: UCP 382	Health: 100/100	Class: Unknown
Attribute Pts Available: 0	Mana: 50	
Intelligence: 5	Strength: 2	Charisma: 1
Adaptability: 6	Stamina: 2	Luck: 2
Constitution: 2	Agility: 3	Health Regen: 6/m
Will Power: 3	Dexterity: 3	Mana Regen: 5/m

A prompt appeared below the stats.

Human #1,512,241,003 would you like to change your designation? Y/N

Allistor rolled his eyes upward at the question, looking to see if there was a 'tag' above his head with that ridiculously long number. If there was, he couldn't see it. And there wasn't one visible above any of his family

8

members' heads either.   He clicked "Yes" and a new prompt appeared.

Please state clearly your new designation.

He said, "Allistor," while picturing the spelling of his name.   One advantage of the unusual spelling of his name was that even in games with millions of players, nobody ever beat him to his own name.   A quick check of his status screen showed his designation had been updated. He took a minute to review his other stats, finding that if he focused on any one of them, more detail would appear in a secondary screen that was an opaque green.   Most of the stats were pretty clear, standard for many of the MMORPGs he'd played. A few caught his attention, though.

He focused on Adaptability. The detail read: *Inhabitants of backward or undeveloped worlds such as UCP 382 often have difficulty adjusting to the new realities of membership in the Collective. Those with an initial adaptability rating of three or lower often perish in the early days of assimilation. Higher adaptability scores enable one to better assess new situations and surroundings, identify potential dangers and benefits, and adjust themselves or their actions in order to achieve a more positive outcome.*

He was moving on to read about Constitution when George stopped staring at his own screen to address his son. "Any chance you can explain all of this to us old farts, kiddo?" He winked at his wife and daughter, trying to lighten the mood a bit.

"Sure!" Allistor was happy to help. Especially since he'd caught so much grief over the years for always being in his VR worlds. His dad actually enjoyed VR games as well, but he was a first person shooter guy, not an RPG gamer.

His mother cut him off before he could say more. "Let's go back inside and talk. This sky… scares me." She gazed nervously up at the sky, pushing Leah toward the door with quick steps.

Back in the house, they all took seats in the family room. Allistor was just beginning to explain about attributes, having them each pull up their health bars, when his phone went off. It was a text from a guildmate in his current VRMMORPG. A moment later, his sister's phone went off too. Their father shook his head, and neither of them answered. But it was comforting to know the network was still working.

For the next half hour, Allistor walked his family through their entire stat sheets, teaching them about how attributes could be used to boost each other, and how to specialize in certain classes or play styles. And he learned a good bit himself. For instance – Constitution was a factor in several things. Overall health pool and regeneration rate. Resistance to extreme heat or cold, poison resistance, and physical damage resistance.

His research also showed him that the attributes point scores weren't based on 'human' norms. The numbers were calculated based on the average base starting stats of all the species within the Collective. So if a two in strength was slightly below the human average, it was much lower than the Collective average. Humans in general ranked low in almost every attribute compared to their new neighbors.

There were obvious differences in his family's stats. His father was heavy on Strength and Constitution, while his mother favored Intelligence and Will Power. Leah only had a one in Adaptability, but she had fives in Agility, Stamina, and Dexterity.

As they talked, Allistor's attention was repeatedly drawn to a timer that remained in the upper right corner of his visual field even when he waved away his stats. It was just over seventy-one hours and counting down. The original message had said that Earth had three days to prepare. But prepare for what?

"Hey guys, you all see that timer? Something big's gonna happen in three days. Maybe the something that's gonna kill 90% of the human race. The voice said to read the 'Details' tab. So I say let's all focus on that and read up. Right now. So we know sooner rather than later what it is we're preparing for."

They all settled back in their seats as they located the correct tab and began to read.

Welcome to the Collective! Your world has been found (barely) worthy of membership. Mainly for its natural resources. Being in the outer reaches of the Collective's territory, repeated travel to and from your world and the Nexus worlds would have been cost prohibitive. So the Collective initiated a supernova of your system's sun, harvesting its power and using a portion of it to relocate planet UCP 382 to a more accessible location.

Citizens of the Nexus worlds will be offered the right to purchase lands and resources on UCP 382 once the planet has been stabilized. However, in the interest of fair play, the Collective does not simply seize a planet and sell off its parts. The inhabitants of the planet are given an opportunity to prove their worth and earn a share of their homeworld. This can be achieved via many paths.

In the case of UCP 382, simply surviving the reduction of human population will entitle you to land and resources sufficient to survive the remainder of your lifetime. Improving your attributes through completion of quests, intensive training, and/or killing of other life forms will increase your chances of survival.

Conquest of territory is another means by which you may improve your station within the Collective and ensure a comfortable life on this planet or another. Collective citizens from other Nexus planets are required to wait one year from the date of assimilation before they can bid on UCP 382. This 'stabilization period' allows you and your fellow 'Earthlings' time to develop yourselves, your skills and abilities, and to secure as much of the planet as you can for yourselves. Once the bidding is opened, you may elect to retain what you hold or sell some portion of it on the open market.

Fame is another means of achieving status within the Collective. Your activities may be monitored by off-world citizens as you grow and attempt to seize assets. Some will be watching in anticipation of taking advantage of you post-stabilization. Others will seek to aid you with gifts of useful items or knowledge to further their own entertainment. Heroic deeds will earn you Fame points, just as cruel and immoral deeds will earn you Infamy points. Both Fame and Infamy, upon reaching a high enough level, can ensure a place for you among certain societies.

Lastly, as it has always been and always will be, fiscal success can secure your future. Accumulating large quantities of currency in many forms may allow you to purchase a territory of your liking on your planet or others. Your 'Earth' currencies shall remain static through the stabilization period for purposes of planetary commerce between yourselves. Each unit of measure will be accompanied on your interface with its real-time equivalent in Collective currency, called klax or K's for short. For example, an ounce of pure water is currently valued at 10 klax. An ounce of gold is worth 1,100 klax today. Be warned, prices and values vary greatly from world to world. And dishonest entrepreneurs abound.

All of these paths can be traveled alone or in groups. There is sometimes strength in numbers. But choosing the wrong companions can slow you down or hold you back. So choose wisely.

Mandatory Quest Accepted: Survive One Year Reward: Variable experience. Land Grant – size variable. Ten Thousand klax.
Congratulations! If you've read this far, you might just be among the survivors. Work hard, get stronger, and build your area of influence.
The better your performance, the greater the reward.

Below this summary was a series of additional tabs. There were dozens of them. Some were deeper explanations of territory rights, fame, currency conversion rates, and other information from the text above. Allistor noted them and moved on, looking for information on the three-day countdown. Leah began to freak out after reading through the notice. "We're dead! This is it - game over! I don't want to get eaten by some alien. Just kill me now!"

Allistor tuned her out as their mother tried to calm her.

He finally found what he wanted under a tab labeled "Stabilization Procedures." Opening up the tab and reading the information within, he began to tremble.

Stabilization of UPC 382 will commence three solar days from assimilation date. Priority One: Reduce human population to sustainable levels.
Estimated optimum population reduction: Ninety-one point five percent.

Priority Two: Reduce environmental contaminants. Estimated industrial infrastructure reduction necessary: Eighty-five percent.
Focus on destruction of facilities harvesting or consuming fossil fuels.

"They're going to alter the planet to suit their needs," he said, catching his parents' attention. "They consider us a contaminant. That's why they plan to kill most of us. And they're going to take out our factories and power plants because they create pollution. We'll be back in the stone-age."

*****

Allistor was roused from his memories by another blast of sound from the void titan. The sixty-foot-tall behemoth was now several hundred yards past his location, still flattening everything in its path as it pursued his neighbors. It most closely resembled a mythical mountain troll featured in so many fantasy games. All muscle and no brains, the things disliked bright light, preferring to hunt at dawn and dusk. They had horrible night vision and were easily distracted. Which had been the only weakness he and his neighbors had found so far. A few brave souls with guns could distract and lead the creature away from vulnerable groups in hiding.

He could no longer make out the faces of those still fighting, but he could see that even in the last minute or so that he'd been zoned out, their numbers had declined. He hoped that meant that some had escaped.

14

Not wanting to do it, but knowing he'd be unable to live with himself if he didn't, Allistor went to check on the woman and her child. The rubble half-wall they'd hidden beneath was crushed into gravel where the monster's foot had landed. He didn't immediately see any evidence of blood, which he took as a good sign. Maybe they'd found a hole deep enough to save them.

He kicked at some of the larger stones, then shifted a bent and twisted metal beam slightly. A week ago, he'd never have been able to move the thing. But he and his father had taken the warnings seriously and worked nearly nonstop to develop their bodies and increase their physical attributes. His Strength, just a two on day one, had doubled to a four. Same for his Stamina. A four in Strength made him, as best they had been able to figure, on par with a chimpanzee when it came to muscle mass. Which would be roughly double the strength of a normal human male. Most recently he'd been pushing his body by lifting stacks of tires over and over again. In most of his games, players started with a uniform ten points in each attribute across the board. This System was different. Starting attributes were based on each person's actual strengths and weaknesses, as compared somehow to the other beings in the system. Humans were physically weak compared to most sentient beings, so an average male like Allistor began with a Strength stat of two.

Below the beam was a displaced manhole cover. Allistor's hopes soared! If she had managed to find the open manhole in time, it was possible they had survived the passing of the giant. Another few seconds of searching amid the rubble, and he found the hole. It was partially collapsed, but still open. Keeping his head back from the opening, he called out in a hoarse whisper-shout. "Hello? Are you down there?"

He waited and listened, carefully avoiding sticking his head over the opening to look inside. That was a lesson learned the hard way on the first day of stabilization. Creatures had spontaneously appeared across the globe when the three-day countdown hit zero. Nightmare creatures that should not have existed even in the worst horror vids. One of them had materialized in his basement. It proceeded to wreak havoc among the items stored down there, searching for human prey. His sister had heard the noise the same time as the others, but she had been closer to the basement door. As Allistor ran to stop her, she opened the door and flicked on the light switch. A tentacled arm wrapped around her torso and yanked her downward with such force that he'd heard her spine snap, cutting off her scream of terror and pain.

Blinking away the tears caused by that memory, Allistor heard the echo of his voice from below, but no other sound. His hopes for their survival plummeted. There hadn't really been time for them to move out of earshot in the tunnel. Her failure to respond didn't bode well. He tried again, "Are you hurt? I can help you. The titan has moved on; it's safe to come out." He cringed at that last statement. There really wasn't anyplace safe anymore, above or below ground.

A soft and wet rustling sound drifted up out of the hole. Allistor instantly fell back away from the opening, then scooted on his butt still farther. He knew that sound. He'd heard it in his basement. Made by one of those things called an Octopoid that had taken his sister.

That was it. If the woman and her daughter were down there with that thing, there was nothing he could do for them. They were gone. Likely their corpses were tucked in some corner waiting to be consumed.

Anger flashed within him. He was sick of these things killing his people. His family, his friends. It had taken two days and half a dozen close calls, but he and his father had figured out how to kill the thing that ate Leah.

They were sensitive to fire, for one thing. And acid, especially in powder form. Regular old Comet cleaning powder ate away at their skin quite effectively. And their bodies were vulnerable at each of the spots where a tentacle connected with its trunk. A lucky knife throw from Allistor as the thing charged up the stairs toward them had struck it in what he thought of as its armpit, causing it to scream and thrash before falling back down the stairs.

They'd learned that like most of the newly arrived terrors that were steadily wiping out the human race, it was sensitive to the scent of blood. Allistor looked around, finding a broken and slightly bent length of rebar close by. He pressed the bend down against his leg, mostly straightening it back out. Then he used his improved strength to apply pressure as he rapidly scraped one end back and forth across the side of the steel beam until it had sharpened to a point.

Taking a deep breath, he looked down at the hole a few feet away. "They were the last humans you're gonna kill." He dragged the rough point across the back of his hand, drawing blood. His interface flashed with a red negative five, indicating he'd taken damage. Waiting until a decent amount had pooled, he flicked his hand toward the manhole. Droplets sprayed across the ground, with just a few making it down into the darkness. But he knew it would be enough.

He carefully moved around through the debris until he was on the opposite side of the hole. Crouching down behind a mound of rubble and metal, he put the back of his hand to his mouth and sucked the blood from it. Keeping his mouth on it to prevent more open bleeding, he waited. After a few moments, the bleeding stopped, and he watched as the small wound began to heal over.

The wet sound returned quickly. The scraping of scales against the concrete sides of the tunnel below. A moment later first one, then a second tentacle reached up and grasped the edge of the manhole. A third emerged and wandered back and forth around the edge, searching for prey. When it found nothing moving, the creature's octopus-like head emerged to look around with two of its bulbous eyes that swiveled in protruding sockets. It sniffed the air, turning toward the line of blood droplets in the dust. One tentacle reached out to touch the nearest droplet, returning to the creature's maw, where a purple tongue flashed out and tasted the blood. It gave a gurgling purr as it lifted itself the rest of the way to the surface.

The moment its torso cleared the hole, Allistor lunged. He drove the point of the rebar spear into the uppermost tentacle joint, twisting it violently as it penetrated the thing's rubbery flesh, scoring a critical backstab. It screamed and fell forward, off balance with the lower half of its body still in the hole.

Allistor jerked the threaded rebar free, sending a spray of purplish blood and the reek of ammonia into the air as it shredded more of the thing's flesh and muscle on its way out, disabling the tentacle. Then he rammed the makeshift rebar spear back into its torso, right at the base of what he assumed was its soft skull. He put all his weight into the thrust, pinning the nasty-smelling thing to the ground. This strike also earned him bonus damage, hitting an incapacitated opponent in the back.

Octopoid Reaver
Level 6
Health: 460/2,000

It wasn't exactly like an earth octopus. Generally humanoid in shape, it had six tentacle arms like an octopus, flexible and strong, covered with suction cups that each held a tiny but razor-sharp hook inside. But the octopoid's other two limbs were stubby legs that ended in small feet. These legs helped it ambulate across solid ground much faster than an octopus would be able to. Mainly a water creature, the amphibian had gills on either side of its bulbous head. But it also had lungs that allowed it to function on dry land.

The five working tentacles blindly thrashed and grabbed at him. One of its four eyes rotated backward to focus on him, and the tentacles quickly became more effective. One of them wrapped around his boot, tugging hard in an attempt to tip his weight off the spear.

In answer, Allistor roared his rage at the beast and twisted the spear inside its body. He lunged his own body forward, taking the spear shaft with him and changing the angle to widen the hole in the creature's body. It convulsed, causing the one tentacle to release his boot while another whipped across his back, tearing his shirt and a good amount of his flesh as it passed.

He leapt up, using the spear shaft like a vaulter's pole to push himself higher, and used gravity and muscle both as he slammed the heels of his boots into the back of the monster's head. It caved in with crunch of cartilage and a wet squelching sound. The tentacles flapped about for a moment, then went still.

A little green number flashed +*2300* in the upper left corner of his interface. That was the experience gained for killing the beast. More surprisingly, another number, this one a golden +*150*, flashed up right after. Those were

fame points.   Someone somewhere must have been
watching his fight. Another notification popped up next.

You have learned the skill: Spearwielder.
*Using the sharp end of your weapon to puncture
your enemy has taught you the value of a sharp weapon
with reach. Continue to use stabbing weapons to increase
your skill level.*

Bending to loot the corpse, he received twenty klax
– about average for monsters of that level. Though the
world's trading currencies remained as they had been pre-
assimilation, rewards for kills and completed quests, as
well as payments for items sold on the open market, were
paid in klax.

The creature also yielded four pieces of octopoid
hide, ten barbed hooks, and two octopoid eyes. The hide
could be used for crafting armor or weapons, or so the
description said. So far Allistor had not met anyone who
had learned much about crafting. The hooks would make
good fish hooks. And he had no idea what to do with the
eyes. But he dutifully put all the items in his pack, his
gaming experience telling him that as long as he had room
for it, he should take it all. Even if the eyes were useless
for crafting, they might make a tasty cooking ingredient or
good bait for fishing.

Lifting his makeshift spear, he *Examined* it.
Examine was a skill he'd learned on day one of the
stabilization. He'd been staring at one of the creatures that
roamed the street outside when suddenly an information
block appeared on his interface, along with a notification
that he'd learned *Examination, Level 1.*

Makeshift Iron Rebar Spear
Quality: Common
Durability: 230/300

Damage: 300 piercing/100 blunt
Bonus damage: 100 tearing

The spear was heavy, and not an ideal weapon. Even with his improved strength, he'd not be able to throw it far. But it was a good heavy bludgeoning weapon. Though the threads had roughed up his hands a bit as he'd pressed it into the ground. An idea struck him. Pulling one of the pieces of hide from his bag, he used his teeth to tear off a long strip. He wrapped the hide tightly around the rebar near the butt end, where he'd held it. Just as he was finishing the wrap and searching for something to tie it off with, the hide seemed to seal itself to the metal, and another notification popped up.

You have learned the crafting skill:
Weaponsmithing!

With this skill, you will be able to combine materials to create viable weapons. Existing weapon schematics can be purchased on the open market, or from smiths at Journeyman level or higher. You have earned additional skill points for creating a viable weapon from scratch using makeshift components you found lying around and a little creative thinking.

Allistor blinked a few times as he read the prompt, then he stared at the spear in his hand. The description hadn't changed, but now with the new skill, he could conceive of ways that the weapon might be improved by further sharpening the point, tempering the metal, sharpening the threads to increase tearing damage, and adding a weighted butt cap for smash damage.

"Holy shit!" He did a little dance as he held the spear at arm's length. "I can make weapons!"

*****

21

"You open the door, and it leads to a small, dark room with stone walls."

"I umm… what do you call it? I roll for a perception check." A twenty-sided clear crystal dice rolls across the table, landing with the number 17 facing upward.

"Hel, you notice a gold ring on the floor in the center of the room."

"Really, Loki? Just like that? A gold ring out of nowhere?"

Loki rolled his eyes at her. "Don't blame me. This is a human game. I didn't make the rules. Though I like the possibilities generated by the random dice rolls."

"You mean you like being able to control the dice rolls and thus the direction of the game." Hel glared at him, scooping up the dice. "There's nothing random about this game with you."

Loki chuckled. "Fair enough. Let us take a break and check in on these humans."

A wave of his hand brought up a three-dimensional hologram of the planet currently labeled UCP 382 hovering above the gaming table. The planet spun slowly, showing the observers each of the continents and oceans as it turned. Loki moved his hand toward the display and tapped the continent known as North America. The view zoomed in so that the continent filled the display, except for a stream of information scrolling along the right side.

"The extermination of the humans seems to be going well. The focused attacks on the major cities has eliminated fifty-five percent of the population in this first week. The ones in charge of this continent actually did some of our work for us, detonating nuclear blasts in hopes of containing the spread of the void titans and drakes we set to spawn there."

Hel zoomed in on the area that had once been New York City. It was now a blasted wasteland with only some steel skeletons of broken buildings to suggest it had once been a city of millions. "We'll need to seed some of the slimes and silicoid fungus to absorb the radiation and return these areas to habitable status.

"Already done." Loki pointed to a section of the info feed which stopped scrolling. "Still, it will take more than the solar year Stabilization period for the land to be viable again. Maybe as much as two years. There are several similar spots where their primitive nuclear power plants have malfunctioned and contaminated large tracts of land."

"These human creatures seem to have no concern for their planet. Short-sighted of them, really. It's good that we claimed their world when we did. Another century or two and they might have destroyed it."

Baldur, who had been observing the game quietly, said, "I believe they lost their way when they stopped believing in us. This new god that so many of them adopted was one of fear and revenge, fire and brimstone. They lost sight of honor and duty, the glory of battle and rightful plunder. Strength of arm and stout heart were replaced with politics and greed. Men and women have forgotten the ways to Valhalla. And I believe that was *your doing,* Loki." He scowled at the deceiver through the mist that drifted throughout the room. The alien beings preferred a moist environment.

Members of a race so old that none but themselves even knew its name, they were effectively immortal. Their people were born on a planet that orbited one of the universe's first stars. They had long ago discovered the *Neutrocosm* and harnessed its powers, and they had the ability to alter their forms at will. But in these casual settings, they preferred their natural, vaguely amphibian forms.

"That may be." Loki breathed a puff of mist at his brother- the species' equivalent of a 'talk to the hand' gesture. "But the weak and foolish deserve their fate."

The three watched the display as Loki spun the view westward into a mountainous region. "These areas, where fewer cities grew and people lived closer to nature, the humans have fared better. There are some true warriors here. With survival instincts that will serve them well. Some remember the old ways, others have learned from the games we sent them. The human race is not totally without merit."

Not true gods, they lacked omnipotence or omniscience. But to the simpler life forms of the universe, like the humans they visited every few thousand years, the powers they displayed seemed godlike. And their names became legend. Creatures of myth in whatever lands they visited. Most of their race had become bored with planetary life, and either let themselves perish or assumed forms that allowed them to travel the stars, seeking adventure or knowledge of the universe's origins. Some few had remained, forming the System and gathering worlds into the Nexus. Fostering younger species with potential.

Loki scanned the scrolling information on the display, then pointed a tentacle-like finger and stopped it, highlighting one section. "Here is an interesting one. Abnormally high initial *Adaptability* of six, and *Intelligence* of five, yet he seems to have chosen to develop his *Strength,* having already doubled it in a matter of just a few days."

They watched in silence as Loki zoomed in on a young human male battling an octopoid – one of the low-level creatures regularly pulled from the Menagerie and transported to newly claimed and overpopulated worlds. A distant cousin of the gathered beings, they were semi-intelligent and quite deadly.

"See how he improvises a weapon? This one will go far." Baldur admired the young man's spirit. He applauded when the human defeated the octopoid and earned a new skill. His approval automatically awarded some Fame Points to the young man.

"He is young and foolish. If this trash doesn't kill him, another will soon enough. He believes his limited knowledge of our System makes him stronger than he truly is." Hel spat on the floor in disgust.

Loki tilted his head to one side, watching as the octopoid died. "He is clever. Thinks fast on his feet. This one will bear watching."

"Shall we send him another, stronger opponent?" Hel's smile was pure evil.

"No!" Baldur slammed a fist on the table, causing the mist to swirl in a reflection of his anger. "You will adhere to the rules, Hel. And you, Loki." He looked at the scrolling information as he spoke. "This man must already face the void titan that killed his parents and most of his townspeople in the last hour. That opponent is more than three times his level. That is enough. The humans and other species of this world must be given their fair chance to survive, grow and thrive. Any interference will be looked upon as an act of defiance by Odin and myself. Judgment will be swift and severe."

"Thrive? By the end of Stabilization, they will be living like dogs in caves and old ruins, killing and eating each other to survive. Most cannot even make fire! And they do not understand the System or its power. They do not even have a word for the *Neutrocosm*." Hel's voice was filled with contempt.

"They are close." Loki held up a finger. "They may not know the word, but they have touched on the concept in their stories and their science. They speak of 'The Force' and 'Magic' in their popular tales. And minuscule machines they call 'nanotech'. Given a little more time, they might have made that final leap to discover and eventually manipulate the *Neutrocosm.*"

"And now that we have brought them into the System, their awareness of it has already increased greatly. This young man, for example, has embraced the concept of training by action. Greatly increasing his strength in a matter of days through extensive strenuous physical activity. Granted, at such low levels, the dramatic increases are easy. But the fact that he has embraced the System is what is important. Let us see if he continues to improve. And whether he shares this knowledge with others."

Baldur paused to give Hel a significant look. "Over the past few millennia, there have been a rare few humans born with the ability to sense the *Neutrocosm,* even manipulate it in some small ways. But in their greed and ambition for power or fame, or perhaps their wisdom in the case of Merlin, they kept the knowledge to themselves. In Merlin's time, the human race was little more than rutting livestock. Able to speak, make fire, farm and trade, but little else. Warlike, but only able to damage each other on a small scale with primitive weapons in petty wars for territory. If he had spread his knowledge to the uneducated masses at that time, the race might have wiped itself out."

"And now, we're wiping them out!" Loki grinned. "And you're hoping that the knowledge will save some of them."

"That is indeed my hope. Humankind has long been a favorite of mine," Baldur agreed.

Chapter Two

Salvation

Allistor took a minute or two to bask in the glory of his new skill, and then he got back down to business. This new system now governing Earth didn't forgive slackers or people who stood around admiring themselves for too long.

Knowing what he would find, but needing to check anyway, he took hold of his spear and dropped down into the manhole. Producing a work light from his bag, he strapped it onto his forehead and scanned both directions. He could see the scrapes in the muck at the bottom of the tunnel indicating that the octopoid had come from his left. Assuming the only way the woman and her daughter could have gone and lived was the opposite direction, he went right.

He caught himself ducking down unconsciously, though there was no need. The storm drain tunnel ceiling was at least seven feet high, providing plenty of room for him to walk upright. Straightening his back and gripping his new spear in both hands, he moved down the tunnel to a junction. Shining his light on the floor, he noted a small footprint pointing toward the junction. "They're alive?" he murmured to himself.

Looking left and right again, it wasn't clear from the footprint which way they might have gone. He took a chance that, based on only finding one in his basement, octopoids were solitary creatures that didn't run in packs.

"Hello? Lady? Are you there?" he called out once in each direction. Echoes of his own voice were the only answer he received. He crouched down low and examined the first several feet in each direction but found no tracks. Then his gamer instincts took over.

"She went right the first time, let's assume she'd do it again. Everyone knows once you pick a direction you should keep it up. Until you can't." With a last look down the left tunnel, he went right. He moved as quickly as he could while scanning the floor for any hint that they'd come this way. Maybe fifty yards down the tunnel, he froze. A chittering sound echoed faintly from the darkness outside the range of his light. He gripped his weapon tightly and spread his feet, preparing to battle whatever monster emerged from the dark.

What he heard next sent him sprinting forward. A little girl's scream of fear bounced off the rounded concrete walls. "Aaaaahh! Mommy! Rats!"

Allistor's light finally reached the little girl, who was huddled up against her mother, the two of them pressed against one wall of the tunnel as half a dozen rat-like creatures surrounded them. The mother looked up at him, only able to see his rough outline behind the light shining in her eyes. "Please, help us." She gasped. Her voice was weak, and she looked to be on her last legs. She held a kitchen knife in one hand, her grip so tight her knuckles were white.

Without even thinking, Allistor jabbed forward, skewering one of the rat things. It died instantly. He turned and swung the spear with the rat-thing on the end like a golf club, smashing another of the creatures down the tunnel and clearing the first corpse from the end. The remaining four backed up as he moved to stand between them and the other humans.

Vermin Scout
Level 2
Health 250/250

They were larger than normal rats, at least the ones Allistor had seen before the assimilation. These were the size of overfed housecats, with wicked-looking claws and incisors as long as his fingers. Their eyes were bloodshot with bright red pupils.

One of them lunged at him, leaping into the air with surprising speed and strength. He didn't have time to bring his weapon to bear, and his instinct was to dodge. But his brain screwed with his instinct, reminding him that the unprotected females were behind him. The hesitation allowed the nasty thing to latch onto his thigh with its razor claws, then chomp down with its teeth. Allistor screamed, his voice nearly as high-pitched as the little girl's, as the thing removed a solid chunk of his jeans and the flesh of his leg and swallowed it whole.

Letting go of his weapon with his left hand, he grabbed the thing by the neck and yanked it off him. The claws did more damage as he ripped them free, and red numbers flashed across his interface. He throttled the thing, shaking it while squeezing with all his considerable strength. Its neck snapped, and it stopped struggling. He hurled it at the remaining three vermin. They looked at him, then at the corpse, and decided on the easier meal. One of them grabbed hold of its dead brethren and began to drag it away into the darkness. The other two followed, walking backward and baring their teeth at Allistor.

When he could no longer hear them scurrying away, he waved away the experience notifications on his interface and turned to face the woman behind him. He had one hand clamped to the wound on his leg, trying to stop the flow of blood. She looked down as she said, "Thank you... Allistor, right?" She didn't wait for confirmation. "You're hurt. We need to stop the bleeding."

Reaching into her own bag, she pulled out a small jar and a rag. Then she said, "Take off your belt and wrap it around your leg, twist it tight.

Allistor shook his head. His health bar was down to seventy percent and was ticking downward slowly. A blinking icon on his interface indicated a bleeding debuff. "Later. Those things were called scouts. Which means there are probably more of them down here somewhere. Let's get you out of here, then we can fix my leg."

She nodded and took the frightened little girl by the hand. With Allistor's light leading the way, the three of them walked side by side back to the junction and went left.

"I'm sorry," Allistor said as he limped along. "I don't think I know your name."

She smiled unsteadily, her teeth white against her tear and dirt-stained face. "I'm not surprised. I know your mother, but the last time I saw you in person was at one of your little league games. You were maybe... ten? But your mom has... *had*... your picture on her desk. I'm Nancy. And this little bundle of snot and tears is Chloe." She smiled as Chloe wiped her runny nose on a dirty sleeve, leaving streaks of snot-crusted dirt across her face.

"Nice to meet you... err... again." Allistor couldn't shake hands, with one on his leg and the other holding his weapon. Chloe gave a halfhearted wave, looking over her shoulder fearfully. They picked up the pace a bit, moving as fast as Allistor could with his injured leg. It was only a few minutes before they reached the ladder leading up to the manhole.

Nancy went first, her knife in hand as she struggled to climb the ladder that was bolted into the wall. She popped her head up and looked around carefully before continuing up. Next Chloe scampered up the ladder with surprising dexterity. She was frightened and clearly anxious to get away from the rats and back into the sunlight.

Allistor passed his spear up to Nancy, then climbed himself. That necessitated removing his hand from his wound, relieving the pressure, and allowing the blood to pump more freely. He'd lost a good bit since the battle, and he was going to need to stop the flow soon or risk losing consciousness.

Upon reaching the top, they paused while he let Nancy treat his wound. He used his belt to restrict the circulation in his leg while she poured some water on it, then applied the salve she carried in a jar. Afterward, she tied a rag around his thigh tightly enough to keep pressure on the wound without cutting off blood flow completely. Then she made him turn around so she could put some of the salve on his back.

"What did this?" she asked.

Chloe made a face and said, "Ew."

"Octopoid. Came up out of that hole right after you went in. You got *very* lucky you went the direction you did. I figured it had killed you. Lured it up here for a little vengeance."

Nancy shuddered. "Those things are horrible. I'm glad you killed it. And that it didn't see us. That would have been bad."

Allistor studied the terrain as she worked on his back. Whatever was in that salve was working wonders.

32

The sting of the hooks was completely gone, and it felt cool on his skin. "What is that stuff?"

"Hmmm?" Nancy looked down at her hand. "Oh, a little something I mixed up. Gardening is my hobby, and I've somehow picked up a skill called *Herbology*. It tells me what some of my plants can do when I focus on them. And when I started mixing them together, I learned *Alchemy*, too. The description for this stuff says it helps with coagulation to stop bleeds, prevents infections, and heals for 5 points per minute over ten minutes."

"That's awesome! I just learned *Weaponsmithing*. Totally by accident. This new world... it's a lot like the virtual games I've played."

Nancy grinned behind his back. "I played my share of those as a kid. That was a long time ago, though. Still, you're right. This *does* feel familiar."

Allistor wasn't sure where in the town they were. All the usual landmarks had been crushed to rubble and ruins by the monstrosity that had invaded their town that morning. Not a single wholly undamaged building still stood. The thing was like a petulant child smashing a sandcastle on the beach.

"I saw some others leading that titan toward the river. We could follow, see if they've found a safe place?" he offered.

Nancy looked down at Chloe, who was sitting on the ground with her knees to her chest, rocking back and forth slightly. The child was clearly exhausted, and Nancy wasn't looking much better. "I'll have to carry her. She's had about all she can take."

Allistor shook his head. "What level are you?"

33

Nancy replied, "I am almost level two."

"You're obviously a tough lady, but you look exhausted. I'm guessing you couldn't carry her a hundred yards. I'll take her. She can ride on my shoulders."

Nancy gave him a grateful smile and nodded. As he squatted down, she lifted the little girl and placed her atop his shoulders. When he straightened, he gave a little hop to adjust her weight evenly, and they were ready to go. Allistor set off in the general direction the titan had headed.

Both adults kept wary eyes on their surroundings. Likely the recent passing of the sixty-foot monster had scared away any other predators, at least temporarily. But hard lessons had been learned over the past few days. Friends and neighbors who acted foolishly or even less than vigilantly had perished in nasty ways.

And while the Earthlings got experience for killing the newly spawned creatures sent by the Collective and were able to loot them for items of value… the creatures themselves seem to grow stronger by consuming their prey. Every human they consumed made them just a little bit harder to kill.

As they walked, Nancy tried to make small talk. Very quiet small talk. "So… your family?"

Allistor did his best not to let his voice betray the sorrow that crushed him right then. "Gone," was all that he managed to push out in response. Nancy nodded with understanding.

"I'm sorry. I lost Michael, too. And Chloe's big brother, Chris."

Allistor knew he should offer condolences, but he just didn't have it in him. Losing Leah on that first day had been traumatic enough. But it had only been hours since his mother and father perished. He hadn't really even had time to process it.

They continued on in silence until they reached the river. There had been two bridges large enough for vehicle traffic, and a smaller stone footbridge that crossed a narrow spot where the water dropped into a natural defile thirty feet below. Both the larger bridges were damaged, one with the center section completely gone, the other bent and twisted. But the footbridge seemed to have escaped the giant's attention so far. None of the trees in the forest on the other side had been damaged.

Allistor led them across, spear at the ready as he scoured the opposite bank looking for monsters. They were high enough above the water that he doubted they had to worry about octopoids or other aquatic menaces.

His attention proved worthwhile as he spotted a squat, burly creature emerging from the shrubs not far from the end of the bridge. He froze, gripping Chloe's leg with one hand hoping she would understand and remain still herself. Nancy bumped into his back, then went still herself as she followed his gaze.

Wolvite
Level 3
Health 850/850

The thing was aptly named. It resembled a wolverine in size and form, its body low to the ground atop four short but powerful legs with wicked, taloned paws. Its head was angled, as with most predators, from its widest point at the ears to a narrowing face that ended in a snout full of teeth. Its eyes were jet black, void of any emotion. Sniffing the air with its head raised revealed a heavily muscled chest and neck. This creature was a natural tank if ever there was one. Able to take and dish out horrible damaging blows.

Allistor hoped it would pass on by. They were downwind of it, and still far enough away that it might not notice them. He and his father had learned when one of them wandered into their back yard and attempted to break into the kitchen that the wolvite's eyesight was poor, but that their sense of smell was incredible. They had barely managed to kill it.

This one made a snuffling noise as it searched the various scents brought to it on the breeze. All three humans were holding their breath, watching the monster as its head swayed back and forth, sampling the breeze. It chuffed a couple times, sounding almost thoughtful. Then with a slow turn of its head, its gaze fell directly on Allistor.

The growl that emerged from deep in its chest seemed to resonate through the stone of the bridge. It shifted its body so that it faced the humans and began to waddle toward the bridgehead. Allistor acted fast, pushing Chloe's legs up and over his shoulder to dump her into her mother's arms. Then he stepped forward, spear at the ready.

"Come on then, just move along. No easy lunch here. You come onto this bridge, fella, and I'll be forced to kill you." He wished he felt as confident as he sounded, trying to dissuade the wolvite from attacking. He took several steps forward, to put some distance between himself and the ladies behind him.

The wolvite ignored his words, ambling along at a sedate but steady pace as it continued to approach. Its head

36

shifted to look at Chloe when she whimpered and clutched at her mother's leg.

"Hyah! Hyah!" He half-thrust the spear at the creature, trying to drive it off. This time it focused its gaze on him but didn't slow. Its lips raised in a snarl, revealing the rows of sharp teeth beneath.

When it was within a dozen feet of him, it lowered its head and charged. The slowly ambling predator was suddenly as swift as the wind as it closed the distance between them. Teeth bared and eyes still a dead black, the image was horrifying.

Again, mostly out of instinct. He brandished his spear at the charging beast. Holding it like a two-handed paddle, he thrust the butt end toward the oncoming hairy missile. It connected with a loud *crack* as the momentum of both creature and weapon combined for an effective blow. The rebar struck the creature just to the side of its snout, peeling back skin and delivering a stunning blow. The wolvite backed up a couple steps, shaking its head and briefly whining like an injured dog. Allistor stepped toward it, using his body momentum to jab the point of the spear into the creature's side. The tip bit deep into flesh, causing another whimper of pain from the wolvite. Allistor mercilessly twisted the rebar as he pulled it free, doing extra damage.

Wolvite
Level 3
Health 500/850

The nasty creature shrugged off the wound and lunged for him. Its jaws snapped shut just short of his shin as he dodged backward. As he tried to bring his weapon to bear to block it, the monster used its forward momentum to barrel into him.

37

Knocked off balance, Allistor fell forward atop the wolvite's back. It jerked around with shocking speed and clamped down on his left triceps. Shaking its head savagely, its teeth tore at his flesh even as he tried to roll away. Blood sprayed as it clamped down even harder, and Allistor's health bar dropped to sixty percent.

Nancy rushed to his aid, screaming as she plunged her kitchen knife into the wolvite's exposed neck. Again and again, she slammed the knife in up to the hilt. Blood sprayed, coating both Allistor and Nancy. He felt the pressure lesson on his arm and tried to pull free. The pain nearly caused him to pass out.

With some difficulty, he managed to use his free hand to jam the end of the spear between the creature's jaws and lever them open. It growled and resisted, shaking its head again and breaking several of its teeth against the rebar. But the fight was quickly going out of the little beast as its lifeblood poured from the neck wounds.

His arm free, Allistor managed to get to his feet. He swung the butt end of the spear down atop the creatures head, intending to crush its skull. The tough little bastard took the hit but didn't die. Its thick skull protected it from the blow.

Allistor reversed his weapon and thrust the spear point down into the wolvite's neck. He pushed until the spear burst from its body somewhere underneath and scraped against the stone of the bridge. The monster struggled briefly, its tiny brain inside the thick skull refusing to acknowledge its death. When it went still, several alerts popped up on Allistor's interface.

The first was a green experience notification showing *+1400*

The next two made him pause for a moment, still breathing hard from the exertion.

You have learned the skill: Blunt Weapon.
Using the butt end of your weapon to crush vermin and crack a wolvite skull has taught you the value of a heavy weapon with room to swing.
Continue to use blunt weapons to increase your skill level.

Level Up! You are now Level 4. You have earned two attribute points.

Allistor felt lightheaded, his legs giving way beneath him. He sat on the ground, releasing the rebar spear to fall to the stone with a clang. He could feel the wet blood soaking his shirt along his left side.

Nancy was there, her own hands covered in blood from the wounds she inflicted on the wolvite. She quickly wiped her hands on a relatively clean section of his shirt, then clamped them down around his arm, trying to stop the bleeding. A moment later, she looked at him, confused. She pulled her hands away and stared at his arm. Then she looked at his back.

"Your... wounds have closed." She eyed him with suspicion. "How?"

He was barely conscious. Though the wounds had closed when he leveled up, and his health meter on his interface showed him at 100%, the healing did not instantly replace the blood that he'd lost over the last hour.

He and his father had learned this lesson early, fighting the octopoid that had killed Leah. His father was badly injured, the thing having managed to wrap three tentacles around him in the tight confines of the basement. George had been nearly dead when Allistor finally took a hatchet to the thing's face and killed it. They had both leveled up, and George's ragged wounds had closed. But he hadn't really recovered from the blood loss and Stamina drain until he ate and drank, and rested for about ten minutes.

Allistor heard himself mumbling to Nancy, but he wasn't sure if he was making any sense. A moment later, he felt cool water in his mouth and swallowed. This perked him up enough to open his eyes.

He was on his back, looking up at the faces of Nancy and Chloe. The little girl was crying, her tears dripping onto his face. Nancy was trying to force-feed him something. Trusting the woman, he opened his mouth. Something soft and sugary touched his tongue, and he managed to chew and swallow. When he was able to focus more, he saw that she was holding a Ho-Ho package with one hand, pushing the second of the two treats into his mouth with the other. He tried to thank her, but his mouth was full.

He lay there for several minutes, recovering his stamina, lost blood, and his senses. The sugary calories of the chocolate snack cakes processed quickly through his system. Nancy gave him several more swallows of water to help wash them down. Five minutes after the fight ended, he was sitting up and shaking his head.

"That sucked," he said, raising his arm to look at the spot where the wolvite had clamped down. There wasn't even a scar. Just a faint itch. Looking up at Nancy, he said, "Thank you. I was pretty sure I was dead, there. You killed that thing before it could finish eating me, then saved with me Ho-Hos."

She laughed at the crooked grin he gave her, still not quite himself. "I didn't kill it. I just distracted it so it would let go of you. You shish-kabob'd the thing."

He shook his head. "No, I just sped things up. It was dying. You should have gotten some experience…" his voice drifted off as she nodded.

"Yup! I'm level two now." She puffed out her chest with pride, and he couldn't help but stare for a moment. She noticed and didn't seem to mind.

Blinking a few times, he said, "Congrats on the ding!" making her smile yet again.

She helped him to his feet as resilient little Chloe, having calmed a good bit after eating ho-hos herself, looked him up and down. "You look like shit," she observed matter-of-factly. He chuckled as her mother admonished her.

"Chloe! Language! I'm sorry; her brother taught her some bad habits."

The girl shrugged, not the least bit repentant. "Well, he does. He's not very good at fighting. He keeps letting things bite him."

Nancy couldn't help but laugh at this, and a moment later Allistor joined her. "You know, you're right, little lady. I should have thought of that myself. From now on I'll do my best not to let things bite me." He mussed her hair a bit, and she stuck her tongue out at him.

He bent to loot the wolvite, receiving twenty klax, several wolvite teeth and claws, and two pieces of wolvite hide. He was surprised a moment later when Nancy also bent to loot the creature. "You can loot it too?"

"Apparently so. I got twenty klax and some body parts. You?"

"The same. That's interesting. So we both damaged it, and we both got loot. Good to know." He wondered for the hundredth time about the mechanics of this new world as they got themselves together and continued across the bridge.

Following a walking trail through what had once been a state park, they remained vigilant. For the dozenth time in the last several hours, Allistor wished for the guns that had been inside the family home when it was crushed. Being near the outskirts of town and having almost no warning when the titan appeared, he and his parents hadn't had time to retrieve their weapons. They'd barely gotten out of the house with the clothes on their backs when it stomped on their kitchen, then kicked the rest of the house into smithereens.

Shaking off the grim memory, Allistor focused on the path ahead. They were still moving in the general direction of the titan. He could feel the slight trembles in the ground that accompanied its footsteps. They didn't seem to be gaining on it, though. Which might be an indication that the survivors had managed to lead it away at a rapid pace. He hoped they figured out how to lose it and double back. Otherwise, the remaining townspeople might be scattered across a wide area, making it easier for the smaller and more numerous monsters to pick them off.

"At least being in the trees, we don't have to worry about the flying monsters," Nancy ventured. Neither of them had spoken in several minutes. Allistor looked up at the canopy above, the sunlight breaking through in a thousand small gaps between branches and leaves. But none were large enough to admit the nasty flying lizard things that had plagued the town on the first day.

"Thank God for small favors," he replied, returning his gaze to the surrounding terrain. There was no shortage of new dangers here on the ground. Though he'd not seen them himself, there were reports of mutant canine things with six legs. Vicious reptiles with two small forelegs and the bodies of snakes a dozen feet long and longer. Along with the octopoids, the vermin, the flying lizards, wolvites, the titan, and who knew what else the Collective was throwing at them, Earth had become a death trap.

A rustle in the brush to their left caught his attention. They picked up their pace as he kept his focus locked on that location. A moment later, a small brown fuzzy bunny leapt from the brush onto the path.

Chloe instantly stopped and reversed direction, making for the cute critter. "Squee! Mommy, can we keep the bunny? It's soooo cute!" Suddenly full of energy, the child trotted toward the woodland creature.

Nancy set off after her, hissing. "Chloe! Get back here! No!" The little girl was maybe ten feet from the bunny when it turned to retreat into the brush.

It never got the chance.

A silvery-green blur shot out from the brush in front of it, resolving into the head of a serpent as it clamped down on the squealing bunny. Almost as fast as it had come, the head withdrew and disappeared into the foliage.

Chloe skidded to a halt, falling on her butt and crying as her mom scooped her up and retreated. "I hate this place, Momma!" she sobbed.

"I know, baby. I know." Nancy stroked her head and rocked her from side to side as she walked. Allistor, keeping one eye on the shrubbery, couldn't agree more.

The trio continued down the path, keeping as close to the center as possible. When Chloe had calmed a bit, Allistor hoisted her back onto his shoulders to give Nancy a break. With his strength, the child's weight was nothing to him.

Ten minutes later, Allistor began to salivate as he detected the scent of smoke and roasting meat. They picked up the pace a bit, hoping they'd found the group of survivors they sought. The flicker of flames could be seen through the trees just around a bend in the path. Allistor thought he saw a cabin of some kind. A vague childhood memory hinted at the possibility of a picnic area along the path here.

As they rounded the bend, Allistor's growling stomach heaved and his mouth went dry. The roasting smell that had seemed so attractive was, in fact, the odor from a funeral pyre. Half a dozen bodies burned atop a makeshift stack of lumber and firewood. Five people stood nearby, talking quietly. When they saw Allistor and company, they went silent.

"Nancy? Is that you?" A woman stepped forward. Chloe began to wiggle atop Allistor's shoulders, demanding to be let down. "Auntie Meg!" The moment she touched the ground she sprinted toward the woman, who took a knee and opened her arms for a hug as Chloe launched herself at her, squeezing tight.

Now that he heard the name, Allistor recognized Meg – she ran a diner near the highway exit. The man behind her was her husband, Sam, an ex-Marine and line cook at the diner. He made the best chocolate chip pancakes, which were featured in some of Allistor's favorite childhood memories.

Allistor held up a hand in greeting. "Meg, Sam. Good to see you made it!" He slowed as the others gathered around. He recognized a kid he'd gone to high school with. Robert Edward Dudley. He mainly remembered the guy because he'd detested being called "Bob" and insisted people use his full name. The guy had been an athlete and one of the smarter kids in school. Allistor gave him a 'bro nod' and received one in return.

The others were strangers to Allistor and didn't introduce themselves.

Meg stood, holding Chloe in her arms. "Nancy, I'm so glad to see you. We've... lost so many. And Chloe is the only little one I've seen since that thing hit town. How did you manage?"

Nancy nodded toward Allistor. "He saved our bacon. More than once now."

Allistor shook his head. "She's being modest. She went all stabby-stabby on a wolvite and saved me from having my arm chewed off."

Nancy changed the subject. "What happened here?" She indicated the funeral pyre.

Sam's voice was rough with grief. "My sister, her husband and kids. They were out here camping already, missed all the bad shit in town. We came out here to find them, get them to the rally point. When we got here, we found..." He didn't say any more. The blood spatters on the nearby picnic table and restroom cubicle told the story.

Robert Edward kicked the dirt and said, "Damned dog mutants. Six of them. We killed them when we got here, but it was too late."

Meg whispered to Nancy. "Sam's niece was Robert Edward's girlfriend." The two men just stared at the ground, grieving.

After a few moments, Sam added, "We burned the bodies so none of the monsters out here could eat them." Allistor thought it was a good idea, less because he was worried about strangers' bodies being desecrated, more because it would have made the monsters stronger. Looking at the sorrow on the faces around him, he kept that thought to himself.

"You mentioned a rally point?" he asked Sam.

The man shook himself and raised his head. "Yeah. The caves here in the park. Sandy over there," he pointed to a woman Allistor didn't know, "is one of the rangers here. She does... she *did* tours of the caves before the world went to shit. There's solar power and a few natural springs for water. The entrance is wider than I'd like, but we can maybe build a wall or something to block it off."

Allistor had been in the caves once as a kid. But he'd been bored and anxious to get back to his games, and he hadn't really paid attention. "Is there enough room for the whole town in there?" He immediately regretted the question when he saw the looks everyone gave him. "Right. Sorry. About how many do you think are left?"

Meg said, "If we're lucky, about twenty of us. That we know of, anyway. Might be a few others that got out. Or found a place to hide."

Nancy spoke up. "Just FYI... don't hide in the storm sewer tunnels. Nasty vermin colony down there." The others all nodded, accepting the information as just one more way their new world was screwed up.

Sam looked around. The fire was burning low and would be out soon enough. "Let's head for the caves. The others will join us there. Sheriff Chatfield and a few others were leading the titan away. The rest are supposed to be securing the caves. They've all got guns, but so far I haven't heard any shots since we took out these canids."

The group gathered together and followed Sam and Sandy. Rather than continue down the meandering hiking path, they cut through the dense forest in a more or less straight line toward the caves. Nancy and Chloe were herded to the middle of the group with Meg, while Allistor and Robert Edward took up the rear. They went without speaking, trying not to draw the attention of more predators.

It was less than twenty minutes before they reached the cave entrance. Sandy, intimately familiar with the area since she was the park ranger, had led them down into a gully where a quiet stream burbled its way down toward the river. They walked in the stream about a hundred yards uphill before exiting onto some flat boulders. Allistor assumed it was an attempt to disguise their scent from any monsters that might track them. Somehow he doubted it would work.

The inside of the cave was well lit. Wires ran down out of the ceiling from somewhere above ground where the solar array was located, into a junction box, then out again in several directions, lighting the various branches of the cave system.

They found Sean, the sheriff's deputy, crouched behind a boulder maybe twenty feet back from the entry. When he saw them step inside, he stood up and lowered his shotgun, looking relieved. He still wore his uniform, though it was stained with blood in several places. "Good to see you, Sam. The others are working their way through checking for monsters." He jerked a thumb over his shoulder. "Have a seat. If you go back there now, you might get shot by mistake."

Allistor gladly obliged, fatigued from the day's stresses. He'd nearly been killed several times, lost more blood than was healthy, lost both parents, and he didn't even know yet how many friends and neighbors. Physically and mentally worn down, he sat on the floor of the cave, leaned his back against the wall, and closed his eyes.

Chapter Three

Newbtastic

The sound of a shotgun blast echoing off the cave walls woke Allistor. He came to his senses in time to hear Chloe scream and several others begin to shout. He turned toward the cave entrance but saw nothing. It was dark outside. And the shouting was coming from behind him.

Looking toward the back of the cave, he saw a disaster. Dozens of vermin were swarming around the human survivors. Biting and clawing at legs and feet. A man Allistor didn't know was on his back, thrashing about as three of the rat things chewed on his face and arms.

Allistor ran toward the downed man, stabbing one of the vermin as soon as he got within reach. His spear passed through its body and into another, killing both. A swift kick knocked the third vermin off the man and sent it careening off a cave wall. He stuck out a hand to help the man up, but he didn't accept it. A closer look showed the man was blinded, both eyes having been chewed by the vermin. Allistor grabbed the man and dragged him toward the front of the cave with one hand, keeping the other on his weapon.

When he'd cleared the melee, he dropped the man and turned back to the battle. He saw Nancy slashing at a nimbly dodging oversized rat with her knife, scoring a hit here and there as Chloe huddled behind her. Sam was taking careful aim with his pistol, then blew one of the nasty things out of existence. Sean's shotgun sounded again, and a swath of the vermin dissolved into pink mist and chunks of flesh. Allistor picked one and Examined it.

Vermin Gatherer
Level 3
Health 220/400

Meg, oddly enough, seemed to be the most effective of the melee fighters in the group. She swung a long-handled frying pan like a home run hitter, smashing in the faces of vermin after vermin. Cursing them with each stroke. "Take *that,* you ratty-assed little shit!"

Rejoining the fray, Allistor swung his own spear, crushing the rat creature that was threatening Nancy. Then he stabbed the rebar spear forward at a low angle across the cave floor, skewering two more. He paused to scrape them against a boulder to clear his weapon, then stalked forward. He smiled to himself as he remembered Chloe's admonishment not to get bitten.

Another shotgun blast scattered the last clustered group of the mobs, leaving only a few for Allistor, Meg, Nancy, and Robert Edward to dispose of. Robert Edward wasn't using any weapon other than his feet, stomping the life from any vermin that held still long enough.

When it was over, each of them looted the rats they had helped to kill, identified by a faint glow only they could see. Except for Nancy, who had moved to the fallen man to try and help him.

Already, his face was swelling, puffing up with a sickly green pallor that indicated infection. He was sweating and coughing, his teeth clenched in pain. Nancy tried to wrap a bandage around his head to cover his eyes, but he fought her. Managing to grab hold of one of her wrists, he begged, "Kill me. I'm dead anyway. A blind man can't survive here." He groaned in pain as a swelling pustule near his eye burst. "Make it quick. Please."

Nancy looked up at the group, all of whom had gathered around her. One by one they all nodded. She lifted her knife and pointed it at his throat, then paused. After a moment she lowered it again. "I... can't."

Allistor didn't hesitate. He stepped forward and slammed the point of his spear up under the prone man's sternum and straight into his heart. The man stiffened and groaned in pain, then went still. A green number flashed up on his interface; *+3500*.

I got experience for killing another human? His mouth dropped open, and he nearly said something aloud about it to the others. But it occurred to him that when things got rough, it might be better that they not know their fellow humans' deaths might level them up.

Sam looked at the dead man. "He was one of the guys who went to clear the caves?"

Sean nodded. "His name was Alan."

"Shit." Meg's response was succinct and shared by everyone. "They must have disturbed another colony? Or is it possible they're from the same colony as the one in the storm drains?"

Sandy replied. "No, we're a good two miles north of town and the storm drains there. And the cave system only goes north from where we're standing. I don't think they connect anywhere."

Allistor added, "One of those octopoids spawned in our basement. There was no way for it to get in there. Maybe these vermin things did the same here in the cave."

Sean, still looking toward the back of the cave said, "I didn't hear any shots. From back there, I mean. Before the vermin attacked. Just Alan shouting and running toward me with those things all over him."

Sam looked at him, a frown bunching his eyebrows together. "You think the vermin got the others who went back there." It wasn't a question.

"Do we go look?" Sean didn't sound as if he *wanted* to go look at all. Neither did anyone else. No one spoke.

Meg broke the silence. "We can't afford to lose more people. If they're dead, we can't help them. If they're okay, they'll come out on their own. They took most of the guns with them, and that's a big loss for us. But I don't think even retrieving the guns is worth sending people back there."

Sandy put an arm around Meg. "We can't stay here. Even if this place is clear now, Allistor brings up a good point. Something else could spawn back there. And there's way too much territory for us to guard. Miles of tunnels and caverns. Too many ways for something to get to us. We need someplace smaller that we can make safe."

The others took a moment to consider, and there were murmurs of agreement. They began to make ready to move. Allistor, having no belongings to gather, volunteered to help deal with the body. When he approached it, he saw the same glowing aura around it that appeared on monsters he killed.

Not wanting to loot the body, but curious about what he would receive, he surreptitiously reached down and placed his hand on the dead man's chest. The loot window popped up. He received twenty-five klax, an empty pistol with two empty magazines, an ammo belt with shotgun shells, a Swiss army knife, and a scroll.

All of the items that appeared in his hands quickly went into his nearly-full bag, except the knife, which he put in his pocket. When Sean approached, the other half of the burial detail, Allistor asked, "Did he have family? Still living, I mean?"

Sean shook his head. "No, he didn't. In a way, he was one of the lucky ones. He didn't lose anybody special this week."

The two of them easily lifted the corpse and carried it gently outside. It was full dark now, and Allistor found himself a little disoriented. He'd intended to get a short rest, not sleep several hours.

Setting the body on a flat boulder near the cave entrance, they began to gather firewood. They stacked it in a three-foot-wide pile about six feet long, making sure the inside held plenty of kindling and brush that would burn quickly. When they were done, they set the body atop the pyre but didn't light it. They'd do that when the party was ready to leave.

Stepping back inside, they found everyone packed and ready but sitting around talking quietly. Allistor moved to stand with Nancy, asking, "What's going on?"

She rolled her eyes and looked embarrassed. "We got all ready to go, and then realized we don't know *where* to go."

Allistor looked around. The remaining survivors were gathered in groups of two and three, talking quietly and gesturing, occasionally pointing in a direction. He moved to the middle of the cavern and cleared his throat loudly. When he had everyone's attention, he said, "I think we should all put our heads together and figure out our next steps. The first question seems to be where we should go. And I would submit that we should also discuss whether to try and go there in the dark."

The small groups gathered around him as he spoke. Sean was the first to respond. "That's a good point. Regardless of where we go, I don't think I like the idea of walking through the forest at night."

Sam agreed. "Allistor's right. I think we should find a way to secure just this room, and hunker down till daylight. Anyone disagree?" He waited, but no one spoke up. "Fine. We stay the rest of the night. Hopefully, the others get back from dealing with the titan by then. Next question, or rather first question, where do we go?"

Sandy said, "There's a Park Service station about ten miles from here. It's a log cabin, with solar power, well water, and a working bathroom. But it would be a little cramped for all of us."

"If it's even still there," Sam added.

Allistor raised his hand. Then, feeling silly, just spoke. "When my pop was mayor, he used to take me to work with him at city hall sometimes. I was a kid and got bored easily. Used to explore the building. There's a basement level that they used for jail cells when they first built the place back in the 1800s. It's two levels down and cut right into the bedrock. I remember there being a long hall with six or seven cells on each side."

Meg was nodding along. "I remember that! When I was little my teacher took us on a tour down there. It had one of those old toilets with a pull-chain. So there must have been water at one point. And it wouldn't hurt us to take a look around town. See what we can salvage in the way of food and clothes, weapons, whatever."

Sam looked around the group. "Anybody got any better suggestions?" Again, no one spoke up. "So our choices are the ranger's cabin or the old city hall basement. Raise your hand for the cabin."

No hands went up.

"Right. The basement it is. We'll head out at first light. I'll take a watch on the entrance. Need somebody to watch the back." He nodded at Sean who raised a hand to volunteer. "The rest of you, get some sleep."

Allistor, having just slept about six hours as best he could tell, didn't feel like resting. He wanted to speak with Sam. Since the 'stabilization period' had started and the monsters began showing up, he had mostly huddled in his home with his family. There had been a few town meetings during the three-day countdown, mostly to talk about whether their situation was real, and to try and make some basic plans for survival. Nobody really had any idea what to expect.

Now, with some time on his hands, he wanted to compare notes with the marine to see what he could learn.

"Sam? Feel like some company? I was hoping we could talk."

"Sure, kid. Grab a seat." He indicated one of the 'stones' next to the one he was perched on. They were man-made, formed into a rough semicircle where people had sat to listen to Sandy and the other rangers give cave safety lessons before tours.

Allistor sat and got right to the point. "So, have you read all the info that they gave us in our interfaces? All the stuff about attributes, experience, and skills?"

Sam nodded. "Me and Meg, we went through it all. Been training a little bit. Killed enough monsters to make third tier so far."

Allistor was glad to hear it. "Level three," he corrected the older man. "And that's great! So, I sort of accidentally picked up a skill this morning. Weaponsmithing. I had to leave our house without any weapons and had to improvise. I made this." He handed the spear to Sam, who looked it over and handed it back. "It gave me the skill. I also got one for stabbing, and one for blunt weapons for using this thing as a club."

Sam turned his gaze to his wife. "Meg and I both got the Cooking skill on day one. Raised mine up to Apprentice level already. Had to feed all the folks who came to hang out at the diner to talk. The food we make gives bonuses to a few of those attribute things."

Allistor smiled at him. "Those are called buffs. They beef up… what? Stamina? Constitution?"

Sam nodded. "Those, and Health regeneration. And Meg can make a tea that increases Will Power."

"Sweet! If we ever have any casters, that'll come in handy."

Sam looked confused. "Casters?"

"Magic users. Wizards, Sorcerers, anybody who casts spells."

"Are you shittin' me? Wizards? C'mon, man. A lot has changed this week. Some freaky shit has happened for sure. Stuff I'd never have dreamed possible. But most of it has been aliens coming here. We humans seem pretty much the same. Are you trying to tell me that some of us can somehow magically do… well, magic?"

Before he answered that, Allistor asked, "Have you been doing anything to train yourself? Improve your stats at all?"

Sam shook his head. "Not so much. Your pop told us you and he were training to get stronger. I'm sorry he's gone, by the way. He was a good man."

Allistor did his best to keep the tears from his eyes as the crushing grief settled over him. He'd been on the move almost every moment since their deaths, and he hadn't taken time to deal with it. "Thanks. And yeah, it was his idea. I figured out that this new system the Collective has put us in works a lot like the VR games I've played all my life. So we focused on increasing attributes like Strength. Trained really hard every day."

He handed the spear back to Sam. "This is, was, standard rebar. Try and bend it."

Sam took it in both hands and tried to bend it. Though he was past his prime, his bulging biceps still showed through his shirt as he put some effort into it. Allistor took it back, set it across his knee, and bent the bar into a rough C shape.

Sam's eyes widened. "Holy shit, boy!" he reached out and took the bent spear. As if he thought it was some kind of trick, he tried to straighten the metal back out. Again, he failed. Allistor retrieved it and took a minute to work it back into shape.

"So… you're super strong? Just from training for a few days."

Allistor shook his head. "It was intense training. And I'm no superhero or anything. Currently, I'm about twice as strong as I was last week." He paused and let Sam absorb that. Continuing on, he said, "Now, back to

57

wizards. It stands to reason that just like I can develop Strength and Stamina, someone like my mom, who started with high Will Power and Intelligence stats, could develop them as well. And the most direct benefit of that is an improved ability to cast spells."

"Huh." Sam's eyes unfocused as he pulled up his stats. "My highest numbers are in Constitution and Strength."

Allistor said, "Have you been applying the attribute points you received when you leveled up each time?"

Sam shook his head, returning his focus to Allistor. "Nope. Me and Meg talked about it, but we didn't understand enough to know how to do it right. She figured better safe than sorry. You know about this stuff?"

"Yep. I mean, not this system exactly. I'm doing some guessing here. But it's a lot like other systems I've used. And I read as much as I could. At level three you should have six points available to assign. Two for each level. You see them?"

Sam took a moment, then confirmed he saw them. Allistor continued, "Okay, so you said you started with higher numbers in Strength and Constitution. If you want to be a melee sort of fighter going forward, somebody who can take and dish out a lot of damage, then you continue to put points into those attributes. On the other hand, if you wanted to become a wizard, for example, you'd start loading up Intelligence and Will Power."

Sam got the idea very quickly. The two of them talked for a while about the various attributes. Sean, who had been listening from across the room, joined them. He asked a few questions and listened while he watched the back of the cave. Allistor noticed a few others who were listening rather than sleeping. He and the others started speaking in normal voices rather than trying to be quiet. The more these people knew, the more likely they were to survive.

When he had them all caught up, he added a few twists. "So, getting the free points isn't the only way you can improve. My pop and I worked out nonstop for days, and I raised both my Stamina and my Strength by a point just from that. So what you do in the world now impacts who and what you are more than ever before. Pop's Constitution went up after he took a lot of hits from the octopoid in our basement and didn't die."

He looked around at the folks who were now obviously following the conversation. "Any of you pick up any skills like my *Weaponsmithing* or Sam's *Cooking*?" He knew about Nancy's skills, but he didn't feel it was his place to share them.

Sean raised a hand. "I got one called *Engineering* while I was working on the car."

A woman Allistor didn't know but vaguely recognized spoke up as well. "*First Aid.* I'm a physician's assistant. I wasn't doing anything in particular when the notice popped up."

Allistor thought about it for a second. "It might just be that you have the knowledge in your head, and the system recognized it. Or maybe… if you had helped some injured folks earlier, and they reached a certain level of healing? I'm not sure."

She seemed to agree with the last part of that. "Makes sense. Thank you."

A small woman in her fifties that Allistor hadn't even seen sitting behind Sandy raised a hand. "*Tailoring.* I was mending my husband's favorite jeans after a dog thing bit through the leg." She pointed at Allistor. "I can fix your clothes for you, if you like. It looks like many things have been chewing on you." She gave him a little smile, and Chloe giggled somewhere in the background.

Allistor grinned at her. "Indeed they have. Thank you. But I'm not sure they're worth the effort. I'll probably just replace these. I have no particular attachment to them... I'm sorry, I don't know your name."

"Mrs. Chen. You can call me Lilly." She had a kind smile that reminded Allistor of his mom. "And I'd like to try anyway. Like you said, the best way to level a skill is practice, right?"

Allistor nodded, conceding the point. "You're right. As soon as I find replacements, they're all yours."

Robert Edward shyly raised his hand. "I got one called *Reproduction*."

Sean scratched his head. "*Reproduction*, huh. Like making copies of stuff? What were you doing when you got the notice?"

When Robert Edward blushed, the physician's assistant snorted. "I think he means *Reproduction* like making more humans."

It took Sean a moment as everyone grinned at him. When he caught on, his eyes widened. "Oh. Oh! So you were... Ohhhhh." He winked at Robert Edward, who looked like he wanted to be pretty much anywhere else at that moment. Sandy gave him a good swat on the behind and a wink, making him blush even more deeply.

Allistor heard the faint voice of Chloe in the background asking, "What was he doing, Momma?" followed by a hushing sound from Nancy.

"Anybody else?" Sam asked, trying to hide his smile.

Nancy spoke up. "I've learned *Alchemy* and *Herbology*. From working in my garden."

Sandy raised her hand, still giving Robert Edward a flirty smile. "I have one called *Tracking*, and another called *Woodworking* that I got while making a walking staff." She put special emphasis on 'wood', never taking her eyes off Robert Edward. The man lowered his eyes and coughed.

When nobody else spoke up, Allistor said, "Nancy, you should speak with our resident doctor here. There should be a way the two of you can combine your skills to speed up healing or increase how much of a heal we get from bandages or potions and such. Maybe include Meg and Sam. The ingredients that give buffs to the food they make might help you as well. And vice versa."

Sam looked at his watch. "We can do that tomorrow, once we're someplace safe. For now, get some sleep folks. Maybe assign your attribute points now that we have a better idea what they do. We might need some boosts to get to safety tomorrow.

As the others laid themselves down or zoned out to mess with their attributes, Allistor took a spot in a corner behind the sitting stones. Out of sight of most of the group, he reached into his bag and removed the scroll he'd looted from Alan. Keeping it out of sight, he used *Examine* on it.

Scroll of Levitate
Item Quality: Uncommon
Single Use Item
Opening and reading the spell on this scroll will imbue upon the reader the knowledge of the

Levitate spell. This channeled spell will allow the caster to lift and move objects with magic. Can be cast on self or others. Higher skill levels will increase caster's control over the target. Length of spell depends on available mana pool.
Effectiveness and duration increase with higher Intelligence and Will Power attributes.

Allistor practically drooled as he read the description of the item.

His first instinct as a gamer was to open and read the scroll. *Levitation* was an awesome power. When cast on himself, with the proper control, he might be able to actually fly. Eventually. But he could do tons of other cool stuff as well.

When the initial rush of loot adrenaline subsided, he took a moment to reconsider. He had focused all of his attribute points on *Strength* and *Stamina* before that day. With his current stats, the spell would be wasted on him. Better to find someone with high *Intelligence* and *Will Power* and give it to them.

But what if that person didn't make it? Was it smart to potentially waste a valuable scroll on a practical stranger who might die tomorrow in the forest, or next week from some low-level monster? Maybe it was smarter to just hold onto it for now.

Thinking again about using it himself, he pulled up his stats. He'd started with a reasonably high (for a human) score of five in *Intelligence* on day one. And though his focus had been on developing his *Strength* and *Stamina*, raising each by a point through hard work, and assigning one free attribute point to each to bring them up to fours, *Intelligence* was still his highest stat, other than

Adaptability, which was at six. He'd also put one point in *Constitution* after seeing his father's health pool go way up when he'd raised that skill.

He began to think about scale. When it came to humans, and how they performed within the Collective's stat-based system, how good was an *Intelligence* of five? He and his father had figured out that a four in *Strength* was roughly twice the human norm. Did that mean his five in *Intelligence* made him two times smarter than the average bear? He didn't think so. And his *Will Power* score was still a three. So if he elected to go with a caster build, he'd need to raise that.

If he were honest with himself, his starting stats had favored a caster build, to begin with. He'd followed his father in developing his more physical aspects because the twos that he started with had seemed pitiful at the time. It was also a simple and clear way to test out ways to improve

Designation: Allistor	Level: 4	Experience: 520/15,000
Planet of Origin: UCP 382	Health: 250/250	Class: Unknown
Attribute Pts Available: 3	Mana: 50	
Intelligence: 5	Strength: 4	Charisma: 1
Adaptability: 6	Stamina: 4	Luck: 2
Constitution: 3	Agility: 3	Health Regen: 10/m
Will Power: 3	Dexterity: 3	Mana Regen: 5/m

himself.

Tempted to spend his three remaining points to raise his *Will Power* and *Intelligence*, he decided to hold off. He put the scroll away and leaned his back against the wall. Despite his extended nap earlier, it wasn't long before he fell asleep once again.

Chapter Four

No Place Like Home

Morning brought a bustle of activity. The group gathered all their supplies and prepared to set out for town. There was a brief discussion of staying in the caves, since nothing else had tried to attack during the night. But the arguments of the previous evening held, and none of the men who'd led the titan away had shown up. So the group set out.

Once again, Sandy led them on a straight path through the forest, avoiding the hiking path until just before they reached the footbridge that led across the river into town. There were a few gasps as they emerged from the trees and viewed the town. Most of them had been too busy running from the titan to get a good look at the extent of destruction the thing had caused. Not one building remained whole. They could still see the church steeple, but the rest of that structure was caved in. The water tower, strangely enough, was intact. Though one of its iron support legs was bent.

Chloe whimpered into her mother's shoulder. "Momma, it's all gone. Our house."

Nancy patted her back and hugged her close. "I know, baby. But we're going to find a new home. A nice safe one."

Sean and Robert Edward moved forward first, crossing the bridge and securing the other side. When they signaled it was clear, the others followed as quickly as they could. They gathered in the shadow of a brick wall - a remainder of what had been the elementary school.

Sam spoke just loudly enough for the others to hear over the sound of the river rushing by. "Alright. We make for City Hall. It's only three blocks. Keep low, and pay attention. There might be… what did you call them, Allistor? Mobs?" Allistor nodded once. "Mobs. Bad things. Call out if you see something. Try not to fire a weapon unless we have to. I don't want to attract every damn mob in town."

He and Allistor took the lead. Sam wielded a machete, while Allistor held his rebar spear. The others waited a few seconds, then followed along single file. Sean brought up the rear.

They skirted around the side of the elementary school, picking their way through the rubble past what had been a convenience store. Meg hissed at her husband and pointed toward the store. There were several cans of soda and plastic drink bottles scattered about. Sam nodded in understanding, and the group fanned out. They searched the rubble as best they could, grabbing anything intact that could be of use. Drinks, food, even some band-aids, air fresheners, a single cheap plastic flashlight and some batteries, and a couple of fake fire logs.

Chloe found quite a bit of candy and sweets, which her mother let her gather up, with a very quiet lecture on sharing with the others. They found a bunch of plastic bags to help carry their supplies and distributed the weight among the group.

Every time a plastic bag rustled as they moved along, Allistor found himself cringing and wishing for a bag of holding or inventory bag like he got in most RPG games. The kind that could store twenty or fifty items without adding weight. And didn't make any noise when you walked. He resolved to find a way to check out the 'open market' that the system info had spoken about. Maybe he could buy one there.

They approached City Hall from behind. There was a small park at the rear of the building, less than an acre of green grass with a gazebo, some mature trees, and a fountain in the middle. The building itself was surprisingly intact, compared to other buildings in town. It was clear the titan had stepped directly onto or into the three-story building. The entire center of it was obliterated, the roof completely gone, and sections of the interior burned out. But the stone walls on either end had remained. The east end wall was two stories high, the west end only one.

Unfortunately, the stairway leading down to lower levels was buried under a pile of stone and scorched wood.

Sam took a look, prodding at some of the debris with his foot. "It would take us days to move all of this. And I'm not sure it wouldn't collapse on us."

Meg was looking at the west wall. "I... remember there was an old coal furnace down there. And a coal chute. One of the kids tried to climb up in it and got all dirty." She had been walking toward the outside of the wall as she spoke. After a while, she pointed to a square section of the wall where the stone was a different color than the rest. "I'm pretty sure this is it."

Allistor nodded and stepped in front of her. He jammed the tip of his spear into the mortar between two of the stones. Levering it back and forth, he pried out some of it. Getting closer, he used the sharp point to scrape at the mortar. When he'd made a deep groove, he shoved the point in again and levered out a stone.

He stepped back so that Meg could take a look. Behind the stone was a metal plate. She tapped on it with a knuckle, and a hollow clank could be heard.

66

"Yep! I think this is it." She turned to smile at him. With one rock gone, Allistor was able to reach in and pull the others free with his bare hands. The noise had the others nervously searching the area while he worked. Within just a few minutes, he had exposed what they now could see was an iron door about three feet square. There must have once been a lever used to secure it and pull it open, but it had been removed when they covered the door with stone.

Allistor used his spear tip again, pushing it between the metal door and its frame where the lever had been. Prying it open caused the metal hinges to squeal so loudly that they all dropped into a crouch and held their breaths.

Not wanting to have to make the noise more than once, he continued. Grabbing it with both hands he yanked it all the way open. The rusted hinges protested but complied. A look inside showed a narrow metal shaft sloping down at a very steep angle. Allistor couldn't see the bottom. Coal dust tickled his nose.

The group waited in silence for a while, expecting some of the new monsters to appear. When none did, Sam stuck his head in the door and shined a flashlight downward. His voice echoed as he said, "It goes down maybe fifteen feet. I can't see anything but the floor right under the shaft."

"We don't have a rope. How are we going to get down there?" Sean asked.

Allistor grimaced. "Never go adventuring without a rope," he mumbled to himself.

Meg stepped forward and looked down the shaft. "I could shimmy down there without falling. I think," she offered.

Sam shook his head. "We don't know what's down there. And we'd have no way to bring you back up. We need a rope. Preferably a rope ladder."

"Hardware store's across town. Might find some rope there. I could go take a look?" Robert Edward offered.

Meg smiled at him but shook her head. "Can't have you wandering off alone." She thought for a minute. "There should be a ton of power cords and extension cords in this building. Maybe we can find enough to use?"

The entire group moved back into City Hall and began to poke around. The rooms up against the end walls were partially intact. They grabbed up anything that might be tied together to make a rope. In a custodian's closet, they found a plastic chair and a six-foot folding ladder. There were also several dozen rolls of toilet paper, which Meg took a few of with a grin. "This might be the best thing we've found all day."

They scooped up a few tools they found on a shelf and a can of spray lubricant. Sean grabbed that up. "For the hinges."

Five minutes later they were all back at the chute. Sam and Allistor began knotting cords together, using their improved strength to pull them tight and test them. Sean sprayed the hinges while the others watched and waited.

When they were done, they had nearly thirty feet of cord-rope. The two men played a quick game of tug-of-war to test whether it would hold. Meg volunteered again to go down. And again, Sam refused. "We're sending Sean. He's armed, and he knows how to clear a room." Sean nodded, and there was no argument, even from Meg.

Allistor anchored the makeshift rope around his waist, then dropped the rest of the coil down the shaft.

Robert Edward assisted Sean in getting his legs into the shaft, then gripped one arm as he took hold of the rope. When he felt secure, Sean let go of Robert Edward and began to lower himself down. The multiple knots gave him decent hand and footholds as he worked his way down.

In less than a minute, Allistor felt the tension on the line go slack. A whisper came up from below. "I'm down. Hang on."

They all waited anxiously as Sean explored the room below. Allistor actually jumped a bit when he called up. "All clear. Lots of junk down here, but there's enough room."

Meg, looking dubiously at the rope, called down in a loud whisper. "Any doors leading out?"

"Yeah. But both are blocked with furniture and crap."

Robert Edward stepped toward the shaft. "I can help him move that. I put a point in strength last night."

So they repeated the process, helping him into the shaft and down. While they waited for the two men below to try and find a way out, Allistor looked to Sam. "I can hold this while everyone else goes down, but…"

Sam nodded. "We need an anchor. Especially if this is going to be the only way up or down." He went back around the wall to poke around inside the building.

Five minutes later he returned carrying a six-foot length of broken wood beam. "We can tie onto this. Set it across the hole with one end stuck in the ground. It's sturdy enough."

There was a crash from below, and a cloud of coal dust erupted from the shaft. Everyone took a few steps back as the breeze pushed it away. Sean called up, "We're okay!" causing Meg to chuckle. There was another sound of creaking hinges, then silence.

The group up top shuffled around and fidgeted, anxious to hear what was going on. None dared call out, in case something non-human was alive down there. Several minutes passed, and then Sam stuck his head into the shaft. Allistor could see him clenching his fists, resisting the urge to call out. They hadn't heard anything that sounded like a battle, or screams of pain. So he held his tongue.

Allistor nearly shit himself when Sean walked around the corner of the building and called out, "Hey guys!" as he waved at them. He had a huge grin on his face, bright white teeth standing out from his coal-dust-covered face.

Meg threw a water bottle at him, cursing under her breath about giving old ladies a heart attack. The bottle bounced off his chest, and he caught it on the rebound. "Thanks!" After taking a swig and spitting it back out, he took a long drink.

"We found another way. Obviously. There's a stair that leads down to the jail level. From there, we found a tunnel. The other end comes out in the basement of the sheriff's office." He pointed in that general direction. The sheriff's office was situated next door to City Hall, on the side opposite of where they stood. "I worked there two years and didn't even know it *had* a basement. Anyway, the basement is still intact, and we found a way out."

Allistor quickly pulled the cord-rope up out of the shaft and closed the metal door. The hinges complained much less after having been lubricated. When he'd secured the rope over one shoulder, he nodded to Sean, who turned and led them around the back of the building

70

toward what had been the sheriff's office. As they walked, he said, "I have to warn you, it's kind of creepy down there. Smells, too."

As soon as he said that, Meg grabbed Sandy and the two of them ducked back into the city hall custodian's closet. The two ladies grabbed a mop and bucket on wheels and raided the shelves for various other cleaning supplies. Rejoining the group, Meg handed the heavy bucket full of bleach bottles and such to Allistor. She winked at him, saying, "It's handy having a strong young man around."

From the front of the group, Sam called back, "I heard that!" without turning around.

The group reached the entrance to their new home just a minute later. There was a pair of metal doors built into the ground at a forty-five-degree angle, like storm cellar doors you might find on a farm. One of the doors was open and stairs led downward. Sam turned on his flashlight and followed Sean down. He turned to Allistor on his way down. "Close that door behind us, and see if there's a way to bolt it shut."

One by one the group descended, Sam illuminating the stairs for them. Allistor closed the door behind himself, and sure enough, there was a simple slide bolt to lock them. Upon reaching the bottom of the stairs, he found they were in a very basic concrete-walled room with an old wood stove, a rough-hewn wooden table and chairs, and an empty rifle rack on the wall. In one corner was an eight-by-eight-foot holding cell with iron bars and two long benches, one against each concrete wall.

Sean led them through a door and into a tunnel cut right into the rock around it. The ceiling was high enough for everyone to walk upright, but the tunnel was only about three feet wide. They walked single-file, following the light in front. Allistor kept one hand on the wall to his left as a guide. The stone was rough and very, very dusty.

About fifty feet from the entrance, Sean stepped out of the tunnel into the large room filled with jail cells that Allistor remembered. It wasn't as large as he'd pictured it in his head, but he'd only been about ten years old last time he was here. And Sean wasn't kidding about the smell. It was a combination of old dust, mold, and maybe a rotting rat carcass or something.

There was a wide open space in the center of the room. Along the walls to his left and right were rows of cells. He quickly counted – each wall sported six cells. They were cut right into the stone, each with a wooden door that sported a single small window about five feet off the floor. In one corner was the bathroom that Meg had mentioned, complete with the antique pull-cord toilet with the tank mounted just below the ceiling. Meg was already moving toward it. She gave the chain an experimental tug, but nothing happened.

She looked at Sean. "Think you could get this working, Mister *Engineering*?"

The deputy shrugged. "I could check the pipes upstairs. Maybe it's just a simple matter of reconnecting it. If the water lines between here and the water tower aren't damaged, it should work fine."

Meg gave him a look, and said, "The sooner the better, young man."

Nancy and Chloe had lit half a dozen candles and placed them on the floor across the room, providing some light. Sean took Sam's flashlight and headed up the stairs to the next level, the one where they'd emerged from the coal chute.   They could hear him banging around up there a few moments later.

There was no furniture of any kind in the main room. But the cells each had a bench carved out of stone against the back wall. Nancy and the lady Allistor thought of as "Doc", began assigning cells and passing out blankets. There weren't enough for everyone, so Chloe and the ladies got priority.

Meg, Sandy, and Lilly were already pouring bleach on the floor and scrubbing at the stone. They recruited Robert Edward to assist them. Sandy handed him two empty one-gallon bleach bottles and sent him upstairs to find water. "Put those sexy muscles to good use."

With nothing much to contribute, Allistor returned back down the tunnel. He lifted the bulky table, turned it sideways, and carried it back down the tunnel. Then he returned for the chairs. Next, he tried the interior stairs leading up from the holding cell area to the sheriff's station. He got about halfway up before the pile of twisted metal and concrete blocked his way.

Not wanting to risk a cave-in by digging, he went back down and out the way they'd come in. Stepping into what was left of the ground floor of the station, he began to pick through the rubble looking for useful items.

He found six boxes of ammo for his shotgun, and several hundred rounds of .40 and 9mm – standard issue for most cops. He also found three more shotguns, though one of them was useless, the barrel bent.   He kept it anyway, in case one of them developed some skill in blacksmithing and could repair it. After some more digging, he found two battery-powered lanterns, a mostly intact first aid cabinet, a pair of pink furry handcuffs that he made a mental note to ask Sean about, several sets of black fatigues, and three big black duffel bags with the sheriff dept. logo on them. Filling them with all that he found, he took a few more minutes to search. He noted several chairs that were still intact and would be worth coming back for. And he found three thin, narrow foam mattresses that must have been in the holding cells up here. Not great, but better than sleeping on stone.

Just as he was about to leave, he spotted a shiny set of keys on the floor. Picking them up, he saw that they were car keys. A quick scan of the area showed him a patrol car half a block away. The front end was crushed, the engine block protruding from the hood. But the vehicle was still intact from the dashboard back.

Allistor grabbed the least-filled of the duffels and transferred its contents to the other two. Then he jogged over to the car, unlocked the trunk first, and nearly shouted for joy. Inside were two more shotguns, an AR-15 style rifle, two armored vests, several flares, six packets that each contained one of the light foil blankets, and ammo for each of the weapons. There was also an empty coffee thermos, and a pair of combat-style boots, size ten. Too small for Allistor, but somebody might be able to use them.

Cramming all but the vests into the duffel, he put one of the vests on and looped his arm through the other. Then he lifted the bag, returned to gather up the other two, and headed back downstairs with his loot.

He ran into Sam on his way down. The man took one look at him and began to laugh. "I was just coming up to do the same thing. Did you leave anything up there?

Allistor grinned. "Just big stuff. There are some chairs, a few mattresses, stuff like that. Let me drop this stuff off, and I'll come help." He continued through the tunnel and deposited everything on the table. Reaching into the duffel he'd filled from the trunk, he grabbed a handful of the blankets. "Nancy? Thought these might be useful. And we're bringing some furniture down next."

Seeing Chloe approaching, he added, "There are lots of guns in there."

Nancy took the hint and nodded her thanks. She was distracting the little girl with the shiny foil blankets when he left the room.

Back up top, he found Sam moving two of the mattresses over near the stairs. The two of them got to work hauling anything that looked useful. Twenty minutes later there were six more chairs, three mattresses, two sets of shelves, several crates that could be tilted on end and used as tables in the cells, one intact metal desk, and a second table all arranged in their new quarters.

Since there were more cells than people, Doc, who Allistor had learned was named Amanda, had commandeered one of them to be used as their medical facility. It was the one closest to the bathroom, which would hopefully also be their water supply. She had them place the extra table in there to be used as a bed for patients. At least until they could find a better one. She set up the first aid cabinet, rolled in one of the chairs, and declared their "ER" open for business.

Sean came back downstairs and was instantly greeted by Meg. "Well?"

He smiled and shook his head. "It'll take some work to get this one running again." He paused to take in the disappointed look on her face. "But don't worry. We found a working bathroom up there. There's no light, so take a candle with you. There's a mop sink up there too…"

Meg had a candle in hand and was dashing up the stairs before he'd even finished talking. Nancy and Chloe drifted up the stairs behind her. Sean went to examine the pipes above the toilet.

It was approaching noon, and Allistor's stomach reminded him he hadn't eaten much since the day before. He'd snacked on a jerky stick from the convenience store as they walked, but that was it. He was reaching into his bag, an old backpack he'd grabbed out of habit as he evacuated his house the morning before, when he noticed the shelves had been stocked with food and drink.

Putting his bag back on his back, he helped himself to a candy bar, another stick of jerky, and a bottle of water. There wasn't much in the way of real food in a convenience store, especially if one didn't have a microwave.

He took a seat at the table and tried to relax as he ate. Amanda joined him, snacking on a bag of sour cream and onion chips and a soda. When she saw what he was eating, she grinned. "Not exactly the breakfast of champions."

"Yeah. Hopefully this afternoon we can find some real food. Maybe a few intact refrigerators or basement freezers. Though without power, nothing will last long. We're going to need to start hunting for food. Or raising livestock."

"Or maybe buy some on this 'open market' the system info mentions," Amanda added.

Meg joined them, taking a break from cleaning. "We need a way to cook. Maybe a propane stove? Or somebody's grill? There's got to be at least a few intact propane tanks around."

Allistor nodded. "I'll make that my next priority. We've got enough bottled water for a few days, and running water upstairs, for now. This junk food will last us a couple days too. But we are going to need real food ASAP. We had a grill behind my house. It's not far. I'll check there first."

His meal complete, he hefted his spear and headed out. Checking in with Sam on the way, he told him roughly where he'd be scavenging. Sam nodded. "Be careful out there. You're the highest level among us right now, but those monsters are no joke."

Allistor exited the cellar doors behind the sheriff's office and turned west. He moved as quietly as he could, using debris piles as cover. His family home was only a short walk from City Hall. Actually, everything in the town proper was a short walk. The entire town was only about a dozen blocks long. Most of the citizens lived out on farms or one of the three subdivisions that had sprouted up between the town and the interstate.

Main Street consisted of mostly retail spaces. City Hall and the sheriff's office were near the center of town, and there was the library at one end. The rest of Main Street had been restaurants, a coffee shop, bakery, florist, three bars, a bookstore, a mom and pop grocery, department store, hardware store, a music shop that sold both records and instruments, a feed store, a used car dealership, two gas stations (one on either end of town), and several empty buildings.

On the blocks off Main Street, there had mostly been homes on quarter to half-acre lots with old oak trees and green lawns. Old homes built in the early 1900s when the town was growing. Some had been replaced over the years, but many were craftsmen homes, built to last. Mixed in were a couple of small parks, schools, and

77

assorted businesses like the convenience store they'd already looted.

Allistor noticed for the first time that few of the trees had been damaged. It was as if the titan had been programmed to target man-made structures and leave the natural features intact.

He passed behind the former car dealership on his way home. Most of the vehicles on the lot had been crushed or flipped over. But a couple pickups and an old Mustang looked intact. More importantly, he spotted a flatbed trailer on the back lot. With two axles and a ramp that folded off the back, the thing was capable of carrying the weight of a car. Allistor thought about all the heavy objects he wanted to retrieve – the grill, some beds, or at least mattresses, maybe a couple of chest freezers. The trailer would allow him to make one trip.

Testing his strength, he lifted the hitch on the front end and tried to pull the trailer forward. It resisted initially, then slowly began to move. Once he got it going, it wasn't much of an effort to pull it behind him. Of course, things would be different with more weight on it. And it was awkward walking backward. Especially when he needed to keep an eye out for mobs.

What he needed was a harness of some kind.

Poking around in the rubble of the dealership, he found a pile of old tire chains. And a set of jumper cables. He also found a metal box full of car keys with numbered tags. He set that aside where he could find it again, planning to spend some time finding the keys for the working vehicles. He would have preferred to use one of the trucks to pull the trailer, but until they knew more about the monsters roaming the town, he didn't want the sound of an engine attracting attention.

Taking the chains with him back to the trailer, he took about ten minutes to improvise a sort of harness by hooking them to the frame of the trailer and creating two loops. He could slide his arms through those loops and hitch them over his shoulders. In this manner, he could pull the thing walking forward, even lean into it to decrease the strain on his back.

You have learned the skill: Improvisation
Finding a creative way to use materials found in the wild to improvise a useful tool has unlocked the Improvisation skill. Your high Adaptability attribute provides a 20% bonus to skill level advancement.

Allistor pulled the trailer with him, moving slowly and maneuvering around the debris in the road. It took another ten minutes to reach what was left of his home. He dropped the chains and left the trailer in the street out front. Then he walked up the driveway, stepping carefully over a shattered roof truss and piles of broken bricks.

First things first. He needed to look for his parents' bodies. He knew where his mother should be. She'd been in the yard next to the tree, having just fled out the front door with Allistor. A splintered two-by-four propelled by the force of the titan's kick had impaled her from behind. The wound was instantly fatal, and he didn't think she'd felt much pain.

Despite the giant monster bearing down on them, he had turned and stared in shock, his body frozen in place. He heard his father's anguished shout as he called out his wife's name. Turning from his mother, he found his father just in time to see him crushed by a huge section of the two-story front wall of their brick house. The moments after that were mostly a blank for Allistor. He'd eventually turned and fled, one among many as his frantic neighbors joined him.

Standing under the oak tree in the center of his front yard, he stared at the ground. The only sign of his mother was a patch of blood-stained grass. There were paw prints in the bloodied soil. Tears rolled down his face as he imagined his mother's corpse being consumed by monsters.

Moving to the still mostly intact wall that had crushed his father, he debated with himself. The bricks formed an effective burial mound, and there was no evidence they had been disturbed. He said a quick prayer over his father's grave and stepped away.

Allistor walked into the devastated structure. Nothing taller than six feet remained intact. Turning to look at the street, he could see the cone-shaped dispersal pattern of all the bits of his house that had been launched outward as the titan lifted its foot and stepped forward.

Turning toward the back of the house, he was pleased to find his father's gas grill still intact on the rear patio. He stepped through the debris to retrieve it, wheeling it around the side of the house and loading it onto the trailer. Next, he went to their shed, which sat at the back of their yard, and was still mostly intact. Some incidental contact from the titan had made it lean drastically to one side.

He grabbed everything useful from inside the shed. Several lengths of rope, his father's tools and workbench with clamps, more lengths of chain. There were boxes of nails and screws, and a hydraulic nail gun, which he left behind. He grabbed a full-sized axe and a hatchet, as well as a gas-powered chainsaw. When he lifted that, he had visions of slicing through the titan's tendons and making the thing fall on its face.

Once he had loaded all those items onto the trailer, he went back to the house. He found most of the kitchen was smushed flat. The titan had stepped directly on top of that room. The doorway to the basement was gone, but after he cleared some debris, he found the stairs still intact. Moving downward, he sighed in relief. The basement was nearly untouched. Still in disarray after the octopoid's rampage, but undamaged by the weight of the titan. The only visible damage was a foot of water from leaking pipes above. He made a mental note to organize a group to turn off all the water valves in town.

Descending into the water, he waded over to his highest priority item. The gun safe. His father was a collector of rifles and shotguns. The safe was three feet wide and seven feet tall. Inside were two racks, upper and lower, filled with weapons. A shelf under each held boxes of ammunition. More ammunition was stacked on top of the safe.

Laying an old blanket out on the even older sofa, he began to stack the weapons. Then he rolled up the blanket and used some twine to tie it into a bundle. While he had the twine, he looped some around his spear near both ends, the line between allowing him to sling it over his shoulder, almost like a bow. The ammo all went into his father's old footlocker. Grabbing the footlocker by its end handle with one hand, and with the bundle of weapons under his other arm, he began to ascend the stairs.

Just two steps up, he froze. A snuffling sound from above came to him. Followed by the sound of shifting debris in the kitchen. He stood completely still, holding his breath as he listened. The snuffling grew closer. If something had caught his scent, it would appear at the stop of the stairs any second.

He very carefully retreated down the one step he'd already climbed, then quietly set down the chest and bundle. Unfortunately, the rifles clacked together inside the bundle as he set them down, and a startled growl echoed down from above. He quickly unslung his spear and held it at the ready.

A canine head with a bloody snout appeared at the top of the steps. Standing in the sunlight, Allistor doubted it could see him well in the comparative darkness of the basement. He took a second to Examine it.

Canid
Level 4
Health 650/650

It was basically a wolf, but with six legs. Comparative in size to a Siberian wolf, its shoulders stood about waist high to Allistor. The beast's entire body bulged with muscle. Its eyes were crystal blue with red irises, the color combination giving him chills as he stared at the thing.

A low growl grew in the canid's chest, getting louder as it crouched low and bared its fangs. Allistor's pulse raced and his mouth went dry as the canid took a step forward, beginning a slow creep down the stairs above him. He raised his spear and spoke to it.

"Are you the one that ate my mom? Is that her blood? You're gonna pay for that. Come get me!"

Allistor jabbed the spear in the monster's direction, knowing it was well out of range. He wanted to show it he wasn't afraid, though he very much was. He thought he remembered something about dogs being able to sense fear. And he didn't want to give it the satisfaction.

The growl increased to a slavering snarl as it took another step down. Now only eight steps separated the two combatants. The canid sprang forward, jaws aimed directly for Allistor's head. He managed to dodge to one side and club the flying wolf-thing with the butt end of his spear. It yelped in pain as it flew past him and splashed into the water.

Faster than Allistor would have imagined possible, it was back on its feet and lunging at him. He didn't have time to dodge, and it barreled into him. The canid's forepaws struck his chest, driving him back to fall against the stairs. He managed to get his spear between him and the thing's chest, holding back its snapping jaws.

Still, it clawed at his legs with its back and middle sets of feet, trying to find purchase to push forward and eat his face. He heard his jeans rip and felt his flesh tearing under the onslaught. His health bar decreased by about twenty percent.

Planting one elbow against the stair beneath him, he used the spear to lever the thing to one side as he pushed himself up. The canid crashed against the stair railing, causing it to crack and give way as it and the beast fell over into the water.

This time, the canid was slower to recover as its legs were tangled in the railing's balusters. Allistor regained his feet and stabbed at the canid's face with the spear. It managed to pull its head to one side, leaving the spear to puncture its shoulder instead. Making the most of the strike, Allistor twisted the metal, the sharpened threads of the rebar tearing at muscle as he ripped it free. The canid yelped and tried to retreat, its legs still fouled by the railing.

Allistor leaped from the bottom step, turned the spear and swung it like a club down onto the thing's skull. The blow pushed its head underwater, stunning it briefly. That was all Allistor needed. He reversed the spear again and drove the point down into its neck right below its left ear. Using his weight, he pressed down, pushing the point deeper into its flesh and holding its head below the water. "This is for my mom!" he growled at the creature as he pressed downward.

The canid thrashed weakly, concussed, losing blood and unable to breathe. Allistor held it in place until it stopped moving altogether and a green *+3000* flashed on his interface. He also got a notification that he'd increased his blunt weapon skill by one point.

Breathing hard, he tried his best to be still and listen for any other mobs above. Canids were known to move in packs. He looked down at himself as he listened. His legs and belly were bleeding profusely from dozens of long scratches. A blood stain was pooling around him, his blood mingling with that of the canid.

After half a minute with no sounds from above, he bent to loot the wolf. He received thirty klax, a wolf pelt, four pieces of canid meat, and a set a canid fangs.

Unsure how to stop the bleeding, he sat down on one of the steps and began ripping his already tattered shirt into strips. He tied several of them around his legs over the top of the scratches, trying to restrict the blood loss. By the time he was done, his health bar was down to sixty percent, still ticking downward due to the bleed debuff, and he was starting to feel weak. He pulled a piece of jerky from his bag and took a few bites. Allistor hoped this new Earth was like his games, and eating would heal him more quickly.

After ten minutes, he felt better. Though his makeshift bandages were soaked through, he didn't see any blood dripping anymore. Bending to lift just the bundle of weapons, he walked it to the top of the stairs before returning to retrieve the chest of ammo. Back on the ground level, he set the bundle atop the chest and lifted both, walking slowly out to the trailer. When they were securely stowed, he took some time to look around again. He noticed as he stood there that his health bar was moving slowly back toward full on its own. He was now at eighty percent health.

Where the garage used to be, he found the chest freezer they stored their meat and ice cream in. It was still closed and latched, though one side was dented. It had been a full day since the power went out, but Allistor figured if the freezer had remained closed, the meat inside should still be good. Opening it, he quickly pulled out the melted canisters of ice cream. A few pokes at the meat on top showed it to still be mostly frozen. He closed and latched the freezer.

Looking around in the debris, he found an old metal hand truck. Sliding it under the freezer, he tilted it up and wheeled it out to the trailer. Not having the strength to lift the full freezer, he put down the ramp and wheeled it up on the hand truck. Stowing both safely in the middle of the trailer bed, he folded up the ramp and sat down. The sun had moved across the sky, and he estimated it to be about three o'clock. As he thought about the time, a clock appeared on his interface, the numerals stating it was 2:38 pm.

Resigned to the job ahead of him, Allistor took a deep breath and got back to his feet. He moved to the front of the trailer and donned the chain harness. When he leaned into the chains and pushed with his legs, nothing happened. He backed up a step, then lunged forward, the chains jerking taught as he strained to get some momentum. The trailer rocked forward slightly, then settled back again.

Turning to face the trailer, he crouched down and grabbed hold of the hitch. Leaning back, he pushed with his legs while pulling with his arms and torso. This time the trailer moved slightly, rolling toward him. He backpedaled, pulling with all he had until the trailer was rolling steadily. Then he let go, turned back again, and picked up the slack as he pulled against the harness, keeping the momentum going.

Slowly but surely, he kept the load moving as he threaded his way back the same way he'd come. When he left the street to cut across the grass behind City Hall, the soft earth slowed his progress. But he dug in and kept pulling until the trailer reached the cellar doors of their new shelter.

With his stamina nearly drained, he unhitched himself and sat on the stairs. Producing a water bottle from his pack, he took a few big swallows and leaned back on his elbows. As he was resting, Sam appeared from the tunnel.

"Hey, Allistor. I was just going out to look for you. We gathered all the food we could from the diner, but it wasn't much. Some hot dogs, prepackaged pies…"

When Allistor grinned at him, he stopped talking. "What?"

"I found some stuff. Anybody else down there that could help unload? I'm kinda beat." He jerked a thumb over his shoulder. Sam climbed a few of the stairs and looked at the trailer loaded with salvaged items.

"You... pulled that thing? From where?" Sam's mouth hung open.

"Found it at the car lot. Pulled it to my house. That part was easy. After I loaded it up, well that was not so easy."

"No shit." Sam shook his head. "I'll fetch the others. Be right back."

Two minutes later, Sam returned with Robert Edward, Meg, Sean, Amanda, and Lilly. They all made astonished noises as they saw the load and realized what Allistor had done. When Meg opened the freezer, she started to laugh. Looking at Sam, she said, "Get that grill and this freezer down there first. We need to cook all of this meat right now before it goes bad. This is... this is two weeks' worth of food for all of us if we mix in some vegetables and things."

Allistor sat and watched as the group unloaded everything and moved it inside. The hand truck was a big help when moving the freezer down the stairs.

When Sean lifted the still-dripping bundle of weapons, he gave Allistor a disappointed look. "All of these will have to be cleaned now."

Allistor shrugged. "Yeah, I'm sorry. The basement was flooded, and a canid attacked me as I was bringing those up the stairs. I dropped them in the water."

Sean looked at the shredded condition of Allistor's front and nodded. "No worries. We can share the work. Have them all cleaned and ready by morning."

Ten minutes later, the trailer was empty, and everyone was inside. Amanda had returned to demand he come to the medical bay and get looked at. "We don't want any of those getting infected. Though they already look like they've been healing for days."

"Yeah, it seems like my health bar fills up more quickly than I actually heal. Like, I'm at one hundred percent now, and these wounds have closed, the bleeding stopped. But the scars are still healing. And when I lose a lot of blood, it takes a while to replenish, even after my health shows one hundred percent."

"We'll figure it out." Amanda patted his shoulder. "Just like everything else."

Not wanting to be surprised by any more monsters for the day, Allistor closed and barred the metal doors. As soon as he did, another message popped up on his interface.

Congratulations! You have created and secured a Stronghold.

A secure Stronghold is vital to survival. Claiming a property as a Stronghold prevents any new monsters from spawning within its boundaries. In addition, the structure itself can be improved to increase its defense rating, resource production, and available facilities. Facilities may include sleeping quarters, dining hall, kitchen, market interface, tavern, merchant shops, defensive weapon emplacements, et cetera.

Would you like to claim this Stronghold? Yes/No

He looked at Amanda. "Are you seeing this?"

"Seeing what?"

"The system is offering me a chance to claim this place as a stronghold. Like a home base. Keeps mobs from spawning inside, among other things."

"Well, hell yes! What are you waiting for?" She put her hands on her hips and looked at him as if he were stupid.

"I'm... I mean, nobody elected me boss or anything. I'm no leader. I'm not sure I should be the one to claim this place."

She continued to stare at him, making him feel like a child who insisted Santa Claus was real. "It was your idea to come here. You're the highest level of any of us so far. And you've just brought us two weeks' food and the means to cook and store it."

When he didn't respond, she turned and shouted down the tunnel, "Hey, guys! Anybody get that message about making this place a stronghold?"

"What!?" Several voices echoed back down the tunnel. Followed by footsteps. A minute later most of the group joined them. All but Nancy and Chloe, who volunteered to watch over the grilling.

Sam asked, "What's this about a stronghold?"

Allistor filled them all in, reading the message that was still displayed on his interface.

Amanda jumped in as soon as he was done. "He's concerned that he's not the one to claim it. Doesn't think he's leader material."

Meg snorted. "Just do it, Allistor. For one thing, I trust you. I think everyone here does, too. You took the time to save Nancy and Chloe, fighting monsters in a tunnel when you could have just kept running. Coming here was your idea, and it was a good one." She waited while heads nodded. "You are the one teaching us how this new world works, and you're the only one who got the message. So clearly the system thinks you've done something to merit your own stronghold."

Sam added, "It may be that we can create more strongholds in the days to come. Or expand this one so that the whole town becomes one. But for tonight, I'll rest a lot better knowing no beasties are going to appear in my cell and murder me in my sleep."

Allistor grinned, feeling better about the choice. He mentally clicked "Yes" on his interface. Then all hell broke loose.

Horns sounded out of nowhere, scaring the pants off of everyone. A golden glow surrounded them, the floors, walls, and ceiling all going nearly transparent. Meg grabbed hold of Sam's arm to steady herself as the others lifted their feet one at a time as if to reassure themselves the floor was still there. Chloe's squeal and Nancy's voice echoed from the tunnel, "What the hell is happening?"

Meanwhile, Allistor's interface was flooded with new information. There was a screen with basic stronghold summary information. Name – which was blank – rough size, number of people, and rough resource listing. At the bottom were a bunch of tabs for detailed descriptions.

"Whoa!" Allistor said. "This is like a guild management tab for guild leaders. It's asking me for all kinds of information." He was mentally poking at tabs as he spoke. The others looked at him, waiting for more information.

Meg bit her lip for about half a minute, then with a slightly snarky tone, asked, "I see. Anything in there about why this place is suddenly see-thru?"

Allistor was hitting tab after tab looking for precisely that. When he opened the *Physical Structure* tab, his eyes widened. After a quick read through the information, he said, "It looks like I can change the structure of this place. Move it above ground or deeper underground. Add walls, buildings, assign spaces. All of it costs something called system points. And I have the ability to open a market interface. It says we can sell resources for system points to make improvements."

The questions started rolling in all at once. "What kind of buildings? What resources? Can you build a decent bathroom with a shower?" That last one had been Meg.

Allistor was feeling a little overwhelmed. He sat down on the opaque stairs behind him, causing a few of the others to flinch for a second as if worried he'd fall through. He was mumbling to himself as he read through the list of facilities available and their point cost. "I wish I could share this with all of you, so I don't have to read it all off."

As soon as he said it, another tab opened. It was an authorization screen.

Do you wish to allow other citizens to access the Stronghold interface? Yes/No

He instantly selected "Yes" and another message popped up.

Please list the citizens you wish to authorize and indicate their access level.

A list of all the people inside the stronghold popped up. Next to them were columns of boxes. The first column was labeled *Review Only*. The next columns from left to right were *Review and Recommend, Review and Modify,* and *Full Authority.*

When he read these choices to the others, Meg was first to speak. "Just mark all of us for the recommend one. Can't have everybody making changes and spending points all willy-nilly. We need to agree as a group and have one person make any changes. Anybody got a problem with that?"

When nobody spoke up, Allistor checked the *Review and Recommend* boxes for everybody but Chloe, whom he wasn't sure could even read yet. When that was done, he said, "How 'bout we go take seats at the table and review these choices?"

They all filed back into the tunnel and returned to the main room. The furniture had not faded out like the rest of the structure, and it looked kind of funny just hovering in space. Nancy was moving the half-dozen burgers that were on the grill onto a paper plate and turning off the grill as Amanda filled her in.

When they were all at the table, the discussion began.

Allistor started it off. "Okay, it says here on the summary tab that we currently have one hundred thousand system points that we earned by creating the stronghold. Then there's a listing for *Possible Individual Contributions.* I don't know the source for those, but it says there's another six thousand and change available.

Lilly spoke up. "I'll start checking on that. Keep going. I can multitask."

Allister smiled at her and continued. "Thank you, Lilly. Let's tackle some easy stuff first. We need to name this place. Do we want to go with the town name? Or if you guys plan to create individual strongholds, we can go with a different name."

Meg shook her head. "I have no plans for my own stronghold. Though I'd eventually like my own house, if we can expand this place. But I don't want to use the town name, either. This town died along with most of the people that made it what it was. This is a new world, with new rules. I say we find a new name."

Nancy raised a hand. "I second that. Everybody?" They all raised a hand, and the vote was unanimous. Even Chloe's hand went up, though she looked confused as to why.

Sean spoke next. "Not to derail things, but those burgers smell amazing, and I'm starving. Can we eat while we talk?"

Meg and Sam jumped up. They had located some unopened loaves of sliced bread and buns, along with bottles of ketchup, mustard, and relish. There were also two tall stacks of paper plates that they'd used for catering and some plastic ware. In moments they'd set the table and began passing out warm burgers for everyone.

"Alright," Allistor said around a delicious mouthful of beef. "I'm open to suggestions for the name. Maybe *New Haven* or *Base Camp*? Or... anything that doesn't have a number like UCP 382 or whatever they're calling earth now."

Sam snorted. "How 'bout *Terra*"? We call this place something that'll piss them off."

Nancy shook her head. Looking at Chloe as she spoke. "I understand your anger, but I don't think purposely pissing them off is wise. We're trying to survive here."

Chastened, Sam nodded his head. "Sorry."

Lilly offered, "I've always liked the word *Utopia.*"

A few around the table nodded their heads. Sean wasn't one of them. "This place is far from that. At least, so far. Since we're underground, how 'bout something like *The Anthill* or *The Warren*?"

"Warren! Like the cozy houses where fluffy bunnies live! I like that!" Chloe clapped her hands together.

Everyone looked at each other and sort of shrugged. Allistor smiled at Chloe. "The Warren it is, then." He mentally filled in the name next to the appropriate prompt. The interface updated accordingly.

Sean, showing his bent toward *Engineering*, went next. "Speaking of underground, I'm thinking that for now at least, we should keep this place underground. If that titan is still walking around, having the only standing building in town would make us an obvious target. And we wouldn't have to spend points on walls. That way we can maximize what we build down here. We can always move above ground later."

Meg agreed. "As long as we can build all we need down here, that's fine with me."

Lilly cried "Aha!" then looked embarrassed as everyone stared at her. Blushing slightly, she said, "I figured out the contributions thing. It seems that we can contribute by converting our experience points into system points at a rate of two to one. That's one system point for every two experience points. The max experience points we can trade is the amount we've earned toward our next level. And the contributions can be structured as a donation or a loan."

"Awesome. That explains a lot. Thank you, Lilly."
Allistor thumped the table with a flat hand. He was
beginning to get into this whole base building thing.
"Okay, so for now, let's just focus on the points we already
have. I don't want to ask for contributions yet. I think we
all need to level ourselves as quickly as possible. And
there has to be a way for this place to earn its own points.
We just have to figure out what that is."

He smiled as he saw Lilly's eyes go vacant again.

He located the tab *Available Plans* that listed the
possible structures and their cost. Calling everyone else's
attention to it, he waited while they all reviewed the
options. He sincerely wished they had pencils and papers
to make lists of their own. Then a thought occurred to him.

"Hey guys, I want to test something. Look near the
top left, where the *Underground* option is listed. If you
would, everybody but Sam and Sean, check that box. You
two, check the *Surface Structure* box.

He watched his own interface as they all did as he
requested. As each person voted, the number of votes for
each would increase. They were color coded yellow, which
according to the key at the bottom of the screen, was for
recommendations.

"Can you all see this?" he asked.

Amanda chuckled. "That's cool. The votes show
up next to each choice. That'll make things easier,
especially if we ever expand to a much larger group. We
won't have to gather everyone together and count hands."

Allistor leaned back in his chair, relaxing slightly.

"Okay, folks. There are a few things we have to
have, that I think we all agree on." He mentally ticked the

boxes as he read them off, so the others could follow along. "We need a clean water source. When I went to my house, the broken pipes had flooded the basement. I assume every building in town is hemorrhaging water as well. Unless we cover the whole town and shut off all the water meters, the supply in the tower won't last long. The cost listed for water is five thousand points." The others all nodded their heads or made agreeable noises.

"Next, we need places to sleep. Each sleeping quarters costs two thousand points. I say we make a dozen for now. There are ten of us here now, but we may find other survivors. And I'm guessing Sam and Meg will pair up? Same with Nancy and Chloe?" Both pairs nodded again.

"So that's twenty-nine thousand points spent. As somebody who, as Chloe put it, keeps letting things bite me... I would also suggest a proper infirmary. That's four thousand. We need a kitchen, obviously. And cold storage for all that meat and whatever other food we can find. Together those are also four thousand. We can make the kitchen bigger later if we need to."

He looked around the table. Nobody was speaking up or making faces at him. "Please guys, if you have opinions, speak up. Especially if you disagree."

When he got nothing but amused grins in response, he kept going. "Okay, since several of us have picked up skills, and I expect will pick up more – I got a new one called *Improvisation* today, by the way – I suggest a crafting hall. If it's anything like I expect, there will be workbenches and such inside for us to use to improve our skills. And trust me, we're going to want to improve them. Make weapons, better armor, healing salves, and such. The cost is a little high - ten thousand points - but I think it would pay off."

Sam spoke up. "I agree, but can we set that one as an option? I want to make sure this place is secure first and foremost. I mean, in theory, we could just sit at this table and craft if we had to, at least to start with. Right?"

"Good point, sir!" Allistor was thrilled to have input. "We'll save that as an option if we have the points. And since you brought it up, let's look at available defenses."

They all took a minute to look over the options. Allistor favored *Reinforced Gates*, which said it provided strong, lockable gates with a set amount of defense points, which could be increased at will by upgrading with system points. There was also an option called *Proximity Alert* that he suspected were sensors that would warn them if beasties approached.

After it seemed everyone had made their choices, he reviewed the boxes that were checked. Everyone had selected *Reinforced Gates*. *Proximity Alert* was third most popular after one called *Escape Hatch* that he had skipped over when he was reading. He quickly found and read the description. It provided a 'back door' with a secret exit in case the Stronghold was overrun. After that, fourth place went to *Traps*, which allowed the installation of traps inside and outside the gate.

"Okay, has everybody finished choosing?" He looked around the table and got a chorus of yeses. "Right. Then in order of popularity, the first three cost ten thousand, ten thousand, and twelve thousand. *Traps* is five thousand. There are some other votes, but only singles and doubles. So if we go with all of those, that's thirty-seven thousand, plus the thirty-seven thousand we already assigned, for a total of seventy-four of the hundred thousand we have available. Not bad." He grinned at the group.

Sandy, the park ranger, asked, "Is electricity an option?" Immediately, they all began searching.

"Yes!" Meg shouted. Then her shoulders sagged. "But damn, it's expensive. Twenty thousand."

"It might be worth it," Amanda argued. "I mean, think of all the things we could salvage that run on electricity. Refrigerators, lights, battery chargers for radios and lanterns, sewing machines, power tools, and I could maybe salvage some medical equipment like an x-ray machine or ultrasound eventually."

By the time she was done, everyone seemed in agreement. But Allistor wasn't ready to pull that trigger yet.

"Let's assume that's our top choice for now. But I want to do more research. Like, how quickly we can earn more points. And what else we might not be thinking of right now." He looked around the table before his gaze rested on Meg. "For example, has anyone looked to see if the sleeping quarters include bathrooms or showers?"

"Oh, shit. No, I didn't. Anyone else?" Meg looked around, then her gaze went blank as she started her own research.

Lilly raised her hand. "I've been reading about the system points. It seems that there are a few ways for a Stronghold to earn them. The most popular seems to be through the sale of resources. Like, we could sell a few of the weapons you brought back. Or some of the meat. The points earned depend on the value of the item. But it's a one-to-one exchange rate with klax. So you can also just purchase system points directly with Stronghold treasury funds. And before you ask, we have zero treasury funds right now." She paused for a moment, looking at her interface.

98

"Okay, another way is by defending against attacks. If something, or several somethings, or *someone* attacks us and we kill them, then we get the usual experience points, and the Stronghold gets the same number of system points. We get a lesser number of points if we drive them away." She looked at them and added, "Yeah, this includes if other humans attack us. Or any sentient aliens after the stabilization is over."

She let that sink in for a moment, then moved on. "There's also skill improvements. If one of us improves a crafting skill, for example, while we're inside this place, it will earn some system points. More if one of us discovers a new recipe, creates a legendary weapon, invents a new gadget, that kind of thing. There is a formula I don't yet understand."

Meg waited for her to finish, then added. "Yes, each of the sleeping quarters comes with a main room, one bedroom with a bathroom and choice of tub or shower. There are two-bedroom quarters that cost an extra thousand and still only have one bathroom. Also, you can add kitchens and other rooms, most cost a thousand each."

Allistor thought about it for a minute. "Alright, two things. First, regarding the sleeping quarters. Let's just say that the stronghold will provide the basic quarters, one bed and a bath. If an individual wants to do so, they can pay for it themselves. Any objections?"

Nobody spoke up, so he moved on. "Right. Next, I think we should take some more time for research. I propose we go with the choices we've made, saving both the electricity and the crafting hall as options for now. I'll execute the seventy-four thousand worth of options, and we'll all spend the evening thinking and reading. I intend to look at the value of selling some of our items and whether it's a good trade. And get familiar with the pricing of things on the open market. My guess is, there will be things we can salvage that will be rare or unique to the market and might fetch pretty good prices." He watched as dollar signs began to twinkle in the others' widening eyes.

"Then, first thing in the morning, we'll get together and see what info everyone can add before making more hard decisions." He raised his hand. "This time I'm gonna need input from everybody. Sound like a good plan?"

Every hand at the table went up. Allistor turned his focus to his interface and executed their first choices. The reinforced gates, back door, sensor system, traps, clean water source, dozen sleeping quarters, kitchen and cold storage, and infirmary.

A bold red prompt asked him if he was sure about those choices. When he clicked on "Yes" the golden glow returned to the floor, walls and ceilings. The lines began to blur and shift, and Allistor wasn't the only one who began to feel a little woozy. Amanda had her eyes shut tight and had a death grip on the table. Meg was once again holding onto Sam. Chloe crawled into Nancy's lap and scrunched her eyes tightly closed as Nancy held her.

When it was all over, the place looked nothing like it had before. It was as if the system had hollowed out a small underground town. They sat in the middle of a large open circle next to a small fountain. A cavern had been hollowed out around them, with a twenty-foot-high domed ceiling. Around them stood several small stone buildings with doors and windows.

To his right, Allistor saw a ramp that sloped up to the familiar-looking metal cellar doors. Only now they were much larger and thicker, and they stood upright at a ninety-degree angle from the floor. There was some kind of natural light, but no source was evident. He looked at

Amanda and said, "Well, that solves the light issue. No lanterns needed."

The group began to fan out and explore the buildings. Those closest in around the edge of the circle turned out to be the kitchen, which came with a dining area sized for about twenty people and the cold storage walk-in; the infirmary with a waiting area, an office, three exam rooms, a triage area and some storage; and two bathrooms, one with a bathtub and one a shower. In between them was a small octagonal building with a window on each surface. The market interface.

Behind those three buildings were a dozen smaller ones. The sleeping quarters. They were arranged in a semicircle behind the kitchen and infirmary. If the cavern was a giant pie, the buildings took up roughly the northeast quarter of the whole.

Exploration revealed that all of their possessions had been placed in appropriate places. The grill was now situated behind the kitchen, right next to a back door. The shelves and all the food they held were in the cold storage room. Along with additional built-in shelves that came with the room. The pile of blankets and weapons, as well as the tables, chairs, mattresses, and the rest were deposited in the circle. The system had apparently decided to leave it up to the humans to redistribute them.

Nancy and Chloe chose the sleeping quarters farthest from the door. Amanda and Lilly chose the next two. Sam and Meg picked the next one. Allistor chose the one closest to the door, with Sean and Robert Edward choosing the next two - their unspoken intent to be the first line of defense between the gates and the others. Sandy, sneaking a covert glance at Robert Edward, chose the quarters next to his.

101

They gave the mattresses to the ladies and Meg and Sam, helping them move those into their quarters. They agreed to retrieve more of them the following day. Everybody grabbed a blanket, and Meg tossed each person a roll of toilet paper with a smile. With a good bit of studying ahead of them, they each retired to their quarters. Allistor had just taken a shower and settled himself on his bedroom floor. He was using his backpack as a temporary pillow, berating himself for not grabbing a few of those while he was out. He was feeling comfy in a pair of the sheriff's black fatigues and had just opened up his interface to begin checking out the open market information when he dozed off.

Chapter Five

Working the System

Allistor woke with both an urgent need to urinate and a sore back. Sleeping on the cold stone did not agree with him. A quick look at his interface told him it was 3 am. He'd fallen asleep early, exhausted, and slept a full eight hours. With his morning ablutions completed, he left his quarters and went back to the big table out in the circle. He sat there and pulled up the open market research, figuring he was much less likely to fall asleep again sitting up.

The first thing he checked on was food pricing. If they failed to salvage more food in the coming days, and were unlucky in hunting, he wanted to know what kinds of food were available and what they cost.

When he did a simple search for 'consumables' the results list was hundreds of thousands of items long. He narrowed it to 'food', and the list cut down to just under a hundred thousand. He decided to go the other direction and get very specific. "Food items safe for human consumption." This time the list was just over a hundred items.

Scrolling down, he saw 'loaf of bread' for five klax. A single piece of canid meat like the ones he had looted was ten klax. On the other hand, a beef patty like the ones they'd eaten for dinner was thirty klax.

"So... earth beef is a semi-valuable commodity. Good to know. We need to get our hands on some cows," he mumbled as he continued to scroll. Luxury items like a bottle of cabernet were as much as a hundred klax. Again, something they might be able to salvage in large numbers.

Lots of people kept wine in their basements. And there was a winery about ten miles from town. If they could get one of the trucks working and safely raid that place, they'd be instantly wealthy.

Next, he looked up weapons. These items were listed differently than the common consumables. They were all set up with a bid structure. The seller set the minimum bid and the time available to bid. There wasn't much in the way of earth-style gunpowder and lead firearms. There was a surprising array of alien weapons available. From plasma weapons to some kind of pressure-driven flechette weapons. There was even one that shot pellets of acid, accurate up to one hundred yards. That one cost ten thousand klax, minimum.

But he only found a dozen or so familiar guns from earth. There were ten handguns listed, all but one between five and seven hundred klax. All had been placed within the last day, and bids were ongoing. One genius that he assumed was some human had listed a Glock 9mm, one of the most common handguns on the planet, for five thousand klax. Maybe he had been the first to list a gun and was trying to set the market.

The rifles went for considerably more. The minimum bid for a basic M-16 was a thousand klax, and the one listed currently had a high bid of fifteen hundred. With thirty rounds of ammo included. Allistor made a mental note to follow that one.

The highest bid on any of the rifles was for an antique Winchester. There was an eloquent description of the weapon and its history in the American West. It emphasized the age of the weapon and its rarity on earth. The high bid on that one was four thousand klax, and it had only been available about six hours. It seemed rarity added value in the Collective just as it did on earth.

Allistor began to do some math. He was extremely reluctant to sell any of their weapons as they might need them for defense. Or hunting. But if they managed to salvage a good supply of them... he might try to generate some system points. Especially if it meant they could have both electricity and a crafting hall. And he thought it might be a good idea to purchase a few alien weapons that might do more damage to creatures like the titan.

He slapped his forehead as an idea struck him. He did a search for Earth vehicles. There wasn't a single one listed. When he searched for ground vehicles, the least expensive result was a solar-powered two-wheeled motorcycle thing that listed for ten thousand klax. The lowest priced enclosed passenger vehicle was currently bidding at sixteen thousand. He pictured an auction of the classic Mustang he'd seen at the lot. With a write-up like the Winchester seller had created, he might pay for some serious upgrades to the Stronghold.

Closing the market information, he made finding the proper vehicle keys at the car lot a priority alongside mattresses and pillows, wine bottles, and cows. The new gates were large enough that he could drive the vehicles right down into the cavern and park them. The trailer too. He began to feel the tingles of greed take hold. After all, what was more fun than epic loot? If he could be the first to sell an Earth car and make a killing before others noticed and followed along, it would give them a good solid start.

The idea excited him so much he had to restrain himself from going out in the dark to find the keys and retrieve the Mustang. He had to remind himself that on the first day of stabilization, the creatures that roamed the streets at night were much scarier than during the day. He remembered lying in bed listening to the screams of those who'd been foolish enough to venture out, or even just leave their windows open.

His interface told him it was now nearly 5 am. It would be getting light soon enough. He'd recruit somebody to go with him. For the third time since they'd come down here, he wished for paper and pencil. Planning would be so much easier if he could make a list or three. Maybe one of the group could be convinced to loot City Hall for some office supplies.

As he let his thoughts drift, the burbling sound of the fountain caught his attention. He hadn't really paid much attention to it when it first appeared. He got up and walked over to it. The thing was maybe twenty feet in diameter, with a thick stone outer wall that made a good bench to sit on. The stone appeared to be some form of marble that glowed faintly. The centerpiece was a creature Allistor had never seen before. It was bipedal with feathered wings extending out from its back. The face was vaguely amphibian, a hint of gills at its neck. The water poured out of its mouth, splashing down into a bowl formed by cupped hands before falling into the pool below.

He sat there enjoying the pleasant sound of the water and thinking about nothing in particular. Until he noticed a ripple in the pool. He stared, following the small wave as it grew and dispersed. Then another ripple formed. Allistor thought he'd felt a vibration. Alarms began to go off in his head. A moment later, a third ripple. Larger this time. And he'd definitely felt a tremor in the stone beneath him.

Jumping to his feet, he began to shout, "Up! Get up! I think the titan's back! Everybody up! Get some weapons!"

He was running toward the line of sleeping quarters when the proximity alarms started going off. The sound was a deep gong, pitched low enough to vibrate the stone beneath his feet. The sound was loud enough to hurt his ears, which he covered with his hands as he dashed toward his quarters. He'd left both his pack and his spear in his room.

Inside his little abode, the sound was only slightly less deafening. He spun around, looking for his gear and snatching it up. Then he opened his interface and shouted, "How do you turn off that damn alarm?"

Instantly a defense management screen popped up. There was an alarm button flashing bright red every second or so. He focused on that, and several options came up. The first was to cancel the alarm. The second was to silence it, but leave it active. He chose that option when he noticed a sort of rough map of the area above with a range meter running on both the x and y-axis, to a classic radar readout. It showed a red dot moving toward the south through the town. It wasn't moving directly toward them but would pass by too close for comfort.

As the annoying gong faded to silence, he heard the others calling out to each other. He jogged outside and motioned for everyone to gather at the table. Each of them, except Chloe, held some kind of weapon.

By this time they'd all felt the vibration of the titan's footsteps and had no doubt what they meant. Allistor tried to share his sensor monitoring screen with the group, and he found he could do so just by focusing on an individual and thinking 'share screen'. When he'd included them all, they grew silent as they watched the dot move in their general direction.

Dust trickled down from the ceiling above as the six-story-tall monstrosity drew closer. Allistor took comfort in the fact that it seemed to be moving in a straight line, rather than a meandering pattern that might mean it was following their scent or tracking them somehow.

It was passing within about fifty yards of their gates when it stopped moving. A burst of gunfire echoed through the pre-dawn silence, penetrating their gate and reaching their ears. Sam began to run toward the gates. "That's gotta be our guys. God help them if that thing has been following them all this time!"

Allistor was right behind him as he reached the gates. Instead of the slide bolt that had been on the original doors, there was a thick beam made of steel about the thickness of Allistor's thigh. It looked like it weighed a literal ton. But when Sam grabbed it and tugged, it slid easily along its track. When it cleared the left-hand door, Sam pulled it open just far enough to stick his head out. Another tremor passed through them as the thing began to move again. Its new direction sent it directly away from their gates.

Sam pulled his head back in. "I saw Michael and Ramon! They're heading toward the forest. What the hell are they thinking?"

Meg said, "Doesn't matter. We need to help them. They led that thing away from us once already. We owe them."

"No question," Sam said. "But we don't all need to go."

Allistor stepped forward. "I'll go. I saw those guys shooting at it yesterday morning. They weren't doing any damage. Maybe the spear will get its attention."

Sam said, "I'm going too," causing Meg to gasp.

"No offense, old man. But you aren't exactly a spring chicken anymore." Sean smiled to take the sting out of his words. "Let one of us younger specimens go tease the giant death machine thing."

Sam glared at the deputy, then nodded. He stepped back from the door without a word. Allistor could see it was killing him to stay behind. He put a hand on the man's shoulder. "You'll need to be ready to lock these doors if that thing turns around."

Not waiting for a reply, he dropped his pack and dashed out the door. Sean and Robert Edward were right behind him, each with a rifle in hand. Sean also carried a long blade of some kind in his belt.

They ran as fast as they could toward the towering monster. It never noticed them, solely intent on the prey in front of it. Allistor held a finger up to his mouth, signaling for silence as they approached. Both men lowered their rifles, and Sean slung his over his shoulder before drawing the sword. Allistor took the lead, dashing up behind the titan and ramming his spear into its ankle with all of his strength and speed.

The spear broke the skin and pushed its way in among sensitive tendons and nerves. The beast roared in pain, the foghorn sound making trees lean backward in its path. Its momentum forced it to take another step forward on its injured foot. As that foot began to move forward, Allistor ripped the rebar spear free, tearing nerve and tendon alike. The titan roared again and stumbled.

Sean took advantage of the distraction. Running up to the same foot, he slashed at the back of the ankle, which was as high as he could reach, with the sword. He made contact very near the spot Allistor's spear had struck. The tear in the titan's skin widened as Sean pounded at it with the blade. Dark, thick ichor leaked from the wounds. It smelled of rotted meat and sulfur.

As the monster came to a halt and began to turn, Allistor struck again with his spear. Robert Edward was farther back, down on one knee with his rifle aimed high. A single shot rang out, and the titan flinched. "Direct hit!" Robert Edward yelled. "Right in the eye!"

Sean backpedaled a bit to keep from getting stomped on as the titan pivoted. Spotting the other humans, he shouted "Michael! Ramon! There's a safe place back behind us. We've got this thing! You guys get in there. Sam's waiting. He has cheeseburgers and beer!"

The older of the two men waved at Sean and began running right toward the titan, which was turning its back on them to deal with Allistor and company. The two men shouted their thanks as they passed by and continued on toward the stronghold.

The giant had lifted its injured foot and placed it back down a good distance to Allistor's left as it spun around. He could see it favoring that foot. With the thing still focused on turning around, Allistor struck again. This time in the uninjured foot. He drove the spear point between two of its toes with all the strength and weight he could muster.

There was a nasty-sounding squelch, and the rebar sank deep into the titan's foot. Thick black blood welled up around the wound. Allistor kept pushing, levering and twisting the rebar around to inflict as much damage as possible. With its weight on that foot, it took a while for the titan to be able to shift and lift the foot. Allistor made it pay for the delay. When he felt the foot begin to move, he yanked the spear free and ran backward just as a massive hand swept past where he'd been standing.

The titan's roar of frustration and pain nearly deafened him. Sean, who'd been running toward the first injured foot to continue his assault, dropped his sword and covered his ears with his hands. Unwilling to let go of his own weapon, Allistor had to just grit his teeth and suffer. He turned and ran past the giant's foot, away from the stronghold. He hoped to turn it around and lead it away again.

Dashing about fifty yards behind the thing, he turned and started shouting. He thought about firing a shot from his handgun, but it wouldn't do any damage, and he didn't want to waste ammo. As it turned out, he didn't need to. The taunt was more than enough. His toe-shot had well and truly annoyed the monster. He *Examined* it as it turned again.

> *Void Titan*
> *Level 10*
> *Health 4,600/8,000*

"Holy shit! Almost half its health is gone?" He stared at it for a moment longer and then retreated farther. It had made its lumbering turn and was moving toward him. A shout from Sean caught his attention. The deputy was running up to the damaged heel with his shotgun in hand. Allistor saw him jam the barrel up against the wound they had opened and pull the trigger. He was instantly covered in a back spray of titan flesh and black ichor.

The monster faltered again, making a sort of pained whining sound rather than a roar. It dragged the injured foot a bit as it tried to step forward and the damaged muscles and tendons didn't respond. Suddenly off balance, its momentum made it stumble forward onto one knee. Both hands went down in front of it to stop its fall.

Michael and Ramon, seeing this, stopped their flight and turned around. They raced back toward the monster, guns up and ready. Robert Edward, who had retreated inside, and Sandy, both shot out of the gates behind them, intent on joining the fight.

As the void titan's hands had hit the ground not far from Allistor, he too charged forward. He jammed his spear into the inside of one wrist, hoping it had veins similar to a human wrist that he could open. The flesh was softer here than on the feet, and his weapon sank deep. A notification popped up on his interface.

Critical hit! You have hit a vulnerable point on an incapacitated enemy.

Allistor waved away the notice and pulled his spear free. Black blood pumped from the ragged wound, so he shoved the weapon in again close by. He twisted as he ripped it back out, then retreated back the way he'd come.

Behind the titan, he could see Sean pumping round after round into the sole of the injured foot. The barrel was inches from its flesh, and based on the amount of black blood spraying around him, he was creating a good-sized hole.

Still backpedaling, and despite the fear and adrenaline pumping through him, Allistor had to laugh when he saw the brown-skinned Adonis he assumed was Ramon dash between the downed titan's legs and fire several rounds up into its crotch. Based on the squealing sound it made, the monster definitely felt that. The Hispanic man laughed, shouting, "The bigger they are, the harder they ball!"

Allistor's laughter died in his throat a moment later when the titan lunged forward, stretching out both long arms and reaching for him as its belly impacted the earth. Allistor dodged to his left, turning to sprint away at an angle, hoping to avoid being smashed. An impact on the ground right behind him sent him stumbling forward to fall on his face. The debris pile he landed in lacerated his face and neck, a sharp metal edge jabbing into his cheekbone just below his eye.

Scrambling to his feet and ignoring the damage, he turned to see titan flesh blocking his entire field of vision. The hand and arm had slammed to earth literally two feet behind him. A broken steel beam with a jagged tip now protruded up through its arm just below the wrist. The thing had impaled its arm in its bid to squash him. Already it was struggling to free the limb and try again.

Void Titan
Level 10
Health 1,460/8,000

They were doing it! Slowly but surely they were doing enough damage that they might bring this monster down!

Allistor started shouting, "Kill it! Kill it! Hit it with everything you've got!" like a maniac as he ran toward the prone body. Since its arm was extended and trapped for a moment, he ran for the most vulnerable spot he could think of.

Its armpit.

The smell when he reached it nearly overpowered him. Clamping his mouth shut and holding his breath, he slammed his spear into the exposed flesh covered in matted hair. The spear penetrated all the way up to where his hands held the shaft. As he twisted and levered it around,

113

he instinctively took a breath. The stench overwhelmed him, and he yanked the spear free as he bent to empty his stomach's contents. He felt dizzy and had to plant the butt of the spear in the ground and use it as support. Another deep breath inflicted more of the stench on him, and he retched some more. Behind him, the creature began to roll, but he didn't notice.

A moment later he was knocked from his feet as the hairy armpit rolled over the top of him. Black blood poured onto him from the spear wound that was now above his head. He was sure he was about to die, and he thought maybe that was okay if only he didn't have to take another foul breath.

The spear didn't budge as he fell, and his hands released the shaft, which remained upright. On the ground, he rolled to his back and saw his spear standing upright like a tent pole, the sharp end embedded in the titan's armpit again, the blunt end stuck in the ground. The thing had rolled right onto it. Allistor screamed as the hairy armpit flesh pushed further down the spear shaft, threatening to crush him.

He retched again, some of the black blood having gotten in his mouth when he screamed. The matted armpit hair pressed down against him, smothering him even as he rolled to one side to spit out the blood.

A moment later, the pressing weight that threatened to crush him lifted away. He risked a glance upward, seeing the armpit rising, taking his spear with it. Scrambling to his feet, he leapt up to grab the shaft but missed. It continued to rise out of his reach as the titan rolled away from him. Another spasm wracked his body, and he retched again, the last contents of his stomach, including some of the black ichor, splattering the ground at his feet.

Weaponless, he looked around the debris piles that surrounded him. He found several good-sized rocks, which he flung at the titan's back with all the strength he could summon. They simply bounced off, having no effect. He needed a real weapon.

The steel beam caught his eye. Covered in black blood, it was the one that had impaled the titan's arm. Too big for him to lift even with his improved *Strength*, it set his frenzied mind on the right track.

Searching the pile, he found an eight-foot-long metal pole about four inches wide. He grabbed hold and yanked it, intending to use it just like his spear. But when he pulled, it resisted. He set his feet and pulled hard, the thing finally breaking free. The bottom end was encased in a thick chunk of concrete. About to discard it and find another weapon, he turned to see the titan still on its belly.

"Come on, blunt weapon skill!" He grunted as he hefted the heavy pole with the concrete end over his shoulder. He spat a few more times, trying to clear the nastiness from his mouth as he ran toward the titan's head. The eye closest to him was the one that Robert Edward had shot out earlier. The monster didn't see him coming as he picked up speed. Now at a full run, he lifted the pole above his head, concrete end trailing behind him. As he reached the head, he leapt up and slammed the pole forward like a massive sledgehammer. The combined weight of his body mass and the concrete, assisted with his momentum and every muscle he put into the effort struck the titan's temple.

There was a cracking sound as the thing's skull dented in slightly. The concrete bulb at the end of the pole cracked, and several pieces fell free. Allistor's momentum slammed his own body into the side of the thing's head. It was like running full speed into a brick wall. He was knocked backward, disoriented for a moment. His left elbow stung and didn't seem to be working properly.

He lay there for a moment, hearing gunshots somewhere to his left. A moment later there was a very human scream that cut short. Allistor rolled onto his side and struggled to his feet. His left arm was definitely broken. Looking up at the titan, he was staring directly at the side of its head. He could see a small indentation where he'd struck the thing, but the blow hadn't even broken the skin.

Lifting the pole with just his right hand, he tucked it up under his arm like a jousting lance. "Just die, dammit!" he gasped at the titan as he rushed forward. He used his momentum to jam the end of the pole into the monster's ear. Its end was rounded, not sharp like his spear, but the pole was hollow. It dug into the much softer flesh inside the thing's ear and broke the skin. Allistor gripped as hard as he could and leaned into it, pushing the hollow tube deeper. When he lost his grip, he backed up and pressed his shoulder against the back end of the pole where some concrete still clung to it. He slammed himself forward like it was a tackling dummy. Something popped, and the pole shot forward at least a foot. Continuing to push, he moved forward with it until the pole struck something more solid and stopped.

Once again, messages filled his interface. A green *+18,000* floated across as Allistor realized the monster was dead, and he let himself collapse to the ground. Cradling his broken arm, he coughed and spat, still trying to clear his mouth of the nastiness. He instinctively reached for his bag, looking for his water bottle, but it wasn't there. He'd left the bag back in the stronghold when he charged out.

His back against the monster's head, he reached up with his right hand and took hold of the pole that protruded

116

from the ear. He used it to help himself to his feet. Disoriented, he looked around for the stronghold gates, but he couldn't see them. As he fought to gather his wits, a series of golden numbers flashed across his interface. Fame points. It occurred to him to wonder why more than one set of them had flashed by, but he blinked the thought away and focused on trying to walk. His legs were a little unsteady, but he managed to stumble around the debris and make his way toward the titan's feet.

Several seconds later, he was able to look past the corpse and see that the others had exited the gates and were walking toward him. Amanda caught sight of him and dashed forward, Nancy right behind her. The two of them scooped him up, each one ducking under a shoulder and supporting him as they walked him back toward the group. Each step sent pain lancing through his arm, but he just gritted his teeth and tried to accept the pain. Nancy coughed once and said, "What the hell is that smell?" Amanda appeared to be holding her breath.

Sam was laughing and hopping up and down as they approached. "You killed it! I can't believe you did it! Holy shit, man!" He reached out to shake Allistor's hand, noticed he was covered in ichor about the same time he caught wind of the stench, and changed his mind. "Way to go, guys!"

Allistor turned to see Ramon and Michael walked toward them. Ramon had a grim look on his face. Allistor looked past the two men at the monster. "Where… where are the others? Sean?" he asked as the two ladies set him down in the grass and started to work on him.

Michael shook his head. "When it began to thrash and rolled over, they were too close. It crushed the three of them."

"Oh, god." Nancy began to cry. She set down the jar of salve she'd been opening and bowed her head. "I've known Sandy since grade school. We just keep losing people! Why are they doing this?" Her shoulders shook as she sobbed. Chloe came running over and wrapped her little arms around her mother's neck.

Amanda grimly kept working. She poked at his elbow and tried to straighten it, causing him to hiss in pain. "It's broken," he informed her through gritted teeth.

"No shit, captain obvious. I'll put it in a sling for now. Let's hope the system has a quick way to heal it."

Meg and Sam were holding each other as they faced Ramon and Michael. She asked quietly. "All three of them? Gone? Sandy, Sean, Robert Edward?" Ramon nodded his head, not speaking. They'd all lost too many people over the last week. A sort of numbness had set in.

Sam broke the silence. "We need to burn their bodies. And do something about this beast. We can't have it rotting outside our doors. Or let it be eaten by other beasts and making them stronger." He looked at Allistor. "You need to loot it."

Allistor turned his head toward the titan's corpse. It was indeed glowing, indicating he needed to loot it. The foot was only a dozen or so feet away, but there was no way he was getting to his feet. Michael and Ramon stepped over and touched the corpse, receiving their share of the loot. Michael's eyes widened. "Holy shit. I got two hundred klax!"

Ramon said, "Yeah, me too. And something called *void crystals*."

Seeing that Allistor was struggling to rise, the two men returned and lifted him up. Together they carried him

118

over to the corpse and let him touch it with his good hand. Allistor's interface filled up again, but he mentally waved away all the notifications. As they carried him back to the group, he begged, "Please... anyone have any water? I... got some of that black shit in my mouth."

"And everywhere else," Meg added, handing him a water bottle. "You're not coming inside like that. Stink the place up for a week. We're going to have to hose you down out here or dunk you in the river or something." The look on her face spoke volumes. She included Nancy, Amanda, Ramon and Michael in her condemnation, all of them now slathered in the stuff from helping Allistor.

Allistor emptied the bottle one mouthful at a time, swishing the water around before spitting it out and taking another. The taste lingered, but he swallowed the last few mouthfuls, needing the water.

After a quick discussion, Ramon and Michael lifted Allistor and carried him toward the tree line. There was a creek close by that fed into the river. Nancy and Amanda followed as Lilly took charge of Chloe.

The hundred yards or so they had to walk past the tree line were pure torture for Allistor. Each jostle sent pain spiking up his arm. When they reached the creek, the two men just walked right into it, wading out to the center where it was maybe four feet deep. They lowered Allistor so that his feet touched bottom, and held him steady while the two women scooped up sand from the bottom and scrubbed at him.

When he was reasonably clean, they all moved him to the shallows and left him there as they cleaned themselves. Allistor dunked his head into the water several times, blinking his eyes and taking in big mouthfuls of water for further rinsing. Eventually, the smell faded.

119

When everyone was reasonably clean, they helped Allistor to his feet. He was feeling stronger now, his body having had some time to recover. He was able to walk along with them.

Arriving back at the stronghold, he was escorted inside by Amanda who directed him straight to the infirmary. Ramon and Michael followed along, both having some injuries that needed tending. By the time she finished bandaging and splinting Allistor's wounds, the two men were both sound asleep. After two full days of fighting and dodging that monster, nobody blamed them.

Allistor sat at the table by the fountain, going through his notifications. The experience from the kill had bumped him up to level five. He'd picked up skill levels in *Piercing Weapon*, as well as *Blunt Weapon* and *Improvisation* for his use of the pole weapon. The fame points had been awarded by several different factions, hence the multiple golden numbers that had crossed his interface. He'd never heard of any of the factions, but nine of them had awarded him fame points. He wondered if that meant they were watching him. Or just that anyone who killed a void titan was okay in their book.

The notification he was most excited about was an award of system points. Since the titan had entered the perimeter of their sensor net and attacked Stronghold citizens, killing it had counted as a successful defense of the Stronghold. Which had been awarded eighteen thousand system points! They now had enough to get both electricity and the crafting hall, with several thousand points left over.

Since they'd all agreed the night before, he went ahead and opened his Stronghold interface and spent points on electricity and a crafting hall. Once again the golden light filled the cavern, and the changes were complete. The hall formed next to the infirmary, a two-story structure with a double-door front entry.

Taking some jerky from his bag, he began to munch on it. He'd rested for a good while, but he needed food and drink to speed up the healing on his elbow. Amanda had promised to search the market for magic bandages or other instant heal options. Apparently, there were variants to healing in the new world. Lost blood could be regenerated quickly – a matter of minutes if you rested and ate. Superficial wounds could be closed instantly if, for example, you leveled up. But more serious injuries like broken bones or lost digits would take more time to heal.

Regardless, it would happen much faster than it would have two weeks ago on old earth. Already the pain was dulling and the swelling had gone down some. Allistor waited for the others to emerge from the infirmary, and they all walked together back outside for the funeral.

The funeral pyre was built, and the bodies resting atop it by the time Allistor and the others emerged from the Stronghold. The body of the titan was nowhere to be seen. Allistor looked at Sam, the obvious question apparent on his face.

Sam shrugged. "Lilly asked us to help her cut some skin from it, something about using it as armor. When we'd peeled off enough to build a damned tent, the corpse faded into dust."

As the sun cleared the treetops to the east, they lit the funeral pyre. The bodies were consumed by the flames as they all stood quietly. A few tears were shed, but most were too numb or too lost in memories of their own loved ones. Allistor felt a building anger. Too many innocent people had died. Including all of his family. He'd only known the three who just died a few days, but he thought of them as friends. And they died fighting next to him.

Who the hell decided that 90% of the human race needed to be killed off? What gave them that kind of authority? And what kind of an ass would drop a level ten giant killing machine in a newbie zone in the first week of stabilization?

Finally, as the fire burned low, they turned and re-entered the Stronghold. As Sam closed and barred the doors, Meg muttered, "It's a shame. I think Sandy fancied Robert Edward."

Allistor stomped his way back to the fountain, the anger still building.

Chapter Six

Pie R Round

Back in the town center, as he thought of it, Allistor called a meeting. The others gathered around the tables that were still set up there and took seats. He paced back and forth as he considered what he wanted to say.

"First, I want to say thank you to Michael and Ramon. I don't know how you guys did it, but you kept that thing off the rest of us for two days." He waited as the others all chimed in with thanks and pats on the back.

"I'm just a kid. I didn't know a whole lot about the world we lived in last week. This new world, though. This I know at least something about. Its rules and mechanics are a lot like the VR MMORPG games that I've played all my life." He looked around the room, hoping someone would chime in. Apparently, there weren't other gamers among the survivors.

"One thing I can tell you is this. The people... the beings running this 'system' as they call it, are cruel. They gave us three days to read up and prepare for the stabilization period and warned us that they were going to kill off 90% of the human race. Fair enough. But then they drop the equivalent of a nuke on our little town just a few days in. That titan was two or three times the level of any of us here, and resistant to all of our weapons. You just don't massacre all the newbies in your starter zone! You have to at least give them a chance to..." His voice drifted off as he noted the puzzled looks on several faces.

With a sigh, he said. "That thing was overkill. In any fair system, we should have had much more time to get stronger and learn how to live within this system before something like that wandered into town. The octopoids, canids, the other things roaming around at night, those were even a bit of a stretch. We should have started out fighting fluffy horned bunnies and angry mutant frogs or something."

Now he was getting nods of agreement. "In light of this, I think we have to push ourselves harder than we have been. I'm talking boot camp combined with midterm cram sessions combined with trade school. All at once. We need to build our bodies and our skills. We need to craft, or buy, better weapons and armor. We need to get ready for whatever nasty surprise they send us next. And the one after that. And when our year is up and the stabilization is over, we need to be strong enough to go find those dicks and get some payback!"

He slammed his fists on the table and looked around. He didn't get the rousing cheers of agreement he hoped for, probably because his *Charisma* only had one point. But most were nodding their heads and slapping the table. Nancy was giving him a dirty look, her hands over Chloe's ears. Chloe was giggling.

Attribute level increase! Your Charisma attribute has increased by +1

Allistor waved away the notice. "I'm sorry, Nancy. I'll try to watch my language. But I'm afraid in this new world, Chloe's childhood is going to be much shorter than any of us would like." Lilly put an arm around Nancy's shoulder, giving a quick squeeze for support.

Then she spoke up. "In case you folks who were outside didn't notice, we have electricity! And the crafting hall." She pointed to the new building. "Both will go a long way toward helping us grow."

Meg chimed in, "Then let's get outside and start rounding up useful items. Appliances, medical equipment, tools. We've got lots of space down here. Let's grab what we can while we can!"

Allistor held up a hand. "I was thinking about just that this morning. I want to go to the car lot and find the keys for the two trucks and the Mustang that are still intact. We'll bring them back here. I'm going to sell the Mustang on the open market. From the research I've done, it should bring us a butt- … err, a great big pile of money." He winked at Chloe.

"We can hook one of the trucks up to the trailer and use both trucks to gather what we can use. A group of us will go out together. There is strength in numbers."

He looked at Michael and Ramon. "From the snoring that was happening in the infirmary earlier, you two need some sleep. There are several unclaimed sleeping quarters." He paused as they all thought about the three friends they just lost. "You two grab a place and get some sleep. You've got the rest of the day off."

Michael nodded. "Thanks. But… I have to ask. Who put you in charge?"

Allistor opened his mouth, then shut it again. "You are absolutely right. Nobody did. And maybe one of you is better qualified. The system chose me to establish this Stronghold, but we're not really sure why. So if one of you thinks you'd rather lead…" He opened his arms in a gesture that encompassed the entire table.

"I'll do it! I wanna be boss!" Chloe shouted, raising her hand and wiggling her fingers. Nancy hushed her but was smiling at her irrepressible child.

Allistor grinned at her as well. "Anybody else?"

Michael shook his head. "I don't want the job. And I meant no offense. Just trying to catch up." Ramon nodded his agreement.

Sam spoke up. "Allistor has done a fine job so far. I vote we let him keep doing it until he screws up or someone else steps up." He raised his hand, and one by one the others did too.

Allistor was half disappointed. He had mixed feelings about running the community. On the one hand, town building was one of the things he loved to do in his games. But here, the lives lost were real, and the deaths were permanent. It was a huge responsibility.

"Alright. I need two of you to come with me to the car lot. We'll figure out the proper keys and bring the vehicles back here. Hook up the trailer, put the Mustang on the market, and then get to salvaging. Also, it would be good if somebody could go upstairs and search the sheriff's station and City Hall for some paper and writing utensils? Organizing everyone and everything would be much simpler if we could write stuff down."

Sam and Meg volunteered to go with him. Lilly and Amanda said they'd go upstairs and poke around. He warned everyone to stay on their toes.

Nancy and Chloe walked out with them, closing and locking the doors behind them. They promised to wait on the ramp and let folks back in.

*****

An hour after they left, Allistor, Sam and Meg were back with the vehicles. It hadn't taken long to identify the keys and get the vehicles moving. Sam had come up with the idea to siphon the gas from any of the disabled vehicles that still had an intact tank. So both trucks and the Mustang had full tanks.

They'd stopped on the way back to explore a couple of houses, including Sam and Meg's place right behind the diner. The truck Sam was driving held a refrigerator from their basement, a gun safe, a bunch more food, as well as most of a set of real plates and bowls and silverware. Meg's truck was piled high with mattresses, blankets, pillows, and various other household items. Sam had tried to bring the pool table from their basement, but Meg wouldn't have it.

When Nancy opened the gates, they drove all three vehicles down the ramp and into the main cavern. Parking near the fountain, they quickly unloaded. Amanda and Lilly had scored dozens of legal pads, pens, pencils, and other supplies. They'd also brought down more toilet paper and paper towels.

Allistor took some time as the unloading was happening to figure out how to list the Mustang. He'd been going over a 'pitch' in his head and thought he had a good one. Dictating it into the market's description box, he poured it on thick. The rarity, history, the thrill of the ride, the roar of the engine. Then he set the minimum bid at fifteen thousand klax.

That done, he turned his attention to the salvage operation. Gathering all that were close by, he grabbed a pen and pad and asked, "Okay, let's talk about priority items. And where we might find them."

Sam started it off. "Radios. I'd feel a lot better if we could talk to each other while we're out. The sheriffs had radios that would work for miles. We need to round up as many as we can. And the base system and chargers."

Amanda added, "Medical equipment and supplies. All we can find. Machines, surgical supplies, drugs, bandages, all of it."

Meg said, "Food, obviously. Anything in bottles, jars, sealed plastic, basically anything still edible that will keep. And we have the cold storage and electricity now. So we can keep meat, vegetables and such viable for a good while."

Allistor wrote it all down. "Okay, good. I'd like to add that we should keep an eye out for items of value. To be sold on the market. Gold, gems, rare items like that Mustang. Anything that other people will pay klax for. We can convert them to system points to grow this place." He wrote down *wine* on his list. "I want to take a trip to the winery soon. Hope it's intact. Wine sells for good prices. Plus we can hold some back for personal use." He grinned at them. "But the most important thing is to keep an eye out for threats. I think maybe the titan scared off most of the lesser monsters. But now that it's gone, they'll almost certainly return."

Lilly asked, "What if we run across other survivors?"

Allistor hadn't considered that. "I'm not sure. I think if you know them, or they're townspeople, bring them here. Anybody else, be suspicious. I'm not saying shoot on sight. But don't disclose the existence or location of our Stronghold. Let's say we take them to a neutral place... say the church. The steeple is still there, so there's at least some kind of shelter. Leave them there and report in here. At least until we get the radios up and running."

They talked for a while longer, then broke up into two groups. Allistor was going with Amanda to find medical supplies, Sam, Meg, and Lilly were going to start hunting for the radios, and both teams would grab any useful items they found.

Allistor drove his pickup out and hooked it up to the trailer. They were going to start at the doctor's office here in town. But after, they'd be going the four miles to the regional hospital to see if it was still operating and grab whatever equipment they could if it wasn't.

Once again, they left Nancy and Chloe behind, along with the two men who were sleeping, to guard the Stronghold. Allistor needed to figure out a way to secure the doors from outside, so they didn't need to leave someone behind all the time. He was already missing Sean's *Engineering* skill. Maybe he could pick it up himself or convince one of the others.

He parked the truck in an alley behind what had been the doctor's office. It was part of a row of storefronts just off Main Street. The roof was gone, and the glass front was shattered and twisted. But the three other walls remained - at least the lower six or seven feet of them.

The inside was scattered with debris. The carpet was squishy, soaked by a broken pipe somewhere in the building. Allistor stalked through all the rooms, making sure the place was clear, and went to go find the water meter and shut it off while Amanda grabbed whatever supplies she wanted.

He located the meter out back, along with six others for the strip of tenants. After shutting off the water for all of them, he rejoined Amanda. She'd found a rolling cart and was loading up boxes of bandages. There was already a large box of medications, mostly samples, on the cart. She pointed to an adjustable exam bed in one of the rooms. "Do you think you can move that?"

Allistor walked over and tested it. He grabbed hold and tried tilting it on its side. When it didn't budge, he crouched down and looked at the base. There were brackets holding it secure to the floor. They were simple bolts. Not having any tools with him, he tried grabbing hold and twisting the bolt head. He squeezed as hard as he could with his thumb and forefinger, then twisted. No joy.

"I'll have to come back with tools and unbolt it. I'll bring one of the guys with me. It looks heavy, but two of us should be able to lift it."

Amanda nodded then pointed to a stainless steel cabinet with glass doors. "How about that?"

Allistor took hold of either side of the cabinet and pulled. It came away from the wall without issue. He carefully hefted it, walking backward then sideways out the door. He set it down outside. Looking at the truck and the trailer, he shook his head. "If we just set this up there, all the glass will be broken by the time we get back."

Going back inside, he found two sofas in the waiting area. He was tempted to take them back but settled for pulling all the cushions off them. He lined the bed of the pickup with the cushions, then lifted the cabinet up and set it down atop them.

After some poking around, he found several rolls of duct tape in the shop next door. He used the tape to secure the cabinet to keep it from sliding back and forth. Amanda filled in the open spaces in the bed with small boxes of medical supplies, piles of robes and scrubs, anything relatively soft.

Once she'd pulled everything she wanted, other than the bed, from the doc's office, they jumped back in the truck and headed out of town. It was slow going, having to drive around, and sometimes over, the debris. Once they cleared town though, the roads became much clearer. They had to stop once for Allistor to clear a few fallen trees from the road. There was clear evidence the titan had passed that way – a path of devastated trees and brush stretched away on either side of the road.

The hospital was deserted. Abandoned vehicles were scattered about the parking lot. Some of them with broken windows and blood spatter. Several of the ground floor windows were shattered, including the automated doors that led to the ER. Clearly, something had attacked this place. Several somethings.

Allistor parked the truck right in front of the ER doors and got out. He gripped his spear and checked the .45 holstered on his hip. He could feel the shotgun strapped over his shoulder. Amanda was holding her shotgun like she knew how to use it.

The two of them exchanged a look, then stepped through the broken glass. The ER was a disaster zone, furniture and supplies were strewn everywhere, and blood stains covered the floor and walls.

They stopped to listen, holding very still for a solid minute. When they heard no movement, Amanda lowered her weapon and began pointing. She knew this ER and had worked here for years. Leaning close to Allistor, she whispered, "Down this hall to the left is a portable X-ray we used to move from bay to bay. We need that. And a crash cart - if there's one still intact. Also a few of these beds wouldn't hurt. They're on wheels. If you'll do that, I'll go raid the pharmacy."

Allistor shook his head. "We're not in a rush here. I don't want you wandering off alone. Something or things might still be roaming the halls. Which is the priority?"

Amanda glanced fearfully over her shoulder, then gave him a look, and he could tell she was trying to decide if he was being sexist. He cut her off at the pass. "I know you can take care of yourself. I saw you handle that shotgun. You know how to shoot, right?"

She nodded her head. "My pop took us hunting as kids."

"Right. So you're just as capable as I am. Maybe more. But look around. See all the bloody prints? Some kind of pack of monsters must have done this. We need to stick together."

With a sigh, she relaxed. "Sorry. Old habits." She looked around. "The drugs are the priority. Antibiotics especially. Let's hit the pharmacy first. We can grab this stuff on the way back."

So he followed her as she crept down one hall, then another. He insisted on checking each room they passed, then closing the door as quietly as possible. The last thing he wanted was mobs sneaking up on them from behind. He realized his pulse was racing, and his shirt was soaked with sweat. There was a definite feeling of being prey, watched by a predator waiting for the right moment to strike.

Ten minutes later, Amanda was crawling through the broken service window of the pharmacy to unlock the door for him. He found a rolling laundry hamper out in the hall and dumped its bloody contents. Rolling it inside, he pushed it down the aisles behind Amanda as she cleared the shelves of useful drugs.

"I'm skipping all of the cancer drugs, that kind of thing. I think with this new system, those aren't going to be a problem. I'm focusing on infections and pain reduction."

Allistor asked. "What about poison cures? Do they have that kind of thing in here?"

She thought about it, searching the shelf in front of her. "Not exactly. There are emetics, charcoal treatments, that kind of thing. But I'll grab whatever's here."

"Anybody have any chronic problems that you know of? Diabetes, arthritis?" he asked.

"No. But it wouldn't hurt to grab some of those drugs as well. Straight insulin would have to be refrigerated, but we have electricity now. And it has a short shelf life. Still, we'll throw some in. There should be a few small coolers in here somewhere."

Allistor left the hamper with her and went in search of coolers. Naturally, he found them right next to the wall cooler that held the insulin. He took a cooler, removed some slightly cool gel packs from the bottom of the wall cooler, and then put them and a double handful of insulin vials into the little cooler. Closing it up, he returned to Amanda. The hamper was about half full when he set the insulin inside. "I grabbed a bunch of insulin. Anything else you want from the refrigerated section, dear?" he winked at her.

Snorting, she said, "Let me go look."

Allistor stood there, reading labels on the boxes in front of him, not understanding what they meant at all. Two minutes later she returned with another cooler. "They had some common antivenoms in there. Rattlesnakes and such. Can't hurt to have them. I'm guessing all the normal Earth beasties are still out there in the woods, too."

When she'd taken what looked like enough drugs to serve an army, they left the pharmacy. Amanda led him to a huge linen closet where they grabbed more scrubs, a couple of white doctor's coats, and filled the rest of the hamper with clean sheets and towels. There were two more hampers sitting in there, so they grabbed those as well. Allistor pushed one and pulled another as Amanda pushed the third. They cleaned out the linens, then moved to the surgical supplies. Amanda loaded armfuls of prepacked surgical kits, suture kits, and boxes of gloves and masks. She grabbed a couple one-gallon bottles of liquid soap as well. And a case of the sanitary paper sheets they put over patients during surgery.

Leaving that wing, Allistor continued to close each door as they passed. He wanted to preserve as much as possible, in case they ever needed to come back for more. Or expanded enough to claim this place as a stronghold. It would be nearly perfect with some walls around it. But they were far from that point right now.

They found a custodian's closet with tons of cleaning supplies, so they loaded half a hamper with cleaning fluids, sponges, brushes, etc.

On the way out, Amanda stopped. "The cafeteria. They probably have a ton of food. They have these great Salisbury steaks…"

Allistor grimaced. "It won't smell good in there. Has to be all rotten by now."

Amanda rolled her eyes. "This place had a backup generator, dummy! Assuming the power went out when that giant took out the power lines, they still would have had a few days of juice here, powering critical systems. It would have come on automatically. And the kitchen counts as critical systems. Gotta feed the patients and staff, right?"

Getting excited now, Allistor followed her to the cafeteria, their little train of hampers rolling along. Again, he checked and secured each room they passed. It took a while, but after four turns and a long corridor of offices, they reached the cafeteria.

He was suddenly much less excited. Tables and chairs were scattered everywhere and covered in blood. The windows were smashed, the glass on the inside. Which meant something had come through them from outside.

Leaving the two full hampers where they were, he pulled one toward the buffet line and the swinging doors behind it. Amanda followed behind, shotgun ready.

Allistor peered through the small window in one of the doors. The kitchen hadn't been spared whatever massacre happened here. Pots and pans and tableware were scattered everywhere. He watched for a while, seeing no movement. A loud rap on the door didn't rouse anything either. He was about to step through and turned to make sure Amanda was ready when he saw movement.

Eyes wide, he tracked the movement as a huge cat emerged from behind a vending machine near the corner. It was easily two hundred pounds of teeth and muscle. It stared at him with red eyes, not blinking once as it crouched and watched them. Its long tail swished back and forth.

Lanx
Level 5
Health 1,200/1,200

Seeing the direction of his stare, Amanda turned and gasped. The sound seemed to trigger the feline, and its back legs began to twitch and a low growl emanated from its chest. Allistor knew that movement. He'd seen the

135

family housecat do that hundreds of times, right before it attacked whatever toy they were dangling in front of it.

He raised his spear and whispered, "Get ready. It's going to attack."

The buffet line was between them and the lanx. So it was going to have to either charge around one side or leap over the top. The glass sneeze-protector thing mounted above the buffet topped out at about five and a half feet. An easy hop for a cat that size.

The lanx agreed. With a burst of speed, it crossed the room, pushing fallen chairs aside in its rush toward them. With a last bound, it soared up and over the buffet, jaws wide and front claws extended.

Allistor raised his spear, jabbing into the cat's gut as it cleared the hurdle. He'd been aiming for its chest but misjudged the speed and height. As the spear penetrated the now screaming big cat's belly and sank into its innards, its front paws struck Allistor in the chest and razor-sharp claws raked at him. The weight knocked him backward into the swinging doors, which gave way as he fell.

The weight of the impact pushed the spear entirely through the cat's body, the tip bursting through its back just above its hips. It scrabbled and thrashed, biting at Allistor and slashing at him with its claws. He was pinned beneath it, using both hands to try and grab its forelegs and stop the damage.

Amanda finished the thing. She jammed her shotgun barrel right against its head, pushing it clear of Allistor before pulling the trigger. The shotgun, being an 'old Earth' weapon, typically wouldn't do catastrophic damage to one of these new monsters. Maybe two hundred points per shot at normal range. But this close, when she fired, physics won out and the head exploded, coating both of them in blood and brain bits. No matter how much health a monster had, losing its head meant death.

Cursing to himself, Allistor shoved the cat off and got to his feet. He immediately scanned the kitchen, then the cafeteria, looking for more lanxes. He wasn't sure if they were solitary hunters like the lynx, or pack hunters like lions. When nothing else showed itself, he relaxed a bit.

Amanda bent down and looted the corpse. She received thirty klax, six pieces of lanx meat, a lanx pelt, claws, teeth, and six pieces of lanx leather.

Taking a look at him, she said, "Chloe's right. You do seem to have this thing about letting stuff bite you." She touched his shoulder gently.

He looked down at her hand and saw that the cat had managed to bite down on his shoulder at some point. He hadn't even noticed as he struggled with it. But he definitely felt the tears in his chest and arms.

Amanda said, "Let's get you cleaned up." Then looking down at herself, covered in blood and brains, added, "And me too. There are some showers down the hall. Can you walk?"

"Yeah. My legs are fine. But I need to eat something. It'll heal most of this."

She nodded and looked around. First, she found a rag to clean off her hands, handing it to him when she was done. Opening a small glass cooler sitting atop the counter, she pulled out a slice of pecan pie. "This doesn't need refrigerating, so it will still be good even if the power went out on day one."

Allistor accepted the gift and munched on it as she led him toward the locker room. He took bites of the pie in between room clearings as he checked and secured each one along the way, finishing it as they walked across the locker room toward the showers in the back. Unabashed, she began to strip as they walked, stepping naked into the shower and turning the water to full hot. She didn't bother to close the curtain behind her. Allistor stared until she turned and caught him at it. She smirked at him, still standing there covered in blood, and said, "Strip. I'm a PA; you've got nothin' I haven't seen before," before resuming her shower.

Allistor did as he was told, leaving his bloody and shredded clothes on the floor. He stepped into the shower and turned the dial to hot before pulling it out. The water came out ice cold. He jumped and squeaked, glaring at Amanda. She burst out laughing.

"Apparently the water heater has been off for a while," she managed to say.

"Why didn't you tell me?" he grumped at her, stepping back under the water with a clenched jaw.

"And miss out on seeing you squeal like a little girl?" She finished her shower and stepped over to a pile of towels. It took all his self-control to keep from staring again. He focused on cleaning himself quickly, making liberal use of the liquid soap dispenser on the wall. When he shut off the water and turned, a towel hit him in the face. "Nice butt! Now get dried off. There are scrubs that should fit you out here," she said as she walked through the door into the locker room.

By the time he was dried and had retrieved his jeans and boots, she had set aside some scrubs for him. He dressed and slipped his boots back on. Folding his jeans, he wrapped them in the wet towel he'd just used. "I want to keep these," he explained. She nodded and went back to gather her own clothes.

She found them a bag to carry their bloodied clothes in, and they returned to the kitchen. Allistor opened the walk-in refrigerator to find that it was indeed still cold. And the ice in the ice machine was only partially melted. "The power must have just gone out in the last few hours." He bowed his head in her direction. "Good call!"

He was about to load a few hundred pounds of burgers and Salisbury steaks into the hamper when Amanda called out. "This one's on wheels."

He emerged from the walk-in to see her standing in front of a double-width stainless freezer. Inside were pre-made desserts like cheesecake, carrot cake, and key lime pie. Shelves of them.

With a sigh of regret, he said, "We need the meat more than these tasty treats. Let's take them out and fill this thing with meat."

Amanda began removing the pies, setting them on a long prep counter behind her. Allistor grabbed boxes of meat and began refilling the shelves. When it was full, he looked around again. Behind him, Amanda was filling the hamper with desserts. She grinned and said, "They're still frozen enough to last until we get back. Then we can put them in cold storage. They'll be good for a week or two."

Allistor didn't even want to argue. Cheesecake was one of his favorite things. Instead, he asked, "What about pots and pans and knives and stuff?"

She thought about it. "We can grab a few, I guess. I think Meg has the pots and pans pretty well covered from the diner. But let's take as many of the knives as we can."

They loaded those in with the desserts, and then Amanda said, "There's a door back there that goes directly outside to a loading dock. Instead of pushing all this stuff back through the building, why not just go get the truck. We can load up some tables and chairs and stuff, too."

Allistor agreed, hesitantly. "I'll run and get the truck. Do me a favor? If you hear *anything* that's not me, get inside the walk-in and hold it closed?"

"Deal. I'm gonna raid the spices, sugar, and flour and stuff while you're doing that. Grab lots of coffee and tea, too."

He gave her a brief hug, not sure why, then dashed out of the room. He got lost once on the way back to the truck but realized all he had to do was backtrack and follow the corridors with all the doors closed. He was back in the ER a few minutes later and took time to push two of the heavy gurneys outside and set them on their sides on the trailer. He pulled around the back of the building and found the sign that said "Food Service" with an arrow pointing to the loading dock. He pulled the trailer right up to the edge, then got out and knocked three times on the door.

Amanda had heard him coming and opened it immediately. They wheeled the three hampers up onto the trailer, then the refrigerator. Right away, Allistor noticed an issue.

"Shit. I forgot to bring rope. Gotta figure out a way to keep this stuff secure as we move."

Amanda grinned at him. "The roof! Plenty of rope on the roof."

He looked at her with one eyebrow raised questioningly.

"There's a rig up there that they use to wash the windows. It's basically a bench with ropes at either end hooked to an electric pulley system. We could actually probably make use of that, too."

He snorted. "You just want to make me run up six floors of stairs and carry all that crap down."

She shook her head. "First, I'm going with you. No telling what's up there, and I've already had to save your ass once today." A wink took the sting out of her words. "Second, you won't have to carry it down. It's mostly rope. Just *lower it down.*"

He did an exaggerated facepalm. "Another good call. What would I do without you?"

She poked him in the gut. "Well, in about three days you'd be getting shat out by that lanx."

Rolling his eyes and shaking his head, he replied, "I'm assuming we're gonna need some tools to disconnect that pulley?"

"Yup! There's a maintenance shop on the lower level. Let's go."

She led him to the nearest stairwell and down one floor. They passed by the morgue, and he made *VERY* sure that door was secured. Beyond the visions of walking corpses, he didn't want any more critters getting in there and consuming whatever bodies might be inside. And very soon, with the power off, it was going to start to smell.

In the maintenance shop, they found at least two of every kind of tool Allistor could imagine. Metal wrenches, channel locks, sockets, power tools, hammers, and hacksaws. There was even a massive wooden workbench that made him drool, and two portable, folding workbenches next to two extendable ladders. They also found several large canvas duffle bags. He discovered a few spools of wire and thick twine that would help him secure stuff on the trailer if the rope didn't do it. And one entire wall was stacked high with bags of salt for winter. After filling four bags, there were still more tools Allistor wanted. And in the corner, he found an actual anvil! Dreams of *Weaponsmithing* danced through his head.

"We need something to carry more of these things in. Something big, preferably with wheels. I want to take as much as we can. Hell, I'll even take these metal shelves if I can."

Amanda tapped her chin. "There are the steel autopsy tables in the morgue. They're on wheels and have a shelf underneath. We could pile these bags on there. They'd make good rails on the trailer, too."

He shook his head. "Bigger. Heavier."

She shrugged. "We'll have to look around."

He grabbed a socket wrench, channel locks, a hammer, and some pliers and they made their way to the roof. With his improved strength and stamina, the walk up the seven levels from the basement to the roof was almost effortless.

Out on the roof, he immediately saw what Amanda had meant. There was a sort of mini-crane on a swivel bolted to the roof. Standing six feet high with an electric motor and two pulleys, it could be turned toward any of the four sides of the building and used to lower the ropes that supported the bench. The bench with the rope coiled atop it lay nearby.

One look at the base of the crane and Allistor said, "We'll have to come back for this. The bolts are welded.

142

And somebody with more knowledge than me is going to have to figure out how to disconnect the electrical wires in a way that lets us reconnect it later." She stared at the bolts and didn't disagree.

"But we can take the rope!" He stepped forward and examined the bench. It was basically just three two-by-six boards screwed to three slats underneath. The rope passed through two holes in each end and was knotted underneath. The knots were sealed with something transparent. There was no way to untie them.

"No worries." Allistor simply lifted the bench with the two hundred feet or so of rope coiled atop it and looked around. "Which side is the cafeteria?"

Amanda pointed east, and he walked to the edge and dropped the bench off the side. A moment later there was a crash as the bench hit the ground. Dusting off his hands, he said, "That was easy!" She just gave him a half-smile and headed for the door.

Back downstairs, they returned to the maintenance room. He reluctantly agreed to use one of the morgue carts to load up the bags they'd filled. Since they couldn't push it up the stairs, she directed them toward the lower level loading dock. This was where funeral homes came to pick up the bodies and supplies were delivered.

As soon as they walked out onto the dock, Allistor whooped for joy! Which caused Amanda to jump and nearly wet herself. When she turned on him, he was already gone. Headed to the far side of the dock where three large grey plastic bins with wheels sat. Each of them was about three feet wide and five feet long.

"Ew! They use those to collect the trash!" she called out. "Do you *know* how nasty hospital trash can be?"

He shrugged, peering down inside the nearest one and sniffing. "They're not so bad. We can line them with plastic. I saw some tarps in there. And I'm putting tools in here, not food."

She made a disgusted face but went to help him. They pushed the three bins back to the maintenance room and filled them until they creaked under the weight. Then Allistor laid a ladder across the top of one, and a workbench atop each of the others. Once again, they made a train down to the loading dock. Leaving their loot there, they returned to the main floor.

"Okay, show me these machines you want."

Amanda led him to the portable X-ray machine first. It was nothing fancy, and not particularly heavy. The equipment to print the X-rays was much heavier and less portable. Allistor was able to disconnect it all, as most of it was just 'plug and play', and load it onto a gurney, which he pushed outside along with the X-ray unit itself. They grabbed a portable defibrillator on the way out. Along with several networked pads that the staff used to pull records and such. "For when you run out of pencils and paper," she poked at him.

As Allistor ran back through the corridors to get the truck, Amanda added a few last-minute items to the pile outside. Six of the posts they used to hang plasma bags, boxes of tubing and needles, blood pressure cuffs, stethoscopes, and other assorted supplies. Finally, she ran into a breakroom and emerged with a pillowcase filled with the trashy romance novels the nurses kept stashed in there. And a gallon-sized jar of lollypops for Chloe.

Allistor retrieved the rope and used some of it to secure the refrigerator and other items already on the trailer. Then he slowly pulled around to the ER to load and secure those items. Amanda hopped into the truck and they pulled around to the loading dock for the bins of tools. When they were done, there wasn't a square foot of free space on the back of the trailer, and the truck bed was piled high. Amanda volunteered to drive, and Allistor rode on the trailer, prepared to stabilize anything that shook loose.

She started moving slowly, creeping along over the single speed bump between them and the road. When nothing fell off, she picked up some speed on the road. The first three and a half miles she cruised along at about 30mph. When they reached the outskirts of town she slowed way down and threaded her way through the debris. Reaching the stronghold gates, she honked the horn once, and Nancy let them in.

As they passed, she told them that Sam and Meg had already returned twice with their truck filled with stuff. They were inside when Amanda parked in front of the kitchen. For the next half hour, the group unloaded and stowed all the loot amid surprised exclamations, laughter, and much congratulation.

Sam was especially appreciative of the many and varied pies. When he saw them, a wide smile appeared on his face. Seeing that smile, a suspicious Meg walked over and looked into the bin. "Oh, no you don't!" She got in front of him and physically pushed him away from the cart. "We're going to need a lock for the refrigerator!"

Allistor laughed and said, "Just leave some cheesecake out where I can get to it!" Still chuckling, he caught Sam's attention. "This might make you happy." He led the man up onto the trailer bed and unwrapped the rope around the refrigerator. When he opened it, he made an "Aaah, AHHH, aaah!" sound like angels crooning over a miracle. Sam's eyes widened and his smile returned. "Beef!" he shouted!

The two of them wheeled the massive fridge off the trailer and into the kitchen, where Meg promptly began transferring the treasure trove of meat into the cold storage. As they watched, Sam caught him up on their foraging trip.

"We got four radios and the base station. Not great, but should be enough for now. Found two more deputy's cars and got some more weapons and ammo. More vests, too. We hit the hardware store and loaded up all kinds of stuff. There's still more there we can pick up later. With those bins you brought back, we can carry all kinds of stuff. And I don't think it would be that hard to build rails for the trailer."

He looked out the window at the Mustang parked near the fountain. "Found lots of other vehicles that are still intact. But no keys. So either we need to spend more time searching out the keys, or learn how to hotwire them. If we can find the keys, there's a very pretty 1969 Corvette at my buddy Frank's house. He lives about a mile outside of town. He also has a tractor. I was thinking we might try to grow a crop outside at some point. And we could use it to clear the roads eventually."

"Good thinking all around!" Allistor patted the man on the back. "This has been a very productive day. I know it's still early, but I'm beat. I say we close up for the day, finish sorting through everything, and then celebrate!"

Chapter Seven

Zombiecue

The celebration went well into the night. Steaks were grilled, pies were consumed, and bottles of spirits opened. Ramon and Michael woke in time to join the celebration, looking refreshed and healthy. Allistor's wounds from the lanx had fully healed as well. The group ate, drank, laughed, and told stories.

Meg had found a radio, and to their surprise, a few stations were still transmitting! Though there were no live voices. It seemed as if they were running pre-programmed tracks. But that didn't matter. Several of the group got up and danced. Ramon, who'd hit a bottle of rum pretty hard, didn't have the balance to get up and dance, so he showed off his chair-dancing moves, over which Chloe giggled and clapped, trying to imitate him.

Amanda hauled Allistor onto his feet and dragged him over to dance with the others. Then she mocked his dance moves with a sparkle in her eye. "You should maybe stick to lifting heavy things and killing stuff." Her smile was wide and warm. When a slow song came on, she latched onto him and put her head on his shoulder.

With quite a bit of rum in him as well, Allistor was doing his best not to cross a line he wasn't sure he'd been invited to cross. So he whispered at the top of her head. "Thank you for saving my cute butt today. I'd have you as my wingman anytime."

Her only response was to lower her hand from his shoulder to give his butt a squeeze.

*****

The next morning he woke up with a pounding headache. When he blinked his eyes open, he found Amanda's face inches from his own, drooling on his chest. Grinning to himself, he closed his eyes again. He had no urgent need to be up and about. Though he would need to find the bathroom soon.

He pushed a strand of hair from her face as he watched her sleep. He guessed she was about thirty years old, with long, ebony hair that glistened in the light. He didn't remember much about the events of the previous night, but he didn't regret finding himself where he was this morning.

Eventually, she rolled onto her back and began to snore. He took the opportunity to get up and use the bathroom. He was just finishing a shower when she joined him. It was a good hour before they emerged to seek breakfast and start the day. And Allistor found he was quite hungry.

Meg was in the kitchen with Sam. The smells of pancakes, bacon, eggs, and sautéed onions drifted out to the dining area. Allistor tried to volunteer to help, but he was chased from the kitchen by Meg and her spatula.

Nancy and Chloe were already sitting at one of the foraged cafeteria tables with Ramon and Lilly occupying the other two seats. Amanda took a chair at an empty table and Allistor joined her. A moment later, Michael entered and sat with them. Allistor scooched his seat close to Amanda's and pulled over two more chairs so Meg and Sam could join them. Everybody but Chloe seemed to have a hangover.

Breakfast was delicious and served in large helpings. Allistor devoured a stack of four pancakes, several strips of bacon, three sausages smothered in onions, and a couple rolls. There was water, sweet tea, and orange juice to wash it all down.

With their hugely successful salvage operation the day before, they had plenty of food to last them several weeks. When folks were done eating, Allistor suggested a plan for the day.

"Hey, everybody. I was thinking this would be a good day to stay inside. Amanda has a whole infirmary to organize. We have a crafting hall just begging to be used and a ton of materials. I was hoping everyone would want to focus a bit on their skills, and maybe find out what we can make, or build, to improve our circumstances here."

This was met with general approval. He looked at Ramon and Michael. "You guys weren't here for the quick and dirty tutorial the other day. I imagine you've been pretty occupied by that titan since it arrived. If you'd like, we can spend some time this morning catching you up?"

Both men agreed, and after helping Meg clean up the breakfast dishes, they went outside to sit at the big wooden table that still occupied a space near the fountain.

Allistor spent about an hour going through everything they had learned, pausing for questions or to hear input from the men. Ramon popped up with a skill he'd learned. "I keep a journal. I've written in it every day since I was a kid. The other day when we thought we'd lost the titan and stopped for a while, I was recording the day's events. A message popped up that I'd earned the *Scribe* skill. That made me curious, so I tried something else. Took out my knife and started whittling at a piece of firewood. After about twenty minutes I earned *Woodworking*."

Michael added. "I've only gotten one so far. *Marksman*. I shot so many damned rounds at that monster. On the second day, the notification came up when a shot went right into its mouth."

"Good! All useful skills that I don't think any of the rest of us have. My hope is that we'll all develop skills that complement each other and benefit the community. For example, do either of you know anything about engines or machines? Sean had earned the Engineering skill, and obviously, now we've lost that again."

Ramon clapped his hands together. "I studied engineering in school. Give me something to work on, and I'll level up that bad boy like crazy."

Allistor told him about the hospital, the generator, the crane on the roof. "I'm not sure what else is there that would be worth checking out. But for today, Amanda might need help setting up her medical machines."

Ramon hopped up and headed for the infirmary. Michael looked at Allistor. "What've you got for me?"

"Dunno. What are you good at? Or more importantly, what do you *like* to do?"

Michael looked over his shoulder to make sure Ramon was gone. "I didn't say anything before because I didn't want to make Ramon feel bad. But I was a huge gamer as a kid. I recognized what this was almost on the first day. So I've been 'playing' it like a game. As for skills – I was thinking I could try something cool. Like enchanting. Maybe combine it with blacksmithing to make badass armor." He grinned at the look on Allistor's face.

"Right on, man!" Allistor gave him a fist-bump. "I'm glad to have another gamer in the group! You can help me push everyone else in the right directions. Not with their choices, that's totally up to them. But motivate them to get better at whatever path they choose."

"I can dig that, my friend." Michael leaned forward, his elbows on the table. "So what's your build? What are you thinking?"

The two of them chatted for another half hour, sharing their stats and talking about possible skill trees. Neither of them had the first clue how to trigger a skill like Enchanting, though.

Finally, Michael just said, "Maybe I can find a scroll on the market or something."

The two of them both moved over to the open market trade building and approached the window. When they did, the windows turned out to be holo-screens with prompts that allowed you to search for items. There was a setup required with both biometric and retinal scans to confirm identity.

It seemed one could *list* items on the market and browse using just their interface. But to *purchase* something, one had to physically contact the kiosk. Once a purchase was made, the item would either appear on a shelf behind the display, or a larger door would open and allow the buyer to remove the item (like a car, for instance).

Both men scanned for scrolls. Allistor took a more general approach, searching for *skill training scrolls* to get a general idea of availability and cost. He had a few hundred klax from his various kills, and he was ready to spend them on scrolls.

Michael went with a much narrower search. He started with *beginner enchanting scrolls*. When that turned up nothing, he tried a few other keyword combinations.

Both men were discouraged by the results. Michael finally found a scroll that would teach him a skill called *"Power Infusion"* which, best he could tell, was the System's version of Enchanting. But the scroll was expensive. Six hundred klax. And every gamer knew that Enchanting was one of the most expensive skills to level. The material costs were generally prohibitive. If it cost six hundred klax just to learn...

Meanwhile, Allistor was discovering a similar issue. All the scrolls he looked at were expensive. On a whim, he did a search of a Levitate scroll and found it was worth two thousand klax. That was big money, but not big enough to make him sell it. He'd try to improve his *Weaponsmithing* the old-fashioned way first. Plain old hard work and experimentation.

While he was at the screen, he checked his account. The display told him he had three hundred and ten personal klax, and two thousand five hundred klax in the Stronghold account, over which he was the sole authorized individual.

That reminded him. He added Michael and Ramon to the *Review and Recommend* list, so that they could review what had been done and make recommendations in the next upgrade discussion.

Authorizing individuals put him in mind of his old guilds. He asked Michael, who was still perusing the market, whether he'd spent much time in a guild.

"Yup. Ran one for a few years. Wasn't a big deal. Mostly a social guild. We did some raiding, but it was hard to get everyone's schedules sync'd when they're not hardcore. We were lucky to do one a month."

Allistor felt his pain. "You think we could form one here? Now? I mean like, officially. Through the system."

"Maybe? But why would you want to?" Michael stepped away from the market window and looked at him. "Why sign yourself up for all that hassle?"

Allistor grinned. "Actually, I was thinking of signing YOU up for all that hassle. I'm already somehow in charge of the Stronghold. But I was thinking if we expanded... Like if we also made the hospital a Stronghold, with one of you as its boss. And a few others around town in strategic spots. We could fold them all into one guild."

He could see Michael wasn't convinced. So he added. "I mean, maybe it comes with perks like guild chat. We could talk to each other at a distance anytime. No need for radios."

Michael looked less skeptical, but he wasn't biting yet. Allistor left him to think about it. There wasn't an urgent need for a guild yet.

They were just taking seats again when the proximity alert went off. Allistor pulled up his interface and the map that went with the alarms. The radar-like screen showed multiple red dots moving from the forest almost directly toward their front gates. He tried to count the dots, but they kept merging and crossing over each other. His best guess was a dozen of them.

As he turned off the audible alert, the others began to emerge from the various buildings, weapons in hand. As one they moved toward the gates. There were few words. Meg said, "I can't tell how many."

Ramon responded, "Lots. It's either a pack of canids or vermin, or a group of human survivors."

When the dots paused and began to mill about at the spot where the titan had died, Allistor said, "It looks like a pack. Sniffing around where we killed the titan. Probably followed its scent."

As they reached the gate, Michael shook his head. He spoke quietly. "Nope. We came from the other direction with the titan. But they might be following our scents from when we went out to the creek to wash off. Though how they could pick us up over the stench of that thing, I don't know." Allistor grimaced at the memory of the combined armpit and blood stench.

Meg whispered, "Maybe the smell of the titan will scare them off? You know, like small predators fear big predators?"

They all waited impatiently, standing at the gates with weapons ready while staring at their interface maps. The dots all meandered around in roughly the same area for a while. Then one dot ranged toward them. It moved maybe twenty yards, then paused. A moment later, the other dots all moved in unison, following the first. Which moved right up to their gates.

Allistor put an ear to the metal, as did most of the others. He could hear scratching and snuffling on the other side. A series of yips told him what was out there.

"Motioning for everyone to step back down the ramp, he waited for them to gather close. "Canids, I think. There was evidence that a pack of something killed everyone at the hospital. This might be the same one."

"So what do we do?" Lilly's eyes were wide with fear. She'd seen what a few canids did to the unfortunate family at the campsite.

Allistor said, "There are eight of us that can fight. No offense, Chloe." He smiled at the little girl holding her mom's hand.

154

She smiled back and shrugged. "I know, I'm little."

Allistor continued. "So they outnumber us by about half. We can't just open the gates and charge out there. We might win with the weapons we have, but I doubt we could do so without losing somebody."

Sam said, "We could use the trucks. Run over a few of them to even the odds?" Several people nodded their heads at that.

"The trucks, yeah. But I don't think we'd actually be able to run them over. And when we open the gates, they'll charge in." Allistor thought about it. "What if we use the trucks, and the trailer, as sort of a defensive wall?" He pointed toward the gates. "We could turn the trailer on its side right in front of the gates. Then when we open them, the canids have to go around it to one side or the other. We park the trucks across both gaps. We'll be up in the beds firing down at the canids."

He paused as he pictured it. "Nancy, Chloe, and Meg can be in one cab. Lilly and Amanda in the other. You keep the windows up on the side closest to the gates. Shoot out the window on the other side at anything that gets past us. Meanwhile, Sam and Ramon are in one truck bed, myself and Michael in the other. We should be able to mow them down pretty quickly, with less chance of anyone getting hurt."

Nancy asked, "And if all of them go in one direction? That truck will get overwhelmed."

Allistor nodded. "Then we go with Sam's plan. The other truck will haul ass over and try to run down a few of them. Guns blazing. We'll keep the engines running. That way if things go badly, the ladies can gun it and drive us away from the pack so we can regroup.

Maybe take shelter in the kitchen. Make them come through the windows at us."

Meg said, "Or we could just do that to start with. Open the gates and fight from inside the kitchen."

Sam shook his head. "None of us can outrun those things all the way to the kitchen."

Michael raised a hand and waited for everyone to be silent. "I think I have an idea." He pointed over to their right. "The holding cell. The spaces between bars are narrow. I doubt those things could squeeze through. We go in there, fire at them through the bars. Keep the trucks close by in case some of them disperse through the cavern and we have to go after them. But I'm betting we could massacre them from inside there."

They all looked surprised at how simple it was. Sam added, "We could coordinate fire. Only shoot uninjured ones the first couple volleys. Then when they're all wounded, finish them off."

Meg took a step toward the kitchen. "I have another idea. Sam, get a couple of those flares." She took off running toward the kitchen as Sam went in search of her flares. Meg returned a minute later in one of the trucks, with a jug of cooking oil and a blanket. She rolled the blanket up into a sort of log and placed it on the floor against the bars nearest the gates. Then she poured a puddle of the oil between the blanket and the ramp. It was a narrow puddle front to back but stretched about twenty feet across from left to right. They all watched as oil began to spread and soak into the blanket.

Sam returned with the flares and the other truck. Seeing what she'd done, he chuckled to himself. "Meg loves those zombie movies. She cheers when they lure them all together and light them on fire."

Meg nodded enthusiastically with a big smile on her face. "Zombiecue!"

Nancy touched her shoulder. "But these things are going to be alive. They're going to scream and bleed and..." she looked at Chloe, concern written all over her face.

Meg took her hand. "I think maybe you and Chloe should be in one of the trucks. Hunkered down so they don't see you. You can play the radio or something." Nancy hugged her, grateful.

Their plan agreed upon, everybody took their places. Allistor volunteered to open the gates. He was still the highest level among them, with the largest health pool. He wasn't going to open the gates, exactly. Just unlock them and haul ass. With all the scratching on the outside, he was sure the canids could open the gates on their own. His plan was to be safely inside the holding cell, or at least close to it, by the time the first canid got in.

Meg stood next to the door, a roll of duct tape in hand, one end already wrapped around the door frame. They didn't have keys to the cell, so they were going to tape it shut and keep the canids away from their makeshift latch.

As Nancy shut herself and Chloe in the truck's cab and locked it, Allistor approached the gate. He took a moment to listen again, even going so far as to yell at the canids outside to get them riled up. Taking three deep breaths and exhaling quickly, he unbarred the gates and took off.

He sprinted like he was running from, well... a pack of wolves. The others quietly cheered him on as he practically flew down the ramp. The three men in the group were on the far left of the cell, high-powered rifles already up and aiming past Allistor toward the gate. The first mob that stuck its nose through was dead meat.

Allistor reached the cell just as the doors began to push open. Sam fired first, his rifle shattering a canid's face as soon as it poked through the widening gap. Ramon and Michael each fired a moment later, hitting another of the canids and downing it.

As Meg slammed the door shut behind Allistor and began quickly wrapping the tape around, he lifted his own shotgun and shoved it through the bars. He sighted on the foremost canid rushing toward him. Waiting until it was only about twenty feet away, he fired. Its front left leg and a good section of its chest were blown off. The thing faceplanted, and its momentum caused it to roll ass over teakettle, landing on its back. Allistor fired again, this time into its exposed belly.

> **Canid Hunter**
> **Level 6**
> **Health: 110/650**

It wasn't dead, but it was no longer a threat. Allistor moved to the next target, leaving that one to bleed to death. A quick scan showed him that over half of the canids were already down, either dead or wounded. His friends had been firing nonstop, downing one after another. He chose one that was almost at the bars of the cell and fired into its face.

As it fell wounded, Meg flicked a flare to life and tossed it through the bars onto the oil. There was a brief delay, then a *whoomph!* as the oil caught fire. Four of the wounded canids, and two that were so far untouched, were within the area of the puddle. All of them caught fire as well. The yipping and whining of the canids was hard to hear. Allistor was a dog lover, as most people were, but these canids were here to kill them.

The sound of breaking glass and high-pitched scream of a little girl caused them all to swivel towards the truck. The back half of a canid stuck out the passenger window of the truck, its four back feet scratching away the paint on the door trying to gain purchase and push through. Michael fired his rifle, the round tearing through the rearmost hip of the thing. Ramon fired half a second later, punching through its innards between the middle and back sets of legs. Another gunshot rang out inside the cab, and the thing quit moving. The only sound was Chloe sobbing.

Allistor scanned the area. He counted corpses and found thirteen, including the one hanging out of the truck. One canid, its body afire, was bolting across the cavern toward the sleeping quarters. He could see both Michael and Ramon taking aim.

A quick check of his interface didn't show any red dots, other than the one. Which disappeared a few seconds after Michael fired. Nothing but green dots inside and out.

Meg frantically cut the duct tape and rushed to the truck. She yanked the dead canid free of the window and stuck her head inside. "Oh my god. Chloe. *AMANDA!* Oh my god."

Amanda was right behind her. She pulled open the door and grabbed Chloe. The girl had lacerations on her face and forehead and was drenched in blood. She set Chloe down and checked her over. After a few seconds, Amanda shouted. "She's okay! She's okay! Most of the blood is not hers. She's got some deep cuts, but she'll heal."

Nancy crawled out of the cab and dropped her shotgun as she bent to scoop up her baby. She and Amanda ran toward the infirmary, Ramon right behind them. Unconscious, Chloe's arms and legs flapped limply as they ran.

Allistor ran too but in the other direction. He ran to the gates, pulled the two canid corpses inside, then closed and barred the doors. He bent to loot the canids, but couldn't. He hadn't shot either of them. Returning to the cell area, he looted the two that he'd killed. He told Sam about looting the two by the doors, then watched the fire carefully as the oil burned away.

When all the corpses were looted, they faded away. The group moved back to the fountain area, quietly waiting for news about Chloe. They were encouraged when they heard the girl crying after a few minutes. Eventually, Amanda came out.

"She's okay. Understandably traumatized. Nancy said the thing actually bit down on her head. Most of the scratches were from claws. But that thing's teeth nearly punctured her skull. She's eating some pie and drinking juice. With some rest, she should be fine by morning. I'm hoping when she heals, it won't leave any scars."

She looked at Allistor, who removed his shirt so they could all see. Most of the cuts and scratches they'd seem him suffer had healed without any trace of scarring. But the recent deep bite on his shoulder from the lanx was still visible. He tried to reassure them. "This is from yesterday. It looked way worse when it happened."

Having received the good news, the others all went back to their individual business, in the infirmary, the crafting hall, the kitchen. Allistor sat at the table, staring at his hands. Michael rapped knuckles on the wood to get his attention. "You know, something just occurred to me."

"What's that? That we should have had Chloe someplace safer?"

"What? No. She should have been fine where she was. Things rarely go according to plan. Probably even less often in this new world that's trying its best to kill us." He paused until Allistor looked up at him.

"What's just occurred to me, is that in this world, this 'system'... we're the damn NPCs." His face was grim as he watched Allistor absorb that thought. The look of horror on his face pretty well matched what Michael was feeling.

"Think about it. We're NPCs in the pre-alpha testing mode. Where the AI that runs the game is putting us through our paces, developing backstory, molding the world to prepare it for the arrival of players. In a year, when stabilization is over, the beta testers will come first. To test the waters. Then we'll be flooded with millions of players who'll think nothing of snuffing out the lives of one of us NPCs. Or a whole town's worth."

Realizing he was breathing hard, he stopped talking for a moment. Allistor was staring at his hands as he clenched and unclenched them. "That's why the damn level ten giant town killer showed up here in a newbie zone. Because they're not looking at us as players who deserve a fair shake. We're friggin' disposable NPCs."

Allistor looked up, his eyes blazing. "And they'll come and claim land. Levy taxes on the poor unfortunate NPCs who managed to survive the genocide and remain here. Use us for cheap labor or flat out slaves in their mines and lumber yards. Use us to fight their battles like the worthless fodder they see us as?"

Michael nodded. "I mean, you seem like an okay guy. But how well did you treat NPCs when you were gaming? I can't say I'm proud of the way I treated them. Can't even count how many I killed to complete a quest or as part of a conquest battle."

Both men paused as numbers flashed up on their interfaces. The first was a golden *+500* followed immediately by a crimson red *-1,000.*

"What the hell?" Michael asked, his eyes tracking the bigger number.

"Fame points." Allistor's voice was cold and emotionless. "And I'm guessing Infamy points. Different factions. I'd bet money that the Fame points come from some faction that believes in preserving the life or integrity of newly acquired worlds. Maybe they just don't like killing. Or they object to the way things are being run around here. And the Infamy points would be from the ones who brought us here and planned this whole thing. Or those who are itching to come and take over. The ones who, as you've pointed out, don't give a shit about us NPCs. Sentenced billions of us to death. We're probably getting a little too uppity for them."

He looked up at the ceiling. Slamming his fists on the table, he shouted. "I got news for you! We humans, we don't give up that easy. We're violent, and smart, and cruel, and inventive, and most of all we adapt! We'll find a way to survive your genocide! We'll claim the planet for ourselves, and we'll make you pay in blood and tears for every inch of it you try to take! Then, when we're strong enough, we'll come find you. We'll take your planets from you. One by one, inch by inch if we have to! We'll be the ones deciding that billions of your people deserve to die. Only we'll have a reason! It's called vengeance!"

His throat was raw from screaming at the ceiling. The others had all come outside to see what the yelling was about. Allistor looked around, suddenly feeling tired. He sat back down. Looking at Michael, he said, "You tell them."

*****

Allistor woke early the next morning. He'd gone to bed alone after brooding for much of the evening. His rage hadn't subsided any. If anything, watching the others react to Michael's realization had made him angrier. These poor people had been through so much. And their ordeal was only just beginning. Not being gamers, they hadn't understood the horror of being an NPC. Michael had tried to explain it. But unless you'd been a player and seen the treatment NPCs received, or did some mistreating yourself, you just couldn't understand it fully. He was afraid that at the end of the year, they'd find out the hard way.

If they survived that long.

Resolved to live up to the threats he'd made, he started the day by focusing on his own growth. The stronger he was himself, the more he could help the others to grow. And protect them while they learned.

So first, he assigned his available attribute points. At level five he'd picked up two more, giving him five points. He put two into *Intelligence* and three into *Will Power*.

Immediately he noticed that his mana pool increased. From the fifty points that it had been to four hundred. He felt more clear-headed as well. Connections he hadn't quite made before were obvious to him now.

Next, he pulled out the *Levitate* scroll and opened it. The moment he started to read, the knowledge of how to cast the spell flooded into his mind. But as he reflected on it, it wasn't just the mechanics of casting the spell. He better-understood gravity and how to counteract it. He knew more about force and resistance, about density and momentum. All of the knowledge of the physical laws of the universe that were directly involved in levitating an object became clearer to him."

As the scroll disintegrated in his hand, he muttered to himself, "Damn. No wonder these things are so valuable. I was expecting to learn a chant or a hand motion or something. Not get a friggin degree in physics."

His spear sat leaning against the wall near the door. To test his new spell, he focused on the weapon and thought *levitate* at it as hard as he could. The butt of the spear lifted off the ground, but the point remained leaning against the wall, scraping along the stone as it rose. Unsure how to direct it, Allistor pointed a finger and moved it to one side, motioning the spear away from the wall as it floated a few inches above the floor. The butt end moved, and the spear point began to screech back down the wall until the spear was laying horizontal. It continued to move away from the wall until he stopped it.

"So... when I lift something odd-shaped like this, it doesn't automatically remain upright. Makes sense. Its natural resting position is horizontal. I'm only negating the gravity to a certain extent."

Allistor tried another motion, this time twisting his wrist roughly ninety degrees as he pointed. The spear point rose so that it was nearly vertical. He mentally released it, and it fell to the ground with a clang of metal on stone.

The flood of understanding decided a few things for him. He opened the market interface and checked on the status of the Mustang. The bid was over twenty thousand klax, and there were still almost twenty-four hours to go. There were three messages attached to bids from brokers offering top dollar for more rare items in a direct sale. Allistor smiled to himself. He didn't know how to do a direct sale, but he'd find out. For those times when they needed funds quickly. Being careful not to say it aloud for whoever was watching him, he thought, *That's right. I'll send you shit I don't need, and you'll send me the funds I need to make sure you never set foot on my world!*

The next thing he looked into was a bag of holding. He wanted to see if the system had something equivalent. He was beginning to believe that the legends and stories of his home had somehow been directly influenced by the Collective. To prime his race for entry into the system. Since so many tales and games included some sort of interdimensional storage, he assumed it would be a real thing on this new Earth. And he desperately wanted one.

His initial search, *bag of holding* came up with nothing useful. Bags of many shapes and sizes, but all ordinary. Nothing interdimensional. So he tried different combinations of descriptive terms until he ran across what he wanted.

They were called *Personal Pocket Dimension Accessories* and came in many forms including bags. And they weren't all that expensive.

The first he found was a ring. With a boring if accurate name.

PPD Ring
Quality: Good
Capacity: 100

This personal pocket dimension ring will store up to one hundred individual items in a secure private space. Items stored within will be preserved in a dimensional lock, unaffected by time. The physical weight of each object stored will be reduced to .001% of normal. Identical items such as currency or mass-produced items will stack within a single storage slot. Items within the storage inventory may not be removed by anyone other than the user. The item itself cannot be bound to the user, and thus may be stolen.

There were several other forms of PPDs, including bags, bracelets, charms, even undergarments. Some with greater capacity, some with less. But the ring was the most reasonably priced at two hundred klax. He purchased one for himself using his personal funds. After a moment's thought, he purchased eight more using Stronghold funds. They had gained more than enough just from defeating the canids inside the Stronghold to pay for the rings. Leaving his quarters, he went directly to the market kiosk and logged in. A box appeared on the shelf behind the holo-display. When he retrieved and opened it, there were nine PPD rings inside.

He put one on his finger and *Examined* it. The description was exactly the same as the one the market interface gave. As a test, he touched his spear to the ring, and it disappeared. An inventory interface popped up, and he saw the spear occupying one slot in a ten by ten grid.

Several of the others were seated in the dining room having breakfast. He put some scrambled eggs and toast on a plate and sat to eat. When everyone was together, he stood up.

"Good morning, folks. First, I'd like to apologize for my rant yesterday. I must have seemed like a lunatic. I let my anger get the better of me, and I am sorry."

He didn't wait for replies. Either they'd let it slide or they wouldn't. Instead, he held up the box. "And I'll apologize for another thing while I'm at it. I made a command decision just now and spent sixteen hundred klax of Stronghold funds on these."

He opened the box and began to hand them out. Chloe smiled prettily and blushed as he presented her ring with a flourish. He was glad to see no evidence of scarring on her face.

Each of them stared at the gift as he handed it to them.

Michael was predictably first. "Shit! You found bags of holding!"

When the others began to ask what that was, Michael launched into a description of the storage devices and why they were so handy to have around. He picked up a slice of bacon and touched it to his ring, making it disappear. Then he said, "Imagine you had a thousand strips of bacon. You could put them all in your ring, they'd only take up one slot, and would weigh almost nothing. Oh! And they'd never go bad. You could pull one out a year later and it would be as delicious as the day it was cooked."

Sam scooted away from Meg slightly before asking, "So I could store ten cheesecakes in here?" Meg reached over and slapped the back of his head.

Michael laughed. "Or a hundred. And a hundred perfectly grilled steaks. Doesn't matter. I'd have to read up a little about the limitations… but it's possible you could store something as large as a car. Uh, don't try that until we're sure. Might destroy the ring and lose you whatever else you had stored in there. For now, let's just stick with nothing bigger than... a beach ball."

*****

Morning found Allistor once again alone. He was beginning to think the night with Amanda was either a one-time thing, the result of too much rum, or both. She hadn't seemed uncomfortable around him at all afterwards, but then they hadn't really been alone to talk.

The previous day had been dedicated to organization and preparation. Folks worked on their skills – developing the ones they'd already earned or attempting to achieve new ones. Michael had managed to pick up *Blacksmithing* by taking the bent shotgun apart, putting the barrel in the furnace that came with the crafting hall, and then using a heavy hammer to pound at it atop the anvil Allistor had found. The crafting hall had come with an anvil as well, but Michael had said he trusted the one he knew had been made on Earth.

Allistor had spent some time on his *Weaponsmithing*. He took the now-ruined shotgun from Michael when he was through with it and heated it again. He took turns heating and pounding at it until he had the rough approximation of a blade. It was maybe thirty inches long, double-edged with a thick spine. The point was a little blunt – Allistor had been concerned about it being too pointy and the tip breaking off.

When it had cooled, he took a file and began to sharpen the blade edges. After more than an hour working his way across the length of both edges, he went to work on the handle. Using another piece of the octopoid hide, he

168

wrapped it around the handle. The moment it was tight, Allistor got a notification.

Your Weaponsmithing skill has increased by +1!

He *Examined* the weapon.

Basic Sword, One-handed
Quality: Common
Durability: 400/400
Damage: 200 slashing, 200 piercing

Then another notification came.

Your Improvisation skill his increased by +1
You took a ruined cast-off weapon and repurposed it into a viable blade.

At the end of the day, almost everyone had improved a skill at least once. Several interesting items had been crafted. The most popular of which was some beef jerky made by Sam that provided a buff of +1 to Stamina for three hours.

Lilly had added *Leatherworking* to her *Tailoring* by creating a simple sheath for Allistor's sword. She had also taken a few of the canid hides and created several pairs of bracers. This had leveled both her *Tailoring* and *Leatherworking*. First, she'd sacrificed one of the hospital towels, cutting off pieces in a pattern that would match up to the bracers. Then she cut the leather into the same pattern, only slightly larger. And cut several thin strips of leather to use as laces. Setting the towel pieces inside the leather, she stitched them together to provide a soft lining and a small bit of additional protection. Then she ran the laces loosely through holes up and down either end of the leather in a crisscross pattern much like one would lace a shoe. She used Ramon as her guinea pig. Sliding his hand through and tightening the laces. She tied off the end, making sure the fit was snug. He moved and flexed his arm, saying it felt great. It was a little difficult to remove after being tightened, but with her helping, he was able to tug it off. She made a few modifications, and Ramon declared it perfect. She went on to make enough for everyone, even little Chloe.

Today Allistor planned to make them enough funds to expand their holdings, purchase better weapons, and do whatever else they needed to do to make absolutely certain they thrived on this new world. The auction on the Mustang was less than an hour from its end, and the high bid was thirty-eight thousand klax. There were still no other earth cars listed. He intended to take advantage of that for as long as possible.

Sitting with Sam at breakfast, he said, "How 'bout we go find your friend's Corvette?"

Sam nodded, his mouth full of bacon. He mumbled something unintelligible.

Turning to Michael, he said, "You and Ramon feel up to a road trip? There was a bench grinder in the hospital maintenance shop that I didn't have time to unbolt. Might be some other useful items as well. But more importantly, I'd like you to check out the winery. If you can, bring back a truckload of their best wine. Each bottle might sell for as much as we paid for each of these rings. We'll list a couple of cases first. If they become popular, we'll restrict the sale to single bottles, and charge more!" He grinned at them.

"Right. Crafty stuff, then drunky stuff. Got it!" Ramon agreed. He stepped into the crafting hall where they'd stored all their tools and materials. A few minutes later he returned with a tool bag and two radios. He handed one radio to Sam. "The winery is ten miles out, but these radios are supposed to be able to cover the whole county. We can test that out today."

Sam said, "If you get the chance to grab one of their box trucks, do it. Load it up and bring it back. The keys should be somewhere in the office. If not a truck, any usable vehicle would be good."

Both trucks set off, Lilly waving at them as she waited to close the gates behind them. Allistor let Sam drive, since he knew where Frank's house was. It only took a few minutes to reach the place once they got out of the debris-strewn streets of town. Both men were glad to see the house and separate three-car garage were intact.

Sam pulled up the long driveway and got out of the truck. Rifle in hand, he waited for Allistor to join him. The two approached the front door. It was standing slightly ajar, which wasn't a good sign. Allistor went through the door first, his shotgun a more effective short-range weapon than Sam's rifle.

The inside of the house was a mess. Not total chaos like the cafeteria had been, but the sofa was shredded, a china cabinet knocked over, and the dishes broken. They found what they assumed was all that was left of Frank – a large splattering of blood on the kitchen floor and cabinets. An S&W .45 lay on the floor nearby, locked open. Frank had managed to empty the magazine before he died. There were canid prints in the blood leading out the back door. Allistor closed the door and locked it, then did the same at the front door. The two men cleared the house, checking the basement and upper floors. When they were sure it was all clear, Sam went right to a cabinet next to the fridge. He grabbed a key ring and looked at Allistor. "The garage."

The garage was thankfully undisturbed. And there was a treasure trove inside! The Corvette sat covered in the rightmost bay. Next to it was a long workbench covered in tools, with a six-foot-high multi-tiered Snap-On toolbox on wheels. The rest of that wall of the garage was built-in metal cabinets.

On the other side of the Corvette, in the middle bay, sat a pair of ATV's. One was a single-seater, the other one of the big Gators that could seat four and some gear on a rack at the back. Allistor drooled. These would be great for scouting missions, or small retrievals of specific items. The last bay held a full-sized pickup, another useful vehicle.

He looked over at Sam, whose face was much less enthused. He was looking at the ATVs with a tear in his eye.

"Frank was a good friend?" Allistor asked.

"The best. Known him all my life. Went to school together, played ball together. Even enlisted together, though we got assigned to different units. We took these ATVs out fishing just a few weeks ago. He got a bite, started yelling about it being the Loch Ness monster. It might have been, cuz it pulled his drunk ass into the water!" Sam half-chuckled, half-sobbed. He laid a hand on the nearest ATV. "Gonna miss ya, my friend."

Allistor didn't know what to do. "Hey, umm… we can just leave this stuff here. We'll find other vehicles-"

"Nope." Sam cut him off. "Frank would want us to have this stuff. If he were alive, he'd want to fight right alongside us. We'll take these and the guns." He pointed to a large safe against the back wall. "Damned armory in there. More underneath the floor. Frank wasn't an actual doomsday prepper, but he was a step away from becoming one. There's a bunker built into the hill out back. More supplies and guns in there. But I'm thinking maybe we

172

leave that alone? Could be a good place to hole up if we need to. Or another Stronghold point?"

Allistor wanted to hug the man. "Agreed. We can maybe load one of the ATVs onto our truck. Come back for the other one after we drive the Corvette back?"

"Nope," Sam said again, smiling this time. "There's a car trailer out back. Frank used it to take the 'Vette to car shows. We can load the car on the trailer. Put an ATV in the back of his truck, one in the back of ours. I'll drive his truck back. We'll empty the safe there. Load it on the trailer behind the car. Too heavy for one of the pickups." He pointed to a wet bar in the corner next to an open bathroom door. "Move that wet bar, there's a trap door. Storage area down below. Maybe a dozen hunting rifles, some handguns, and lots of ammo. Again, maybe we leave it there for now? We've got more guns than we need."

Allistor didn't want to ask, but they needed some sellable rare items. "Any of the guns in the safe an antique? Or something special?"

Sam glared at him for a minute when he realized why Allistor was asking. Then he sighed. "You're right. There's an old flintlock from the early 1800s. It's no good to us. Might as well use it to trade for something that'll help us. There's also an early colt pistol. But... if you don't mind, I'd like to keep that one. To remember him by."

Allistor held up both hands. "Hey, man. Everything here is yours as far as I'm concerned. I'll take whatever you're willing to donate to help the community, and thank you sincerely. But anything here you want for yourself is yours, no question."

Sam put a beefy hand on Allistor's shoulder, tears still threatening to fall from his eyes. "You're a good kid." He sniffed, wiping both eyes with the palm of his hand. "Now, let's go get that trailer moved up here."

"I got that. You uh... spend a little quality time in here. I'll be back in a couple minutes." Allistor left Sam in the garage and walked around back. There was a gravel drive that led around to a wide pad where the trailer was parked. Allistor removed the blocks from under the wheels and the hitch and placed them carefully at the front of the trailer. It was a top of the line transport trailer with steel mesh sides and a winch at the front for pulling cars up onto it. The back end had two small ramps that could be folded out, and a wider ramp in between. All three could be dropped out for loading things like the ATVs or furniture.

He spent a few minutes admiring the thing, giving Sam some time to collect himself. As he waited, a rustling sound reached him. His head jerked around to where he thought the sound had originated. Across the yard that stretched out about fifty yards behind both the house and garage, the tree line was still dark. The sun hadn't risen high enough to clear the trees and shed light through the canopy.

The sound came again, and Allistor unslung the shotgun from his shoulder. A moment later, a dog shot out from the underbrush, heading toward the house. Not a canid, an actual Earth dog. A chocolate lab, Allistor thought. He called out, then whistled. The dog faltered midstride as it turned to look at him.

A second later, three canids emerged from the brush, hot on the trail of the dog. The lab yelped and picked up speed, changing direction toward the garage. Allistor shouted, "Sam! Canids!"

He raised his weapon and sighted on the lead canid. It was twenty yards or so behind the lab, but its superior muscle mass and six legs allowed it to gain on its prey. Allistor led it a bit and fired.

It wasn't an ideal distance for his weapon, but the 12-gauge slug struck the canid in the neck, knocking it off its feet. Allistor chambered another round and took aim at the next one. Before he could fire, Sam's rifle rang out. The canid in Allistor's sights dropped like a stone, dead before it hit the ground. Allistor looked over to see Sam on one knee at the corner of the garage, already working the bolt to chamber another round.

The dog, seeing Sam, barked twice and charged straight toward him. It leapt at him, bowling him over. Allistor raised his weapon, but couldn't get a clear shot at the dog. Instead, he turned his sights on the last canid. This time his slug went wide, hitting the mob in its hindquarters. The impact still knocked it over, but it quickly got back up. Its left rear leg was disabled, but the now maddened beast still had five legs. And it was now targeting Allistor.

He needed to hurry up and dispatch this one so that he could help Sam. He fired three rounds as rapidly as he could, punching into the canid's chest, and finally, its head. When it went down for good, Allistor turned to Sam.

The man was laughing, trying to calm the dog and free his weapon. "Stop it, Max!" he pushed at the excited lab. "I'm glad to see you too! But you brought monsters home with you! Now, sit!"

The lab ceased its lick-attacks at the command and obediently planted his butt on the ground. His tail still wagged furiously, and his tongue hung out to one side as he panted. Sam raised his rifle and scanned the tree line. "Is that all of them?" he called out to Allistor.

"I only saw three. But there might be more out there?"

Sam shook his head, looking down at the lab. "Max doesn't think so. He's too relaxed. Then again, this stupid mutt might not recognize danger if it bit him in the ass." He reached down and patted the dog's head. Max woofed at him softly.

"I take it Max belonged to Frank?"

"Yeah. Just got him a couple years ago. When Sally died, Frank was lonely. Meg saw a litter of lab pups at the grocery store. We got one, and she brought Max to Frank. Our Rufus didn't survive the titan." He continued to pet Max.

Allistor started walking across the lawn. He looted the closest of the canids he'd killed, getting the usual 30 klax, some leather, meat, pelt, teeth. Sam followed him out to loot the one he'd dropped. Allistor really needed to figure out if they could group up and share loot so that one person could loot everything. As he passed Sam's kill headed for the first canid he'd shot, Max began to growl behind him. Allistor turned mid-stride to see what Max was upset about and didn't see the first canid lunge at him.

His first warning was the snarl as it pushed forward, then pain as it latched onto his shin. The razor-sharp teeth clamped down and punctured deep into his leg. It shook its thick, well-muscled neck, shredding his flesh and snapping a bone.

Sam's rifle fired even as Allistor was falling backward, trying to bring his own weapon around. The canid's head exploded, a cone-shaped spray of blood

176

coating the grass behind it. The creature fell back down to the grass, twisting and tearing Allistor's leg as it went. Allistor screamed in pain, looking at the torn flesh and broken bone as he writhed on the ground. Sam came running up and fell to his knees next to him.

"Shit. That's bad. We need to cut off the blood flow or you won't make it back." He unclipped the strap from Allistor's shotgun and wrapped it around his leg above the knee, clipping the two ends together. Then he cinched it as tight as it would go. Allistor grunted in pain again, but he didn't complain. Max sniffed at the wound, then gave it a tentative lick, causing Allistor to nearly pass out. Sam shouldered the dog aside. "Don't help, Max." He was half-grinning as he worked. Happy to see the dog alive.

"Leg's broken, but it's just a fracture. I can see the break. If you don't lose all your blood, you'll be fine. He took his shirt off and wrapped it around Allistor's calf and shin, using the two sleeves to tie it off. "Let's get you into the truck. I'll run you back, and we can return for this stuff later.

Allistor shook his head. "This is good enough. Give me some of that jerky you made. I've got water in my ring. It'll be good enough to keep me going while you hook up the trailer. Let's get this done. I'll sit here and keep watch while you work.

Sam nodded, pulling some jerky out of his own ring and handing it to Allistor. He stomped off toward the trailer, grabbing hold of the tongue and pulling it forward with a little effort. A minute later it disappeared around the other side of the garage and Allistor could hear him hooking it up.

Max had chosen to stay with Allistor, lying next to him in the grass and whining. He kept sniffing at the injured leg and looking sadly at the human next to him. Allistor, still in a lot of pain, petted the dog to reassure him. It helped relax him a bit as he scanned the tree line.

The sound of the Corvette engine firing up was music to his ears. Sam let it run for a minute or two, then he pulled it up onto the trailer and shut it off. There was a bit of clanking and clanging, followed by the sound of first one ATV, then the other being started up and driven up into the trucks.

Roughly ten minutes had passed since Sam had bandaged his leg. Allistor had looted the canid at his feet and was feeling better, the pain receding a bit. The buff from the jerky had him feeling stronger. Still, he could see blood spreading through the shirt's fabric very slowly. He knew he needed to loosen the strap on his thigh soon, to allow a little circulation. But he was hoping the wounds would have closed by now. With a sigh, he loosened the strap. The stains on the shirt grew more quickly. After about thirty seconds, he began to feel dizzy. He quickly tightened the strap again, grunting in pain. He grabbed the bottle and drank some more water.

Max whined, laying his head in Allistor's lap for moral support. Allistor laughed in spite of the pain. He scratched the dog's ears and rubbed his tummy, waiting for Sam to return. Another ten minutes passed in doggy-communing bliss before Sam walked up.

"Everything's loaded. Except the safe. Going to need help to move that." He extended a hand and helped Allistor to his feet.

"I might be able to help." Allistor tested his weight on the injured foot. He didn't feel much pain, as the leg was asleep from lack of circulation. He took a single step forward, and the pain was bearable. After a few more, he said, "Yeah, let's do this."

The two men walked slowly back to the garage, Max frolicking around them and barking happily. Sam just smiled at him and muttered, "Stupid mutt."

When they reached the garage, Allistor saw that the vehicles were loaded, and more than a dozen long guns were stowed in the back of Frank's pickup. Next to the empty gun safe stood a four-wheeled furniture dolly – basically, four lengths of 2x4 bolted in a square with a wheel at each corner. Sam said, "We can wheel it right up the trailer ramp on its side, if you help me tilt it onto the dolly.

Allistor obliged, gritting his teeth against the pain as they first lowered the safe, then pushed it up the ramp together. When they were done, he took a minute to sit on the stool by the workbench and loosen the strap again. This time there seemed to be less blood loss. Or the shirt was just so saturated he couldn't tell the difference.

With everything loaded, Sam boosted him up into the pickup, asking no less than three times if Allistor was sure he was okay to drive. When Allistor finally answered, "Yes, mom, I'll be fine," Sam snorted and let it go.

"You're a tough bastard, I'll give you that." Sam waved at him as he closed the garage doors, then he jumped in Frank's pickup with Max. He pulled forward, the trailer with the Corvette and the gun safe following behind. Allistor pulled in behind them and let out a long sigh, ready to get back to the Warren and crash. He felt a slight twinge as he realized he was about to get some alone time with Amanda.

Chapter Eight

Money for Nothin and Your Skills for Free

The next several days passed uneventfully. Parties went out foraging, occasionally running across mobs. There were injuries, but no fatalities. People worked on their skills, trained their bodies, ate, drank, and got to know each other better.

The Mustang sold for forty-one thousand klax. The Corvette - still the only Earth vehicle on the market - went for an even higher sixty thousand klax. Ramon and Michael had returned with a box truck filled with wine and other usable items, including the grinder which was now installed in the crafting hall. Allistor had sold six cases of the best wine for two thousand klax each. Then he'd stopped putting them up for sale, wanting to allow time for the buyers to spread word about the quality of the wine. In a few more days he'd start putting up single bottles.

The old flintlock hadn't sold. Allistor wasn't sure why, but he intended to modify his write-up and put it back up.

A week after establishing The Warren, they were sitting on over a hundred thousand klax. Everyone had become stronger and more skilled in their professions. They had foraged more food and supplies than they could use in two months. They now had a fleet of three pickup trucks, a box truck, a Humvee, a tractor with several modules, three ATVs and a pair of dirt bikes. Things were looking up.

Allistor called a meeting as everyone was eating lunch. "Okay, folks. You've all been doing a great job! We've got food, cash, weapons, and a safe place to sleep. I think we should spend some of our moolah and make some improvements. The question I have for you is… do we add to the stronghold? Do we buy some scrolls for our various professions? Or do we spend it in some other way?"

Meg spoke up first. "I mean, I think we've got plenty of room here. Do we really need any improvements to this place right now?"

"We could expand upward?" Nancy offered. "Put some walls up. Make it easier to get some sunshine. And it would protect the crops we plant."

Ramon, who had been spending quite a bit of time with Nancy and Chloe, shook his head. "That would be nice. But it presents a danger, too. Walls will draw attention. Until there are more of us, or we're a lot stronger, I think it's better if we remain hidden."

Several around the table muttered agreement. Nancy sighed, but she let it drop. Lilly took her hand. "We can take Chloe topside for a little bit every day. Start with a small garden, maybe? Close to the gates. The sensors will tell us if anything is approaching in plenty of time for us to get back inside."

Chloe had been enchanted with Max from the moment he arrived. And the feeling was mutual. The two had adopted each other and were constantly romping around the cavern together. For most of the week, the only time the girl had been outside was to let Max out to do his business. And her mother had kept her within a few yards of the gates. "She'd love that. Thank you, Lilly." Nancy hugged her.

Michael spoke up. "I'd really like that *Power Infusion* scroll. I've been leveling my *Blacksmithing*, and I can make decent armor now. But being able to enchant it

181

would go a long way toward protecting us while we're outside."

Allistor agreed whole-heartedly. He was hoping the group would lean toward personal improvement. They could always find a new Stronghold if they lost The Warren. As long as they were individually strong, and worked together, they would survive.

"Anybody else have something they want to learn? Or improve? With scrolls, I mean."

Meg raised her hand. "A few more recipes would be good. For food buffs."

Nancy added. "I could use a few alchemy recipes as well. Fast-healing potions especially. And... I need to spend some time outside gathering plants. Or start planting them in that garden. Or both. I can't increase my skill level without ingredients."

Ramon said, "I've been reading about the *Scribe* skill. It seems I can learn to make spell scrolls. But to do so, I have to learn the spell first. So, if there are any affordable spells that would also be useful? I can learn it, write it down, and others can learn it too. We could also sell the scrolls for profit."

Allistor replied. "You bring up a good point there, my friend. Let's talk about our economic system. Within our group, I mean. So far, everyone has been generous in sharing the fruits of their labor. We've worked on sort of an informal barter system, or maybe more of a commune. Anyway, some of you may want to start building individual wealth. To purchase things for yourselves, or even branch out to claim a Stronghold of your own. And I don't want anyone to feel like they're being held back from that." He looked around the table.

"I think we should set a certain goal. A level of development that, when we reach it, we can all begin to focus more on personal gains. Whether that is a certain population level, a certain defense level, whatever it is. Until we reach it, we continue as we are. All the crafting items we loot from kills or forage go into the pot for our crafters to use. In return, they give the fruits of that labor to others who can use them. It makes sense for now as we're all trying to gain and increase our skills."

"Once we reach that point, I propose a percentage of what we loot and forage still goes into the community pot. Say, twenty-five percent? The rest you can all use as you like. Whether that means gifting, trading, selling, or hoarding. There will be no price gouging amongst ourselves. Anything you sell to one of us has to be priced fairly, if not discounted. You can milk the bastards on the open market for every klax you can get." His devilish grin brought some laughter. "Anybody disagree so far?"

Everybody shook their heads no. Sam added, "I think that's more than fair. I myself have no plans to branch out. I'm in this for the long haul. We build a community here, add to it as we can, and defend it with everything we have. A year will pass by quickly, and I hope we control the entire county by then. If not the whole state!" Meg thumped a hand on the table, over and over again. One by one, the others joined in a show of solidarity.

A few more minutes' discussion and they had agreed on the metrics for their economic structure, at least for the balance of the year. Everyone finished lunch and spent some time looking at the market for useful scrolls and giving their list to Allistor.

When they all went back to what they were doing, he began going through the list and searching the market.

He'd been given a total of ten requests for scrolls. Nobody was being greedy, as they were aware of the costs.

He purchased Michael's *Power Infusion* scroll for six hundred klax. And two *Alchemy* recipes for Nancy at a thousand each. One was a *Common Healing Potion,* the other called *Regeneration* that was supposed to speed health, mana, and stamina regeneration to ten times the normal rate for thirty seconds. He found and purchased a druid spell called *"Nature's Boon"* that said it could heal for three hundred health points. It cost a thousand klax, but if it were for real, that could save lives. He'd get Ramon to learn and copy it for everyone.

He purchased ten cooking recipes, having found a bundle for sale for five hundred klax. They all used meat from the invading species they'd been killing - canid, lanx, and octopoid, as well as a few others he hadn't run across yet. He hoped that Sam and Meg would be able to adapt them to beef and pork because they gave some solid buffs.

Allistor also found half a dozen *tailoring* and *leatherworking* patterns. Shirts, pants, boots, a good start for Lilly's crafting. He also found a few for plate armor and chain mail.

For himself, he purchased a couple combat spells. The first was a stun spell called *Restraint* that would incapacitate an opponent for three to ten seconds, depending on an incomprehensible formula that factored in the level of the caster, the target, the *Will Power* of each, etc. The second was a fire spell call *Flame Shot.* From the description, he could cast flame either in fireball form, or just a burst surrounding the target. They were a thousand klax each. He also purchased three copies of a *Weaponsmithing* related scroll called *Metallurgy* that was supposed to give him knowledge of base metals and alloys that should help him improve his crafted items. He'd give the others to Michael and Ramon. They were twelve hundred klax combined.

With Ramon in mind, he purchased the *Scribe* spell, plus two more scrolls for scribes. The first was called *Calligraphy* and it taught some form of lettering that was supposed to enhance the chances of successfully writing a spell and the power of said spell. That was an expensive one at two thousand klax, but if it improved Ramon's scrolls, they'd make that back with just a few transactions. The second was called *The Art of Ink* which cost a thousand klax and was supposed to impart knowledge of the various herbs and powdered ingredients that made up inks that increased the power of the scrolls. It was also supposed to teach the user which colors were best for each type of magic.

Then he purchased a dozen minor spell scrolls for Ramon to practice on. Spells like *Light* which created a small light globe, and *Dowse* which allowed the caster to find nearby sources of water. Another was *Night Vision,* which was pretty self-explanatory. These were all a hundred klax each. He figured they'd be good spells for Ramon to reproduce and for everyone in the group to learn.

He found a spell called *Grow* for Nancy that would allow her to speed up the growth rate and size of whatever she planted. And a formula for fertilizer.

Lastly, he found a spell called *Internal Analysis* that, from the description, would allow Amanda to be her own MRI and X-ray machine. It would allow her to look inside a patient to assess their injuries better.

It almost felt like cheating, purchasing all these spells and the ability to reproduce them. As he considered how much of a cheat it would be in a game, he realized two things. First, this was real life. And if he had to cheat to survive and keep his people alive, he'd damn well cheat. And second, the amounts he was paying for these spells would normally be well beyond the means of a low-level player. The broken aspect of this system was actually the ability to sell rare items for massive moolah, and being among the first to discover and exploit it.

Completing his transactions, he retrieved the dozens of scrolls from the kiosk window and began making his rounds, passing them out. Ramon actually hugged him when he dumped the pile of scrolls on a workbench in front of him. Michael chuckled like an evil overlord gloating over his plan for world domination.

Amanda chose a more active form of thanks. When she read the description of the *Internal Analysis* spell, she instantly opened and learned it. Sitting patiently on her exam table, Allistor watched her zone out and noticed a faint flash in her eyes. He also detected a sort of wavy distortion field around her that resembled the heat waves you might see in a desert. He reached out to touch it, but it faded before he came in contact.

She turned to him, saying, "Thank you, lover. Now strip!"

Allistor chuckled as he started to pull his shirt off. "I wonder if Nancy and Lilly are gonna thank me this way..." She smacked the back of his head.

"You wish. I'm gonna test out this new spell. You're my guinea pig."

Pausing in the act of undoing his belt, he stopped disrobing. She could look through his chest. No reason to put his bare butt on the cold table for no good reason. "Fine. Go for it."

Amanda mumbled something, then her eyes began to glow again. She stared directly into his chest for a minute or so. Then she took his hand and raised it, examining the hand, wrist, arm, and then shoulder. "Interesting," she mumbled as she moved upward to stare into his head. Allistor felt a little creeped out.

"What's interesting in my head?" He was actually a little nervous she'd found a tumor or something.

"Hmmm... what?" She blinked, and the light left her eyes. "Oh. No. Not in your head. As far as I could see it's empty." She smirked at him as he rolled his eyes. "No, what was interesting is your elbow and your shoulder. Though they have fully healed, and healed quickly because of whatever the system does to us, I could see the remodeling of the bone. Both the break in your elbow and the dents that lanx put in your shoulder. Remodeling can often make a bone stronger than it was before the break. So... letting things bite you all the time, as Chloe would put it, might actually be making you stronger."

She thought for a while, puttering around with his hand. "Makes sense, really. I mean, if you suddenly dumped five points into Strength and had the muscle mass to leap over a building, you'd need the bone structure to survive the landing. Assuming it didn't kill you, each time you damaged yourself, you'd heal up and get stronger."

She set down his hand and cast the spell again. This time looking through his jeans where he'd broken his leg. "Works through clothes, no problem." She touched his thigh as she leaned down to get a closer look. "And there's remodeling here as well. I wonder... I'd like to be using this spell on someone when they increase their constitution. Fascinating."

She handed him his shirt. "As for the other thing, the thank you, come by my quarters tonight and we'll talk about it." She saw him grin and start to take his shirt back off. Holding up a hand she said, "Easy there, killer. You've got more scrolls to deliver." and pushed him off the table. She shooed him out of the infirmary, already grabbing a pad to take some notes.

Before he left, he paused at the door and asked, "Can you do me a favor?"

"What do you think tonight's going to be?" She snorted.

He chose to ignore the jab. "I noticed a sort of... wavy field around you when you learned that spell. I have a couple here for myself. Can you watch me once with normal eyes, and once with that spell going?"

Instantly interested, she motioned for him to hop back on the table. Telling him to wait a second, she left the room and came back with a video camera mounted on her forehead with a head strap. "I plan to use this for surgeries and such. So if something goes wrong, I can see what it was. If I *ever get to do any*. With the healing system here, I might be better off just working with Meg and learning recipes for snacks that cure cancer and heal shotgun wounds in two minutes." She sounded more than a little bitter.

"Tell you what. Next time I get all bit up, I'll try 'n' make it back here quick for some stitches." He looked at her. "Or uh, cardiac surgery or something. Put my heart in your hands!" He put a hand over his heart and made a puppy dog face.

"Fool. Grab your first spell and let's do this." Her words were harsh, but her tone was amused. Allistor grabbed his Metallurgy scroll. After looking up at her to confirm she was ready, he opened it and began to read. Again, he felt the rush of knowledge flood his mind. Information on types of metal and where they can generally be found from a geological standpoint, how they react to heat and cold and pressure and stress. Ways to combine them with specific ingredients to make them stronger or more pliable. Formulas for alloys.

When it was over, he looked at Amanda. She was staring at him, sort of. Her focus was on the air around him. "That was cool!" She gasped. You were right. Some kind of distortion field around you. I touched it. There was no heat, but I got a shock. Like a static charge. And I felt a sort of... warning in my head. To stay back." She rubbed her fingers together as if testing the texture of something. "Fingers are asleep."

"Ha! I was about to do the same with you a few minutes ago. Glad it was *you* that was the guinea pig instead." His smile was probably wider than it should have been, considering his hopes for later.

She didn't seem to notice. "Alright, magic boy. Let's do it again! This time I'll use my spell to watch.

He removed his *Restraint* scroll and opened it. This time the process was much faster. He knew instinctively that much of the knowledge he needed for this spell had already been imparted by the *Levitate* scroll. Gravity, density, force, momentum. There was some additional information about the formula used to determine if the spell would succeed against targets of higher or lower levels with various attributes. He ignored all of that and focused on Amanda.

She was biting her lower lip as she stared at him. "Fascinating."

"Wanna clue me in?"

"Well, you know how we've been wondering how this new system works? How we can beef ourselves up or do magic, heal in minutes?"

"Yeahhhh…"

"I'm seeing… for lack of a better term, I'm gonna call them critters. No, maybe nanobots is a better description. When you activated that scroll, a field of millions – maybe billions – of the things coalesced around you. Mostly around your head. I could see them inside you. And now that I know to look for them, I can see them in your bloodstream. And your bones. Clustered more densely around where you've healed."

She picked up a scalpel from the nearby instrument table and grabbed his hand. "Hold still." Before he could object, she sliced one of his fingers nearly to the bone. She held his hand still as he protested.

"Hey! Dammit, woman. How 'bout a little warning?"

"Quit whining. I'll kiss it better later. Now hush and let me watch."

After a minute or so, she said, "They're gathering but only slowly. Grab some jerky from your ring and eat it. Drink some water, too."

He did as instructed, focusing on the whole 'kissing it better' aspect of what she'd said. A few seconds after he washed down the first bite of jerky, she began to clap her hands happily. "There it is! Whatever the mechanic is that triggers the healing increase from food and drink, it just kicked in. The critters are swarming around your finger now. I can actually see the skin starting to knit itself closed. This is *awesome!*"

He stared at his finger. He could see the bleeding slow, then stop. A minute or so later, the wound had closed to create a thin pink scar. A minute more, and the scar was gone.

Allistor looked up at Amanda. Still holding the scalpel in her hand, she was looking from him to it and back again. He yanked his hand away. "Ohhh, no you don't! Put that thing down. I've guinea pig'd enough for one day."

She gave him a pouty face. "Spoilsport. But thank you. I got two skill points out of that!"

Damn. Now he was reconsidering. Skill points were hard to come by. And pain was temporary. "Uhm, that's awesome. If you cut me again, will it get you more points?" He held his hand back out.

She shook her head. "Probably not. At least not until I think of a new way to approach this. But thank you for being willing." She gave him a brief kiss. "I may ask you to be my piggy again later."

Shaking his head, he left her to review her video and make notes. He delivered the rest of the scrolls and chatted with each of the recipients for a few minutes. He watched each one as they learned their spells. And though he knew better, he tried to touch Nancy as she was learning one of the *Alchemy* recipes.

When Chloe saw him get shocked, she giggled. Then she tried it herself, putting an end to her laughter. "Ow! Dammit!" When she realized what she'd said, her eyes got big, and she covered her mouth with both hands.

Allistor winked at the little girl and was about to say he wouldn't tell, when Nancy said, "I heard that, young

191

lady!" Chloe speedily retreated outside, Max bounding after her.

Allistor chuckled. "Mom radar. Never fails. My mother used to catch me doing stuff from blocks away." He shared a smile with Nancy.

He'd informed each recipient that there would be a meeting at lunchtime. When they were all gathered, he asked Amanda to share what she'd learned by watching him. She quickly laid it out for them in simple terms. Immediately there was a flood of questions. He held up both hands to quieten them.

"I have one more spell to learn for myself. You can all watch. I warn you - don't try to touch me. The result is shocking." He grinned at his own joke. Nobody else did.

He pulled out his *Flame Shot* scroll, opened it and read it. He didn't see the looks on everyone's faces as he was distracted by the information upload. This time it was more extensive as most of the information was new. He learned at what temperature the air around him would ignite, and how bad that would be for him. He absorbed information on combustible materials and their ignition points. Vectors and intercept courses for hitting moving targets. How to control whether heat built up almost instantly or more slowly. And how to keep it contained in a pressurized space for maximum benefit. The latter would, in theory, allow him to appear to hold a ball of flame in his hand without being burned.

When he refocused his eyes, the others were staring at him. Amanda was once again using her spell to look inside him. A few folks had been distracted by her glowing eyes.

To get their attention, and to show off a little bit if he was honest, he raised a finger and shot a short burst of flame into the air.

"Show-off!" Michael accused him, though he was laughing when he said it.

"That was cool!" Chloe shouted, standing up in her chair. "Teach me!"

"Over my dead body." Nancy pushed her back down onto her bottom.

Sam cleared his throat. "So, we have these things. Whether they're nanobots or midichlorians from Star Wars or friggin' Whovians, whatever you wanna call them-"

"Whos," Meg interrupted him.

"What?" A flustered Sam looked at her, annoyed.

"Whovians are people that run around with trench coats and very long scarves saying, 'It's bigger on the inside.' You're thinking of the tiny little people that Horton heard, which are whos."

Chloe smiled and nodded her head. "They live in Whoville!"

Properly chastised, Sam continued. "Fine. Whos. Or damned Tweedlebugs. Whatever." He waited for Meg to correct him again, but she just smiled. "So these things are inside us now? Like, all the time?" He rubbed his chest as if he had acid reflux.

"As far as I can tell," Amanda confirmed. "And not just inside us. I think they're all around us, all the time. And we only see them when they congregate around us in a high density to heal or upload info."

Lilly said, "So we can like, use the force?"

"I'm not sure what to call it," Allistor admitted. "It has struck me that a lot of the games and movies from the last couple decades have born a strong resemblance to what we're experiencing now. I'm starting to suspect there was some kind of seeding of information on Earth to sort of prep us for all of this. Though I don't know why our evil overlords bothered if they were just going to wipe us out anyway."

"Not all of us." Ramon held up a finger to emphasize his point. "They're keeping ten percent of us. Which is roughly a billion humans. They must see some value in us. Even if it's only for entertainment." His eyes unfocused for a second. "Whoa. I just got fifty Fame Points."

Amanda said, "I'm going to study this. Learn as much as I can. Maybe there's some kind of book or something on the market that will answer our questions. I mean, we can't be the first world to be assimilated, right? Others must have asked and answered these questions before us."

A few more minutes of speculation and the group dispersed again. Chloe leapt off of her chair and called to Max as she dashed off behind the crafting house. "Let's go find some whos!" The dog barked happily and bounded after the little girl.

Chapter Nine

Fluffy Bunnies

Another week passed as the group did their best to level up skills. The scrolls Allistor purchased had given everyone a boost - the knowledge they gained helping them to better understand what materials they needed and how to use them.

Lilly was making cloth and leather items that had better stats than before – some with as much as +3 in one attribute, or bonuses in two or three attributes at once. Michael was making uncommon quality chain mail shirts for everyone with *Stamina* and *Constitution* bumps.

Ramon had learned all of the spells from the scrolls he was given, and he was having reasonable success in duplicating them. Everyone had learned the *Light* and *Night Vision* spells. Most had also learned the healing spell *Nature's Boon* from copies that Ramon had made. Sam and Chloe didn't have the necessary attributes to learn the spell – Sam because his *Intelligence* and *Will Power* were both at two, and Chloe because she was too young. Or so they assumed, since her attributes weren't showing up yet. Or she didn't understand what Nancy asked her. She was just learning to read.

Nancy and Ramon had spent a good deal of time together outside the stronghold gathering herbs and other ingredients. Her for her potions, him for his inks. When Lilly and Nancy took Chloe outside for a little gardening time, Ramon usually joined them. There was even talk of establishing a greenhouse when they finally agreed to start building topside. Nancy had researched it, and the building cost was comparatively low. Half the cost of the crafting hall.

Allistor had been doing a lot of thinking as he continued to forage through the week. He'd taken to using the winery's truck, moving farther and farther out of town in search of usable food items, other needed supplies, and rare items that might be worth selling. He'd been thinking about the various ways he power leveled his avatars in his favorite games.

The most obvious and common way was running dungeons. Putting together a party and just grinding through a dungeon for xp and loot. He hadn't run across any dark portals or gateways that looked like a dungeon entrance. But his first meeting with Nancy and Chloe had been on his mind.

The vermin that they'd killed when he found them had been called scouts. That, combined with the fact that they'd been patrolling a tunnel, seemed dungeony enough for him. He'd fled from the tunnels then, having only his rebar spear as a weapon. But with the improved stats that he and his people had now, the better armor and weapons, and their ability to do AoE damage, crowd control, and heal each other, he thought it was worth a shot.

And they needed to do it soon. If the vermin hadn't been killing things and leveling themselves up, his people would soon be a much higher level than the mobs. And if the system here worked like most games, they wouldn't be worth much experience.

He returned to the Warren with a full load in the box truck. He'd found an old 1966 Harley Davidson Shovelhead with pristine red tank and fenders. The kind of bike he'd dreamed of as a teenager. He planned to get at least thirty thousand klax for it.

In the truck with the Harley were two more dirt bikes for their collection, six five-gallon cans of gas, two queen-sized bed frames with mattress and box springs, a water cooler with a dozen full bottles, and ten more cases of wine from the winery. There was also a load of lumber, wire, and nails. And a little surprise for Chloe that he'd run across behind the barn where he'd found the Shovelhead.

Parking the truck, he called Nancy and Ramon over. After whispering to the two of them for a few moments, Ramon nodded his head and went to get Sam. Nancy smiled and hugged Allistor before walking off to find and distract Chloe. She and Lilly would take her out for some extended gardening time.

Ramon and Sam returned with Michael and Meg, all of them grinning like fools. They got to work unloading the truck, then picked a spot near the back of the cavern and got busy. A short discussion, a division of labor, and the sounds of sawing and hammering commenced.

As they worked, Allistor pushed the Harley over to the market kiosk and got to work on the auction listing. He wished for the hundredth time that month for the internet to still be working. He loved Harleys, but couldn't be sure of the correct model year of the bike. And it would have been helpful to have some factual historical information on the company. Still, he did the best he could, then he uploaded the listing and rolled the bike inside. He'd learned that the kiosk would do a full scan of the bike and offer 3-D holo-images as well as detailed dimensions and other information like fuel source, tank capacity, and estimated range on a full tank. If he'd done that with the Mustang, it might have sold for even more. Lesson learned.

When Ramon and company were finished with their little project, they radioed Nancy that they needed her help. Allistor grabbed Amanda from the infirmary so she could participate. Two minutes later, Nancy and Lilly brought Chloe back inside. Ramon pretended to be upset. "Sam was doing some woodworking, and he cut himself pretty bad. He could use one of your potions!" He winked at Nancy and pointed toward the back wall where Sam was laying on the floor, playing injured.

Taking the hint, she took off at a jog toward Sam. Ramon scooped up Chloe, and the rest of the group followed. As Sam theatrically moaned and groaned, hamming it up for Chloe's benefit, Ramon set her down. She looked on, her face scrunched up in worry, until Nancy declared Sam all healed and told him to stop being such a big baby.

When Sam got to his feet, he said, "I was just working on the hutch here, and the dam-…er, the gosh-darn saw slipped. Thanks for making it all better, Nancy."

Chloe's eyes widened. Her focus, previously on the wounded Sam, moved past him to the wooden structure behind him. Max, his nose having alerted him to new visitors long ago, was sniffing around it, tail wagging. He gave a muted woof as he poked his nose at it. "Hutch? Like… for bunnies?"

Meg looked to Allistor, who nodded. "Well, we figured since we called this place the Warren, it should have some fluffy bunnies, right?" She opened a trap door in the top of the wooden box Allistor had brought back, and pulled out a soft, fuzzy brown rabbit. Bending down, she handed it to Chloe. The girl squealed in delight and hugged the furry beast to her chest. *"It's SO CUTE!"*

Nancy crouched down so that she was at eye level with her daughter. "If we keep these here, you're going to have to learn how to take care of them. You'll need to feed them, clean up after them, and make sure they don't escape."

Chloe immediately began nodding her head emphatically. "I will, Momma! Max will help me. If any of them gets loose, he can catch them. He's really fast!" The dog perked up at the mention of his name, and he trotted over to poke his nose at the bunny's hindquarters. Lilly handed Chloe a few plants she'd brought in for the rabbits to nibble on.

They took a few minutes to let Chloe feed and name the two bunnies. Male and female. Thumper and Beatrice. Allistor had run across them in the yard behind the barn. The hutch was there, a wooden structure with chicken wire along the front and top, maybe six feet wide and ten feet long. There was a hole busted in one side, and the bunnies were roaming free. He suspected the two were survivors of a larger group, and that something had broken in and helped itself to bunny tartar.

He'd immediately thought of Chloe. They'd make good pets for her to play with and learn to take care of. And if they did what bunnies were famous for, they could be the start of a colony that could be a sustainable food source.

The others had repaired the hole in the hutch, then built a small rabbit run around it. The bunnies could be let out of the hutch to hop about the roughly ten-foot square area. They'd bring in some dirt and maybe some hay later.

As it was suppertime, they all convened around the big table by the fountain. Sam rolled the grill around and threw on some burgers and vegetables while Meg brought out some buns and other fixings. As Sam grilled, Allistor began to share his dungeon idea.

When he was done reasoning it out for them, he asked, "So… who wants to go kill some vermin?"

Hands shot up. Everyone's except Lilly and Nancy. When Lilly said, "It's okay; I can keep Chloe here with me," Nancy's hand went up too.

Sam served the burgers, and they began to plan their first dungeon run.

*****

The next morning they all had a hearty breakfast of pancakes, eggs, and sausage. The food gave them buffs to health regeneration and stamina. They'd finished their plans over dinner the night before, then began to distribute gear.

Nancy's ring was loaded up with healing, mana, and stamina potions. Each of the others carried at least one of each as well. They all had knee-high leather boots and pants that tucked into them. Both pieces gave extra Constitution, upping everyone's health pools. All but Nancy wore power-infused chainmail shirts made by Michael. She claimed it was too cumbersome for her. So Lilly had made her a studded leather shirt with long sleeves and a fleece lining.

Each of them carried a knife with at least a six-inch blade with a leather sheath and belt. Allistor, Sam, and Michael all carried short swords on their other hips. Ramon favored a long katana-like blade sheathed on his back. Each of them also had a rifle or shotgun on their backs, and a handgun strapped to a thigh. And, of course, Allistor carried his trusty rebar spear, slightly improved.

They'd come up with some specialized weapons as they improved their skills. Meg had earned the *Improvisation* skill when she'd used oil to fry the canids by the holding cell. She'd taken her love of the zombicue a few steps further. With a little help from Sam, she'd figured out how to mix up some small napalm-like grenades. They were basically crystal Christmas tree ornaments filled with chemicals and sealed with wax. When she completed the first one, she'd been given a notice that she had the option to name it and file a patent. The cost was one hundred klax, but when she asked Allistor about it, he jumped at the chance. It meant that somebody somewhere down the line would have to pay her for the use of her design.

Her plan for the grenades was to throw them at a group of mobs and let Allistor light them up. She carried matches, a dozen short candles, and a couple of flares just in case he was busy or not around when she used the grenades, or she wanted to set a trap with them. The candles could be set under a hanging ball that, when broken, would drop its contents onto the flame, creating a pool of napalm under a target or group of targets.

Lilly let them out and locked the gates behind them as they headed for the dungeon. Allistor decided to use the same manhole cover he'd gone down before.

Ramon was scribbling on parchment as they walked the few blocks across town. He was creating a new map, trying to earn the *Cartography* skill before they entered the storm tunnels. Once down there, he intended to map the tunnels as they went, in order to level the skill. And to keep them from going in circles.

When they reached the manhole, Allistor went first, followed by Sam. The two men would act as the bulwarks, keeping mobs in melee range at bay while the group burned them down. But the hope was that with all the guns, bombs, and spells the group had at their disposal, they'd murder anything in the tunnels before it got that close.

Behind Allistor and Sam came Meg, Nancy, and Amanda. Meg was ready with guns or bombs, while Nancy and Amanda would primarily heal. Ramon and Michael would bring up the rear, in case anything snuck up from behind.

Sam cast a light globe in front of them, allowing Allistor to save his mana for attack spells. Ramon cast one to follow behind them. The group moved down the tunnel to the first intersection, then right, as Allistor followed his previous route. In a few minutes, they reached the spot where he'd found Nancy. Not pausing to remember, they continued on. At the next intersection, Sam was blindsided by a group of four vermin that rushed out of the side tunnel just as he stepped in front of it. The big marine was knocked off his feet, and the vermin swarmed over the top of him. Allistor *Examined* one of them.

> *Vermin Scout*
> *Level 5*
> *Health 450/450*

Meg screamed, "Sam! Oh god, help him!" and raised her shotgun. The rats were ravaging Sam, taking small chunks of his flesh wherever they could.

Allistor stepped between her and Sam, his back to her as he stabbed one of the rats with his spear. "Wait, Meg!" he shouted. "Don't fire. You'll hit Sam!"

He was tense as he let go of his spear and drew his sword. Two careful swings each eliminated a vermin from atop Sam's struggling form. Sam grabbed the last of the vermin around its neck and throttled it, squeezing until its spine broke and the thing stopped struggling.

Nancy and Amanda both cast heals on Sam as he and Allistor looted the rats. When Allistor noticed none of the others reaching down to loot, he asked, "Did anybody other than Sam and myself get xp from that fight?"

The others all shook their heads no. So they were still on a 'you hit it, you get credit for it' basis. That wouldn't do at all. He leaned against the wall and said, "Everybody look and see what you can find about forming a party that shares experience." His words were clipped, angry with himself for not figuring this out sooner.

Michael was the one to find it. Rather than waste time explaining it to everyone, he just sent Allistor a party invite. Then turned party leadership over to him. Allistor was quickly able to figure out how to add party members, and thirty seconds later it was done.

They moved on, back in formation. Three more times they came across scout parties of three and four vermin each. Allistor tried to mix up their styles, letting different folks fire first, working his team through the easy battles to see how they meshed. Unlike his VR games, his people here were taking things very seriously. There were no attention-deficit cases leaping around tea-bagging things or pew-pewing anything in sight. Respawn wasn't an option. Every one of them knew that a single mistake could cost a life.

As they fought the last group of four, one of them wised up and took off to warn the others. Allistor saw it break off and reached up a hand to cast the *Restraint* spell, but the vermin disappeared around a corner before he could complete the spell.

"Shit! Okay, guys, a scout just got away. Which means we're going to have company soon. Let's find a dead end or a good defensible spot and get ready. This might suck."

They finished and looted the other three rats, then jogged forward. A minute later they came across a metal door with *Shutoff and Redirect* stenciled on it in white block letters. "Here!" Sam said, trying the lever. When it didn't work, he put his shoulder down and rushed the door. With a screech of bending metal, it opened inward. The lock was ruined, but that didn't matter as long as they got inside.

The room wasn't large, about ten feet square. But it was large enough for all seven of them to gather inside. On one wall was a series of monitors and controls, presumably used by the engineers that oversaw the storm system maintenance. For now, it was the Alamo. They were about to be badly outnumbered without any option for retreat.

Sam was nearest the door when a growing sound of chittering and scratching made itself known. He reached for the door to close it, and Allistor whispered, "Wait! Meg, toss one of your grenades out there, just outside the door.

Meg did as instructed, lobbing one of the crystal spheres through the doorway to shatter on the floor about three feet out. Allistor nodded at Sam, who pushed the door closed. With the bent frame and lock, it didn't close flush to the wall. But it was close enough. There were no gaps big enough for one of the vermin to get through.

In just moments, the vermin arrived. A flood of wet smelly fur, teeth, and claws pounded against the door, screeching and growling. Sam put his back against it, and Allistor joined him. The two men, with their improved Strength, held it securely as the horde of vermin outside pushed to get in. When he was sure the tunnel was thick with mobs, Allistor crouched down, held out a finger and sent a gout of flame along the floor through a gap between the door and the frame.

A moment later the oil ignited. All of the vermin who'd trampled through it, or were above it at that moment, went up in flames as well. The screeching outside took on a much higher pitch. The pressure against the door decreased as flaming rat-things ceased trying to get into the room, instead focusing on getting away from the flames.

Allistor shouted over the noise, "Meg! Get another one ready. When I open the door, throw it!" He held up three fingers, then two, then one. Sam leapt away from the door and Allistor yanked it halfway open. Two vermin fell into the room as Meg tossed her crystal grenade through. It struck the face of an already burning vermin and shattered, spraying napalm that was already igniting across the tunnel.

One of the vermin had landed just inside the door, and it was preventing Allistor from closing it. He bent down and grabbed it by a foreleg, yanking it further into the room with one hand as he shoved the door closed with the other. The crazed beast jerked its head forward and clamped down on Allistor's arm with those wicked incisors. Sam resumed his post as Ramon, Michael, and Meg stabbed at the two vermin in the room.

Burning, being stabbed, and bleeding out, the vermin that held Allistor's arm thrashed about. Its razor-sharp teeth savaged his arm, clamping down tighter and driving deep into his flesh. He could feel them scrape against bone as the vermin died. The pain nearly caused him to lose consciousness. His legs buckled, and he fell back against the door. Some part of his mind noted that the metal of the door was getting quite warm. Nancy cast a heal on him, but the teeth remained embedded in his flesh.

Amanda took hold of the dead creature's jaws and attempted to pry them apart. When she failed, Michael took a shot. There was a creak of muscle as the lower jaw moved. Amanda carefully lifted its upper jaw, trying to remove eight-inch long incisors with as little damage as possible to Allistor.

The moment they were free, both Nancy and Amanda cast heals. Allistor felt the pain lessen. The wounds began to close, but he still felt hot and a bit dizzy. One look at the nasty greenish saliva dripping from the other dead vermin's mouth, and he pointed. "P-poison."

Amanda followed his gaze and nodded. "Their saliva must have some kind of poison. Nancy?" She looked at the other healer, who was already pulling a vial from her ring. Taking it and pouring it down Allistor's throat, she whispered, "This should help."

Nothing happened for a few moments. When the potion kicked in, his head began to clear, and the sick feeling in his stomach faded. He was still hot, but he realized that was from the door against his back. All at once, everyone in the room gained a level. The notice flashed across Allistor's interface, along with a flood of experience gains and some Fame Points.

Level up! You are now level 8. You have earned two attribute points.

For the first time, he noticed that the sounds of vermin outside had vanished. Getting back to his feet, he checked his arm. Through the holes in his shirt, he could see the angry red scars of the closing wounds. But he was no longer losing blood.

"Okay, everybody ready? We're going to open this door. Things could get nasty. And as Chloe would say, don't let stuff bite you!"

Sam stepped back, and Allistor pulled the door wide open.

The stench of burnt wet sewer rat and roasted meat nearly overwhelmed them. The tunnel was filled with smoke, and directly in front of the door lay the burnt and mangled bodies of close to twenty vermin. Motion to his left showed two vermin with singed fur dragging away the body of a third. Several of the corpses in front of them had bite and claw marks on them. He imagined them biting and struggling to get free of the flames, damaging their cousins in the process.

The others quickly looted the corpses, and even more notifications crossed his interface. Apparently, as group leader, he was informed of everything that was looted. He waved them away and activated his *Night Vision*. It was hampered slightly by the two light globes that hovered over the group, but he could see the dark outlines of more vermin in the tunnel outside the light's reach. They were retreating, but only slowly.

To encourage them, he sent a fireball hurtling down the tunnel. It impacted a vermin that had already suffered some burn damage, finishing it off. The splash damage lit several others on fire, and a dense mass of the vermin retreated more quickly down the tunnel.

"Shit. There are still a lot of them left." Meg whispered what the others were all thinking.

"We need to follow them. The less time they have to regroup or split up and set ambushes, the safer we'll be." Allistor looked everyone over. "Anybody hurt? We good to go?"

He got thumbs up from the others, and they set off down the tunnel as he pushed his light globe as far ahead of himself as he could. He found out that beyond a certain range, about thirty feet, the spell would fizzle and the light would extinguish. Casting another one, he pushed it out about twenty-five feet. It remained at that range, leading them as they proceeded down the tunnel.

It was a few minutes before they reached another intersection. This was a single branch to their left. A quick inspection of the floor showed bloody footprints going in both directions. But by far, the larger number went straight.

"Looks like three or four went off this way." Sam pointed down the tunnel. "Do we split up and go after them?"

Allistor shook his head. "We stay together. Ramon and Michael, keep an extra sharp eye out behind us. If this group that went left circles back around behind us, we need as much warning as possible."

They continued forward, the vermin gathered in front of them moving back. Allistor watched his mana regeneration carefully, and each time he reached full mana he cast another *Flame Shot* into the seething mass of vermin. As they approached the wounded mobs, he and his team would finish them off with spear and sword. No point in wasting ammo.

Another hundred yards or so, and the tunnel opened into a wide circular chamber roughly twenty yards across. At the back end, there was a grate in the floor where the flow of water dropped away into an outfall. The walls curved upward into a dome, the top of which stood twenty feet above them. Light leaked down from a missing manhole cover at the top. Allistor could see a tree canopy blotting out the sky above.

A quick scan of the room showed about twenty of the vermin left alive. All were burned to some degree, and none was above half health. They were all huddled around a nest constructed of branches, multi-colored fabrics, half of a shopping cart, at least a few human bones, and other debris that had floated down the tunnels. The nest rested against the curved wall, not far from the outfall. Behind the vermin was a much larger, meaner looking specimen. It was the size of a grizzly bear, with a bald, thin, scaly tail at least ten feet long.

Vermin Alpha
Level 10
Health: 6,900/6,900

Allistor whispered, "All right. This is the boss. It'll have some surprises for us, I'm sure. Special abilities to watch out for. Maybe some kind of charge ability. Or a sonic screech that will stun you." He looked around the room. There was no cover of any kind. The floor slanted slightly toward the outfall. That gave Allistor an idea.

He turned and grinned at Meg. "The big fella made the mistake of building his nest out of wood."

Meg's eyes lit up. "Vermincue!" She pulled two more grenades from her ring. "Where do you want them?"

"Well, in a game I'd say we have to kill all the trash vermin before the boss will even attack. But somehow I don't think it'll work that way here. So, everybody, get your guns ready. Don't skimp on ammo. Fire for effect. Meg's gonna hit the big one with her first grenade. It should light the nest on fire. Anything that charges at us, kill it. Try to fire in a zone directly in front of you, and let the folks on either side of you handle their zones. That way we're not all shootin' the same rat."

He looked at Meg. "First one right in the boss's nest. The second one, splatter it about halfway across the floor. It'll spread downward." She nodded, ready to throw.

"Go!"

Meg tossed the crystal ornament grenade like a pro softball pitcher. It soared across the room and impacted the alpha, but it didn't break. Bouncing off the vermin's hide, it struck a nearby branch and exploded. The alpha stood and looked menacingly at them, its red eyes almost glowing with hatred. The thing bared its teeth and looked to be about to make a move when Allistor used his *Flame Shot*. Rather than sending a fireball across the room, he simply created a column of fire that flashed up from the alpha's feet. The napalm that had soaked into the nest caught, and Allistor's small column of flame was increased tenfold.

"Fire!" He raised his shotgun and took aim at the alpha, as it was directly in front of him. He put a slug into its shoulder as it was stepping forward to flee the burning nest. All around him shots rang out. Injured rats were dropping like flies. Meg tossed her second grenade in a high arc, wanting as much splash radius as she could get when it landed.

Ramon, on an adrenaline rush, started shouting, "Yeah! Get some! Take that, rat!"

Michael paused for a moment and looked at him. "Really? Take that, rat?" Shaking his head, he resumed fire.

The alpha sent out a keening sound that hurt the human's ears and sent its remaining minions into a frenzy. They dashed forward, ignoring any injuries they took from flame or gunfire. Their eyes didn't focus at all as if they were mindless balls of teeth and claws being controlled by the alpha.

Allistor didn't mind. It made them easier to kill. Enemies with no sense of self-preservation that simply charged ahead without dodging at all? Perfect! He sent a fireball toward the puddle of napalm in the center of the room just before the vermin zombies reached it. A wide circle of flame erupted, and the seven vermin that were still standing ran right into it.

Leaving them to his group, he turned his focus back on the alpha. It had reached the edge of the nest and was about to leap clear. Allistor cast *Restraint* on it. The boss froze, the muscles of its back legs bunched to jump. He raised his shotgun and took careful aim, putting a slug right into its charred face. The stun wore off as the slug impacted, throwing the alpha off balance. It rolled back into the nest, screaming.

Behind him, he heard Nancy call out. "All the little ones are down! Shoot the big one!"

Smiling, he pumped another slug into the chamber and fired again. Thick, black smoke was billowing up from the nest, making it hard to see the boss. He saw movement within the smoke and fired.

A second later, the alpha exploded out of the smoke, its fur on fire. Both its eyes had been rendered useless by the flames, fluid leaking out of the burnt orbs. It roared in defiance, then oriented on the sounds of weapons fire.

Vermin Alpha
Level 10
Health: 1,190/6,900

Allistor shouted, "Look out!" as the alpha launched itself forward at surprising speed. Jaws open wide, its incisors pointed forward as it charged their position. Most had the presence of mind to dodge left or right. Meg, unfortunately, did two things wrong. First, she screamed.

211

And as the alpha oriented on the sound, she simply backed up, instead of moving out of its way.

The blind alpha's aim wasn't perfect. It clipped Meg's left side as it blasted past her into the wall. But the razor-sharp incisors, each the size of a machete, cut a nasty wound across her left shoulder. The leather and skin opened all the way to the bone. She screamed again and dropped her shotgun as she was knocked off her feet. The alpha didn't notice as it had run full force into the wall and stunned itself.

Regrouping, the party all fired into the prone giant rat, except for Nancy and Amanda, who cast heals on Meg. Nancy dashed forward and grabbed Meg's right arm, dragging her back away from the thrashing alpha.

A whip of the rat's tail caught Nancy in the back of the legs. She fell forward as the rest of the group heard a snapping sound. To her credit, she managed not to scream as she went down. She and Meg lay together in a heap, only about ten feet from the boss.

Allistor couldn't risk one of them being killed. He put away his shotgun and equipped his spear. Shouting at the boss, he ran forward, spear in front of him like a lance. The vermin alpha turned to focus on his voice, its face coming to bear directly at him as it began to keen again.

Allistor fought the urge to cover his ears as the painful waves of sound washed over him. Keeping his eyes on the boss, he launched himself forward, jamming the spear point down the big rat's throat. He twisted and pushed, then yanked the weapon out and drove it back in again. As he pushed the head backward, one of the alpha's foreclaws swiped at his leg. Three deep furrows opened up on his thigh and blood sprayed. Ignoring the pain, he gritted his teeth and leaned into the spear. A moment later there was a *pop!* as his spear point broke through and drove into the alpha's skull. It twitched a few times, then went still.

A scream from Amanda made him spin around, his weight on his injured leg. The pain made him see spots for a moment as he tried to find her.

One of the rats that had charged into the flames had somehow managed to drag itself forward far enough to reach them. A slimy trail of burnt skin and blood stretched out behind it all the way to the flickering flames. It had latched onto Amanda's calf and was trying to drag her off balance.

Michael jammed his sword into the thing's eye, killing it instantly. Then he and Ramon pried the thing's jaw open to free Amanda's leg. Nancy cast a heal on her and handed her a potion. Then she turned and did the same for Allistor.

The fight leveled up everyone but Allistor. He was still a few thousand points from level nine. He sat with his back against the wall as he munched on some of Sam's beef jerky and drank iced tea from a bottle. Though his health bar had only dropped about a quarter from his wounds, he'd lost a good bit of blood. He watched the others loot the remaining bodies as Amanda came to sit next to him. He shared both food and drink with her, smiling when she made a *nom, nom, nom* sound as she chewed the jerky.

"Gotta remember to watch your back," he offered casually.

She took a drink to wash down the jerky and replied, "I was busy trying to heal your dumb ass. Once again you let the beasties bite you."

Chuckling, he said, "Technically, it slashed me." He pointed to the three cuts in his leather pants. Each one was a good six inches long. Lilly was going to need to repair those for him. "You're the one that let herself get bit."

She gave him the evil eye for a moment, then snorted, "I suppose that's true. Hurt like a bitch, too. Hurt worse when they pulled those teeth out."

Allistor nodded in agreement. "Yeah, it always hurts worse on the way out."

They sat for a few more minutes as the others reloaded weapons and finished looting. Allistor rose and looted the boss. He got a hundred fifty klax, four alpha claws, and a scroll!

Putting everything into his ring, he said, "I think that's it, folks. Not much of a dungeon, but it was good experience and good practice." He winked at Michael. "In one of my games, we could all teleport back to home base now. But it looks like we've got a long walk ahead of us. Stay sharp – we don't know if there are more vermin roaming around down here."

Sam added, "At least those ones that took that left turn."

They set off back through the tunnels, Ramon consulting his map as they went and directing them when to turn. They took a few side tunnels they hadn't followed before, just so Ramon could fill in his map. It took them forty minutes to reach the manhole where they'd entered.

Allistor went up first, carefully checking the surrounding debris before climbing the last few rungs of the ladder. He kept watch as the others joined him one by one. Together they walked quietly back to the gates of the Warren, where Lilly let them in.

214

*****

As more days passed, the citizens of the Warren kept busy with foraging and crafting. Four days after the vermin dungeon run, a group of three octopoids wandered into their sensor zone. Allistor took Sam, Lilly, Amanda, and Ramon outside to deal with them. Lilly had missed out on the dungeon and needed some experience. He invited them to group up, and they went to work.

The group made short work of the monsters, firing on them from a distance until they fell. The Stronghold received more system points for a successful defense, and the group got some good experience. Lilly leveled up and was thrilled to get a dozen pieces of octopoid hide. She'd been working with piles of vermin leather for days, and she was getting a little sick of the smell.

The most disturbing happening of the week came when Meg, not wanting to cook vermin meat, had put it up for sale on the open market just for kicks. They'd collected over a hundred pieces of it from the dungeon run. Thinking nobody would want it, she put up twenty pieces and priced them at one klax per piece.

Within minutes, someone had purchased them. And a minute after that, she received a message from the buyer.

We're starving here. There are twenty of us, and we've killed everything we can find close by. If you have any more, please sell it to us.

She burst into Allistor's quarters to relay the message to him. His first reaction was "They must be starving. Who would eat vermin meat if they didn't have to?"

"That's what I was thinking. They must be humans, right? We should try to help them."

"Can you send a message back?"

"I… I don't know?" Meg looked thoughtful. "I don't remember seeing a way to reply."

Allistor walked with her back to the kiosk. "There's a way to do direct sales. When I sold the Mustang, some brokers suggested it. Let's see if we can find them and help."

Meg pulled up her holo display when they reached the kiosk. She found the message, and Allistor pointed out the [reply] button. She quickly dictated the message.

We have more. Can do a direct sale to you. Who are you? And where are you? Maybe we can help?

The reply came back almost instantly.

Oh, thank god. We're survivors from a small town about thirty miles outside of Denver. Half of us are elderly and children. Haven't eaten in two days. How much more can you sell us? Our funds are limited, but we'll take another twenty pieces if you have them?

Meg had tears in her eyes as she read the message. She didn't even look at Allistor before replying.

We have about a hundred more pieces. The price is one klax. Total. I'm Meg. What is your name?

That is very kind of you. My name is Luther. I'm sort of the leader of this group. We figured out how to make a stronghold, and the system chose me. We've been talking about leaving, starting over again somewhere with more food. But we're afraid.

Allistor said, "I know, Meg. They're maybe a day's drive from us. If the roads are clear. We need to call a meeting."

"You do that," Meg said as she transferred the remaining vermin meat to Luther. "I'm going to find them some better food and send it. You already know my vote." She stomped off toward the kitchen as Allistor smiled at her back.

He began calling everyone together. It wasn't hard. Every building in the cavern was within shouting distance. When they'd all gathered at what he now thought of as the meeting table, he caught them up.

Amanda was the first to vote. "We have to go get them. They've got kids starving."

Sam held up a hand. "That's more than double our number here. Even if some of them are kids, it sounds like half of them aren't. What if the adults are trouble?"

There was silence around the table. Even Chloe, whose eyes had brightened at the mention of other kids, sat quietly, petting Max who sat next to her.

Ramon was next to speak. "I have to say, I don't think I could live with myself if we didn't at least check it out. I know it's a long trip. Probably dangerous. But we've been talking about growing this place, right?"

A few heads around the table nodded.

Michael agreed with Ramon. "Yeah. If it was just adults, I might feel differently. Maybe wait and talk to them some more. Or make them figure out how to get to us. But with kids… we have to try."

All eyes turned to Sam, who'd voiced the only objection so far. He shrugged. "I think it's a risk. But

217

every time we go outside these days, it's a risk. I'll want to be *very* sure of what kind of people they are before we bring them back here."

Everyone agreed with that point without hesitation.

"Just as a formality, show of hands in favor of a road trip?" Allistor raised his hand. So did everyone else.

"Fine. We're going. I say three of us should go. Myself, Meg, and Sam the skeptic." He winked at Sam.

"That's not many if they turn out to be trouble," Michael said.

"I'm going too." Amanda slapped a hand on the table. "If there are malnourished kids and seniors there, they might need some medical attention."

With that settled, Sam went to go tell Meg, who was back at the kiosk. The others got to work planning the trip.

The next morning, they were ready to go. The group was taking the box truck, a pickup, and two ATVs. The idea being if the trucks got bogged down somehow, or they got attacked and damaged, they could escape on the ATVs and find shelter.

They loaded tents, crates of food, medical supplies, extra gas, and some weapons into both trucks. Once they reached the other survivors, they could either load them into the box truck or find more vehicles to bring them back in. And they could use the box truck to haul anything cool they scavenged.

Meg had gotten more specifics on their location. Their town was just over two hundred miles away, up on a mountain. On old Earth, that was a trip of three or four hours one way. But if the main roads were blocked or damaged, it might take a full day or more to get that far.

Sam and Meg climbed into the pickup and took the lead. Allistor and Amanda followed in the box truck. They drove up and out of the Warren and were on their way. The group had done a little clearing of Main Street, a bit here and there, so it took them less than ten minutes to get out of town. Sam led the way to the interstate, picking up speed to 30mph. They'd agreed not to go faster on back roads where something might jump out of the woods.

Once they reached the interstate, Sam picked up the pace again. This time they cruised along at 45mph. At this speed, the engines were relatively quiet, and they got decent gas mileage while still making good time. And a wreck at that speed probably wouldn't be fatal.

The first hour of the trip was uneventful. They had to slow down and weave through abandoned cars in a few places. Once Sam had to use the pickup to push a few cars aside to clear the road for the box truck. The few radio stations that had kept transmitting that first week had died out. Sam had told everyone to be on the lookout for a short wave radio set that they might be able to use to speak with other survivors. So far they hadn't located one.

At about the eighty-mile mark, they hit their first real snag. They were passing by a small lake when a massive tortoise-looking thing burst from the water and charged them. There was only a narrow spit of land between the water and the highway shoulder, and the monster covered it quickly. It was the size of a Sherman tank, the top of its spike-covered shell maybe fifteen feet off the ground. A long tail extended out behind it, with a set of three nasty-looking spikes at the end.

Ancient Shellback
Level 22
Health: 130,000/130,000

Thinking quickly, Sam gunned his engine and swerved while Allistor slammed on his brakes. The shellback had been targeting the pickup. With the added speed, Sam had managed to outrun it, the thing's momentum carrying it across the highway and into the median. It slid down the slope, nearly rolling over as its shell caught on a stump. The monster immediately began to right itself and try to turn, but it was more cumbersome than it had been when moving straight forward.

Allistor took advantage and gunned the truck's engine, shooting forward and past the monster before it could right itself. Both trucks sped away, with everyone watching their mirrors to see if the ancient mob followed them.

When it seemed as if they were clear, Amanda let out the breath she'd been holding. "Holy shit, did you see that thing? It was literally a living tank. I wouldn't be surprised if it could shoot fire out its mouth or something!"

"Yeah. Level twenty. That thing was no joke. Probably could have eaten that titan we killed. We'll have to figure a way around it on the way back. Or distract it somehow. It must have been ambushing people here this whole time. Other creatures too, if it's up to level twenty. Unless the system sent it here that way."

They continued another twenty miles along the interstate before it was time to hit the state highways. These were much smaller two-lane roads with trees and the occasional house or patch of businesses along either side. Sam slowed them back down to 30mph and they crept along.

They'd only made it a couple of miles when they encountered an obstacle. A multi-car pileup that included a semi-trailer blocked the road. The vehicles were all burned, their tires useless. There was no way to move the wreckage.

Sam drove the pickup off the shoulder and into the steeply sloped grass that led down to a drainage ditch. He was able to creep around the wreckage and get back on the road. A minute or so later he came walking back around.

"The grass is soft, but if you keep moving, you should be okay. The truck isn't heavily loaded." He hopped into the cab as Amanda scooched over, and Allistor started forward. Sam gently coached him through it as they went off the shoulder into the grass.

"Take a shallow angle, boy. You don't want to start to slide. That's it... good. Now, gun it!"

Allistor did as he was told, and they got back onto the road with only some minor slippage of the tires and flying mud. As they pulled up next to Meg, Sam said, "That's gonna be harder on the way back with a full load. Let's hope it doesn't rain."

They crept along the state road for another five miles or so before they found another pile-up. This one stretched for hundreds of feet, with dozens of cars involved. Crunched car bodies and old bloodstains spoke to fatalities, and probably monster predation afterwards. With no way to get around since even the grassy areas were blocked, they turned around and retreated to the previous intersection.

Sam knew this part of the country well, having lived there most of his life. But without a map, they were just guessing at what roads might take them in the general direction they needed to go. After more than an hour detour, they managed to get back onto the same state highway.

By the time it began to get dark, they'd covered about a hundred and fifty miles. Better than Allistor had expected, actually. They had planned to sleep inside the box truck if they needed to spend a night out on the road. But Sam found a farmhouse with a storm cellar that looked promising. They parked outside, and Sam and Allistor went up to the house. After knocking several times, they let themselves in and explored the house.

Unsurprisingly, they found it in chaos. Bloodstains on the floor with paw prints meandering all around the house. They quietly closed the door behind them and moved around to the storm cellar. Its heavy wooden doors were still intact. Opening just one, they descended the short stairway to the cellar. Allistor cast a light globe, and it illuminated the entire space. Not very large, all four walls were lined with shelves that were in turn filled with jars of fruits and pickles and such. Sam whistled. "We should take some of this with us. I'm sure those people could use it.

Back outside, they unloaded bedrolls and weapons and some food and water. Retreating into the cellar, Allistor secured the doors from the inside with an iron bar. The floor was stone and immaculately clean. Whoever had lived here had obviously put a lot of care into the place. They opened up their bedrolls, took some time to eat and drink quietly, and then settled in to get some sleep.

Allistor was awakened by Amanda in the very early hours of the morning. She had curled up next to him, their bedrolls side by side. Now she poked him a few times in the gut as she placed a hand over his mouth to silence him. When he was fully awake, she pointed at the door, then touched his ear.

He quickly recognized the sound of canids snuffling around outside. The storms doors creaked a bit as one of them must have walked across them. A shuffling sound to his right told him that Sam and/or Meg was awake as well. A moment later he heard the scrape of a gun barrel on stone as one of them lifted their weapon.

They sat there for almost an hour, not making a sound as the monsters roamed above. A few times there were scratches at the doors, even some low growls of frustration. But eventually, the night went silent again as they moved on. Everyone lay back down and did their best to reclaim sleep. It took Allistor another hour before his eyes drifted shut and stayed shut.

He was the first to awaken as the sounds of birdcalls began to increase in frequency and volume, signifying the arrival of daylight. He nudged Amanda a few times, then bent down and kissed her. She patted his face a few times and whispered, "Good morning."

Five minutes later they were all standing at the stairs, guns pointed upward toward the doors. Allistor climbed up and removed the bar, then used it to shove one door upward. He winced as the hinges creaked, but nothing jumped out at him.

They all made their way up, and Meg said, "Gonna hit the head before we go." She and Amanda ventured inside the house as Sam and Allistor picked a convenient tree to relieve themselves upon.

The ladies came back out with two laundry baskets and a large box. They went back down to the cellar and filled all three with jars. Sam found some empty wooden crates, and they filled those too as Allistor made trips up and down the stairs to load them into the trucks. When they were done, they had about sixty jars – more than half of what had been on the shelves. Before they left, Sam closed and barred the cellar doors from above to keep the critters out. They could stop by on the way back and finish clearing out the food. With twenty more mouths to feed, there was no such thing as too much food.

They pulled out of the driveway and back onto the road. Moving along at their safe 30mph pace, it was only a couple hours until they reached the outskirts of the town. It looked like any other small town, only smaller. Maybe half the size of their own town, before it was crushed. By comparison, this one was intact. Mostly. A couple of buildings had burned down, and several homes sported broken windows and open doors.

The Stronghold they were looking for was easily spotted. Right in the center of town, the main thoroughfare was cut off by a twenty-foot-high stone wall with an iron gate. As they approached, faces appeared atop the wall. Sam stopped his truck a good fifty yards back from the gate.

Several of those faces were holding guns.

Chapter Ten

Shoot First, Don't Apologize

The four got out of their trucks, and Meg shouted, "We're looking for Luther. I'm Meg!"

A man atop the gate raised a hand in greeting. "I'm Luther. Glad to see you, Meg! We're going to need you to leave your weapons where you're standing before you come in."

Allistor shook his head. "That's just not going to happen, Luther. My name is Allistor. Did Meg mention me?"

Luther nodded. "Leader of the Warren. I appreciate you coming. I really do. But we've had some… incidents with other survivors."

Allistor looked around at the others. "Luther, I promised to keep these people safe. Much like you probably did for your people. In light of the incidents you just mentioned, how smart would it be for me to just walk them in there without weapons?" He paused for effect. "There are four of us here. You outnumber us five to one. And frankly, I have the ability to cast spells that are much more dangerous than my shotgun. We need to learn to trust each other. I've got a truck full of food here, and an invitation for you to join us at the Warren. But if you're not gonna let us in as we are, we can turn around and head back."

Meg glared at him, but Sam patted her back to calm her. She whispered, "We are *not* leaving these people here to starve."

Allistor whispered back. "I know you want to help them. So do I. But we don't know anything about them. And looking around here, I don't see why they're starving. There are viable vehicles to use here," he motioned all around them. "So they could hunt farther out if all the game in the forest is gone. They have walls, with space inside for gardening. So either they're incompetent, or they're playing us. Either way, they need us. We have the upper hand here. I'm going to make sure it stays that way."

They waited as Luther argued with someone atop the wall. A minute later, Luther called down. "Fine. Come on in."

The gates opened as the four got back into their trucks. Sam led them through the gates into the section of the town that had been walled off. The street just continued through the gates and on toward the back wall. The shops and buildings on either side remained intact, as far as Allistor could tell. People milled around, watching the two trucks. About half carried weapons. And as Luther had described, there were several children and elderly folks in the group.

Turning off their engines, they exited the vehicles. Luther had come down from the wall and was approaching Meg. "I'm sorry about that, Meg. We're all just a little twitchy. We've been attacked twice since we put up this wall. By humans, I mean. Lost some family and friends." He reached out a hand to shake.

"We understand." Meg ignored the hand and hugged the man. "It must have been rough here. Our town was completely destroyed by a sixty-foot-tall asshole giant that stomped it flat. But we haven't had to fight other humans yet."

Amanda interrupted. "We can talk later. These kids look like they're about to pass out. Let's get some food off the truck and into their bellies."

Luther motioned for people to come and help unload. When Allistor opened the back of the box truck, there were gasps of surprise and cries of joy. One old man who looked to be about seventy took the box of jars Allistor handed him with tears in his eyes. "Bless you, son."

Allistor, a lump in his throat keeping him from speaking, just nodded his head.

They unloaded a couple dozen jars of fruit and veggies, and Meg demanded to be shown to the kitchen. She and Sam began cooking burgers that she brought along in her ring. They used one of the recipes that bestowed buffs to Stamina and health regeneration.

Allistor sat in the back of the truck with Luther as Amanda began examining the children one by one. He began to speak quietly to the man.

Luther, I have to ask... why are you and your people going hungry? There are hundreds of miles of forest around you to hunt in. And there have to be other towns close by."

Luther shook his head. "We were doing fine until about two weeks ago. We foraged here in town, just gathering food as we needed it. Got the stronghold set up pretty early. A few of our people already had gardens in their yards, and we used those for fresh vegetables. After a few monster attacks claimed lives, everybody moved inside the walls."

He took a deep breath, then let it out. "Then we got attacked by humans. They walked up to the gates just like you, asking to be let in. Talking about how rough it was out in the wild. I felt sorry for them and opened the gates. Five of our people died before we chased them off. They stayed for three days, looting everything of value in town. We tried going out to stop them – there were ten of them, and we had more fighters than them back then – but we lost two more people in that fight."

Luther's shoulders slumped, and he wrung his hands in his lap. "We decided to just wait. Let them take what they wanted and go. The assholes didn't just take. They destroyed. Started a couple fires. Poured bleach in our gardens. Then their leader said if they caught us outside of town, they'd kill us."

Allistor could guess the rest. "And how long did you wait before you sent out a hunting party?"

"Three days. We were getting low on food. I sent out three men under cover of darkness. They went over the back wall and walked into the forest. About an hour after they left, we heard a bunch of gunshots. The next morning, their bodies were left in the street outside the gate. When a few of us went out to retrieve them, we were gunned down as well." Luther pulled his shirt aside to show a scar below his collarbone. "I was lucky and made it back inside."

Allistor asked, "How many have you lost to these assholes?"

Luther whispered, "Fourteen. Men, women, and children. Including my son."

Allistor was furious. "And how many of them are left? It sounds like you got a few of them."

Luther shrugged. "We've never seen more than ten. We killed a couple. But we haven't seen them in a week. I just don't know."

228

"Do you know where they're holed up? Do they have a stronghold of their own?

Luther nodded. "We recognized some of them. From a town to the south. Their leader is Evan, an asshole sheriff's deputy. Or he was before they fired him. Used to let young girls out of speeding tickets if they… well, you get the idea. He likes power a little too much."

As if summoned, a gunshot rang out. A woman atop the wall shouted, "They're back!"

Luther grabbed his rifle and sprinted toward the wall. Allistor followed. When they reached the top, Allistor saw three men with M16's standing roughly in the same spot they'd parked earlier. About fifty yards out from the gate.

The one in the center shouted. "Luther! I know you guys got visitors this morning! Send them out with whatever goodies they had in those trucks!"

Allistor didn't wait for Luther to respond. "You must be Evan?"

The man nodded. "No need for you to get hurt, whoever you are. Give us your trucks, and you'll be free to walk back to wherever you came from. This town, and everything in it, belongs to us."

Allistor shook his head. "That's not gonna work for me. I drove two hundred miles to see my friend Luther, here. Old friend of the family, ya know? I get here, and the first thing I hear is some asshole named Evan killed his son. You should leave. Now."

Evan smirked up at him. "We've got this place surrounded. Send out your shit, or we'll come in and take it!"

As Evan spoke, Allistor put his shotgun into inventory and pulled out a Mossberg 30.06 with a scope. Just as the man finished speaking he raised the rifle, took aim, and fired. Evan's head exploded. The two men on either side of him stood in shock for a moment. It cost the one to the right his life as Allistor chambered another round and put one through his chest. The third man managed to reach cover.

Luther looked at him wide-eyed. "What the hell did you just do?" he shouted. Both men ducked down as answering fire came from the third man, and at least two others they hadn't seen before.

"I just took out their leader. They'll be confused and disorganized, at least for a while. Maybe even argue amongst themselves about who should be in charge. I'm hoping they retreat long enough for us to get you safely out of here. Assuming you want to come with us?"

Luther's voice was bitter. "It's not like we have much choice, now. They won't stop till we're all dead."

Allister shook his head. "What's different? These guys were always going to kill you. Either by raiding this place, or starving you out. If they thought they could take these walls, they would have already. Now there are two less of them, and their leader is dead. If anything, I improved your position."

The old man that had taken the fruit from Allistor earlier put a hand on Luther's shoulder. "He's right, boy. Another week in here, and we'd starve. Even with the meat these folks sold us. We ain't got the funds to keep buying food." He moved his gaze over to Allistor and grinned. "Nice shot."

Just then Sam joined them up on the wall. "You're here fifteen minutes, and you're already picking fights?"

He winked at Allistor. He peered through a slot in the wall, and said, "One second." Sliding his rifle barrel into the slot, he took aim at something. Letting out a breath, he paused, then squeezed the trigger.

Turning back to them, he said, "The guy with the blue shirt hiding behind the ford. Stuck his head out too far." The grin on his face made Luther shudder. The old man just cackled.

A voice rang out from outside the wall. "You're gonna pay for that! You're all dead!"

Sam shouted, "Stick your head out and tell me that again! One college puke and one old marine sniper just took out almost half your group! I'd take Allistor's advice and leave while you can!"

Nothing but silence answered him. After a few minutes, they straightened up and peered over the top of the wall. There was no sign of movement.

The old man said, "I'm George. Luther's my boy. I want to thank you again for coming here and helping us. Glad to know there're some good folks left in this god-awful new world." He shook hands with both Allistor and Sam. "How 'bout we go get some of that food I smell and talk some more?"

Remembering how hungry these people must be, Allistor felt bad. He'd been wrong; they weren't incompetent. They'd just been bullied into a bad situation. He wanted to kill every single one of the men outside.

As they climbed down, an explosion rocked the gate. Allistor clambered back up and looked out. A man behind a nearby truck had his arm cocked, about to lob a grenade at the gate. Allistor cast *Restraint* on the man. He froze in place, a look of horror on his face. Three seconds later the grenade went off in his hand. What was left of him fell behind the truck.

Three more men broke cover, dashing behind vehicles as they retreated. Sam's rifle put one of them down just as he was about to duck into an alley. George fired at another and struck him in the leg. Allistor missed a shot, and Luther's shot blasted out a storefront window as his target rounded the corner. But the glass deflected the bullet, and the man disappeared.

George said, "Five dead, one wounded. Unless they got a good medic, he's gonna die too."

Sam said, "If I were them, I wouldn't come back."

The four men once again descended the wall. Making their way to an area where several long tables with benches were set up, they joined the back of the chow line. All of the children and seniors had already been served and had taken seats. Though they looked longingly at their plates, none of them touched the food.

The line moved quickly, and soon all but three guards up on the wall had food. A fourth guard piled burgers high on one plate, and then he grabbed a jar of peaches, plates, and forks and headed back up to the wall.

George waited, standing at the end of one table as the others all took a seat. He spoke softly, just loud enough for everyone present to hear. "Let us give thanks for our new friends, and the bounty they have brought us today." He bowed his head, as did everyone but Allistor. His family hadn't been religious, and he was an agnostic. Still, he waited patiently for the others to finish. George raised his head and said, "Let's eat," with a wide smile on his face. He took a seat and dug in.

Allistor was focused on his own delicious burger when Amanda elbowed him in the ribs. Looking up at her, he saw her nod her head down the table. Following her gaze, he saw two little boys that looked so much alike they had to be twins. One of them was cutting his burger in half as the other wrapped his burger in a napkin and stuck it in his bag. Then the two of them began to nibble on half a burger each. When he looked at Amanda, she had tears in her eyes.

Allistor cleared his throat and stood. Looking at the boy who'd pocketed his burger, he said, "What's your name, kid?"

The twin looked guilty. Shrinking down in his seat, his voice squeaky, he said, "Dillon, sir."

Allistor laughed. "Okay, Dillon. Nice to meet you. And please, I'm not old enough to be a 'sir'. Just call me Allistor. I'm here to tell you a few things. First, you're done being hungry. There's no need to save any of this food for later. We've brought lots of food." He paused as the boy sheepishly removed the burger from his bag and set it on his plate.

Allistor looked around at the whole group. His gaze landed on Luther, and he raised his eyebrows, asking a silent question. Luther nodded.

"My friends and I have a stronghold as well. Not like this one, exactly. It's mostly underground. We have all the comforts of home, including electricity. And we would be honored if all of you would come and join us there. We can create more housing units, and maybe even expand to build walls above ground like you have here. More importantly, we have learned how to make ourselves stronger, and how to fight! And there's plenty of food for everyone."

He looked around at the faces looking back at him, trying to gauge their level of interest. Some were nodding their heads, others whispering to neighbors. He added, "We'll stay the night, if you don't mind, and you guys can decide what you want to do in the morning. It's a long trip back, about two hundred miles. And we ran across some obstacles on the way. But we'll get you there safe and sound."

Taking his seat again, he finished his burger as he listened to the chatter around him. Meg was actively lobbying the elders to join them at the Warren. Sam was exchanging war stories with George. Amanda was silent next to him, listening as he was. The general consensus seemed to be that they wanted to leave. Ironically, the fact that Allistor and Sam had killed several of the bullies was working against them. A few folks were feeling confident enough in their odds that now they wanted to stay.

After lunch, Luther offered to take them on a tour of the Stronghold. They obligingly followed him around as he told them about the place, how they'd come about establishing it, and introducing folks as they went. Their story wasn't that different from Allistor's peoples' own experiences. They had actually done quite well for themselves before Evan and his band attacked.

Allistor asked Luther about his people's stats and skills. Luther mentioned that some of the folks had picked up skills by accident, but Allistor could tell he didn't understand the system. So when the tour was complete, he sat Luther and George down at the tables again.

"This new world, it works off a system very similar to virtual reality games I've played my whole life. It lets us build up our strengths quickly, heal quickly when injured, and learn skills faster than we ever could a few months ago. For example, that guy with the grenade? I used a spell I learned called *Restraint* to stun him, forcing him to hold the grenade until it went off." Allistor held up a hand and pointed a finger toward the sky. A small jet of flame shot upward about a foot. "And I learned to do this, as well. If you like, I can share some of this knowledge with you and your people over dinner. And if you join us, you'll have the opportunity to learn much more."

Luther stammered, still absorbing the magic display. "Why... why are you so willing to take us in? We don't have anything of value to bring with us."

Sam shook his head. "You are valuable. You and your people. We need to work together to survive this year and claim as much of Earth as we can before the alien overlords who kidnapped us take over. We need every willing soul to make that happen."

Luther looked blankly at them. Meg asked, "Have you not seen the information about how they moved Earth and all that?" Luther and George both shook their heads.

Allistor sighed. "Alright, before dinner you should have all your people read this." He went on to explain to them where to find the information on their interface. Both men's faces paled as they read. As soon as they were done they got up and began circulating among their people, instructing them as they'd been instructed. The place became more and more quiet as people sat and read.

Allistor spent the rest of the afternoon talking with George and Luther as Sam and Meg began preparing dinner, and Amanda went back to administering to the health of the group.

"We can fit everyone in the box truck if necessary," Allistor was saying to George. "But it would be better if we could grab a working vehicle or two from around here. Ideally something like a camper or a school bus."

George grinned at him. "Take your pick. We got both. More than one of each, actually. There are buses about a mile from here, parked behind the elementary school. And an RV lot not five miles away." He looked around, then pointed at a woman up on the wall. "Katie there used to work there. She'll know where they kept the keys."

Allistor had visions of selling off a whole lot's worth of RVs on the market. He'd settle for just one, for now. "Does this mean you're going with us?"

The two men looked at each other. George spoke for them. "Yeah. I mean, we'll take a vote tonight after dinner. But most all of us have decided to go. A few may want to stay behind, but I don't think they'll have the stones to do it alone. Evan's people are still out there."

Allistor got to his feet. "In that case, how about we go get a couple of those RV's right now? I'll drive. You two can come along. Do we need to bring Katie? Or can she just tell us where to look?"

Ten minutes later the three men were in Meg's pickup and headed out of town. Before they'd even gotten halfway to the RV lot, Allistor spotted a landscaper's trailer in front of a house along the road. It had two commercial-sized riding mowers on it, and several leaf blowers and weed whackers hung on its sides.

Allistor pulled into the driveway. "Help me unload this stuff. We can hitch up the trailer and use it to haul back whatever personal items your people want to bring with them.

The three men had the job done in no time and were back on the road in less than ten minutes with the trailer rolling along behind them. When they reached the RV lot, Allistor said, "Let's take two of the biggest, fanciest ones we can find." The father and son grinned in agreement, and they got to work.

Katie had given them keys to the office, and they let themselves in. There was a sales area with brochures full of shiny images and spec sheets. Luther went to Katie's desk and found an inventory sheet that listed the makes and models of everything on the lot, along with the prices. Not wanting to spend a ton of time on research, they picked the two most expensive vehicles on the list. Allistor found a brochure for that make and model and grabbed it. The info would help him with his market listing.

Luther located the keys, as well as a key to the gas pump behind the office. He also grabbed a hand pump with a hose, since the power was out. He and George located the two RVs and pulled them around to the pump. It took some finagling, but they managed to fill both vehicles' tanks. Allistor had them fill four 55-gallon metal drums with fuel as well and rolled them onto the trailer. It was rare to be able to forage so much gas at once.

George dropped the pump keys through a slot in the office door, and they were off. He took the lead, followed by Luther. Allistor brought up the rear in the pickup. They didn't make any stops on the way back, not wanting to push their luck. The gates opened for them as they approached, then closed behind them as friends and neighbors whistled and cheered at the fancy vehicles. George especially had a good time showing off the top of the line luxury features.

One of them was set up as a standard sleeper camper, with a bedroom in the back, small bathroom, kitchen, and dining/seating area. There were four captain's seats in the front. It could comfortably seat eight or ten people as they rode. The other one was more of a tour bus style, with the same four captain's seats up front, but long benches along either side in the middle. There was still a small kitchen and bathroom in the back. And two fold-out bunks on either side about two-thirds of the way back.

Between the two, they could comfortably transport all of Luther's people. And even let some of them sleep inside overnight. Allistor decided finding a school bus wasn't necessary.

The rest of the afternoon was spent loading up people's belongings. Both RVs had huge storage capacities, their sides lined with doors that opened to reveal capacious compartments for gear. They were filled with bedrolls and suitcases, anything that wouldn't do well out in the rain. The trailer was loaded with crates and plastic containers filled with everything from photo albums to household appliances. There were bags of guns and ammo, boxes of valuables looted from the town that could be sold or traded. Two wooden chests full of kid's toys were loaded up as well.

George had some people strap large tarps and tents to the rails atop the RVs. Then they pulled a trailer from one of the garages that held two snowmobiles. That was hooked to the back of his RV. Allistor laughed at that. The thought of getting around in winter snow hadn't even occurred to him. It was late summer still, and he hadn't thought that far ahead. They'd have to find a few more before the snows came. This close to the mountains, winter was no joke.

The last surprise George sprung on Allistor came after dinner.

They'd gathered everyone together for the meal, leaving the walls unguarded for a time. Meg and Sam had served four giant roasts with potatoes, carrots, and onions. As folks ate their dinners, Allistor explained to all of them about their new world. How attributes worked, ways to obtain skills and level them up. He let Amanda talk about how healing worked, and her discovery of the tiny nanobots, or whatever they were. Allistor convinced Dillon to be his lovely assistant, telling the boy to get up and run. When he was a few steps away, Allistor hit him with *Restraint* and the boy froze mid-stride. When Allistor canceled the spell, Dillon stumbled and fell, causing the other kids to laugh and point. Allistor targeted the most obnoxious of those kids and levitated him up out of his seat. Not letting him down until he apologized.

When the food was gone and the lessons were done, George motioned for Allistor to follow him. They stepped inside a gas station, then turned into the attached garage. Allistor took one look at what was inside and whistled. "Damn, George! With this you could have taken out Evan and all his guys."

George shook his head. "Only if I could have gotten it up on the wall somehow. We didn't want to risk opening the gates long enough to use it."

Inside the garage was a military Humvee. Painted in desert camouflage, it was fully armored and had a fifty caliber machine gun mounted on its roof. When George opened the rear hatch, Allistor saw the back was filled with ammo cans. "Where did you get this?"

George looked slightly uncomfortable. "There was a train wreck right after it all happened. The tracks are five miles north of here, but we heard it and saw the smoke. A few of us went to investigate. There were a bunch more of us back then. The killing hadn't started. Anyway, when we got there, we saw the train was loaded with tanks and vehicles and artillery batteries. Most of them were damaged or half buried. But there were a couple of these babies still intact on a flatbed. We rolled this one down and brought it back."

Allistor looked alarmed. "Did Evan and his guys get the rest?" He didn't like the idea of facing an angry bunch of guys with machine guns when they left.

George shook his head. "As far as we know, they don't even know the wreck is there." Their place is south of us. Don't think they ventured that far. At least, not yet.

Allister's pulse was racing. "Were any of the artillery still intact?

George stroked his chin. "Maybe? I mean, I didn't look all that close. They were all spilled off their rail cars. Might be one or two?"

Allistor hugged the man, lifting him off his feet. "With those, we could even kill a titan! Or the big-ass turtle we have to pass on the way home. Let's go see if Sam knows how to fire cannons!"

George snorted at him. "Son, I was fightin' in the dirt 'n' snow before Sam was a glimmer in his daddy's eye. Artillery can't be all that different now. Between us, I'm sure we can figure it out."

Allistor practically pulled the old man out of the garage, yelling for Sam. When they filled him in, the old marine started laughing. "Oh, *hell yeah!* Let's go find us some big guns!"

They unhitched the trailer from the pickup and emptied its bed. Then Sam and George got in the pickup, and Allistor and two other men followed them in the box truck. All of the food and equipment from the back had been transferred into the RVs.

Twenty minutes after exiting the gates, they turned onto a gravel railroad access road that runs alongside the tracks. Ten minutes after that they came upon the wrecked train. The sun was lowering in the sky, leaving them maybe an hour of daylight. Allistor practically flew from the truck and began to make his way past twisted metal and burned grass.

George led him to where he'd seen the overturned artillery. The flatbed they'd been on had tilted nearly ninety degrees, dumping its load onto the gravel road. Behind it, there were three cars that were more or less intact, just tilted on two wheels. Allistor noted a couple dozen grave markers near the tree line. George saw him looking. "Yeah, we buried all the bodies we could find."

Allistor focused on the downed cannons. Sam informed him that they were 105mm Howitzers as he petted one and practically drooled on it. They worked together to roll the nearest one onto its wheelbase. Sam went over it quickly, pointed to something that Allistor didn't recognize but was obviously bent, and then shook his head. "Nope. Can't fix this. There are probably parts in one of these cars, but we don't have time to search for them."

They moved on to the next one, which Sam pronounced in good condition. Two more were badly damaged, the barrel of one having been partially sheared off by a train wheel. The final one they inspected also met with Sam's approval.

While Sam had been checking out the Howitzers, George had disappeared. When Allistor went looking for him, calling his name, George shouted, "Over here!" He ducked under some wreckage and turned back toward the tracks, following the sound. He found George standing in a field on the other side of the train. He was looking down the incline at another Humvee. "If we can get that one on its feet, it might run. Doesn't look damaged."

Allistor agreed. This one didn't have the gun mounted on the top, but otherwise, it was identical to the other. It had clearly fallen off and rolled a few times, but the armor was only slightly dented. It lay on its passenger side. Allistor shouted for Sam, and the two of them together managed to roll the vehicle back onto its tires. It bounced a few times, the metal frame groaning in complaint. But when George got in and pushed the starter, the engine coughed a few times, then started up. The group cheered as he drove it around the wreck and back up the gravel road next to the pickup.

They spent another ten minutes hooking up the Howitzer trailers to the pickup and the Humvee. Then they began exploring the train. Sam pointed out that the big guns did them no good without ammunition.

The third of the three cars that were still on the tracks near the back had what they needed. Crates upon crates, each with two rounds suspended on wood rails inside and packed with foam. One of the guys backed the box truck up as close as they could to the train car and they formed a line to pass the crates down. Sam took the front of the line, carefully lifting each crate so that others didn't fall. They loaded sixty crates into the box truck before he declared that moving any more of them could be dangerous. That was fine with Allistor. More than a hundred rounds of 105mm badassery meant that the Warren could hold its own against pretty much anything.

A search of the other cars turned up a few crates of M16's and ammo, two large crates each containing a dozen antipersonnel mines, and about a thousand MREs. They also found more than a hundred sets of desert BDUs in various sizes. Allistor insisted they take these as well. If they didn't fit the survivors, he was sure Lilly could make good use of the durable fabric.

The setting sun took away their light, so they abandoned their search and hopped in the trucks. Allistor was a little nervous as he pulled away in the box truck loaded with giant bullets full of explosives. But once his pulse-rate normalized, he began to fantasize about shooting titans in the face. He imagined George and Sam in one of the Humvees comparing notes on firing the big guns. Having never been in the military, he bowed to their experience.

Back at the Stronghold, the survivors all gathered around, eyes wide as the two cannons rolled down the street. The Humvee that Sam was driving turned halfway around so that the gun behind it was pointed southward. The two old men got out of the truck laughing.

Allistor approached, pretty sure he knew what they were planning. When he asked, George held up a binder. "This here manual says the gun has a range of about eight miles. Evan's base is just about ten miles in that direction." He pointed in the same direction as the Howitzer. "Me and Sam had a chat on the way back. We figure we should test fire this bad boy before we hit the road. I mean, to make sure it's okay."

The moment he stopped talking, half a dozen men and every single kid in hearing range volunteered to help. Chuckling to himself, Allistor left them to it. He could learn how to fire the things later. He wanted to spend some quality time with Amanda.

Luther had graciously given them a small house near the wall to sleep in. It had running water, but no electricity. Allistor found her sitting on the sofa in the living room, reading a well-worn magazine by candlelight.

He sat next to her for a while, just relaxing and enjoying the quiet. At least, until a cannon blast shattered the silence about ten minutes later. She looked up in alarm, and he explained what they'd found, finishing with, "So, they just sent a warning shot toward whoever is left of Evan's crew." Amanda rolled her eyes. Snuggling up against his chest, she closed her eyes. He did the same. He and Amanda had claimed the smaller of the two bedrooms in the house, but they never used it. They slept through the night right there on the sofa.

*****

Chapter Eleven

RVs and BFGs

They rose early in the morning. Meg and Sam already had breakfast ready. Simple bacon, sausage, and oatmeal. The kids were given some fruit to help with the malnutrition.

Sam and George had discussed the roadblocks, and George had produced maps taken from the gas station. They were full atlas books, with maps of every state. They put one in each of the RVs and Sam took one with an alternate route marked on it in the lead Humvee. He'd chosen to take the one with the gun on top. Meg rode with him, hoping for the chance to blast something.

As the sun rose, everyone loaded into one of the vehicles, and they opened the gates. One of Luther's men closed them behind the convoy as they left, not wanting the place to get overrun by critters. Then he ran to the top of the wall and lowered himself down atop of one of the RVs. A minute later, they were on their way. A convoy of two RVs, two Humvees, a winery truck, three pickups, and trailers pulling snowmobiles and ATVs along with two cannons in tow. Allistor felt a twinge as he thought how much his father would laugh at the sight.

They kept a faster pace on the way back, now that they had some idea of the condition of the roads. No creature in its right mind would attack such a large noisy convoy, so they worried less about attacks.

A quick stop at the house where'd they'd stopped before, and the group made short work of loading up the rest of the jars from the cellar. Others searched the house and barn for anything useful, and they were soon on their way again. They took side roads to avoid the two large pile-ups, and it was only mid-afternoon when they reached the ancient shellback's lake.

Sam and George, two twelve-year-olds in the bodies of old men, had devised a plan to deal with the monster. They stopped the convoy well short of the lake and gathered everyone together. Meg began sending out party invites to every single survivor there, including the kids. Sam and George unhitched both Howitzers and placed them on the road in front of the lead Humvee. Each of them chose three people to serve as their 'gun crew', and spent a little time showing each one what to do. The gun required one person sighting, one to load, one to feed rounds to the loader, and a crew chief that directed the others and actually pulled the trigger.

The sighting bit was different than normal. Usually, there would be map coordinates for a target miles away. The person sighting needed to know complicated formulas for aiming the weapon to hit that spot. But in this case, they were going to be shooting a target the size of a tank from a couple hundred yards away. Sam sighted in both guns on a spot in the median. The same spot where it had gotten bogged down the other day.

Their plan was simple. They had volunteered Allistor to take one of the ATVs down the road to attract the shellback's attention. When it charged at him, he'd gun his engine and get out of its way as it sped across the road into the median. When it slowed down to turn and pursue him, the two big guns would fire. Meg was up in the gunner's port ready to fire the .50 caliber machine gun. And everyone except the small children had rifles ready. Everyone had instructions that if the big guns didn't take it down, they were to jump into the vehicles and haul butt as fast as they could while Allistor or one of the smaller vehicles distracted it.

Allistor prepared himself. He asked Meg for two of her grenades, in case the thing got too close. His only hope was to blind it and try to avoid getting crushed. The gun crews piled four rounds each next to their guns, with one already loaded. Sam said as fast as the shellback moved, they wouldn't have time for more than three or four shots.

With a quick kiss for luck from Amanda, Allistor hopped on his ATV and rode forward. He honked the annoying little horn a few times to make sure he had the monster's attention. About halfway to the spot where it had attacked before, he saw some telltale swirling of the water. He picked up a little speed, watching the water as his heart pounded.

As predicted, the shellback surged upward from the lake water, crossing the grass as it opened its beak and roared at the bite-sized human who dared taunt it. Allistor gunned the engine and shot forward, the front wheels rising up slightly as the ATV threatened to flip under him. He leaned forward and eased off the throttle slightly, getting all four wheels back on the road as he watched the tank-sized spiked monster hurtle toward him.

It passed behind him, only missing its target by about ten feet. The tail swished toward Allistor's ATV, a last-ditch attempt to crush him. It fell short, but one of the spikes slammed into the rear tire and knocked the small vehicle on its side. Allistor rolled with it, back on his feet in a second. As the shellback slid down the grass into the center of the median, it began to turn. On a whim, Allistor tried casting *Restraint* on it. The thing paused for maybe half a second before resuming its turn.

The two Howitzers fired less than a second apart. The first round impacted the side of the monsters shell, punching through and rocking the thing toward its other side. The second round hit its underside on an angle. It didn't penetrate, but the explosion pushed the thing further onto its side. Allistor tried *Restraint* again, but it had no effect that he could see. The monster was just too many levels above him. He *Examined* it quickly, to see how much damage the guns had done.

Ancient Shellback
Level 22
Health: 97,400/130,000

Allistor nearly leapt from his moving ATV in excitement. Two hits from the big guns had done more than thirty thousand damage! And one hadn't been a direct penetration. Turning his ATV toward the monster as it righted itself and began to turn again, he slowed. A moment later, two more 105mm rounds pounded into the shell. They hit simultaneously. One round punched into its shell, shattering it and sending chunks flying. The other streaked past its head to impact right at the spot where its neck emerged from the shell. This one penetrated deep into soft flesh before exploding. When it did, it was like setting off a firecracker inside a soda bottle. The thing exploded, its neck torn to shreds and its head falling to the ground.

The cheers from the survivors fell off abruptly as their interfaces lit up with notifications. Even spread among two dozen people, the experience from killing a level 22 monster was incredible! The kids jumped from level zero or one to level four and five. All of Luther's adults picked up at least three levels. Allistor himself hit level nine and got halfway to ten. Fame points flooded across all of their screens. The gunners all picked up new skills, and Allistor got something called a *Title*.

Congratulations! You have earned the Title:
Killer of Giants

Shaking his head, he took a moment to recover. The others were getting in their vehicles to join him as he rode the ATV over to loot the monster. When he set his hand on it, more notifications scrolled down his screen. He received three hundred fifty klax, six pieces of shellback armor, two stacks of twenty pieces of shellback meat and one more item.

This one was special. A picture of it appeared on his screen, highlighted in pulsing purple light.

Ancient Shellback's Heart
Item Quality: Extremely Rare
The Ancient Shellback has walked the various worlds of the Nexus for more than a thousand years. It has absorbed the essences of hundreds of species that were unfortunate enough to cross its path. These essences were preserved in the very heart of the monster, combining to form an organ of great value to the elite among GrandMaster crafters.

As the vehicles came to a stop and the others piled out, Allistor pumped his fist in the air. "WE just hit the damned lottery!" he shouted. He described the heart to the others as they all took turns looting the monster. Each of them received a few hundred klax, some meat and armor bits. One of the elder ladies received a scroll. And two of the kids each received an eyeball, much to their delight.

When they'd finished looting, Sam grabbed a knife and a crowbar, telling others to do the same. He began skinning the shellback, explaining to the others how they'd harvested the titan. The shellback didn't smell good, but it was much easier to take than the titan stench. They spent some time harvesting skin and fragments of shell that they managed to break off around the edges of the cannon round impacts. George spent the time cutting the beak off the monster, saying he planned to mount it above his door and spend his old age exaggerating the details of the battle. Two of Luther's men drove the Humvees back and retrieved the Howitzers and the unused rounds.

Looting complete, they piled back into the vehicles and resumed their trip. It was past sunset when they arrived, and the gates to the Warren opened for them. The look on Ramon's face as the convoy passed by him was priceless. After he closed the gates and caught up to them, he teased. "We send you away to retrieve a few strays, and you come back with an army!"

It was late in the evening before everyone was settled. Allistor's first order of business had been to use the Stronghold interface to construct more sleeping quarters. He raised another fifteen, this time on the opposite side of the central fountain. He didn't want to force the two groups to mingle on the first night. There were several couples and families among Luther's group, so fifteen was sufficient to house everyone. Some of them were two and three bedrooms.

Meg took charge of gathering all of the turtle meat and getting it into cold storage. With literally hundreds of pieces of it, she was determined to experiment and create a tasty recipe that provided at least one buff.

Allistor's people helped the newcomers unload their possessions and cart them into their new quarters. Thrilled to have company closer to her own age, Chloe insisted on introducing herself and hugging each of the children. Max was beside himself with all of the attention he was getting from the rugrats, which only lessened slightly when Chloe introduced them all to Beatrice and Thumper.

With the unloading done, they grabbed a quick meal, then put the children to bed. Some of the adults crashed too, having had a very long day.

Meg broke out a makeshift bar - opening several bottles of booze and setting out a case of cold beer. The two groups mingled, introducing themselves and chatting about little things, like the apocalypse.

George took a chair and thumped on the table, taking on the role of storyteller and relating a colorful tale of their journey and the giant turtle battle. He insisted that it was his crew that fired the fatal shot at the shellback. Sam and his team objected good-naturedly, which led to a drinking contest to decide this matter of honor once and for all.

Eventually, everyone retired and the Warren grew quiet. Except for Sam's snoring.

*****

Morning found everyone gathered for breakfast. There was much laughter as the two groups got to know each other better. The folks from Luther's group had lived for weeks with the threat of starvation and murder because of Evan's actions. The relief they felt now was visible in their eyes and their smiles. Powdered eggs, real sausage, and fresh onions didn't hurt either.

When the meal was done, they spent some time as a group discussing the skills people already had, and what they'd like to achieve. Two of Luther's men were former soldiers, another was a mechanic who was willing to take up the Engineering trade. One of the women from the group was a former EMT with five years on the job. She was fascinated by the new healing abilities within the system. Amanda immediately adopted her into the infirmary. Lilly picked up two elderly ladies who already had sewing skills and wanted to contribute.

Nancy and two of the other ladies became the unofficial wardens of the kids during the day. Those from Luther's group that were orphans had already been taken in by others, but the community at large had been helping to take care of them. They saw no reason to change that.

Nancy pushed once again for Allistor to expand the Warren above ground. Put up some walls and allow them to garden safely. With more mouths to feed and more kids to occupy, it was a clear necessity.

Allistor asked her to wait with him and requested Luther and George join them. The four of them went topside and looked around. George admired the garden, which he hadn't seen in the fading light on their way in.

After some brief discussion, Allistor disclosed their extensive Stronghold account and said they would add to it by selling one of the RVs. Luther and George agreed, as long as Allistor promised they'd make a trip up to retrieve a few more. They were a good way for groups to travel long distances that might require overnight stays. If they were going to expand, they'd need that ability.

Allistor opened up his Stronghold interface and authorized the others to see it. Luther was already slightly familiar with it, having built his Stronghold. They discussed the options and chose a modest beginning. After making the selections, and reviewing the cost, he approved the transaction.

The same golden glow that had engulfed the cavern below wrapped around the four humans standing in the middle of the former sheriff's station. When it faded, they were surrounded by stone walls twenty feet high. A rampart ran the entire length of the interior, about five feet below the top of the wall. Switchback stone stairs ran upward from the now smooth ground every hundred feet or so. There was a single gate with two massive metal doors that rose twenty feet from the ground, each one hung with two six-foot long hinges. The perimeter of the wall ran two hundred yards in each direction, meaning it encompassed just under ten acres of land.

Inside the wall, not only had all the debris disappeared, but a few new buildings had risen. Just inside the gate stood a barracks, two stories tall with the main floor sunk four feet below ground level. A ramp led down to the front door. The roof was level with the parapet and would make a great place to mount a Howitzer. The inside consisted of storage space, a kitchen, bathrooms at either end with three stalls each and showers, and a dozen rooms each with two bunks.

Next to the barracks was a motor pool with a six-bay garage and doors large enough to pull the RVs inside. Its rounded roof made it look like an airplane hangar. A side structure that was basically just an extended roof with stone pillars provided space to park a dozen or so trucks underneath.

Each of the four corners sported a watchtower that extended ten feet higher than the wall. The towers were covered with windows facing each of the cardinal points. Inside each was a stairwell leading down and a door facing the ramparts on two sides. A brazier was mounted below the floor level, designed to allow heat to rise without reducing the night vision of the guards.

The largest and most expensive of the structures was toward the back of the compound near the gates leading down to the cavern. Over the top of where their small garden had been located now sat a greenhouse. The one-acre building was built from some kind of metal with clear panels that were more durable than glass.

The group walked inside the building, its entrance a double set of swinging doors. The interior was organized into raised plots filled with soil. Metal framework rose from the corners of each plot, allowing future additions of second and even third levels of growing platforms. The ceiling stretched twenty feet high, sloped slightly to allow snowmelt to drain easily. Sprinkler pipes crisscrossed overhead in a grid, with grow lights extending down from the rafters every thirty feet or so.

Nancy began to tear up as she looked around. "We could grow food for... fifty people in here. A hundred if we're just supplementing meat."

George was impressed. "Damn, son," was all he said aloud. He patted Nancy on the back and said, "I'd love to join you in your work here. My wife loved gardening, and I used to putter around in the garden out back with her."

Nancy hugged the old man. "Of course you can help. Thank you."

Leaving them to their plans for crops, Luther and Allistor left to go examine the garage. There was a long bench along the back side of the bays for tools and such. Below two of the bays was a trench that a mechanic could walk down into. Electric lights hung down from above, and there was a bathroom with a shower. The front of each bay had a metal door on tracks that slid to one side. They all stood open at the moment.

"We could park our entire fleet inside here." Luther gawked at the expansive building.

Allistor shook his head. "We can park some vehicles up here. But until I feel safer, we'll keep some down below. Remember, this place was leveled by a sixty-foot giant that could have stepped right over these walls and crushed every structure here. Who knows if more of them might spawn?"

The walls and structures had cost another forty thousand system points, nearly depleting their available funds. Allistor returned to the kiosk and opened up the RV brochure he had taken. Using it to create a write-up, he listed the one with the full bedroom in the back end. It was the least practical for their needs, and the most likely to attract luxury buyers. He drove the vehicle into the kiosk, concerned at first that only the front bumper would fit through the door. But as the vehicle approached, the door and the building itself seemed to expand to accommodate it. Allistor chuckled as he got out and exited the building, mumbling to himself, "It's bigger on the inside."

The kiosk did its thing, scanning the RV and throwing up stats about dimensions, fuel, range, etc. Allistor added in his description of the comfortable leather seats, marble countertops, and extensive storage. When he thought it sounded properly snooty, he set the minimum bid at fifty thousand klax and started the auction. He set it for three days.

Already planning to retrieve more of them, he would sell the fancy ones and keep the more utilitarian models. The fewer fancy gadgets, the less likely something would malfunction. He wanted his vehicles to be workhorses, not luxury rides.

Just for kicks, he took his stack of shellback meat from his ring. He'd forgotten to give it to Meg, and she wasn't going to notice. He took half the stack and put it up for auction at a thousand klax. If the shellback was as rare as it seemed in the description for its heart, the meat might be valuable too. If so, they could sell a chunk of it and purchase large quantities of something like burgers.

He kept the heart in his ring. He wanted some time to research its potential value. If he put it up for sale and made a hundred thousand klax, then found out it was worth twice or ten times that amount, he'd be kicking himself.

Returning the rest of the shellback meat to his ring, he went back to the fountain and took a seat. He spent some time just watching as folks moved around the cavern. So far there hadn't been any arguments between the different group members, and he hoped it stayed that way. Of course, no large group of humans could live in harmony for long. There would be jealousies, both professional and personal. Disputes over crafting items, or who would go out on foraging expeditions. And if they suffered losses, it was likely blame would be placed. He anticipated all of that. But for now, things were peaceful.

He took a few minutes to go through his notifications from the last few days. He'd mostly waved them away as he was busy dealing with more important things. Primarily they were about experience points awarded and Fame Points received. There was an increase in his *Improvisation* skill that, based on the timing of the notice, seemed to have happened when they used the normally long-range cannons to kill the shellback. He also got a level increase on his *Restraint* skill when he managed to freeze the giant turtlesaur thing for a fraction of a second.

A check of his stats brought him a few surprises. The first was that he hadn't spent any of his attribute points since level five. At level nine now, he had nine points to spend, including the one he had saved. The second surprise was that his title – *Giant Killer* – showed up in crimson red lettering next to his name. He'd have to do some research into what, if any, benefits came with the title.

After a few minutes' thought, he assigned some attribute points. He added three points to *Constitution*, because he still seemed to be getting bit a lot. Two more points went into *Will Power*, and one into *Intelligence*, bringing both up to eight. That left him three more points. Because his low *Charisma* score of two mocked him, he added one point there, and one to *Luck*. The last point he banked for emergencies.

Designation: Allistor, Giant Killer	Level: 9	Experience: 84,700/90,000
Planet of Origin: UCP 382	Health: 2000/2000	Class: Unknown
Attribute Pts Available: 2	Mana: 900	
Intelligence: 8	Strength: 4	Charisma: 3
Adaptability: 6	Stamina: 4	Luck: 3
Constitution: 6	Agility: 3	Health Regen: 100/m
Will Power: 8	Dexterity: 3	Mana Regen: 50/m

Feeling more alert and refreshed, he made his way to the infirmary to find Amanda. He wanted to plan a quiet evening for the two of them at his quarters.

She and her new apprentice were dealing with an emergency medical situation. Or so they made it seem. One of the children sat on the exam table, tears in her eyes as the two women fussed over a scrape on her knee. Allistor rolled his eyes but played along.

"That's some battle wound you got there. Let me guess. An octopoid?"

The girl, maybe seven years old, looked at him wide-eyed for a moment, then shook her head. "Nope. Bobby. We were chasing Max and he tripped me. Not on purpose, though. Accident."

Amanda made a series of flourishing movements with her hands and chanted: "Oh magic critters of UCP382, come to our aid. Heal this child of her battle wounds!" With the end of the chant, she cast a heal spell on the little girl, who watched wide-eyed as her skin healed in seconds. Allistor golf clapped, earning him a dirty look from Amanda as she took a bow. "There you go! All better. Next time, make sure you're faster than Bobby so he can't trip you!"

The little girl hopped off the table and waved, calling, "Thank you!" as she scurried out the door.

Allistor limped into the room, one hand over his right butt cheek. "Oh, miss. I have a boo-boo on my-"

"Don't even think about saying that next word, or you'll have one for real." She cut him off. Her new apprentice covered her mouth to try to hide her laughter.

Allistor stopped limping and changed tactics. He bowed to her, waving his hand with a flourish much like she'd just done during her chant. "Would milady do me the honor of joining me for a quiet evening of snuggling and plotting to take over the world?"

Though she resisted, a small smile escaped. "Idiot. I'll have to check my calendar. With all these new men around, I'm considering my options."

Covering his heart with both hands, he staggered backward. "My lady! You wound me!" Turning to stagger toward the door, he made gasping noises. "I fear… it may be a mortal wound." He listened carefully as he exited and turned to lean against the wall outside. A wide smile broke across his face as he heard the two women laughing.

The woman whose name he didn't remember said, "Lucky you."

Amanda sighed and said, "Yes, lucky me. He's young, strong, not completely stupid, and he doesn't snore. Such a prize." He rolled his eyes and crept away, stepping carefully so as not to alert her that he was still within earshot. When he cleared the building and entered the crafting hall, he got another notification.

You have learned the skill: Sneaking!

He didn't bother to read the rest. Waving it away, he went to see if he could improvise a new weapon with his recently acquired skill increase.

*****

Another week passed in relative peace. Allistor took a party of five back to the RV lot to retrieve three more. One luxury model, and two more functional ones. They also filled more steel drums with gasoline. A drive-by of the Stronghold showed the gates still closed and no sign of activity. Allistor was glad – he hoped to reclaim it as part of their territorial expansion. Luther had come to him more than once, asking about the fate of the Stronghold, and whether Allistor planned to claim it for himself. The situation was awkward. Luther was a prideful man who had been strong enough to gather a larger group than Allistor's and create a stronghold. If not for the interference of Evan and his men, Luther might well be the stronger of the two. Allistor reassured Luther that the Stronghold was his anytime he wanted to void his oath and separate from Allistor's people.

Foraging parties of three and four went out daily, ranging farther and farther. They'd found a distribution warehouse off the interstate that was full of mostly useless items. The foragers did find several dozen winter coats, including some small enough for the children. Another container held thousands of bags of peanuts, like you'd find at a ballpark or on a plane. They tossed a few fifty-pound bags of dry dog food onto the truck for Max and the rabbits.

A howling sound cut short their exploration of the multi-acre warehouse. Rushing back to the truck, they closed the roll-up door and exited the area. Standard procedure was to avoid a fight if a group was potentially outnumbered. And the canids were roaming in larger and larger packs.

Amanda led a group back to the hospital to stock up on more linens and antiseptics. They ran across a smaller pack of canids and managed to kill them with only minor injuries on their side.

The RV that he'd put on the market sold for one hundred sixty thousand klax. He didn't put the next one on the market right away, wanting to make them seem scarcer and thus valuable.

Amanda slept in his quarters more often than not through the week. When he jokingly asked her if she'd finished considering her options and made a choice, she just gave him a funny look and put her head on his shoulder. He let the subject drop.

Though they were scouting and foraging as far as forty miles out in every direction, none of the parties returned with any news of other survivors. There had been a dozen or so reports of evidence of attacks. Some of them recent enough that the blood at the scene wasn't fully dried. But there was no way to tell if it was human blood.

Sam came home triumphant from a foraging trip with a box full of radio equipment. He'd finally located a short wave radio. But after spending a full day setting it up and testing various frequencies, he'd received no replies to his calls. He made it a habit to stop by the crafting hall where they'd set up the radio each day and cycle through the channels, calling for other survivors to respond.

The general consensus was that Ramon and Nancy had a full-fledged romance going. Neither admitted to it if asked, but they weren't fooling anybody. Chloe was growing attached to him as well, suckering him into tea parties and wheedling him into reading to her at bedtime.

A nearby farm had yielded a chicken coop and a dozen chickens, as well as three goats. The coop was set up next to the greenhouse, and the livestock was allowed to roam the enclosure. The areas that weren't paved, which was everywhere but in front of the gate and around the garage, supplied more than enough grass for the goats to browse. The kids sometimes fed them dog food nuggets as a treat. Meg began to offer the kids a klax or two in return for collecting eggs, cleaning out the coop or the rabbit hutch.

Though their sensor network had expanded with the addition of the walls, they still kept two people on guard atop the walls at all times. They patrolled together, keeping each other awake through their shifts.

It was on the twelfth day since they'd brought Luther's group home that they lost their first citizen. Two of Luther's people were on guard duty. A man named Rick and a woman who called herself Candy. The two were walking the parapet and flirting. A guard duty shift was mainly four hours of mind-numbing boredom, since they relied on the sensor system that would alert them to incoming intruders. At night, when visibility was low, the sensors alert would come long before the guards could see anything.

This afternoon, the two were into the third hour of their shift and only keeping a casual watch outside the wall. It never occurred to either of them to glance upward.

That oversight cost Candy her life. A rushing of wind was their only warning before a pair of talons locked onto Candy's head and shoulder and dug in. With a roar of triumph and a few wingbeats, a creature with leathery wings, horns, and a long tail dragged her off the wall and up into the sky.

Rick fired his weapon, trying to hit the creature's wings without injuring the screaming Candy. Shouts could be heard from the direction of the cavern as people came running out to see what was wrong. Rick fired again, rewarded this time with a spray of blood and the sight of the creature faltering with an injured wing. Before he could reload and fire another slug, the creature dropped below the tree line in the general vicinity of the creek.

Shouting in frustration, Rick ran down the stairs and headed for the gates. Allistor and Michael caught up with him as he was pushing one of the doors open.

"What happened?" Allistor grabbed the man and spun him around.

"Did you see that thing? It was a damned dragon! Or, close to it. It took Candy!" Rick shoved the gate open and ran out in the direction the monster had gone. "We need to catch up before it kills her!" Candy screamed, the sound echoing through the trees.

Allistor and Michael followed him out, Sam and Luther not far behind. They ran across the open ground and into the tree line. Thirty seconds later the screaming stopped abruptly. Rick halted, leaning against a tree and panting as he searched the woods ahead. Michael put a hand on the man's shoulder. "I'm sorry, man. She's gone."

Rick shrugged off his hand. "Maybe. Maybe not. Either way, I'm going to find that thing and kill it!" He started off again in the same direction, moving through the trees and brush as quickly as he could. A roar from the monster confirmed their direction a minute or so later.

They emerged from the trees to see the creek right in front of them. Just upstream, the monster was perched on a fallen log. Rick bent over and puked as the dragon took hold of Candy's arm with its jaws and ripped it from her body. Tilting its head upward, it swallowed the limb whole. Allistor Examined the beast.

Forest Drake
Level 12
Health: 8,700/8,700

The creature was maybe thirty feet long from nose to the tail, with a wingspan nearly as wide. Its head was covered in small horns that coalesced at the top of its skull into a ridge that ran the length of its back and down its tail.

As it bit into a lifeless Candy again, Rick shouted a curse and charged at it. His shotgun fired again and again as he got closer. The beast took the hits, bits of green scale chipping off. When he was within reach, the drake flicked its tail at Rick. The impact knocked him off his feet to smash face-first into a tree. Rick's body crumpled limply to the ground.

Allistor cast *Flame Shot* at the monster's face, the fireball screaming toward it and engulfing its head. Having seen that the scales were tough enough to resist Rick's shots, the others all fired their weapons at the drake's head as well. Round after round from Sam, Michael, and Luther pounded into its nose and throat, each doing less damage than normal.

More shots rang out as some of the other survivors caught up. Ramon and two of Luther's guys added their firepower. Allistor was raising his own weapon when he saw the drake take a deep breath.

"Take cover!" he shouted as he cast *Restraint* at the monster. The spell worked, and it froze, its mouth open and chest expanded. He fired one slug straight into its mouth then retreated behind the nearest tree.

When the spell wore off after four seconds, the creature resumed its attack. A molten liquid boiled up from its gullet and spewed outward toward the spot they'd been standing. Everything in its path caught fire.

The drake bellowed in pain and began shaking its head violently. The flames abruptly ceased, and the survivors risked a peek from behind their cover. Smoke rose from the drake's mouth as it thrashed, and blood splattered in every direction. When it opened its mouth to roar, they could see a nasty-looking burned patch in the roof of its mouth.

Resuming fire, they tore into its face and neck. When it raised its head and spread its wings as if to take to the air, a shot from Sam's rifle penetrated its throat just below the jaw. It bellowed again, weakly this time. Allistor cast *Restraint* on it again just before its feet left the ground, and it froze with the wound in its throat exposed. Every man present focused his fire on that weak spot without a word needed. The shotgun slugs and rifle rounds ripped into the damaged flesh, opening the wound further. Each of them got off two shots before the spell wore off.

With a gurgling sound, the monstrous lizard's head fell. Its wings collapsed as its legs buckled, the weight of the creature's body crushing small trees and bushes as it hit the ground. A few of the survivors leveled up, and Allistor got a bit closer to level ten.

They moved forward, the xp gains making them confident the creature was dead. Allistor marveled at it, standing next to the head that, even laying on its side on the ground, was nearly as tall as he was. The drake's menacing jaws were open, and Allistor peered inside, looking past fangs as long as his arm at the burned spot near the back.

Ramon put a hand on his shoulder and spoke from behind him. "I think that last shot you took before it breathed fire is what did that. You punched a hole in its flesh and that liquid fire flowed right up into it. Probably would have fried its brain if it hadn't stopped."

Allistor nodded, imagining how screwed they all would have been if it had been able to continue. The earth in front of the thing wasn't just burned, it was melted.

He touched the drake's head and looted it. The rewards were decent – a hundred klax, a stack of drake hide pieces, two drake teeth that he thought might make excellent weapons, and the drake's heart. This one wasn't purple, but he suspected it might still have some value as a crafting item or cooking ingredient.

They sent a runner back for one of the ATVs, and the rest of them began to harvest what they could from the drake's corpse. When the ATV arrived, several other survivors joined them. Allistor lifted what was left of Candy and set her gently on a sheet someone had brought along. As they wrapped her body, he retrieved Rick's corpse and loaded it onto the ATV. When both bodies were secure, and the harvest was complete, the entire group washed themselves off in the creek and headed back to the

265

Warren. Each of them gathered wood as they walked, and when they reached the clearing outside the walls, they constructed a pyre.

An hour later, the bodies burned and goodbyes spoken, they closed the outer gates behind them and retreated underground for a quiet meal.

Chapter Twelve

The Bear Necessities

"Giant smelly titans, rats the size of grizzly bears, and friggin' dragons? Screw these guys!" Amanda was sitting on Allistor's bed, pulling on her boots. "The bastards running this place need to pay."

Allistor agreed whole-heartedly. Their arbitrary judgment that nine out of ten humans needed to be purged from the planet was unforgivable. But for now, they needed to keep discussions of vengeance at a minimum. They still had no idea when people were watching them. For all he knew, he and Amanda had had an audience during their sexual escapades last night. Though he would like to think he'd have earned some Fame Points if that were the case.

"They absolutely do. But we need to focus on ourselves right now. Get stronger. Learn more. Conquer more territory. Beef up our defenses."

She sighed as she stomped her boots on the floor to settle her feet in them properly. "I know. Time is passing, and we only have a year. I'm studying the little critters that seem to be the key to all the magic and stuff. But I feel like those apes from that old movie, touching the big obelisk and trying to make sense of it."

Allistor pulled her to her feet and hugged her close, kissing the top of her head. "You know that old saying, "Any sufficiently advanced technology is indistinguishable from magic." That Clarke guy was right. You'll figure it out. You're one of the smartest people I know."

She hugged him back briefly, then spun out of his embrace. "Meg might have *real eggs* for breakfast this morning! And Sam said he was going to test out dragon steaks." Allistor's stomach growled at the mention of food. She patted his belly and took off toward the dining area.

Allistor hadn't told her, but after the fight with the dragon, he had decided to go on an extended solo mission. There were several things he wanted to accomplish, and he wanted to do them without risking the lives of any of his friends. As he followed his... *girlfriend?* to breakfast, he mentally ticked off his goals.

He wanted to locate more survivors. He couldn't claim more land if he didn't have the people to hold it. In his mind, he pictured a wide circle of Strongholds with a town or even a city in the center.

He needed to kill some more creatures and reach level ten. Based on the reading he'd done, this would allow him to choose a 'class' based on how he wanted to interact with this new Earth. It was supposed to come with a few class-specific abilities as well.

Allistor also wanted to find another dungeon. The best way to level his people up and make them strong enough to thrive here was to run them through a dungeon where they could kill dozens, if not hundreds, of mobs. Failing that, if he could find more elite creatures like the ancient shellback, they would give good experience as well.

Ideally, he'd like to lead one of those back to the Warren and fight it from the walls. This gave added protection to his people, with the bonus of Stronghold points when they killed it. They got points for the dragon, but only because it attacked Candy atop the walls before flying away.

At breakfast, he told Amanda what he planned. She argued briefly but quickly realized his mind was made up. When they finished the meal, he gave her a hug and a brief kiss and headed for the kitchen, then the parking area.

Checking his inventory quickly, he confirmed he had healing potions, bandages, food and drink for a week. Including half a dozen eggs that Meg had slipped him. There was a rope, because everybody knows you need a rope when adventuring, several kinds of weapons including his trusty rebar spear, one of the radios – which he took out and plugged into the pickup he was taking – a tent, and a frying pan. He'd picked up the cooking skill from Meg when she insisted he help her in the kitchen a few days back. She had decided that everyone in the Warren needed to be able to cook themselves at least a basic meal if they were stuck outside foraging.

He put two extra gas cans in the back of the truck, along with a siphon and hand pump. With that done, he was ready to roll.

A few of the kids who were playing near the cavern gates waved at him as he passed. Max barked happily and trotted along next to the truck until Allistor told him to go back. If the silly mutt got taken by a flying creature, the children would be crushed.

Pulling up to the outer gates, he got out of the truck to open them. It annoyed him to have to either station someone at the gates or open and close them himself each time he went in and out. Rather than open the gates, he leaned against them and opened his Stronghold interface. He'd been meaning to look into this for a while, but he kept getting distracted.

Scrolling through the options for a good couple minutes, he finally found what he wanted. The gates could be opened remotely. Just like with the interface sharing, he could add authorized individuals who would be able to open it. Then he had some options for remote activation method and security settings. The gate could be opened with a specific sound, like a whistle or a tune, or a phrase. It could be set so that the sensors recognized the authorized individuals and opened the gates as they approached. There was a biometric option that required a handprint and eye scan.

With Evan and his murderers in mind, Allistor went all out. He chose the biometric option, combined with a passphrase and the sensor recognition. The three together cost ten thousand system points, but he figured it was worth it. If he was being pursued back to the gate, he likely wouldn't have time to get out, open the gates, drive through, then get out and close them again. He set the system so that it required two of the three be activated. Either sensors and password, sensors and biometric, or biometric and password.

Approving the transaction, he watched as a post grew up from the ground next to the truck. A flat screen with a red handprint on it began flashing at him. He set his hand on it, and there was a brief tingle.

Biometric pattern uploaded: Allistor, Giant Killer. Please set passphrase.

He snorted to himself over the system's use of his title, but said, "Passphrase is Fibble." He decided to use the name of a beloved character from a series he'd read that was based on MMORPGs. It seemed fitting.

Passphrase confirmed. Please list individuals authorized for access and access level.

A list of the Warren's residents popped up. He authorized Sam, Meg, and Luther as full access, and designated the ability for them to add or remove people from the list. Everyone except him.

With that done, the gates opened before him, and he drove through. They obligingly shut behind him as he slowly pulled away. Before he could forget, he picked up the radio and called Sam, giving him the details. When Sam asked, "What's a Fibble?" he just chuckled and said, "I'll see if I can find you a copy of the books sometime."

And just like that, lightning struck! Books! Movies! How much would Earth stories and art sell on the open market? He asked Sam that question, and he could hear the man shaking his head on the other end of the line. "Leave it to you, boy. I'll have our people start looking for hardcover books and intact DVDs and players while they're out. Maybe find a library."

Pleased with himself, he wound his way through the debris on the outskirts of town that hadn't been cleared yet. When he hit the open road, Allistor sped up. The plan was to head roughly southeast a ways. Since Luther had already established a Stronghold near Denver, nearly two hundred miles south by southeast, he figured he would try a city between the two Strongholds. The most obvious choice was Cheyenne.

He might have just traveled down Interstate 25 and reached the city, but he wanted to explore back roads and see what he could see. He knew from experience the only thing he'd run across on the interstate was cattle ranges and the occasional one-light town, truck stop or rest area.

Using one of the atlas books that they'd found, he plotted himself a route that should take him through Medicine Bow national forest and several small towns. Initially, he'd go more south than east.

Setting off at a leisurely pace, Allistor enjoyed the sunshine and the cool air. He stopped occasionally when he saw something that caught his attention. The first was a gun shop out in the middle of nowhere, about fifty miles south of the Warren. The windows were intact, and the front door closed. He pulled into the small parking lot with caution, not getting too close to the building, and honked the horn once. Sitting in the truck for a full minute, he waited for either a response from inside or critters to show up to investigate the noise. When neither happened, he got out and walked up to the shop.

The front door was metal, with a small peephole and a sign that said, "Shoplifters will be shot." He knocked, then tried the handle, but it was locked. Undeterred, he considered this a good sign. Walking around the building, he peered into the small storefront window, which was protected by iron bars. There was enough light filtering in for him to see an entire wall filled with rifles and shotguns, as well as a long glass display case showing off dozens of handguns, knives, and accessories. The shelves nearest the window held hunting bows and crossbows.

Allistor continued around the building, finding a shooting range out back. There was an old Chevy pickup sitting under a carport overhang. The driver's side door was open, and there were blood stains on the seat, door, and concrete. A long gun lay on the ground part way under the truck. Suddenly much more concerned, Allistor drew his own shotgun from his ring and stood perfectly still, listening and watching for any movement. Moving slowly, he stepped up to the driver's door. The blood stains were clearly old, maybe even dating back to the first day of the apocalypse. He imagined the store owner locking up to go be with their family, and being surprised by... something. There were no tracks in the blood to tell him anything.

Sticking his head inside the truck, Allistor grinned to himself. The keys were in the ignition. Not only that, but the key ring held several keys. Crossing his fingers, he put away the shotgun and took the keys. Moving to the back door, he tried one after another until one of them worked!

Allistor opened the door, wincing as it struck a bell hung above. He let the door close and locked it behind him. Re-arming himself with his shotgun, he made his way slowly through each aisle, then checked the back rooms. Pleased to find a clean bathroom, he used the facilities. The tank was only good for one flush, but that was all he needed.

Back out in the main room, he just stood there and drooled for a while. He could arm three times the number of people living at the Warren with just what he could see here. And he'd found a storage room in the back with a locked gate. Peering through the bars he saw dozens of crates and boxes that he assumed held more weapons.

But what he was most excited about were the bows and crossbows. These were effective ranged weapons that packed a punch but made very little noise. In this new world, it seemed like making noise was like ringing the dinner bell.

Moving to the front shelves, his eyes locked on an old Fred Bear compound bow. The lines just spoke to him. Taking it in hand, he tested the weight and the pull. It felt good in his grip. The bow went into his ring along with a hip quiver and twenty arrows. After a moment, he added a second full quiver. There were more Bear Archery bows and one crossbow. He snagged that as well, along with a whole box of bolts.

When that was done, he opened the display case and grabbed a Desert Eagle .50 just because the gun was legendary. He found a couple boxes of the large rounds and put them in storage as well. He helped himself to a pair of nasty looking combat knives with sheaths and put one on his hip. The other he stuck down in his boot.

Looking around the store, there were so many things he wanted. But he tried to stick to useful items. He found a couple camp stoves with small propane tanks. An assortment of fishing poles with various kinds of tackle. He chose three poles and filled a large tackle box with lures, monofilament line, leaders, pliers, sinkers, a couple scaling knives, and anything else that looked useful. Those all went into his ring as well.

Over to one side, he found several traps hung on a wall. Thinking they might be useful if he had to camp outside, he grabbed several, including two huge spring-loaded bear traps. Those he placed in a large duffle that he grabbed off a shelf. They could ride in the back of the truck.

He grabbed another tent, a couple of tarps, half a dozen canteens with belts, a pair of waders, and a floppy camouflage hat that he thought made him look like a sniper. Just for fun, he also took some black and green face paint, a camouflage poncho, and some netting with fake leaves and twigs on it. Those all went into his ring as he imagined himself stalking through the forest after some exotic prey.

He loaded a few rifles into a duffel, then stopped. On a shelf below the gun racks sat a black metal gun case. Unlocking it and flipping it open, he nearly giggled when he saw the Barret .50 rifle inside. He'd never fired one before, or even seen one in person. But the Barret M107 was a legend unto itself. Allistor took the floppy hat out of his ring and put it on before lifting the rifle from its case. The weapon was heavy, maybe thirty pounds. He unfolded the bipod legs under the barrel and set them on top of the display case. Pointing the weapon out the window, he put his shoulder to it and uncapped the scope. It seemed like he could make out the needles on a pine tree about a hundred miles away.

Stepping away from the weapon, he did a little touchdown dance where he stood. "Da daaa… nana na! Ohhhh yeahh!" he sang to himself as he danced. "Who can shoot a beastie from a mile away? I can!"

Finished with his celebration, he recapped the scope, lifted the weapon and put it away. As he was fastening the clips on the case, he noticed a matching case, much smaller, sitting next to it on the shelf. Opening that one, he found a factory-made suppressor. It was almost enough to make him cry. He could sit on a roof or atop his walls and shoot at monsters a thousand yards away and barely make any sound. He knew the suppressor wasn't an actual 'silencer' as many people referred to it. It cut the sound of the gun's report considerably, but it didn't make it silent.

Still, he was thrilled with this find. This was easily a ten or fifteen thousand dollar rifle, and its value to him was incalculable. If they had this rifle atop their walls, no dragon would be safe within five hundred yards of them. This was a weapon meant to punch through vehicle armor or bullet-proof glass. The damage it would do to a flesh and blood monster would almost certainly be fatal.

Both cases went into his ring. Looking around the shop, he was seriously considering loading up the truck and returning to the Warren. It would take most of the day, but the value of all of this…

A light bulb went off in his head. He was on this trip to try and establish locations for more Strongholds. Why couldn't this be one of them? It was a good fifty miles from the Warren, near the top of a mountain with a commanding view of the valley below. It would give him control of the road outside if he needed it.

Opening up his Stronghold interface, he began looking for a tab that would allow him to claim a second Stronghold. He knew it was there somewhere, as part of the quest to survive the year was to claim territory. One could not manage a large territory from a single point. It was why the military's ground forces always established forward operating bases.

When he found it, he thumped the glass countertop and clicked the button to establish a second Stronghold. A message flashed up on the screen.

This structure does not meet the physical requirements of a Stronghold. Would you like to establish an Outpost?

"Well, I do believe I would," he mumbled to himself as he flipped over to read the information on Outposts. They were basically smaller than the Strongholds, with a lot fewer options. By claiming it, he would be awarded ten thousand Outpost points, which traded at a 1:1 ration with klax, just like Stronghold points.

He looked at the available options. There was a wall, ten feet high. The same water and power options as the Warren, along with a communications option that would allow outpost residents to communicate via a holo-terminal with the Stronghold or network of Strongholds and Outposts it was tied to.

He was almost giddy with excitement at this point. First, he clicked *Yes* to establish the Outpost. Then he added the wall, expanding it so that it encompassed the parking lot and stopped about ten feet off the road in the front, and ran about fifty yards back behind the building. He chose the electricity option, and all the lights came on. A pump outside began refilling the toilet tank from a well in the back, saving him from having to buy the water option. He added the remote gate activation, and the sensor network, which he was pleased to find extended across the road outside. So he'd know any time someone passed by this place. Or stopped there.

Lastly, he added the communication option. With that, he pushed the button to accept the transaction, spending the whole ten thousand points that came with the Outpost as well as twenty thousand of the Warren's points. The expenditure didn't even faze him. They had another RV to sell, and he had a feeling the books and artwork were going to be huge sellers.

As the golden glow surrounded him, he thought about how he would explain it to Luther and the others. He especially didn't want Luther to feel like he was being usurped from his former leadership position.

When the glow faded, the place looked different. Instead of the wooden and block structure that had stood here before, the thing was solid stone. The big storefront window was now three much smaller windows, and three more appeared on the other side of the door. The front door was still metal, though now it looked much more substantial. And the glass back door was metal now as well. The place was clearly built for defense.

The inside remained mostly the same, though there was now a stairway leading to a basement level. Allistor didn't think that had been there before. Stepping down the stairs, he found a large room with a kitchen area and a long table. To the left was a hallway with six doors on each side. Further exploration showed him that each door was a ten-foot square sleeping quarters with a stone bed and half bath, much like the ones they'd built in the Warren.

Back upstairs, he took the time to explore the storage space in the back. The gate now opened at his touch, after he identified himself to the biometric scanner. He held off on authorizing others for access to this room. The weapons in the main room were more than sufficient for now. He might want to sell the excess supplies back here.

The storage room occupied one whole half of the building. Wooden crates full of weapons were stacked all the way to the ceiling. To one side was a room that must have previously been the office. Now it was set up as a sort of commander's quarters. It featured a large bed, dresser, desk, footlocker, a small dining table with two chairs, a sofa, and a full bathroom. Allistor was already picturing a romantic getaway with Amanda, a candlelit dinner amongst the mountain of weapons. Grinning to himself, he exited the back area and closed the door behind him.

The other new feature was a pedestal set at one end of the display counter. At the top sat a holoscreen like the ones the kiosk used. He touched the screen, and it began to glow blue.

Would you like to communicate with the Stronghold known as The Warren?

He decided to try a verbal command. "Yes, please call the Warren."

A moment later, Chloe's face appeared on the screen. "Oh! Allistor! Hi!" She beamed at him. "How are you on the TV?"

He chuckled at the little girl. "This is a phone call, Chloe, hun. Is your mom around?" He was trying to figure out where the corresponding holoscreen would have popped up at the other end that Chloe was the first to answer.

"Mom's out in the greenhouse with Ramon," she said. Looking over both shoulders first, she continued in a whisper, "I saw her kissing him this morning. It was oogy!" She scrunched up her face, her nose wrinkling cutely.

"Well, good for her!" Allistor gave her his best smile. "Mommies sometimes need someone to hug and kiss other than their little girls, you know."

Chloe nodded her head. "I guess so. Anyhow, where are you?"

"I'm at a new outpost that I found. It's... like a really cool clubhouse. Are there any grownups around that I could talk with?"

She gave him a brief pouty-face before looking around. "Fine." She waved a hand. "Hey, Auntie Meg? Allistor wants to talk to you. Some kind of grownup special club thing he won't share with me!" She focused on the screen and gave him a dirty look before wandering away.

A moment later, Meg's confused face came into view. "Allistor? What's this thing?" He saw her hand grow larger as she reached out to touch the screen.

"Meg!" His outburst caused her to yank her hand back in surprise. "Sorry. Didn't mean to scare you. I'm at a gun shop about fifty miles south of you. I just figured out how to create an Outpost. And this place is stacked floor to ceiling with weapons and other stuff!"

His enthusiasm had her grinning at the screen. "Hold on, let me get Sam." She looked up and shouted, "Sam! Get out here! Allistor's on the phone!"

A few seconds later, not only Sam but half the survivors were gathered around the pedestal staring at him, all speaking at once. He held up his hands until they got silent, then explained to them all what he'd found, and what he had done. When he was finished, Sam said, "I can see the wall of guns behind ya. Nice find. Might be a good place to hole up while we're out hunting. That's right near the national forest, right?"

Allistor grinned. "Yup! And you have no idea how nice this find is. Hold on a second." He left the pedestal and retrieved the .50 cal case from his ring, setting on the counter. Taking it out of its case, he hurried back to the screen. Standing back as far as he could, he said, "Check *THIS* out!"

When he held the weapon up, more than one of the survivors whistled. Sam said, "Damn, son. I could kill a titan from a mile away with that thing. Farther if it was standin' still!" he paused, then added, "I'll wrassle ya for it!"

"Ha! No chance. This baby is all mine. I might even name her." He smiled as the others laughed. "Anyway, there are twelve bedrooms here plus a kitchen and an eating area, all underground. The place has a wall with metal gates, and metal doors front and back. Based on the thickness of the walls, I think it might survive a friggin' Howitzer attack or two."

He went on to give them more details and told them he was authorizing all the adults for access. "I might establish a few more of these as I move around. I'm headed for Cheyenne, eventually. The plan is to put a full-sized Stronghold there."

The conversation lasted another five minutes or so, then he logged off. On an impulse, he tried to access the market interface using the pedestal. He found he could browse listings, but couldn't buy or sell items there directly. That was okay; he'd given Luther instructions on how to list the second Luxury RV. They'd have plenty of funds soon enough. And he still had more than twenty thousand klax in their account.

Feeling proud of himself at what he'd accomplished, he decided to stay the night at the outpost. The idea of doing a little fishing sounded good to him. A quick trip to the truck to find his atlas, and he was back inside. He estimated his location based on his speed and the time he'd traveled since he crossed the interstate. If he was correct, then the valley below held a freshwater lake. And per the scale on the atlas, it was only a little over a mile away.

After a last minute check of his inventory, he exited the building, then the gates, closing them behind him. The road wound slowly down the mountain he was on, but following it would add miles to his trip. Instead, he crossed the road and stepped into the forest. The downhill slope wasn't steep, and there were plenty of tree branches to use as handholds.

As he descended, he stopped every few minutes to look and listen. These woods were full of wild animals, including predators like bears and wolves, even before Earth was assimilated. Though this was a mostly unpopulated area of a sparsely populated state, the blood around the truck proved the recent presence of predators of one kind or another.

His father had taught him to hunt, to shoot, and what little he knew about tracking. As he neared the lake, he saw more and more game trails, signs of animals passing to and fro. There were clear and recent deer tracks, wolf tracks – the four-legged variety – a set that he thought looked like a wolverine but wasn't sure. More than once he startled a rabbit or squirrel as he crashed through the underbrush. Though his father had taught him the basics, he was by no means stealthy. As he chuckled to himself about it, the thought occurred to him that maybe he could build that skill.

He crouched low, holding still for ten seconds. Then very carefully he lifted one foot and moved it forward. He scanned the ground ahead of him, then slowly placed his foot in a clear spot with no leaves or twigs. Transferring his weight to that foot, he repeated the process. Clear spots were few and far between, so he did his best to choose spots with wet leaves that would make less noise. Each time he had to just hope there were no twigs underneath.

He continued this for about five minutes as he progressed down the last bit of incline toward the lake.

You have learned the skill: Stealth!

Though the result was as expected, the notification still surprised him. He lost focus for a second, his balance going with it. Flailing his arms he struck a tree branch, then stepped sideways onto a fallen stick that snapped loudly.

Snorting, he said, "I wonder if it's possible to have a skill revoked right after you learn it?"

Just for the hell of it, he resumed his stealthy approach to the water's edge. Which is why, when he emerged from behind a sixty-foot cypress tree, he stood facing an octopoid.

The monster had its back to him, standing in the shallows not twenty feet in front of him. Its tentacles were half submerged in the shallow water, undulating back and forth. After a moment, one of them darted forward with a splash, and then emerged with its end wrapped around a fish.

As the fish was being stuffed into the octopoid's maw, Allistor drew the bow from his ring, along with the quiver. Setting the quiver down and leaning it against a low-hanging cypress branch, he slowly withdrew two arrows. He stuck one in the ground next to his foot and nocked the other. Drawing the bow, he took aim.

Octopoid
Level 10
Health 9,000/9,000

As it munched obliviously on bass meat, Allistor focused on the back of its bulbous head and let fly. He was already bending to grab the next arrow as the first sped forward. At that distance, the impact was almost instantaneous.

Allistor hadn't shot a bow in years. In fact, the last time he could remember was at Boy Scout camp. His aim was a little low. The arrow drove into the octopoid's back just below the neck, driving in all the way to the fletching.

As it screeched and stumbled forward from the impact, Allistor nocked the second arrow. He pulled back the string and held for a moment as the monster turned toward him. Its tentacles burst from the water and began to wave in his direction. The next arrow struck a tentacle on its way toward the octopoid's face. The limb was skewered and pinned to the monster's head as that arrow sank deep as well.

You have learned the skill: Archery!

He waved away the notification as he reached into the quiver for a third arrow. This one he fired rapidly, feeling a bit of panic as the mob began to trudge out of the water toward him. The third arrow struck it dead in the center of its chest.

Octopoid
Level 10
Health 5,700/9,000

Even with the sneak attack, the arrows weren't doing much damage. He pulled one more from the quiver and, stepping backward, fired it into the creature's face as it approached. Now the thing was nearly in tentacle range. Dropping the bow to the ground at his side, he withdrew his spear from his ring. Holding it in his right hand, he used his left to draw the sword from its sheath on his hip.

Stepping forward this time, he hurled the heavy rebar spear with all his strength, leaning into the throw. The creature was only about ten feet away, and it had neither the time nor the dexterity to dodge. It tried to grasp the spear with tentacles, but the momentum pushed the weapon into its chest.

As the octopoid floundered, Allistor transferred his sword to his right hand. Continuing his forward momentum, he took two steps into the creature's tentacle range and began to hack at it. The first two tentacles that swung his way were lopped off with ease. The sharp blade passed through the rubbery flesh with a slick sucking sound. But a third tentacle wrapped around his left foot and yanked, sending him onto his back. Two more wrapped around his legs and began to pull him toward the water as the octopoid staggered backward.

Hacking at the limbs repeatedly, he missed once and cut deeply into his own shin. The pain and frustration made him howl. He cast *Restraint* on the creature, followed instantly by a *Flame Shot* in its face. The octopoid froze, its mouth open as Allistor sat up and swung more carefully at the tentacles gripping his legs. He managed to sever two of the three before the stun wore off and the creature screeched at the loss of two more limbs.

Allistor dropped the sword and pulled his shotgun from his ring as the octopoid fell backward into the shallow water and began to pull him in. He hadn't wanted to make so much noise in this wild place, but he also didn't want to drown. Aiming the barrel at the monster's face, he blasted three slugs into it before it died.

He lay there panting, his back on the sand and his feet in the shallow water. Each time the ebb and flow of the lake water moved the octopoid corpse, the claws in the tentacle still wrapped around his thigh jabbed at him through his leather pants. Reaching up to retrieve his sword, he used it to pry all three tentacles from his legs. Removing a healing potion from his ring, he gulped it down and waited for the self-inflicted cut and all the little wounds on his legs to close.

Getting to his feet, he pulled his spear from the monster's chest, retrieved his arrows, and looted the corpse. He received ten pieces of octopoid hide this time. And some octopoid meat, which he quickly tossed far out into the lake. A moment later the water out there frothed up as something big snatched up the offering.

Allistor quickly picked up all his weapons and backed up as that same something headed in his direction.

A small bow wave formed as it rushed toward him just below the surface. He raised his shotgun and continued to back up, visions of some kind of alien shark-gator-piranha hybrid leaping out at him.

What actually emerged from the water wasn't far off. It was a massive lake sturgeon. Or so Allistor assumed. A solid twelve feet long from nose to tail, it powered up out of the deeper water into the shallows. Its wide open mouth had a lower jaw that curved upward as it jutted out. Along its back ran a ridge of spines almost like the dragon's. Its scales were multicolored, and its eyes a dead black. Overall it was one of the ugliest creatures Allistor had ever seen.

Sturgeon Matron
Level 15
Health 12,000/12,000

Allistor watched, weapon at the ready as the enormous fish chomped down on the head and torso of the floating octopoid. With a quick flip, it tilted its head up and swallowed the seven-foot creature whole.

Thrashing about in the shallows, it turned a baleful eye on Allistor, then managed to get itself back into deeper water and disappeared. Nothing but a widening circle of ripples giving any hint that the octopoid or the giant fish had ever been there.

"Right. So... no swimming in the lake." Allistor picked up a stone and skipped it across the water, just to show the big fish who was boss. He was suddenly much less interested in fishing. Still, he was here, and he was the apex predator on land. At least, that's what he told himself as he turned right and walked along the lakeshore, making sure to keep well back from the water's edge. He kept a keen eye on the water as he went.

Eventually, he found a wide stream that tumbled down the rocky mountainside and fed into the lake. Walking upstream, he found a spot where an open level area below a tiny waterfall had formed a pool. The sun shone through the trees, reflecting off the water as the stream burbled along. It was a postcard-perfect spot. Finding a rock to sit on about ten feet back from the pool, he took out his pole and tackle.

Five minutes later he had a green rubbery worm thing and a light sinker on the line and was casting it into the pool. It plopped into the water out near the center, and he gave it a moment to sink a bit. Then he tugged slightly on the line to make the lure wiggle and reeled in the slack slowly. Jiggering it across the water in this manner, he leaned back and relaxed. When the lure reached the shore, he reeled it the rest of the way in and cast it again.

The rock at his back was warmed by the sun, and the sound of the waterfall was soothing. He was dozing off when something big splashed into the pool.

Startled and alert, he sat up and scanned the area. Motion at the waterfall caught his attention as a stone tumbled down to splash into the pool. Following the stream upward with his eyes, he cursed to himself.

Sneaking clumsily down the slope was a grizzly bear cub. It looked to be about six months old as best he could guess. It was actually kind of cute, all fuzzy and stumbling as it worked its way down the rocks. Allistor even had an urge to play with it.

The problem was, where there were grizzly bear cubs, there was usually a mama grizzly. Dropping his pole, he got to his feet. Frantically searching the slope above while trying to keep an eye on his surroundings, he retrieved his rifle. With a grizzly, one needed penetration to get through the hide and the fat for a kill shot.

Working the bolt, he chambered a round and used the scope to search above the cub, which was still approaching the pond. He saw no sign of another bear, which terrified him. He was no longer feeling like the apex predator on this particular land. Sweat trickled down his back, and it wasn't from the warm rock he'd been leaning against.

The cub got itself trapped on an outcropping with no clear way down, and no way to get back up. It let out a weak little distressed-sounding half-roar that tugged at Allistor's heart. Some part of him wanted to climb up there and wrassle with the little fella.

When no answering roar from mama bear sounded, Allistor began to back away downstream, the way he had come. He was hoping he could get mama bear to chase him into the shallows where the big fish might attack. Assuming mama bear wasn't even larger than the fish. Apparently, Earth wildlife also had the ability to level up by killing things. A bear trying to fatten up for hibernation would be eating pretty much nonstop. If she'd managed to kill other critters, she could be bigger, faster, and stronger than any bear previously seen on earth.

That line of thinking was *not* helping. His heart thumped in his chest and now sweat was dripping from his forehead. The little cub remained on the outcrop, crying for its mama. Allistor wanted to be far, far away when she found him.

Now a good hundred yards away, he ducked behind an ancient cottonwood tree and paused to calm himself. He needed to think clearly. Did he really want to potentially trap himself between a grizzly and a giant lake monster? Would it be better for him to just head back uphill and make a run for his outpost? He could get up on the wall and use the .50 cal to take out the bear from a safe position.

Still calling for help, the cub hadn't moved. And still, there was no answer. He took a deep breath and peered around the tree. No sign of any movement at all. He raised his hunting rifle and scoped the slope above again. Then did the same in a wide arc around himself.

The cries of the cub were starting to get to him. After a solid five minutes, he cursed to himself. "You're a damned fool. Gonna get your face ate off. It's a bear cub. It can fend for itself. Or not. Either way, it's not your problem."

Even as he argued against it, he emerged from behind the tree and started back toward the pond. Moving back almost to his previous position, he hid behind the sun-warmed rock he'd been leaning against. From there he watched the cub as it peered over the edge, then changed its mind and tried to climb upward. But it was unable to get any purchase with its claws and failed to make progress. Eventually, it fell on its butt with a growl of complaint.

With a sigh, Allistor began to climb. He picked a path up the rocks that he hoped would allow him to make a hasty retreat if mama showed up. Swearing to himself that he would just knock the little fella off the ledge into the water and leave it at that, he climbed higher, then dropped down a bit to approach the cub from above.

When it saw him coming, the cub reared up on its back legs and growled. It looked like an angry teddy bear, and Allistor smiled at it. "Hey there, fella. What's your name?" he spoke in a soothing voice, the way one would with a strange dog of indeterminate disposition. "What's that? You don't have a name? How 'bout Boo-Boo? No? Well, then I'll just call you Fuzzy for now. Are you hungry, Fuzzy?"

The cub tilted its head to one side as he continued to talk to it. Still on its hind legs, the cub stood about three feet tall. It grunted at him, then huffed a few times. He kept talking as he produced a hot dog from his ring. "Here's a little snack for Fuzzy. Cuz Fuzzy's a good boy, and not gonna try and eat me." He tossed the meat tube down onto the stone at the cub's feet. It dropped to all fours, sniffed once, then scarfed up the treat. A moment later it was back up on its hind legs, waving one paw at Allistor as if saying 'Please, sir, can I have some more?'

Allistor, now just a couple feet above the cub's reach, obliged. He tossed out another hot dog, which the bear caught in its jaws. Unfortunately for the cub, the action overbalanced him, and he fell backward off the rock. It was only a short fall into the water, maybe a dozen feet, but his back thudded against a large rock before he bounced off and splashed into the pool.

Allistor dropped down to the outcropping and peered down into the water, waiting for the cub to resurface. After ten seconds, he got nervous. "Shit. I didn't want to kill the little guy."

Storing his rifle in his ring, he quickly stripped down to just his leather pants, storing boots and the rest in his ring as well. Then with a couple deep breaths, he took two running steps and leaped out over the water. He cleared the boulder that the cub had hit and plunged feet-first into the pool.

The water was quite cold, and he had to fight not to gasp in shock. When he opened his eyes, he found the water quite clear. A quick spin using his arms allowed him to survey the entire pool. The bear cub was maybe thirty feet from him floating several feet below the surface, apparently unconscious.

Allistor kicked his legs, surfacing quickly and taking in a lungful of air. As fast as he could he swam over to the spot he estimated the bear would be and ducked under the surface. A couple strokes downward, and he was able to reach the cub. He grabbed it by the scruff of the neck and kicked upward again. As soon as he was back at the surface, he rolled over onto his back, dragging the cub onto his belly as he kicked with both legs and stroked one-armed over to the nearest shore. Hitting shallow water, he stood and lifted the cub out of the water to set him in the grass.

The cub's body was limp, and it clearly wasn't breathing. He feared he'd accidentally killed it and felt ashamed. With nothing to lose, he lifted the bear back up and gripped it around its belly from behind. He squeezed gently, doing a sort of Heimlich maneuver that did succeed in pushing a good amount of water out of the animal. After a second squeeze, he put the bear cub on its back and used one hand to clamp its jaw shut. With his other hand, he formed the best seal he could around its nose, then blew into it. He tried this several times, watching as the cub's chest rose slightly with each forced breath.

He didn't know how to check a bear's pulse, or even if its heart was in a place where CPR would work. "Come on, little Fuzzy! Don't die on me!" He breathed into the cub's nose again, then shook him.

There was a splutter, then the bear inhaled on his own. A moment later, it did it again. Allistor stepped away as the cub rolled onto its belly and puked out a bunch of water. It took another wheezing breath, then mewled like a kitten in pain. Fuzzy tried to get his feet under him and failed. Allistor didn't know what to do except sit and watch, give him some time to recover. He nervously scanned the forest around them, still expecting mama bear to make an appearance.

After several minutes of retching and labored breathing, Fuzzy seemed to grow stronger. Allistor figured it was the system's rapid healing. "That's right, buddy. Get your feet under you." Allistor spoke softly, aware that the bear could hear him just fine.

As a sort of apology, he removed a piece of grilled turtle steak from his ring and tossed it to the cub, who couldn't quite reach it where it landed. With a growl, he got unsteadily to his feet and moved forward enough to take the steak. Then he plopped back down and began to gnaw on it. By the time he was finished, he was breathing much better.

"Right, then. Good to meet you, Fuzzmiester. I'm sorry about drowning you. Was only trying to help. Now run along back to your mama bear. I'm gonna retrieve my fishing pole and head home."

He waved at the bear as he began his walk around the pond to retrieve his gear. When he had everything packed away in the tackle box and both box and pole stored in his ring, he turned to find Fuzzy standing right behind him, looking up with his tongue hanging out to one side like a dog. When he jumped in fright, the cub hopped backward as well.

"Shit! Don't sneak up on me like that! You nearly gave me a heart attack, Fuzzy, old chap." Allistor sat down on the rock and looked at the bear, who was sniffing the air between them. Bears had a nose several hundred times more sensitive than a human's. But even with that sniffer,

Allistor doubted Fuzzy could smell what was in his ring of holding.

"Hungry little bugger, aren't you? Has your mama not been feeding you?" A thought struck him. "Is your mama gone? Did she get killed? Or maybe you just got separated?" The bear stared at him, head tilting from side to side as he spoke.

"No, not separated. She'd be able to follow your scent. I'm guessing something bigger and badder than mama found your den, huh?"

Fuzzy chuffed at him, sitting on his butt and raising one paw. Allistor shook his head and tossed him the last of his hot dogs.

"Well slap my ass and call me Grizzly Adams," Allistor mumbled to himself as he watched the tube steak disappear. This time, when he was done eating, Fuzzy walked right up and shoved his nose into Allistor's outstretched hand. After a second, he licked the ring. "I'll be damned. Can you smell what's inside there? Or does my hand just smell like meat?"

A moment later Fuzzy jumped up onto the rock and moved behind Allistor. Squeezing in between him and the warm rock he'd leaned his back on, the bear huffed once and dropped on its belly. His eyes closed, and he snorted, adjusting slightly to make himself more comfortable. Allistor sat there, surprised at the sudden acceptance from the wild predator. A few minutes later, Fuzzy began to snore.

"I don't blame you. I could use a nap, too."

Since the bear didn't seem to be in any hurry to move, or much concerned about predators, Allistor produced his pole and resumed his fishing as the bear cub snored against his back. His pants slowly dried in the warm sunlight, and it felt good on his skin as well. The wet bear didn't smell all that great, but then Fuzzy might be thinking the same of him.

Two hours later, he'd managed to catch a grand total of three bass, each a foot long or less. Normally he'd just throw them back, but he thought Fuzzy might enjoy them. When he stood to stretch his legs, the bear woke up. He immediately sniffed out the fish but didn't touch them. Sitting on his haunches, Fuzzy looked up at Allistor and huffed.

"Go ahead, buddy. Those are for you."

The moment he spoke, the cub ripped into the first fish. He ate all but the tails of all three fish. "I'm not sure, but I think you probably shouldn't have eaten the bones, Fuzzyboy. But you seem alright, so we'll assume I'm wrong." Allistor patted the cub on the head, then scratched his ears. Fuzzy growled happily, leaning into the attention.

"Did I somehow just become your mama?"

Allistor thought back to all the games where he'd played a hunter, druid, or wizard type class that possessed skills enabling the player to tame pets or familiars. With a grin, he pictured going into battle with an octopoid alongside a great big grizzly bear. "Bear tank for the win!"

Looking at the sky, he said, "Time to head back, buddy. I want to be safe inside those walls before dark." He got up and started hiking up the hill in the general direction of the Outpost. A rustling behind him let him know that Fuzzy was following. Each time he stopped and turned around, the bear would stop and stare at him. After half a dozen times, he just kept going.

An hour later he reached the road and spotted the Outpost a short distance uphill. Trudging along, he turned to find that the bear wasn't there. He scanned the tree line and found Fuzzy was ghosting along inside the tree line, keeping pace with him. Shrugging his shoulders, he continued up the road and opened the gate. Turning to look for the bear, he didn't see any movement. With a smile, he dropped a turtle steak just inside the gates and walked to sit by the front door of the building.

It was less than a minute before Fuzzy stepped gingerly onto the pavement, sniffing it as he did. Deciding it wasn't going to bite him, he trotted across and scooped up the meat. When he sat to gnaw on it, Allistor closed the gates behind him.

"You can't come inside, little buddy. I don't want to be cleaning up after you rampage through and knock everything over. You'll be just fine out here tonight."

As he was about to go inside, the memory of the drake flying off with Candy hit him. "On second thought, how 'bout we make you a little bed out back?"

He went inside and grabbed a flannel blanket from one of the shelves. Going back out, he found Fuzzy had finished his steak and was sniffing around. Allistor called out. "Follow me, Fuzzy." Waving the blanket, he walked around the corner toward the back of the building. He paused at the next corner, turning to see if the cub followed. A moment later the teddy bear face poked around the corner. Seeing him, it pulled back. Then a few seconds later the cub leapt out from behind the building, snorting and charging at him.

Laughing at the game of tag, Allistor rounded the second corner and hopped up into the pickup truck's bed.

He ducked down so just his eyes and forehead stuck up over the gate, and waited.

Ten seconds later Fuzzy's nose slowly emerged around the corner. The bear sniffed a few times, then took a peek. Not seeing Allistor, the cub snuck around the corner stepping lightly with his back bowed up like a cat's.

When he got close to the truck, following Allistor with his nose, Allistor jumped up and raised his hands "Hah!" he shouted.

Fuzzy pissed on the concrete as he rolled over backward trying to get away. He regained his feet and scooted back around the corner, wailing.

Allistor instantly felt bad. "I'm sorry, buddy!" he called out. He climbed down and sat on the back bumper, waiting for the cub to return. After ten minutes, he pulled a candy bar out of his ring and unwrapped it. He just stood there holding it as the chocolate began to melt between his fingers. Another minute or so passed, then the nose reappeared around the corner.

Allister spoke softly. "I'm sorry, Fuzzy. I shouldn't have scared you like that. I've got a treat here for you. Come and get it."

The bear slunk around the corner, belly low to the ground. He watched Allistor for a few moments, then walked forward as his nose twitched. Allistor held out his hand as he crouched down to the bear's level. Fuzzy licked at the candy bar, then gently took it out of his hands. He chewed awkwardly a couple times, then dropped it onto the concrete and began to lick at it.

Mimicking the cub, Allistor licked the melted chocolate off his own fingers. Then as Fuzzy worked on his treat, he lowered the truck's tailgate and unfolded the blanket partway. Setting the blanket in the truck bed, he waited for Fuzzy to finish. When he was done, Allistor bent and carefully lifted the cub up into the bed, setting him on the blanket. He scratched the nervous cub's ears for a while until he calmed down and settled his head down on the blanket. Allistor flipped the other half up and over the bear cub, cocooning him in.

"Sleep well, little buddy. Stay here, okay? You'll be warm enough, and protected under this carport roof."

Allistor felt silly, mothering the bear cub. Using his passphrase to open the back door, he went inside and closed it behind him. A few minutes later he came back out with a small pot filled with water and set that in the truck before going back inside and closing the door.

Chapter Thirteen

The Park is the Thing

Allistor spent some time in the back room going through inventory as the sun set and darkness fell over the Outpost. Every hour or so he peeked out the back door to check on the cub, who was snoring contentedly, still wrapped in the blanket.

When he crawled into bed in the commander's quarters several hours later, he had fashioned a harness of sorts. If he was going to keep the bear with him, he'd need to be able to control it to some extent. The heavy rope harness looked much like a standard dog harness that wound under the chest and around the torso. Snorting at the ridiculousness of walking a bear cub like a dog on a leash, Allistor rolled over and went to sleep.

The sound of howling canids or wolves woke him in the wee hours of the morning. He got up and went out back to check on Fuzzy. The cub was awake and alert, huddled in his blanket and breathing rapidly. He patted the bear's head. "Don't worry, Fuzzy. They won't get in here."

Still, he sat with the cub until the howling receded, scratching his head and whispering. At some point, both man and cub fell back asleep.

As the sun came up, Allistor awoke in the back of the truck, blanket and bear both draped across his chest. He shivered as he slid out from under them and the cold air hit him. Needing to pee, he went inside and used the facilities. When he returned, Fuzzy was out of the truck, having dragged his blanket with him. He trotted over to Allistor, tripping over the blanket twice, and plopped down in front of him. He licked his bear lips, staring deep into Allistor's eyes.

Congratulations! *You have learned the skill:*
Taming
By showing kindness to a helpless animal and tending to its needs, you have earned its trust and loyalty. The animal has bound itself to you as your companion. For more information, please review the 'Companions' section of your interface.

And there it was. Allistor had himself a pet. Not like Max, but a bound pet that he could level up and take into combat with him. And right now his fuzzy bear was looking at him hungrily. "You are going to be hard to feed when you get bigger." He sighed, removing another turtle steak and tossing it to Fuzzy.

He grabbed the blanket and headed for his pickup. Fuzzy followed after scarfing down breakfast. Allistor laid the blanket across the passenger seat, and Fuzzy obligingly leapt and pulled himself up. Circling a couple times like a dog, he plopped down on the blanket and snorted.

Allistor got in, turned the truck around and drove out the gates, closing them behind him. Fuzzy sat up and moved around unsteadily as the truck's motion initially confused him. But when they got going down the road, he calmed and laid his head back down. Allistor spoke to him as if he were a human riding along.

"Well, it's just you and me, buddy. Off to explore the world, hunt exotic beasts, capture territory, and *take over the world! Muah ha ha!"* He did his best Brain impersonation, but Fuzzy wasn't impressed.

About ten miles down the road, the bear cub let loose an obnoxiously loud fart. "What the hell, man? Party foul!" Allistor scolded him as he rolled the truck's windows down. Fuzzy just looked proud of himself. When he caught an interesting scent coming in from the windows, he sat up and stuck his head out. Allistor laughed at the bear that looked just like a dog, head out the window, tongue flapping in the wind as he watched the trees go by and sniffed.

The truck was only moving about 30mph when Fuzzy started to growl. Allistor slowed even further, scanning the trees on either side of the road. Fuzzy's hackles rose, and he bounced his front paws on the seat a couple times. He sent out a tiny roar, then pulled his head inside and sat back against the seat, ducking down. Whatever was out there, he didn't like it.

As they rounded a bend, now only going about 20mph, Allistor spotted the tops of several trees shaking violently just ahead. Whatever was doing it was moving toward the road. He stopped the truck and turned off the engine. Whispering to Fuzzy, he said, "Hold real still and stay quiet, okay? Whatever this is, we're just gonna play dead and let it walk right on by."

Fuzzy relocated himself down into the well below the dashboard. He curled into a ball and set his head on his back leg, looking up at Allistor.

Allistor's attention was drawn back to the road ahead. He could now hear crashing and splintering as underbrush and small trees were demolished. Whatever was moving through the woods was big. Not sixty-foot titan big, or he'd be able to see it already. But bulky enough to push around mature trees.

His mouth dropped open a moment later when a neon green gelatin oozed out onto the highway. It separated as it moved around trees, then came back together on the other side. Allistor could see the corpses of animals large and small suspended within the slime creature. When it was all the way out on the highway, it formed into a rough cube and sat motionless, except for an occasional quiver. Looking more closely, Allistor could see a moose trapped near the 'front' of the slime – the side closest to him – that was still struggling. He watched as it kicked and thrashed its massive rack, getting weaker by the moment. Eventually, it stilled, and Allistor Examined the cube.

Giant Gelatinous Devourer
Level 11
Health 4,000/4,000

Allistor almost laughed. He'd dealt with slimes in the various games over the years. Usually in low-level zones, and in large numbers. They were slow moving and didn't have large health pools, and were most effective when they could surround a prey. Some could bunch their bodies tightly then spring forward for short distances. Others could extend parts of themselves like tentacles to snatch prey or shoot acid or some sticky substance. Once they captured and consumed prey, it would slowly digest within their gelatin.

This one, though, was too big to laugh at. The moose it had just devoured took up less than a quarter of its internal space. The cube had to be ten yards square, and it contained the decomposing bodies of normally fast-moving creatures like a wolf, several rabbits, the moose, and rotting pieces of deer that might have been one or two animals originally.

"So, either you can move fast, or you've been picking up corpses as you go. Either way, you just keep on going, big guy. Move on across the road and find yourself some more tasty treats. Nothing to see here," he mumbled quietly to himself. They were on a downhill slope, and he was hoping gravity would persuade the thing to move away.

No such luck.

The cube vibrated a few times, causing ripples to pass through its body and shifting some of the corpses inside. Then it began to undulate itself up the road in his direction.

Allistor's first inclination was to just back up and flee the thing. But this was just the kind of creature he'd come out here to hunt. Just a couple levels above him, it might be a manageable fight. And it should award some decent xp if he killed it solo.

Opening the truck door, he said, "Stay here, Fuzzy," and got out. He began to walk toward the devourer, which was plodding along steadily. First, he cast *Restraint* on the creature. The result was surprising. It froze into a perfect cube, seeming to harden as the stun took effect. Allistor equipped his shotgun and fired a quick blast, striking the front surface and knocking off a chunk as if it were made of stone. He rapidly fired three more shots, focusing on one corner of the cube. The third shot fractured off maybe ten percent of the creature, the loose bits tumbling onto the road.

But as soon as the stun wore off, the broken pieces liquefied and began to flow back to the main body. Allistor put away the shotgun. Physical attacks just weren't going to work.

Raising a hand, he cast *Flame Shot* and held it as a ball of flame built up in his hand. When it was the size of a basketball, he flung it forward at the slime. The fireball impacted with a sizzle and burned its way deep into the slime's mass before being extinguished. The monster let out a high-pitched keening as if it felt pain from the burns.

Allistor hit it again, this time dropping a column of flame down on top of the devourer. The slime's body seemed to melt away as the flames penetrated. On a whim, he cast *Restraint* again, and the flesh solidified just as before. The hardened gelatin blackened and cracked under the heat still drilling into it from above.

Before the stun would wear off, Allistor equipped his spear and ran forward to slam it into the spot where the first fireball had struck. The hardened gelatin cracked along a line down the center where the fire strike from above had penetrated. With a resounded crack, the devourer's body split in half.

Inside he could see a glowing orb that pulsed slightly. He dashed forward between the two halves just as the stun wore off and the monster began to reform. Reaching down into the slime, he took hold of the orb with both hands. His hands burned as the gelatin ate away at his skin, but he maintained his grip.

With a desperate pull, he freed the orb from the gelatin. When it came free, the lack of resistance threw Allistor off balance, and he fell on his butt. The gelatin all around him vibrated wildly for a moment, then seemed to liquefy. Liquid gelatin flowed across the road and into the ditches on either side. Everything it touched began to hiss and smoke as the acid began to eat away at it, including Allistor's boots! He took two long, leaping steps uphill to get clear of the liquid, then cleaned his boots the best he could in the tall grass.   They'd lost about half their durability, but they were still functional.

Experience flashed across his interface. Not quite enough to level him up to ten, but almost. He also received loot as he held the orb in front of him. A hundred and fifty klax, ten vials of devourer acid, several deteriorated animal hides, a stack of moose meat, and the orb. Allistor examined it as he held it at arms' length.

>*Giant Devourer Core*
>*Item Quality: Uncommon*
>*This core contains the life force of the gelatinous devourer.*

Assuming it had some use as a crafting item, or maybe a power source for alien tech, he dropped it into his ring.

Back in the truck, they waited for the corrosive liquid to fade away before driving across it. The last thing Allistor needed was four damaged or flattened tires out in the middle of nowhere.

They continued southward at a gentle pace, with Fuzzy back up in the passenger seat with his nose out the window. Allistor stopped a few times, once at a driveway that he followed up to a house on a gentle rise. A quick poke-around didn't reveal any useful vehicles or sellable items, but there was a pantry full of canned food. With thoughts of keeping the growing bear fed, he put all the food he could find, along with a can opener, into his ring. He also grabbed two large stainless steel bowls – one for food, one for water. And he found several more blankets to add to Fuzzy's nest.

Moving on down the road, Allistor had driven maybe thirty miles from the Outpost when they came across a direction sign with an arrow pointing to a ranger station. Allistor followed the gravel drive up into the woods and found a log cabin with two ranger's trucks. The trucks were full-sized Suburbans, both painted forest green. Each had a winch on the front and heavy duty tires that would allow the vehicles to go off-road to an extent. Allistor was tempted to trade in his pickup. There was a windmill tower sticking up behind the cabin, squeaking slightly as it spun.

The door of the cabin was open, and Allistor took it as a bad sign. Equipping his shotgun, he approached the door slowly, trying to see inside before he got too close. But the sun was too low in the sky, and the shadows of the surrounding trees left the cabin dark inside.

Taking a deep breath, Allistor pushed the door open with the barrel of this shotgun, then stepped to the side in case anything charged out. After hearing no sounds of any kind for twenty seconds, he stepped back in front of the door and then inside. He kept his weapon in front of him as his eyes adjusted to the lower light.

The main room of the cabin was a combination office and kitchen. There were two desks, an extra chair next to each, a sofa, and a dining table with benches. The kitchen was just a basic wood stove, sink, and several cabinets with a short counter space on either side of the sink. One was taken up by a small microwave. A big coffeepot sat atop the stove, a shelf on the wall above it holding half a dozen mugs.

One of two doors leading off that room led to a full bath. The other led to a large room with a fireplace, two sofas and some chairs, a larger table, and a giant bearskin rug. The grizzly it came from must have been ten feet tall.

Attached to that room were two bedrooms, and a bunk room with three sets of bunk beds. Allistor cleared each room as he went through the house, and an itch started to work at his subconscious. When he finished his search and stood staring at the rug, he realized what it was.

No blood stains, or signs of a battle of any kind. With two trucks out front, there should have been at least two rangers here. If they were still alive, where were they? He doubted they would have left the front door open if they'd gone out hunting.

Remembering the windmill, he tried the nearest light switch. Two table lamps on either end of a sofa turned on. Allistor turned them off again and headed for the door. He made a circuit of the clearing around the cabin, looking for blood or obvious tracks. Finding nothing, he returned to the pickup. Fuzzy was snoring inside, atop his nest of many blankets.

Feeling a little tired himself, Allistor elected to stay the night at the cabin. Lifting the bear in his arms he carried him inside and set him atop the rug. Fuzzy never even opened an eye. Closing the shutters on all the windows, he turned the two lamps back on and stretched out on the sofa and closed his eyes.

Ten minutes later he was back on his feet, poking around in the office. It was too early to sleep. He was just considering lighting the stove to make coffee when he noticed a radio set up on the desk in the back of the room. This far out from civilization, it might be a short-wave radio. He sat in the chair and studied it for a moment, then flicked the power switch. A dial on the right side let him adjust the frequency. Turning it to the one Sam had been using, he pulled the large microphone pedestal toward him. Pressing the button on the bottom, he said, "Heya, Sam, you out there somewhere?"

He released the talk button and waited. When there was no answer after thirty seconds, he tried again. "Sam? Come in, Sam. Uhh... breaker, breaker! Wait, is that for CBs?" He let go of the button again.

"Allistor? Is that you?" Sam's voice was faint. Allistor found the volume button and turned it up.

"Hey, Sam! Yup, it's me. Found a ranger station with a short wave. Decided to camp here for the night. How are things there?"

Sam chuckled. "We're fine. The kids are all excited because some chicks hatched today. They're naming them after cartoon characters. You gonna make another Outpost?"

Allistor hadn't thought about it. "Actually, not a bad idea. There's a kitchen and a windmill for power. The place could sleep ten people pretty easy. There are two nice park service Suburbans here. It's back off the road a good ways..." his voice drifted off as he considered. Then a question occurred to him.

"Wait, chicks? We haven't had that coop long enough for chicks."

Sam's voice sounded amused. "That's what I said. Nancy decided to experiment with the *Grow* spell she uses in the greenhouse. Cast it on a nest of eggs that the hen had been sittin' on for a week. The damned things hatched the next day. Should have been two more weeks."

"That's great! We can speed up egg production that way. Can she do the same thing with the bunnies?"

"She's way ahead of you. Problem is, we couldn't tell if the bunny was pregnant. Amanda had to use her spell to... you know, look inside? Anyhow she found out that she was pregnant, and Nancy zapped her too. The bunny, I mean. Not Amanda."

Allistor rolled his eyes. "So, in a few weeks, we can be knee deep in chickens and bunnies. That'll help feed everybody. I should tell you, I picked up a pet myself. His name is Fuzzy and he's a grizzly cub. About six months old as far as I can tell. The system bonded us together after I fed him, then drowned him, then saved his life and gave him a blanket."

There was a long pause, then Meg's voice came through. "You did *what* now?"

"Hi, Meg! It's a long story. I'll tell you the whole thing when I get back, but we're going to have a growing grizzly to feed. If the kids misbehave, tell them I'll feed them to Fuzzy when I get back!"

"You're terrible!" Meg sounded amused. "Sam says you're gonna make another Outpost?"

"I wasn't going to, but since he suggested it, I'm thinking about it. It's not a bad spot. But I'd have to make it just a basic one. I don't want to spend all our system points on Outposts. My aim is to claim another Stronghold somewhere in Cheyenne. Or maybe Laramie if there's a problem in Cheyenne."

"Why not both?" Meg snorted. In the background, Sam called out "Yeah! Go ahead and grab both!"

Chuckling, Allistor said, "Please pass my congratulations on to Nancy. And tell her I said please don't make any mutant chickens or killer bunnies?"

"You got it! Be safe out there, Allistor. We need you."

"10-4... uhm... over and out?" He switched off the radio and decided he didn't want coffee after all. Just checking in with the others had relaxed him quite a bit. He sat on the sofa near where Fuzzy snored. Pulling up the Outpost interface, he didn't find an option to designate the ranger station as an Outpost.

"Hmm... what was it that allowed me to take the gun shop?"

Last time he'd tried to establish the gun shop as a Stronghold, and the system had offered him an Outpost instead. So he tried it again.

This structure does not meet the physical requirements of a Stronghold. Additionally, this structure is currently occupied by a life form that has a prior claim to your own. To claim the structure, you must kill the prior occupant, convince it to relinquish its claim or banish it from the vicinity for twelve hours.

"Prior occupant?" Allistor looked around the room, suddenly wary. He was sure he'd cleared the place. Still, he got up and searched the rooms again. Finding nothing, he woke Fuzzy. "Hey, buddy. I'm not sure how well you understand me, but I need to know if you smell anybody else here?"

The groggy bear cub tried to roll over and go back to sleep. Allistor picked him up and set him on his feet. "C'mon! Show me what that nose can do." When Fuzzy just looked at him, he tried some one-word commands. "Search! Um... Seek! Track!"

Track must have been a command recognized by the system for pets. Fuzzy's nose went to the floor and he began to follow it around the house. He bumped into one of the tables and knocked the lamp off, then tore a rent in a sofa cushion when he jumped up onto it with his sharp claws. "Right. Mental note. Keep Fuzzy off the furniture." Allistor followed the bear around.

When he reached the kitchen, he stuck his nose against a lower cabinet door and growled. A squeak from within confirmed something was hiding there. He pried the door open with a claw, scratching both the door and the frame. The moment it was open far enough, he jammed his head into the cabinet with lightning speed. A terrified squeak was cut off as whatever it was died.

Allistor suddenly recalled that the system's message had said *life form* rather than specifying a human occupant. He quickly tried again to establish a Stronghold. The exact same message popped up again.

"Good boy, Fuzzy," he said as the bear gulped down the deceased rat. "Do it again. Track!"

The bear cub resumed his search, nose to the floor. Leaving the kitchen he made his way back to the bear rug. After a moment, he shoved his nose under the edge of the rug and pushed at it, revealing a trap door.

"Holy shit, Fuzzy. That was awesome!" Allistor rubbed his ears and tossed him some meat. "Stay up here."

Drawing his .45 in his right hand, he stood behind the trap door and pulled it open. When no shots rang out, he called down, "Anybody home? My name is Allistor. I'm not here to hurt you."

A woman's voice called up. She sounded weak and afraid. "Hello?"

"It's okay. You can come up now. It's safe. Did something attack this place?"

"I... don't think I can make it up there. Been down here for... I'm not even sure how long. A week, maybe more? Haven't had water for two days."

Allistor put away his gun and stepped onto the stairs that led down into the darkness. Halfway down he found a pull string and tugged on it. A light came on, and a woman in a ranger's uniform blinked rapidly before covering her eyes with her hand.

"Sorry." Allistor descended to the cellar floor. "What's your name?"

"I'm Helen. Helen Rodgers. I'm a park ranger here. Or I was when there was still a park service and a park, and..." She drifted off. "Do you have any water?"

"Oh, my god; I'm an idiot!" he pulled a canteen from his ring and handed it to her.

"Thank you... Allister?"

"Allistor, with an o instead of an e. And yes, my parent's might have been high when they named me." He smiled at her as she took several small sips of water. "I have some beef jerky too, if you'd like. Or a candy bar? Granola?"

"Actually a candy bar sounds amazing!" She leaned forward slightly. "I've been living on cold canned beans and granola all week."

He handed her a chocolate bar. "Why have you been down here so long?"

She sat down on a stool and munched on the candy for a moment before answering. "Cliff and I were both here at the station when the monsters started to appear. At first, it was this six-legged dog thing."

"Canids," Allistor supplied helpfully.

"Yeah, OK. Those. First just one, then three. They killed our dog on the first day and kept sniffing around here, trying to get in. We shot several, but more just kept showing up day after day. A week ago, one of them managed to latch onto Cliff's leg. Tore it up really bad. We killed it, but we could already hear more of them howling in the forest. He said he was a dead man anyway with his leg so badly hurt. Told me to hide in the cellar while he tried to lead them away. Maybe if they didn't smell anything anymore, they'd eventually leave the area in search of prey."

She looked down, her candy bar forgotten. "He pulled the rug over the door to hide my scent, then wiped his blood from the floor and headed out. I heard a few shots a little while after he left… then nothing. Until I heard them sniffing around up there." She pointed through the trap door.

"They were inside the cabin. So I made myself as small and quiet as I could and waited. My water should have lasted longer, but I kept getting so thirsty." She sounded as if she was apologizing.

Allistor shook his head. "The door was open when I got here. But I didn't see any sign of canids or any other critters up there. Nothing's been disturbed. Well, not before we got here. Fuzzy has done a little damage."

"Fuzzy?" she asked.

"My pet bear. Bear cub, actually. He adopted me yesterday. He's spent the last couple hours sleeping on that bear rug." He smiled at her. "If you think you have the strength now, I'll help you upstairs and you can meet him."

She nodded and got to her feet. He offered a hand and a shoulder to lean on and helped her climb the ten steps to the main floor. Pretending not to notice the smell of urine and feces down below, he closed the door saying, "Can't have one of us falling down there."

She didn't hear him as she was in the middle of a staring contest with Fuzzy. The bear tilted his head, then sniffed. Not liking what he smelled, he snorted and turned away, walking back toward the kitchen and food smells.

She laughed. "Was that his polite way of saying I need a shower?"

Allistor just grinned. "I haven't had time to teach him manners yet." He helped her to one of the bedrooms that had a bath attached, then closed the door behind him as he left.

While he waited for her to shower, he retrieved the two bowls from his ring, along with a couple cans and the opener. He emptied two cans of spaghettios into one of the bowls and used the sink to fill the other partway with water. Setting both on the floor, he said, "Now don't make a mess, you silly old bear."

Fuzzy promptly stuck out a paw, tipped the food bowl over, and proceeded to lick the pasta and sauce off the floor. He was gentler with the water bowl, lapping the water out without splashing too much.

Half an hour later, Helen emerged in a fresh uniform. She sat on the sofa, only giving the torn cushion a brief glance. "Thank you for coming down there for me. I was in and out a lot the last few days. If you hadn't come, I would have probably just fallen asleep and not woken up."

"Why didn't you try and escape?" Allistor tried to keep his tone gentle.

"I thought about it. Even went up the stairs a few times. But Cliff took our last ammo with him, and I kept imagining being ripped apart by those things. I just couldn't do it."

"Fair enough," Allistor sympathized with her. Just then Fuzzy emerged from the kitchen, using his long tongue to lick the last of the pasta sauce from his muzzle. He walked right up to Helen and gave her another sniff. Seeming to approve this time, he licked her hand once, then went to lay back down on the bear rug."

"Was that some kind of taste test for later?" She smiled at the cub. "He's a young one. Maybe six months. Did you kill his mother?"

Allistor shook his head. "Nope." He sat down on the sofa as well and told her the whole story, starting with the octopoid fight and ending with their bonding. Then, because she didn't understand what he was saying about the system bonding them, he told her all about their new world and what they'd learned about the system.

She absorbed it all without much comment. "I've played a few of those games. When I was a kid." She was in her late thirties as best Allistor could guess. "So, are you like a ranger or a hunter, taming pets to fight for you?"

He grinned. "Ha! No. This was all sort of accidental. I just didn't want him to die alone in the woods, and then he sort of became my responsibility."

They talked for a little while longer until Helen began to yawn. "Hey, you've had a rough week. Get some sleep. I'll sleep out here on the sofa and keep an ear on the door."

She just nodded and returned to the bedroom, closing the door behind her. He leaned down and patted

Fuzzy's side a couple times, then he settled in on the sofa and closed his eyes.

*****

Allistor woke in the morning to a cold wet nose jammed in his face. Sputtering and pushing the fuzzy face away, he sat up. Helen was sitting in a nearby chair, an amused look on her face. "I think he wants to be let out."

Allistor blinked a few times, wiping the sleep from his eyes and looking at his pet. "Is that right, Fuzzster? Are you house-trained already? That was easy!" He got up and went to the cabin door, opening it for the bear. Fuzzy stuck his nose out, checked the air, and then ambled into the bushes.

"Guess that answers the question about whether bears do it in the woods!" Helen giggled at her own joke. Allistor wished he had thought of it first.

"Good one. So, did you sleep well?"

"Like a log! Thank you again for coming to my rescue. I would certainly have died down there in the dark."

"You're most welcome. How 'bout we talk about what's next? I told you about the Warren and my people there. You're welcome to join us if you like."

Helen nodded her head. "I've been thinking about that since I woke up. I've been working in the park for ten years, and I know this area pretty well. If you'd like some company on your little road trip..."

Allistor thought about it. On the one hand, it would be great to have some company. Other than Fuzzy, of course. But it was dangerous, poking his nose around out here. He'd almost died more than once already.

"This isn't a picnic out here. Canids are far from the worst of the monsters we've run into. I'm planning to go into a large city or two, and will more than likely get my face eaten. The safe thing for you to do is take my pickup and go to the Warren. You can stop at the gun shop Outpost on the way and load up weapons and such. I'll take one of the park service trucks here. Those are better for me anyway, as there's more room inside for the bear as he gets bigger."

Helen shook her head. "I'm done with safe. I sat in the dark down there trying to be safe. Safe is just a slow way to die. If you're worried about me pulling my weight, I'm an expert marksman with a decade of experience in the woods. I can track, find berries and nuts and roots for food, and probably teach you quite a bit."

Impressed, Allistor agreed. "I still think we should take one of the park trucks, if that's okay?"

She laughed, slapping his shoulder. "As probably the last official representative of the park service, I hereby authorize you to make full use of department resources. In fact…" She paused and tapped a finger to her chin. "In return for saving my life, I hereby officially grant you ownership of the entire Medicine Bow National Forest!"

A golden glow surrounded them, and chimes filled the air. Helen hunched down in her seat, looking around wildly. "What the hell?"

Allistor's interface lit up with notifications. Ten thousand experience points flashed up on his screen, along with several golden Fame Point numbers in rapid succession. A long notification scrolled up in bright green letters. He waved it aside for a moment, looking at a still-wary Helen.

"What did you just do?"

Confused, she put her hands up and shrugged. "I don't know? I mean, what happened?"

Allistor held up a finger. "Let me read all this stuff. One minute."

He pulled up his interface and the notifications.

First was the experience notification.

Congratulations! You are the first human to secure title to one thousand square miles of territory. Reward: 10,000 experience points; 350,000 klax; Baron's Seal

You have earned the Title: Land Baron
By securing land holdings of one thousand square miles or more, you have earned yourself the title of Land Baron. As a Baron, you have the right to levy taxes on any citizens in residence upon your land. Further, you may sell or grant portions of your land to those who pledge themselves to your service. You may not compel any citizen to pledge to you, but those who refuse can be evicted from your holdings. Further rights and benefits will be bestowed upon completion of the stabilization period.

The next notification was one he'd been waiting for.

Level up! You are now Level 10! You have earned two attribute points.

You are now eligible to choose a Class designation. Available classes are listed in the Class information

317

section. Recommended Classes based on your current attribute levels may also be found there. Choose carefully, as the Class you choose cannot be changed unless or until you reach level fifty.

Allistor held off reading the rest as Helen cleared her throat impatiently. "Um, Helen? Just how big is the park you just gave me?"

Her mouth dropped open. "You mean, when I said that... I mean, I was just fooling around! The system actually *gave you the park?*"

His grin was so wide it made his cheeks hurt, but he couldn't stop smiling. "Yup! Now, what can you tell me about my new Barony?"

"Barony?" She rubbed her face, then slipped into park ranger mode. She motioned for him to follow her as she got up and walked into the office. "The Medicine Bow-Routt National Forest is broken up into several areas in Wyoming and Colorado." She pulled a large rolled up map from a stand next to her desk and opened it up on the table. Pointing as she spoke, she continued. "Totaling roughly 2.9 million acres, it includes open grasslands, old growth forests, three rivers, several mountains, and-" She halted as he held up a hand.

"Did you say a *million* acres?"

"Yep! Even after ten years, I don't think I've seen all of it myself. The best views are from up on the mountains." She moved her finger to a new spot on the map.

Allistor's head was spinning. "That's... in square miles that has to be..."

She already knew the number. "Just over four thousand five hundred square miles."

Allistor sat in one of the chairs. "Your gift just earned me a title. Land Baron. Like in Europe in the middle ages." He looked up at her. "You're my new favorite person on the whole planet!"

She laughed as he leapt from his chair and hugged her, lifting her off her feet. "And all you had to do was carry me up a flight of stairs and feed me a candy bar. I'm a cheap date!"

Setting her back down gently, he stepped back. "I can't believe this. I've been losing sleep worrying about securing enough land for our people by the end of the year. With one wave of your hand, you just guaranteed we'll have enough land to support us for... generations. Millions of us could live and thrive on this much land!"

She shook her head, suddenly serious. "No, not millions. Thousands, certainly. But the ecosystem here is delicate. If you were to kill off all the bison, or the wolves, or alter the path of one of the rivers, it would permanently damage this place. And there's no need to do that. There are enough big cities nearby for people to live in. You need to promise me you'll protect this place, not just the people." The look on her face was stern and implacable.

"Absolutely. You have my oath that as long as I live I will protect these lands as well as the people on them. We may need to hunt the monsters to extinction, but I'll do my best to preserve the natural inhabitants. I grew up camping every weekend and summer that we could. I wouldn't destroy the beauty of this place. And you already know I was planning to take Cheyenne as a Stronghold."

When he gave the oath, a green-blue light swirled around the two of them, and a single chime rang out.

319

Satisfied, Helen nodded her head. "That felt weird. And I got a notice saying we are now Oathbound."

Allistor had gotten the same notice. He was reading the linked information and was already making a mental note to be more careful with oaths. The penalty for breaking them could be anywhere from a fine, to instant death, depending on the gravity of the oath and the consequences to the other Oathbound.

She looked to the door as Fuzzy came wandering back in. There was blood on his snout, and little tufts of what looked like squirrel hair stuck to it. He held his head high as if proud of himself.

"So, Mister Baron Allistor, your Lordship. Have I earned a ticket on your little road trip?"

"Ha! You've earned a ticket on any road trip you want. And my eternal thanks."

"In that case, I'll deal with this notification that popped up earlier." She took a knee in front of him. "I, Helen Rodgers of the National Park Service, hereby pledge my loyalty to you, Lord Allistor."

This time a short blue flash of light surrounded each of them. There were no sounds to accompany the binding. She got back to her feet and said, "I hope you're not going to demand that we all bow to you or service you in kinky ways." She raised an eyebrow at him.

He held up both hands. "No, no. No bowing. No servicing. I think Amanda might object to that. And she knows all the most deadly places to stab a guy."

Just then the radio crackled, and Meg's voice came through. "Allistor? Are you there? What the hell have you done now, boy!?"

He walked over to the radio set and pressed the talk button on the microphone. "I um... I sort of just inherited about forty-five hundred square miles of national forest. It was an accident, I swear." He grinned at the radio as Helen laughed behind him.

"We all just got this message asking if we're willing to pledge our loyalty to Baron Allistor. What kind of game are you playing?" Meg sounded annoyed.

"It wasn't me, Meg! I mean, it was me, I am the Baron now and stuff. But I didn't create that loyalty pledge. The system seems to have generated it automatically for anyone who lives on the land that I control now." He paused, deciding to mess with Meg a bit. "It also tells me I can evict anyone who doesn't want to pledge to me. So you better be real nice to me..."

There was a spluttering on the other end of the line. "You little...! You'll be lucky if I don't beat you about the head with my spatula when you get back!" The laughter in her voice didn't match her words.

"Yup! Love you too, Meg. And I promise you don't have to call me Lord Allistor or kiss my feet or anything. I plan to be a real casual sort of evil overlord."

Michael's voice replaced Meg's. "You lucky bastard! I hear you got yourself a bear pet yesterday, and now you have your own Barony? If there was a leaderboard, I'm betting you'd be at the top right now."

Allistor winced. He hadn't thought of that. "Hey, let's hope there isn't one. You know what happens to the top people on the boards."

There was a pause, then Michael said, "Shit. Yeah, everybody else tries to take them down. Hadn't thought of that."

Allistor was quiet for a few moments. Then he pushed the talk button again. "Listen, guys, I'm going to continue on to Cheyenne and try for that Stronghold. We already own a lot of the land around it now. Also, get together and discuss if you want any upgrades to the Stronghold. We have a buttload of klax in the account now. Let me know what you decide the next time we talk. Also, I obviously won't demand a pledge from any of you. But there might be some benefit to it. So if one of you wants to spend a little time reading up on that?"

Michael replied right away. "Lilly's already done it. She says there are bonuses to crafting skill development, morale, and experience gains. They are supposed to be the benefits to offset the taxes you can charge us now."

"Ha! There will be no taxes. At least, not in this first year. You can consider that an official decree." He could hear some chuckling in the background when Michael keyed his microphone.

"Glad to hear it. We'll get together and talk about upgrades. And I think we'll all be making the pledge. It's not like we can't change our minds later and leave if you turn out to be a tyrant."

Allistor pictured himself on a throne shouting 'Off with their heads!'

"Good to know. And thank you, guys, for the faith you've shown in me so far. This really was an accident. I'll tell you the whole story when I get back. I'm a little worried about the competition coming after you guys, now. The Warren is my headquarters, and effectively the seat of our little Barony. If you can, take a couple people and drive down this way. Stop at the gun shop and grab a bunch more guns and ammo. I'll make this ranger station an Outpost too before I leave. No shortage of klax to convert to system points. I'm going to leave my pickup here and take one of the big ranger's trucks." He smacked himself on the forehead.

"Oh! There's a ranger here with me. Helen. Say hi to everyone, Helen!"

He stepped aside as she bent over the mic and hit the button. "Hello, everyone."

There was a chorus of hellos from the other side as Allistor took the microphone back. "Helen is the one responsible for our recent windfall. So treat her super nice when we get back. Anyway, if you want to swing by here after the gun shop, you can grab the pickup and take it back with you. I'll leave the keys inside the cabin here. You'll all be authorized to enter. This is a good place to spend a night. I'll leave all the food and stuff here. If not, don't sweat it. We can always find more trucks."

They spoke for a few more minutes, and Allistor wrapped up the conversation. "One other thing, guys. The lake below the gun shop has a grumpy sturgeon nearly the size of that shellback. So don't go swimming in there, okay?"

"Got it! We'll swing down there today. Be careful out there, *Lord Allistor.*" Michael signed off.

Helen went to change the sheets, clean up the bedroom, and pack as Allistor opened up his Outpost interface. The button to establish the ranger cabin as an Outpost was a bright and friendly green where it had been grayed out before. He added the usual features – the wall around the clearing, sensors, remote access. The windmill already provided electricity, which also operated the pump in the well beneath the cabin, so he didn't need to spend points on those. He approved the transaction, and the usual golden glow surrounded them as the cabin converted itself to an Outpost. He authorized his crowd to access the doors, then added Helen to the approved list for all the facilities.

By the time he was done, she was ready to go. Fuzzy was napping again, so Allistor nudged him with a foot. "C'mon, buddy. Time to hit the road." He retrieved both of the stainless bowls, tossing the remaining water out the door before returning them to his ring. When he turned around, Fuzzy was nowhere to be seen.

Walking back into the main room, he found the cub with his nose jammed under the sofa, his butt in the air. He pushed at the sofa, trying to squeeze his head underneath to reach something. Thinking it was another rat, Allistor obliged him by grabbing one end of the sofa and lifting it high.

Fuzzy slid forward on his face, his back legs still pushing. He grabbed hold of something green, shook it a few times, then got to his feet and trotted outside. Curious, Allistor followed him out. "What've you got there, Fuzzster?" He reached out a hand for the cub to turn over his prize. Fuzzy turned his back on him and raised a paw at the pickup door, asking to be let in.

"Oh, no you don't. Let me see what you've got there, buddy. I need to make sure it won't make you sick." He leaned down and took hold of one end of the thing. It was made of soft fabric. Fuzzy reluctantly let go, and Allistor got a good look at it.

It was a stuffed toy, about eight inches tall. A little creature of some sort. Bright green with big ears and feet, it had a leather strap across its chest and an underbite with only three crooked teeth. It held a stick in one hand. The thing looked familiar...

"Fibble! Ha! You found a Fibble plushy, Fuzzy. I had one of these as a kid." He held the slobber-covered doll up and waved the arm holding the stick. "Pew! Pew!"

Chuckling, he handed the doll back to Fuzzy, who took it gently in his mouth. Opening the back door of one of the ranger trucks, he said, "Hop up in here, bud. This is our new ride."

Fuzzy approached the door, sniffing at the truck. Then he turned and looked back at the pickup. He walked over and got up on his hind legs, putting both paws against the passenger door. Looking back at Allistor, he chuffed once.

"What's wrong, buddy?" Allistor joined him. A quick glance inside the truck, and he understood. "Your nest!" Allistor opened the truck door and grabbed the pile of blankets from the seat. He transferred them over to the back seat of the Suburban, and Fuzzy happily hopped up and made himself comfortable. He placed the little doll gently on the blankets between his paws and put his head down.

Helen joined Allistor up front a few minutes later, and they hit the road.

Chapter Fourteen

Mall Rats

Helen was driving the truck as she knew the territory. While she navigated the back roads toward Cheyenne, Allistor took some time to review his options for choosing a class.

He quickly eliminated all the warrior classes, as well as most of the melee options. The system had different names than he was used to. But from the descriptions, he eliminated the monk and paladin classes as well. He wanted something with powerful magical abilities, but he wasn't willing to dedicate his life to a deity in return for his powers. Especially since he didn't know anything about the pantheon in this new place.

He thought about the druid class or some hybrid of druid and melee. With Fuzzy as his companion, it made some sense. But the druid class was focused on nature-based abilities that didn't really fit with what he wanted.

Focusing on the Mage and Sorcerer classes, he scrolled down until he found one he thought fit him pretty well. The word *Battlemage* seemed to jump off the screen at him.

Battlemage: *This magic-based hybrid class allows the mage to combine spellcraft with physical attacks. Spells can be channeled through a weapon to increase physical damage or to focus spell power to increase effectiveness. Class-based spells include both offensive and defensive capabilities, single target and area of effect. Main attributes are Will Power and Intelligence, with a* *secondary focus on Strength and Stamina. Luck may play a significant role in this class.*

Allistor squirmed in his seat. *Battlemage* sounded badass! It fit the new path he'd chosen for his attribute build, and the thought of defensive magic was just cool. He pictured casting a bubble of protection over himself and Fuzzy as they were bombarded by fire from a hovering drake.

"Battlemage it is!" he mumbled to himself as he verified that selection. A tingling feeling rushed through his body from his feet upward. A congratulatory message scrolled across his interface, and a new tab labeled *Battlemage Class* highlighted itself.

"What was that?" Helen asked, keeping her eyes scanning the road and trees ahead.

"I reached level ten. Just chose my class. I'm now officially a Battlemage." He deepened his voice and tried to sound like Sam Elliot when he said the word.

Helen snorted. "Sounds very scary." She humored him. "But what does it mean? Can you call down lightning or make fire rain from the sky? Or is that more of a 'make-your-sword-all-sparky' kind of thing?"

"I'm not sure yet, I've been a Battlemage for all of twenty seconds!" he answered, a little defensive. "But from what I've read so far, maybe a bit of both? Plus magic shields!"

Helen nodded her head. "I think I'd go with a Druid class. But I've got a ways to go. I'm only level 4. Being rangers, Cliff and I started out trying not to kill anything we didn't have to. And then, well you already know I spent a week in the cellar."

"No worries. We'll get you leveled up in no time. This little road trip is bound to bring us up against some higher level creatures. And..." He paused to consider for a moment. Looking at Helen, he decided to trust her. "And I haven't told anyone else this yet. But when I've had to kill other humans, I got experience points and loot."

"You've murdered people since this started?" Helen hit the brakes and pulled to the side of the road. She turned to look suspiciously at him.

"You remember I told you about Luther and his Stronghold? Well, this dick named Evan and his guys were attacking the Stronghold. They'd been starving out the group living inside for a week. Stole almost all of their food and trapped them inside, killing several of them in the process." He watched her face as he spoke. When she nodded her head ever-so-slightly, he added. "So I shot Evan in the head, and with a little help, we killed most of his guys. The rest ran away." He elected not to tell her about the artillery round George and Sam sent their way later.

When she still didn't look convinced, he turned in his seat to face her. "I'm not a murderer, Helen. There are people left that seem to have chosen to survive by stealing and robbing others. I'm not one of those, but if one of them comes at me or mine, *I will kill them to keep us safe.* There's no more government to protect us, no more judges. In fact, Evan was an ex-cop, using his skills to gain power over others. And I don't have the resources, or frankly, the desire, to take and keep prisoners. We've been pushed into a new society here. Or rather, a very old one that's much different than what we're used to. If I'm placed in a kill-or-die situation, I will kill. I'm sorry if that is not acceptable to you. We can turn around, and I'll give you back the cabin." He paused for just a second, then grinned. "But I'm keeping the park!"

She laughed, despite herself. "Goofball." Her face grew serious again. "I understand that you did what you did to save people. And I admire that. I've obviously never had to kill anyone before, and hope that I never have to. And you should know that if we come up against hostile humans, I'm not sure I could pull the trigger, no matter how much they might deserve it."

This didn't thrill Allistor, but he understood. "Fair enough. Good with killing monsters, not so much with the bad guys. How do you feel about fluffy bunnies? We're growing a crop of them back at the Warren."

"I'm no vegetarian." Helen gave him a half-smile. "If we gotta snap a bunny's neck to put food on the table, that bunny is toast. Rabbit is quite tasty. But here again... try to get me to eat people, and we're gonna have a problem."

"Ha! I think we can agree on that. And speaking of meat, we'll need to hunt quite a bit to feed the fuzzball in the back seat. He's just about wiped out my protein supply in twenty-four hours."

Helen looked around, focused on a tower sitting atop a nearby hill. Then she pointed in the general direction the road was heading. "In about five miles there's a bridge across a deep creek. Good fishing spot. We stock salmon each year in the park's lakes, and there are always trout."

"Awesome! As long as there isn't one of those friggin' sturgeon in there. That thing creeped me out."

Chuckling, Helen said, "You can fish from up on the bridge if that makes you feel better."

They settled into a comfortable silence as she drove the last few miles to the bridge. In the back seat, Fuzzy polluted the air again, and Helen rolled down the back windows without a word. Allistor wasn't so polite.

"Damn, Fuzzy. You couldn't hold it for a few more minutes? And what the hell have you been eating? Can we feed him some antacids, Helen? Will that hurt him? Cuz I think something's deeply wrong in there somewhere. Like he ate something dead and rotted that also ate something dead and rotted that fed on rancid spam." He kept up a monologue until Helen was laughing and Fuzzy buried his nose under his paws in seeming embarrassment.

Allistor spent a little time looking into his Battlemage class. The choice had come with two new spells. One was *Barrier* and was just what it sounded like. He could cast a magic barrier that blocked both physical and magical attacks. At level one, it could block up to one thousand points of damage.

The second spell was a sort of combination interrupt and damage spell called *Mind Spike*. Again, it was much like it sounded. It seemed the system lacked creativity in its descriptors. The spell sent a sort of mental dagger into the target's brain, doing physical damage and causing intense pain that would interrupt any spellcasting or physical attacks.

When Helen pulled off the road and parked in a gravel area near the base of the bridge, both humans got out and scanned the area. Fuzzy let himself out by crawling awkwardly out a window and dropping to the ground. His nose was in overdrive, checking the scents in every direction. When he casually walked up and dipped a paw into the water, Helen and Allistor relaxed. Helen said, "If there's a predator within a couple miles upwind of us, he'd be able to smell it."

She went to the back of the truck and retrieved a fishing pole while Allistor withdrew his fishing gear from his ring. They both rigged up their poles and split up slightly, standing about thirty feet apart on the creek's bank. Fuzzy, being a grizzly, had some instinctive fishing skills of his own. He politely went downstream about fifty yards to where a rocky spur extended partway out into the creek. Standing in the shallows, he put his nose near the water and waited.

Helen was the first to get a hit. She yanked back on her pole without a word and began reeling with enthusiasm. A minute later she was holding a trout that looked close to two pounds. She didn't tease Allistor, just dropped the fish on a stringer, tied one end to a sapling, and tossed the fish into the shallow water.

A few minutes later a splash downstream indicated Fuzzy had made his move. He'd disappeared under the water for a moment, but his head emerged with a small fish in it. Allistor was too far away to see clearly what it was.

The cub crawled back up onto the spur and plopped down on his belly to eat.

Helen had caught another fish before Allistor finally got a bite. When he reeled his catch in, it was smaller, but still a healthy pound and a half. They spent an hour at the bridge, fishing quietly and just enjoying the morning. When they were done, Fuzzy had caught and eaten three fish, and they had another ten on the stringer. Helen was going to grab a large cooler from the back of the truck, but Allistor stopped her. "I'd rather not be smelling fish all trip. I'll store them in the ring." He did just that, happy to see that they were similar enough to stack in one storage slot.

"I've got to get me one of those!" Helen eyed the ring as each fish disappeared. "Will they stay fresh in there? We didn't even gut them."

Allistor nodded. "It says time doesn't pass inside whatever void they're stored in. So when we take them out they'll be just as fresh as when they went in."

Calling Fuzzy back, Allistor engaged him in a game of tag, running him about the gravel area and into the tall grass in an attempt to dry him off. "Don't want to be smelling wet bear the whole trip, either."

When Fuzzy was reasonably dry, they loaded themselves back in the truck and kept going. If they kept a decent speed, they could be in Cheyenne well before dark. After the sunshine and relaxation of fishing, Allistor found himself dozing off. Fuzzy was snoring happily in the back seat. The third time Allistor's chin hit his chest and he jerked himself awake, Helen said, "It's okay; grab a nap."

Almost as soon as she said it, though, she hit the brakes and slowed quickly. Allistor looked ahead and saw a fallen tree across the road about fifty yards ahead. Opening his door, he said, "No worries. You can stay here, I'll go move the tree. Won't take but a few seconds."

As his feet hit the pavement, Helen said, "That's not a tree."

Blinking the sleep from his eyes, Allistor looked again. The thing was maybe two feet thick and tubular, stretching the full distance across the road and disappearing into the brush on either side. It sure looked like a tree to him.

Until it moved.

A section near the side of the road bent, then straightened again as the whole tree seemed to slide from left to right. Allistor's eyes widened. "Son of a... that's a snake!"

He *Examined* it as Helen responded. "I'm glad you saw that, too. Thought I was seeing things."

Infant Ophidian Queen
Level 12
Health: 7,800/7,800

"Infant? This thing's an infant?" Allistor cursed under his breath, stepped back up into the truck.

"What do you mean, infant?" Helen asked him. Thing's gotta be fifty feet long at least. Nothing in this forest grows that big.

"You haven't learned how to *Examine* things yet?" Allistor asked. When she shook her head, he said, "Okay, stare at the thing for a minute. Really focus on it, and clear your mind."

She did as he said, and after about half a minute, her mouth dropped open. "Holy shit. It does say it's an infant!"

Allistor took a deep breath. "You know how you said you wanted to level up?"

Helen looked at him, mouth still open, and began to shake her head. "Not that badly, I don't."

He chuckled. "Well, our choice is to kill it, or wait here and hope it slithers off the road. But it hasn't moved much. I think it might be sunning itself."

Helen looked at again. "I'm wondering where its head is. And how long its teeth are, and whether they're poisonous, and if they can puncture this truck, and-"

Allistor held up a hand. "All good thoughts. I've been asking myself the same thing. And the inevitable answer is... there's only one way to find out! Let's see if we can get its attention and maybe do some damage at the same time. Drive right over that bad boy!"

Helen stared at him like he was insane, then she said, "You're insane!"

He sent her a party invite, then on a whim, he tried sending one to Fuzzy, too.

Your companion is already a member of your party. Do you wish to remove companion Fuzzy from your party at this time?

Feeling a little 'duh', he mentally selected "No" and the message went away. Helen accepted the invite and raised shaky hands to grip the wheel and put the truck in gear.

As they got closer, she picked up speed. The truck had large tires and a high clearance, designed to move through rough terrain when necessary. But this was going to hurt. Allistor braced himself against the dash.

The wheels struck the snake's body at about 30mph. The entire frame of the truck shivered as the wheels pushed up and over, the weight of the engine pressing down on the flesh of the monster below. Out his side window, Allistor saw the body begin to contort, the strength of the thing actually shifting the truck slightly as the wheels dropped back down on the other side. Helen continued forward, the back wheels striking a moment later, and the back end of the truck rising up.

A second later, the much lighter back end was thrown to the side as the giant snake's body writhed and threw it off. Allistor stretched his neck around to look behind them as Helen wrestled the vehicle back under control. She continued about twenty yards down the road until Allistor called, "Stop!"

She looked in the rearview mirror in time to see a massive head the size of a cow moving toward the back end of the truck. She saw Allistor move his hand and the thing froze. Another hand movement from him, and its face caught fire. It had the head of a viper, spread out at the back like a cobra and narrowing to a V-shaped snout with two nostrils. Its fangs were easily three feet long and covered in something viscous. Just behind its head, maybe four feet down its torso, were a pair of very tiny wings. Obviously vestigial, there was no way the thing would be able to fly. But the wings were flared angrily as it stared at them, its malevolent vertically oriented pupils a sickly yellow.

"Grab your rifle!" he shouted as he jumped out, drawing his shotgun from his ring. "Stay behind the truck, and shoot it in the face! I'm going to distract it."

He managed one shot before the stun wore off the ridiculously large baby ophidian thing and it thrashed in pain from the fire. The slug thumped into the belly of the snake just below its head, the thrashing causing him to miss. He quickly racked another round and fired, hitting the side of its head this time. He heard Helen's rifle fire, and blood spouted from the thing's snout.

Infant Ophidian Queen
Level 12
Health: 5,200/7,800

The massive snake reared up, and up, its head raising more than twenty feet in the air. Then it lunged for him just as he was about to fire another round. He pulled the trigger, not seeing whether he hit it as he leapt to his left away from the truck.

The ophidian was too fast for him. Though it didn't get a fang into him, its massive head still managed to slam into his side, knocking him back in mid-air. Several of his ribs crunched and his right arm went numb before he even hit the ground. His momentum caused him to roll as he skidded down the pavement, losing skin against the rough surface as he went.

336

Another shot rang out, and when Allistor managed to right himself to look back at the snake, it had transferred its focus onto Helen. She was crouched behind her open truck door, using its frame as a rest for her weapon.

Allistor struggled to his feet, bleeding in several places, but not seriously. His health bar was down to 60%, his ribs definitely broken, and he was unable to raise his right arm. Dropping his shotgun, he cast *Restraint* on the mob again. It froze, and Helen took aim then fired directly into its left eye. The socket exploded with blood and vitreous fluid.

Allistor willed his spear from his ring and gripped it in his left hand. He cast *Levitate* and let go of the weapon as it floated upward a few feet. Using his good hand to motion at the weapon, he turned it to face the frozen monster, then sent it shooting forward. His aim wasn't great, but the heavy rebar spear slammed into the side of the snake's head and sank deep.

The stun wore off, and the ophidian's head fell back to earth, the weight of the spear tilting it to one side as it fell nearly three stories. The impact with the pavement pushed the spear deeper into the snake's body, which began to curl and uncurl in a frenzy.

Helen fired again, this time up into the tilted head from underneath, the round from the hunting rifle entering the underside of its jaw and exploding out the top of its nose.

"I think it's dead! The movement is just reflex!" She called out as she stepped from behind the truck door and took a few steps toward the monster.

Allistor knew better. There hadn't been any kill experience flashing across his interface yet. "No! Stop! It's not dead yet!" he screamed at her, his voice hoarse from pain. Even the breath he'd taken for that shout sent pain screaming through him as his ribs poked into his internal organs. Or at least, that's how it felt. He reached out, trying to cast his new *Barrier* spell on her. It seemed to take forever, but a shimmering of the air in front of her told him it worked.

Helen froze, heeding his warning. She raised her rifle again, but she never got to fire. The snake's tail exploded out of the brush at the side of the road, showering Helen and the truck with twigs and leaves before it slammed through his shield into the woman and crushed her against the side of the vehicle.

Allistor cursed as he saw her fall limply to the ground, not able to get enough breath for a scream. He cast *Flame Shot* without even thinking, sending a ball of flame smashing into the monster's face and open mouth. He pulled one of Meg's napalm grenades and tossed it left-handed at the thing's head. It shattered, and liquid fire engulfed the front four feet of the ophidian's head and body.

Seconds later, it stopped thrashing and the expected experience points flashed before his eyes. A quick glance at his party icons showed that Helen was hurt bad but alive. He produced and drank a health potion as he limped around the truck to her. The pain was lessening, but he was pretty sure he'd suffered internal damage. He cast the heal *Nature's Boon* on himself as he moved.

Helen lay unconscious next to the rear wheel of the truck. Her arm was clearly badly broken, sticking out at an odd angle. Her head was bleeding, and blood ran from her mouth as well. She was breathing, but just barely.

Allistor cast *Nature's Boon* on her as well, wishing fervently that Amanda was here. He didn't know if he should try and reset the broken bone, or not. If he just healed her as she was, would it straighten itself out? Or would she be stuck with it in that position?

Starting to get the feeling back in his arm, he pulled another healing potion from his ring and poured it down her throat. He had to gently push her mouth shut to make her swallow, and she ended up coughing some of it out. The pain from the cough brought her back to consciousness.

"Owwww..." was all she said before closing her eyes and lying very still. Allistor cast the healing spell on her again, then began to speak to her.

"You're hurt, but you'll live. I'm not sure how to fix your arm..."

A moment later she screamed as the broken bone snapped back into alignment with a grinding sound. She was instantly unconscious again.

Allistor moved to sit next to her, back against the truck as he took some deep breaths. Sure now that she was going to recover, he cast one more heal on himself. His mana was still about half full, but he wanted to be ready in case something heard the battle and came to investigate.

Realizing his shotgun was laying in the road on the other side of the truck, he pulled another one from his ring and set it in his lap. Pulling some granola bars from his

339

ring, he dropped one on Helen's lap before using his teeth and his good left arm to open his. A few bites later, and he was feeling better. After five minutes, the pain in his ribs was down to a dull throbbing, and he could move his arm freely.

Looking at the still unconscious Helen, he admitted, "Okay, maybe running over the giant angry baby snake queen was a bad idea." He cast one more heal on her, his mana having regenerated some as he ate.

A few minutes later, she blinked and took a panicked breath. He put a hand on her shoulder and spoke softly. "It's okay. You got smushed, but you're gonna live." He patted her shoulder reassuringly as she opened her eyes and looked around, confused.

She eventually focused on him, her reactions a little slow as she was clearly concussed. Spitting some blood out of her mouth, she asked, "Who are you?"

Allistor cursed. Long and colorfully. If she had permanent brain damage… "I'm Allistor. Your friend, Helen."

"Who's Helen?" She looked around as if seeking another person. Allistor sighed, preparing himself to deal with some kind of amnesia.

Just as he was opening his mouth to explain, she barked a laugh. Then she held her head between both hands at the pain it caused. After a moment, she let out a long breath. "Sorry. I was just screwin' with ya." She offered him a pained, lopsided grin.

"Oh, *no way!*" He leaned back. "That was a serious party foul! I thought you were… I was worried… dammit, woman!" He sulked for a few seconds, but the grin on her face just widened.

"Awww! You were worried 'bout lil ol' me? How sweet!" She made a little kissy-face at him, then picked up the granola bar and opened it. "I'm *so* hungry!"

"More like worried I was gonna be stuck with a brain-dead third wheel, dragging down me and Fuzzy the rest of the trip." He grumped at her. She didn't answer, other than to make a few exaggerated nom-nom sounds as she chewed her snack.

When she was done, she looked at him, all innocence and puppy-dog eyes. "You're not really mad at me? I mean, I forgive you for telling me to run over that creature from hell."

He chuckled. "Okay, you have a point. We're even." He got to his feet then reached a hand down to help her up. He pulled a canteen from his ring and handed it to her. "You need to drink to help you heal up. You lost some blood."

As she drank deeply, Allistor heard a curious sniffing noise. Looking through the passenger window, he saw a pile of brown fur scrunched down behind the driver's seat, with a just a nose sticking up above the back seat.

"My hero! Come on out, Fuzzy. The monster's dead. You were a big help!" He opened the door, and the bear cub stared at him, in no big hurry to leave the safety of the truck. "Come on! Out you go, oh fearless grizzly companion!"

Fuzzy attempted to move, but couldn't. He looked at Allistor again and huffed.

"What? Are you stuck down there?" Allistor reached in, pushing his hand between the back of the driver's seat and the bear's shoulder. He tugged gently, but the cub was wedged in there tightly.

Moving forward to the driver's seat, he reached underneath and triggered the release, sliding the seat forward. A grunt from Fuzzy, and the cub freed himself. He tumbled out onto the road as Allistor moved the seat back again.

Looking down at his bear cub, he said, "You grew! Fuzzy, you must have leveled up when we killed the snake! No wonder you were stuck down in there."

Fuzzy mostly ignored him, strolling over to the snake's corpse and growling the whole way. When he reached its head, he sniffed it thoroughly, then licked some of the exposed and burned flesh. He took a tentative bite, pulling away some stringy bits with his teeth.

Rolling his eyes, Allistor motioned for Helen to follow him. He touched the snake's head, looting it. She followed his example and her eyes went vacant as she reviewed her loot notifications. "This is cool! And I leveled up to six, by the way!"

Allistor congratulated her as he reviewed his own loot. Two hundred klax, six stacks of infant ophidian queen meat, twenty pieces each. Four stacks of infant ophidian queen hide, one envenomed fang (he assumed Helen received the other), and as he had begun to expect when killing these bigger monsters, her heart.

When he saw that she was done inspecting her loot, he pulled out a knife. "We need to skin this thing. Take as much as we can with us. A little bonus we discovered a while back. I assume you got some hide in your loot?"

"Yup. A whole bunch! Which, I guess when you look at the size of this thing, isn't a big surprise."

"Well, we can harvest even more. I'm assuming as a ranger you've skinned a snake before?"

Her answer was to walk up to the head and drive her own knife into the flesh under its chin. "This thing is huge. We're not going to be able to skin it like a normal snake."

He agreed. He watched as she made a long slit that extended several feet down the ophidian's belly. Then made a cross-cut at the top, making a T under its chin. She stopped and looked at him. "How big should these pieces be?"

"I don't know? Um… when my mom used to sew she bought fabric in yards? Does that help?"

Helen nodded once and resumed carving at the corpse. Allistor left her to it, moving to the monster's jaw. The two venomous fangs were gone, but inside the jaw were two ridges, upper and lower, that each held dozens of much smaller (by comparison) teeth. Each of these was six to ten inches long and razor-sharp. Carefully grabbing hold of one, he used his knife to pry it loose. Hoping they could be used to create some kind of weapon with his *Improvisation* and *Weaponsmithing* skills, he removed the teeth one by one.

When he was done, he went to check on Helen. She'd cut and peeled six long strips of skin from the body. Each was about two feet wide and ten feet long. Her hands and forearms were covered in blood, and she was sweating. As he watched, she unconsciously wiped some sweat from the tip of her nose with a bloody hand, then cursed when she realized what she'd done.

"That should be more than enough, I would think." He watched as she rolled up each strip into a neat tube of snakeskin, then he stepped up next to her and pulled the canteen from her belt. He motioned for her to hold out her hands as he slowly poured out the water for her to wash. When she was mostly clean, she thanked him and took the canteen back for a drink.

Fuzzy, meanwhile, had taken full advantage of the freshly exposed snake meat, pulling huge bites of the stuff from the body and chowing down. His muzzle was slick with blood, and his belly seemed to be getting rounder.

"Enough, pigbear!" Allistor bumped him in the side with a knee. Clean yourself up before you get in the truck!" Fuzzy obediently stepped away from the corpse, sitting on his haunches and commencing to clean his face and paws by licking them, much as a cat would do.

Leaving him to it, he walked back toward the truck. Helen was standing next to it on the driver's side, looking down. When he saw what she was looking at, he laughed.

"Yeah, there's a Helen-shaped dent right there. It's like one of those old cartoons!" he giggled slightly. When he saw the look she shot him, it erupted into uncontrollable laughter. He managed to gasp out, "You… got… pancaked!"

Eventually, she stopped glaring at him and chuckled. "It hurt. A lot." Then she started laughing as well.

She laughed even harder when he said, "Who are you?"

Finished with his cleanup, Fuzzy ambled over to stare at the two humans who were making strange noises and holding their bellies as if they were sick. When he tilted his head to one side and made a questioning chuff, both humans laughed even harder, rendered helpless by the fuzzy cuteness.

Eventually, they got themselves sorted out and back into the truck. Back at the wheel, Helen took them the rest of the way down one back road after another until they reached the outskirts of Cheyenne.

She'd brought them in from the northwest quadrant of the city, along a road with a sign that named it as Hwy 211. "We're close to the Air Force base here. I figured you might want to check that out as a potential Stronghold." She nodded out the window with her chin, directing his gaze. When he looked in the indicated direction, he didn't see much of anything.

"Um… I didn't know there was a base here. Aren't Air Force bases mostly runways and hangars and better-than-average military housing? I was thinking something sturdy, like maybe an old stone building, a steel high rise, or a stadium or something."

Helen coughed once. "Warren air base is… was a missile base, my friend. Like, silos, bunkers, that sort of thing. Sturdy enough for you?"

"Hell yes!" He offered her a fist to bump. "But…
um, if there are bunkers, there might be survivors. Are we
going to get shot if we trespass on the base?"

She stopped the truck. "Well, shit. Good question.
I mean, we have this official truck, and I'm a ranger, so
maybe they'll wait and ask questions before they shoot?"

Allistor looked at her skeptically. "You don't look
like a ranger." She had put on jeans and a flannel shirt
before they left that morning. "Any chance they'd be
listening in on that radio?" He pointed to the microphone
on a curled cord clipped to the dash next to the steering
wheel.

She thought about it for a minute. "They might be -
if they're scanning channels. As for the ranger bit, stay
right there." She threw the truck into park and jumped out,
walking around back to retrieve her bag. Pulling out a
folded uniform, she said, "No peeking!" and turned her
back to him as she stripped down to change. Allistor
turned to face forward, and he did his best not to look.
Which meant he only peeked a couple times. Quickly. Just
glances, really.

When she returned to the driver's seat all uniformed
up, she grabbed the radio and began calling out. "United
States Park Ranger Rodgers to F.E. Warren Air Force base
personnel, is anyone listening, over?"

They listed for a response, but there was only static.
She said, "We're close enough that if they're listening, they
can hear us."

She repeated the message a few times, adding in
phrases like "We're in your back yard, looking for

survivors." When there was still no response, she changed channels and repeated her message. After she'd gone through a dozen channels, she stowed the microphone and sighed. "If they were listening, they should have heard us on at least one of those channels."

Allistor shrugged. "What do you want to do? Drive on and see what happens? Look for another place and maybe try the radio again?"

She drummed her fingers on the steering wheel for a bit, then said, "If there were survivors, chances are the buildings we'd want are locked down. So even if we don't get shot, we probably can't get in. I mean, they're designed to withstand nuclear strikes 'n such."

Allistor nodded. "Right. So that's that, then. Let's find ourselves a good safe spot for the night, and once that's established we can spend the rest of the afternoon exploring and foraging. Maybe we can find an even better place."

Helen looked askance at him, but she put the truck back in gear. "I might know a good place. Over by the airport." She drove down a couple more roads, which remained mostly clear. There were some abandoned cars blocking parts of them in a few places. Some accidents with a few burned out cars, but for the most part, the city just looked like everybody bailed.

They crossed over Interstate 25 headed east, and Allistor could see the airport control tower. "You're not actually taking me to the airport, just to mess with me, right?"

"Nope! Relax, we're almost there. I think you might like this." A moment later she turned off the road into a parking lot. There in front of them was a big, sexy shopping mall. The sign out front read Frontier Mall. He could see a movie theater, a few big box stores, and signs for many more, including a few fast food restaurants and a candy store.

Excited now, he hopped up and down in his seat a bit. "Yesss! Well done! Sturdy structure, clear line of sight all the way around, filled with loot! Now let's hope there's nobody in there to keep us from claiming it. I wonder if it's too big for an Outpost."

She rolled her eyes at him. "Slow down there, hot pants. I thought we were going to try the base again? You know, the place full of *nuclear missiles*? How much could you sell those for on the market?"

Allistor drooled a little bit. "Much. Many klax. Oodles. And if we could figure out how to fire them, nobody would ever screw with us." He thought about it for a second. "Unless of course, the dicks who brought us here have the tech to nullify them. Still, worth a shot. That's why I was thinking Outpost for the mall. That way we could still make the bunkers a Stronghold if we get in."

"Fair enough." She was driving them in a circuit around the mall, looking for any signs of habitation. There were a few dozen cars still parked within view, some with doors wide open or broken windows and old blood stains. Others still closed tight and mostly undamaged. Almost all of them had dents and scratches on them.

As they reached the end of their circuit without coming across any sign of life, friendly or otherwise, Helen pulled up right in front of the double glass doors leading into a major chain store. The two of them exited the truck and spent a little time surveying the area, watching and listening for any motion at all. Other than a few birds, nothing moved. Allistor tried the door and found it unlocked. There were actually two sets of doors, outer and inner. A quick test of the inner doors unsurprisingly showed them to be unlocked as well.

He stepped back outside and opened the back door of the truck, letting Fuzzy out. "Stay behind me, okay, lil buddy? We're going to explore the great big cave."

They all entered the first set of doors, then the second. Fuzzy caught his own reflection in the glass and licked at it, but he made no sound. Allistor scratched his ears to thank him.

Inside the store, they found themselves in men's clothing. Allistor looked around the wide open expanse full of shelves and clothes racks, and fear gripped him. There could be a dozen canids within fifty feet of him, and he'd never see them coming. A quick look at Helen showed a similar worry written all over her face. She whispered, "Maybe this wasn't such a good idea?"

Allistor didn't answer right away. He crouched down in front of Fuzzy and asked, "You smell anything, buddy? I mean, I know you smell lots of things. There's all kinds of perfumes and people scents in this place. But do you smell anything that might eat us?"

Fuzzy looked at him for a moment, then licked his face. The smell of snake corpse was unpleasant, but Allistor took it as a good sign. Standing straight, he looked back at the doors, considering.

"Fuzzy says we're good for now. Grab some belts off that rack over there." He pointed, and Helen moved to comply while he went back to look at the doors. He'd worked retail for a brief period as a kid, and had been responsible for locking similar doors when he worked the evening shift. As he expected, the right side door of each set had a lever you could pull down that dropped a pin into the floor, and another for the top of the frame. He quickly locked both of those, leaving only the left-hand doors. The outer door could only be locked with a key, which was discouraging. But the inner door had a deadbolt-like knob that could be turned on the inside.

Helen arrived with the belts, and Allistor used one to tie the outer door handles together. Then he used a second belt to reinforce the first. He tried the doors, and they barely moved. "It's not perfect, but it'll do for now." Stepping inside, he turned the deadbolt, then just to be safe he wrapped a belt around those handles as well.

"You realize you just cut us off from our escape route?" Helen snarked at him, nudging him with an elbow.

"Yeah. But I can't have things sneaking in behind us from outside. Let's clear this place and lock it down." Allistor raised his shotgun and took the lead as he walked to the main exit into the mall itself. Here they found a roll-down gate that stretched the entire twelve-foot width of the doorway. Allistor found a metal pole with a hooked end leaning against one wall and used it to pull the gate down. It made a huge racket and scared Fuzzy into backing up and hiding inside a circular rack of ladies coats. Once the gate was down, one needed a key to lock it.

Allistor shrugged. "Good enough for the moment. Anything tries to get in, we'll definitely hear it."

Over the next twenty minutes, they moved through the store, first closing the other set of glass doors exiting the opposite side of the store, then clearing the main floor area and the restrooms, dressing rooms, offices, and finally the stock room. The stock room had two more exits, one a standard metal door, the other a roll-up loading dock door. Both were securely locked.

"If we need to, we can sleep in here tonight. We can secure the door leading out to the store, throw some blankets and pillows down, and sleep in shifts." Helen observed, echoing Allistor's exact train of thought.

"Yep! You read my mind. Okay, let's see if we can find some keys. Check the office first, then start searching the drawers at the cash registers. Some supervisor might have left keys we can use to lock up. Those glass doors won't stop humans with guns or any of the large monsters, but they should be fine for canids and killer rats."

Helen found keys sitting atop the very first desk she checked. Along with a hand-written note dated two weeks earlier.

I'm leaving the store open for anyone who needs it. There are warm clothes, shoes, and other things you might need. The dog-things took my wife and daughter yesterday. I should have brought them here instead of keeping them home. This place, the whole mall, seems clear so far. I'm going out to hunt those things. If you are reading this, make yourself at home, and good luck to you. May the Lord protect you, if he's still watching over us."

Tears flowed down Helen's face as she read the note aloud. Allistor found himself a little choked up as well. He lifted the keys from the desk and cleared his throat. "Maybe he's still alive out there somewhere."

Helen nodded and followed him out of the office. They quickly made the rounds, using the keys to secure all the doors and big gate leading out to the mall. Then they grabbed a couple of chairs and sat near the gate, watching and listening. Fuzzy stuck his nose between the links and sniffed, then just sat down and looked at Allistor.

"I say we wait until tomorrow to try and clear this place," Helen said. She was still bummed by the letter. "That's a lot of open territory for two people to cover."

Allistor nodded. Leaving the gate area, they made their way over to the household section. There were actually four beds set up as displays, along with a few sofas and recliners, dressers, and such. They grabbed a bunch of sheets and blankets and worked together to make a couple of the beds. Then Allistor piled blankets on the floor between them for Fuzzy. The cub wasted no time, a few quick sniffs, and he curled up and closed his eyes.

Mentally tired, Allistor and Helen did some quick shopping. He grabbed a few pairs of jeans, T-shirts, and sweat shorts to sleep in. She returned with similar items, plus a full pair of silk pajamas. "Always wanted a set of these, but rangers don't get paid much." She grinned at him and headed for the dressing room. He changed where he was while she was inside, plopped down into one of the recliners. A quick look at the glass doors showed afternoon sunlight outside.

When Helen rejoined him, they talked for a few hours, sharing stories about family and their past lives. Catching each other up on all the events since the apocalypse began. When Helen yawned widely and caused Allistor to do the same, they retired to their beds for the evening. Allistor said he'd take first watch, but Helen shook her head. "With the doors all locked, we'll hear anything trying to get in. And Fuzzy will let us know if anything gets close. We both need the sleep."

Too tired to argue, Allistor said, "Good enough. Sweet dreams."

It wasn't five minutes before they were both sound asleep.

Chapter Fifteen

Ditch the Twitch

Fuzzy woke them early in the morning, poking his nose at Allistor with the Fibble doll in his mouth, looking to be let outside. Allistor was impressed with the request, though he supposed it was in a bear's nature not to want to shit in its own den. Still, he talked to the cub as if he were a human as they unlocked the set of double doors by the truck. "You just gonna carry that thing around everywhere?" He caught himself waiting for the cub to answer.

After Fuzzy took care of business – apparently bears did it in the woods *and* in parking lots – he fed the growing cub a couple of fish from the day before. While his pet scarfed down the fatty protein, he surveyed the parking lot. There was no sign of canids or anything else. If he knew how to hotwire a vehicle, he could claim a whole fleet for his people. There was a brand new Camaro in the lot that caught his eye. Red with the black dual stripes up the hood and over the top.

Taking the satiated bear back inside and locking the doors, he rejoined Helen in their little recliner sitting area. She'd set some snacks and water out on the coffee table. "Are you ready to try and clear this place?" She smiled at him.

"Nope. But we need to get it done. I didn't hear anything at all last night, did you?"

"Just you and Fuzzy snoring." She tilted her head back and fake-snored loudly. "I think if anything was living in here, you two would have drawn it to us."

Allistor craned his neck around a bookcase to get a look at the gate. "Nothing out there. Maybe we're good. Still, there could be something lurking in the back halls. These malls are full of those."

Finishing their meal, they began to gear up. Allistor was just lowering his shotgun strap over his shoulder when something struck him. He started laughing. "Oh, man."

Helen paused in tying her boots and looked up. "What's so funny?"

He shook his head. "Maybe nothing, hold on a second." He pulled up his interface and selected the Stronghold tab. There it was, the option to claim Frontier Mall as a Stronghold, with a green button ready to go.

"Looks like we can save ourselves the trouble. The system says I can claim this place right now. Which means it's clear. I just remembered the other night when I went to claim the ranger cabin as an Outpost, the system blocked me, saying there were other "occupants" already there. We found you, and a couple rats. I'm going to assume the system meant you."

"So if the system's ready to let you claim this place, we're the only ones here. Nice!" She held out a fist for him to bump. "But what about the missile bunker?"

Allistor nodded thoughtfully. "Yeah, I need to read some more, try to find out if there is anything stopping me from having two Strongholds in a city. Or within some particular geographic radius." He stopped talking and did some reading.

Helen began thinking out loud. "This place would make a good Stronghold, with all the stuff in here we can forage. And there's plenty of space. Maybe we don't need the bunkers."

Allistor stopped reading to answer. "Well, I do want the bunkers, and for more than one reason. I mean, how awesome would it be to have a secure underground facility with our own nuclear missiles! But also, if we don't claim them, how do we know some trigger-happy psychos won't claim the base and nuke us all?"

"And you're not a trigger-happy psycho?" She elbowed him in the ribs gently.

"Ha! Would I know if I was?" His attention shifted to a word that had appeared on his interface as he'd been reading. "One sec; I want to check something."

He shifted his focus from the *Stronghold* tab to one that read *Citadel*. In Allistor's mind, a Citadel was a small town encircled by a wall that included a few score or more shops, homes, a couple taverns, smithy, etc. If he could declare this huge mall a Citadel, then maybe he could also still claim the missile base as a Stronghold.

But when he tried to complete the transaction to claim the mall as a Citadel, a message appeared.

While this structure meets the size and available resource requirements for a Citadel, and your title of Baron entitles you to claim Citadels, you do not have the required population to staff and defend a Citadel at this location at this time.

He relayed this information to Helen, adding, "I think maybe we should go ahead and make this a Stronghold, and just assume that we can upgrade it later when we've found more survivors."

"And hope that you can also claim the missile base. I'm with ya. Let's do this." Helen moved to stand in front of the gate leading to the mall.

Allistor joined her, Fuzzy right next to him, still gripping the Fibble doll. Allistor pulled up the Stronghold interface and pushed the green button.

This time the golden light and chimes that surrounded them lasted much longer. When the light faded, Allistor blinked his eyes and looked around.

The first thing he noticed was that the pull-down gate in front of them had been replaced with double metal doors. The opening was smaller - only about eight feet wide now. Looking around, he noted that all the glass doors had similarly been replaced with swinging gates. All metal-framed drywall walls had become stone.

The fake acoustic ceiling tiles were gone, and the ceiling soared up twenty feet, with high window slits providing natural light to the former sales floor area. Exposed beams and ducts crossed the space above.

The three of them (four if you counted Fibble) walked back toward the stock room. All of the walls creating the small offices had been re-arranged, forming into a large sleeping quarter with its own bath, an attached study, and large kitchen area with two long dining tables. The stock room had been converted to a barracks, rows of stone beds with a chest at the foot of each one, and a large communal bathroom at the back. And the roll-up loading dock door had become a wide metal door that rolled to one side like a barn door.

Fuzzy sniffed around a bit, then lost interest. With a whip of his head, he tossed his green buddy up into the air, then proceeded to chase it, pouncing on the slobber-soaked thing like a kitten before rolling onto his back and dropping it on his belly. All four feet pawed slowly at the air as if he were half-heartedly fending off an attacker.

Chuckling, Helen said, "I can't tell if he thinks he's a dog or a cat. Never seen a bear behave like he does."

Allistor shrugged. "It might be something the system is doing. He seems to… understand what we say. At least on a basic level."

A little more exploration revealed that the two public restrooms off the main floor area had each become a full bath with shower and tub. The dressing rooms had combined into small guest quarters, one by the men's' and one by the ladies', each one attached to one of the bathrooms. The small stock room behind what had been the shoe department was now a conference room with a long table and chairs and a wet bar at one end.

They exited the area and moved out into the mall, Fuzzy and Fibble trotting alongside them. The main section of the mall had been two levels of shops along either side. About halfway down the main wing stood a burbling fountain with what had previously been fake greenery. Now there was lush grass in a ten-foot radius around the fountain, with several tropical ferns and small trees. Directly above, the extensive skylights had remained, allowing the sun to shine down upon the entire walkway.

Each of the old shops on either side of the main hall remained in roughly the same footprint. Glass storefronts had been reduced to smaller windows with shutters, and roll-up chain gates were now solid-looking wooden doors. The shops on the upper promenade had changed more significantly. Now there were two rows of what looked like residential units – single windows and single doors spaced evenly apart approximately every forty feet.

The food court had been turned into a wide open-air dining hall with a commercial kitchen behind it. They looked as if they could serve a small army. As they walked, they found one of the bigger anchor stores had been converted to a two-story crafting hall, and another appeared to be a tavern with sleeping rooms upstairs. The movie theater had remained as it was, hundreds of seats facing a stage with a huge screen.

The largest of the big box stores, located at the other end of the main wing, had become a warehouse, and upon entering they found row after row of large boxes and crates along the left side. The remainder of the space was filled with high shelves stacked to the ceiling with all of the merchandise from the repurposed stores. They even appeared to have been neatly organized by the System – clothes arranged from undergarments to cold weather coats, electronics and components, household goods like pots and pans, even novelty items from a gift store for adults.

Fuzzy's nose led him directly to some shelves filled with gift basket items like summer sausages and fancy cheeses, vacuum-wrapped to preserve them. Allistor and

Helen snagged several of these each, Helen taking pity on the bear cub and opening a turkey sausage for him. The bear promptly forsook his little green buddy, dropping him to the floor to be ignored while he noisily consumed the treat. Allistor also grabbed a couple boxes of fancy chocolates, intending to give one to Amanda, the other to Chloe. Helen helped herself to a large jar of macadamia nuts.

When they had finished a complete circuit of the new Stronghold, they returned to the fountain and sat on its wall. Allistor had grown quiet as they walked, and Helen simply waited for him to share what was on his mind.

Eventually, he said, "We need people. I mean, good people that we can trust to keep this place safe. I'm thinking maybe we should split up the band back at the Warren, put a few of our original group here, and at other Strongholds. Maybe bring Luther here, or send him back to his original Stronghold. But what we really need is to find more survivors."

"Ones that aren't trigger-happy psychos?" Helen smirked at him.

"Hah! Yes, that would be ideal." He looked at her, one eyebrow raised. "How'd you like to run this place? I mean, the mall was your idea, to begin with. It never would have occurred to me to pick this place. I'd have gone with the police station or city hall or something."

She thought about it for a while. "I'd prefer to go back and man the ranger cabin outpost. But if you need me here for a while, I'm okay with that. As long as we find enough people to at least partially fill this place. I'd be creeped out here all alone."

"Well, let's grab the truck and head out to explore the city. Maybe we can find survivors here? I mean, there had to have been something like fifty thousand people living here, right?"

"A little more, I think. But yes, we should be able to find somebody, I think. Unless they all locked themselves down in the bunkers." Helen pointed in the general direction of the missile base.

They exited the mall, finding the wall outside had encompassed the entire land area belonging to the mall. That included the parking lot, stormwater pond, and the grassy areas scattered about the edges. The space was huge! The walls were twenty feet high, with ramps on the back side every few hundred feet. The two massive metal doors that were the only exit Allistor could see swung open as he watched.

Back in the truck, Allistor was driving this time. Helen was literally riding shotgun in the passenger seat, her weapon in her lap as they exited the gate and she scanned their surroundings for threats or signs of life. Fuzzy snored in the back seat, his snout resting atop the green doll between his paws.

Allistor was cruising through the airport, the closest major landmark to the mall. His reasoning being that if he were a survivor here, he'd want a location with a view of the area. The control tower at the airport would show them the entire city. There were no skyscrapers in the city – the tallest buildings being about ten stories high. Most of downtown was low to the ground, the whole city seeming to hunker down against the threat of harsh winter weather that came every year.

A quick stop at the tower turned out to pay off nicely. They spotted movement in two different areas of town. To the south, there was a group of people moving through a neighborhood foraging. They had a horse-drawn wagon that was just beginning to be filled. "Smart," Allistor commented. "Horses make much less noise than engines, and they don't need gas. I should have thought of that."

Helen just nodded, using a pair of binoculars she'd grabbed from one of the controllers' stations to scan the city. She focused in on a faint pillar of smoke. "Looks like a cooking fire over there." She pointed, and Allistor followed, raising his own binoculars that he'd snagged from the gun shop.

Sure enough, there was a trail of smoke so faint he probably would have missed it. It was rising from a warehouse district to the southwest of them. Other buildings blocked their view of the street, and he didn't see any movement atop any of the roofs. "How'd you spot that?"

She lowered her glasses and smirked. "Park ranger, remember? I've spent hundreds of hours atop observation towers looking for fires."

"Oh, right." Allistor blushed slightly, feeling foolish. "So which place do you want to go first?"

Helen didn't even think about it. "The foragers. If it were me, I'd much rather have a trigger-happy psycho and his sexy sidekick approach me while I'm out moving around and alert, than have him approach my home base."

Allistor snorted. "I wouldn't exactly call Fuzzy sexy..." He ducked as she swatted at his head. "But I agree about the foragers. Let's head their way. Make plenty of noise when we get close, so as not to surprise them. Maybe keep the ferocious bear out of sight at first."

Back in the truck, they wound their way through the mostly clear city streets toward the neighborhood where the foragers were operating. When Helen said they were within a few blocks, Allistor gave the truck's horn a friendly double-toot to alert the nearby survivors of their presence. He drove slowly, turning a corner to find the horse and cart about halfway down the block in front of them. None of the people they'd seen before were in sight.

Allistor stopped the truck and turned off the engine. Dropping the keys into his ring, he exited the vehicle. His shotgun slung on his back, he held his hands high and motioned for Helen to do the same. Stepping forward so that he could be clearly seen, he called out. "Hey, guys! I'm Allistor, and this is Helen. We come in peace, and uhh... take me to your leader?"

Helen snorted at the awkward greeting. "My hero."

"You some kind of wise-ass, boy?" A deep voice echoed out from behind a building to their left. Both heads turned in that direction. A large man in a flannel shirt stepped out, rifle raised to his shoulder and pointed at Allistor.

Allistor kept his hands up, his pulse racing now as he had second thoughts about approaching these people. "No, sir! I was just trying to be friendly. If it were me, I'd be suspicious of anyone who approached me like this. Just trying to lighten the mood a bit."

The man stared at him over the rifle's sights, not saying a word. Allistor's mind noted there was no scope mounted on the weapon. Likely the man was either a very good shot or didn't know much about rifles. "As I said, I'm Allistor. What's your name?"

After a moment of glaring, the man said, "Dean." His thick beard barely moved as he spoke.

Allistor waited several seconds for him to say more, but it seemed that was all the information forthcoming. Helen actually chuckled at Allistor's discomfort.

"Nice to meet you, Dean," she called out. "I'm Helen. Park ranger up at Medicine Bow. Allistor here found me and saved my life a few days ago. He's a good guy."

Dean's rifle barrel lowered slightly as he stood straighter. He looked from Helen to Allistor. "What do you want here?"

Allistor lowered his hands slightly, then the rest of the way when he received a nod from Dean. "I'm looking for you, actually. I mean, not you specifically, but survivors. I just established a Stronghold nearby. A safe place to sleep, eat, and live. Now I'm looking for survivors to fill it."

Dean looked at him like he was drunk or slightly stupid. "What? A stronghold?"

Allistor sighed. "How much do you all know about the way the world works now?"

At this, Dean's head jerked to the left and his gaze went to someone across the street that Allistor couldn't see.

A moment later another voice rang out, this one female. "We know enough to get by! Been doing just fine so far." She sounded young, and a little defensive.

"Alright, great! The more you know, the easier life will be over this coming year. My group and I have learned a great deal these last few weeks. I'd be happy to share what we've learned, if you're willing to sit and talk for a while?"

Just then, Fuzzy woke up and moved around in the back seat of the truck. Dean's rifle shot back up and his finger moved to the trigger. "Who else is here with you?" he growled, instantly suspicious.

"Nobody! I mean, no other person. That's Fuzzy. My bear." Allistor winced at how stupid that sounded when he said it out loud. "My companion. That's part of what I can share with you."

"He's adorable!" the female voice was clearer as she stepped out from behind a house. She was short, maybe 5'3" with long blonde hair and large brown eyes. Allistor guessed she was in her late teens. "You said his name is Fuzzy?"

"Annie! I told you to stay behind cover!" Dean shouted without taking the gun's sights off Allistor's chest.

"Sorry, Dean. But I don't think they mean us any harm. They didn't exactly try to sneak up on us." The girl began to walk forward. She held a Glock in her right hand, but it was pointed at the ground as she walked. "In case you didn't hear, my name is Annie. Is it safe to approach Fuzzy?"

Helen nodded at her. "You run the risk of getting drooled on. And I wouldn't try and take the green doll from him. He's very attached to it." She stepped back to the truck slowly, opening the door so Fuzzy could hop out. The bear instantly trotted forward to sniff at the new human.

"Oh, look at him! I want to hug him!" She cried as she bent to let him sniff her hand. Which he did, sitting on his rump and looking up at her expectantly.

Helen said, "Here, give him this," and tossed a piece of snake meat to the girl, who deftly caught it with one hand. She then held it out on the flat of her palm, and Fuzzy gently took it from her.

"Oh, I need one of these!" She giggled as the bear cub scarfed down the meat, making his usual *nom, nom* growly noises.

Dean lowered his weapon again and stepped forward. "Annie, bears are wild animals. Sure, he's real cute right now. But if he gets hungry enough, those claws could take your face off."

Allistor nodded. "He's right, Annie. Fuzzy here is special. He's my companion, and he won't bite you unless I ask him to. Maybe not even then." He grinned down at the cub. "But you shouldn't approach any animal these days. There are some nasty things out here now. I'm sure you've seen some of them?"

Annie's face grew solemn. "Too many. We keep losing people when we come out here to find food and stuff. And once when a monster spawned inside the locker room."

Allistor's eyes perked up. "Spawned. You're a gamer?"

Annie's smile returned, if not as bright as before. "Yup! And I know this whole place seems to work like a VR game now."

"Great! So maybe what I have to tell you won't be so hard to believe. Listen. We spotted you guys from up on the airport tower. There's also a fire going near a warehouse over that way." He pointed in the appropriate direction. "Is that another group? Or is that your home base?"

Dean shook his head. "That's not us. There is another group out there. We've heard gunshots once in a while. But we've kept to ourselves so far. No way to know if they're friendly."

"I hear ya." Allistor understood completely. "I've been exploring for the last few weeks. Run across two other groups, besides Helen here. The first was a good group of people trapped in their own Stronghold by a group of asshat murderers. Most of the asshats are dead now." He looked directly into Dean's eyes as he spoke. "The others have joined me at my Stronghold north of here."

Dean nodded his head. "Glad to hear there are other groups out there. That damned message on the first day said they were going to exterminate us."

Allistor sighed. "They're doing a pretty good job. Sent this giant void titan thing to my town and wiped it out. Killed most of us and stomped everything flat before we managed to kill it. Out of the whole town, there are less than a dozen of us left that we know of."

There was a long stretch of silence as folks remembered their losses.

Finally, Allistor broke the silence. "I don't want to keep you guys from finding what you need here today. If you're short on food, Helen and I have some we can share. How many of you are there, by the way?"

Dean looked suspicious, but Annie answered. "Nine of us, now. There were almost twenty when it started."

Helen patted the young girl on the shoulder. "We've got more than enough food for nine. If Fuzzy doesn't eat it all himself first." This brought a slight smile to Annie's face. But when Helen added, "That is, if you don't mind grilling up some giant snake meat." Annie's smiled disappeared.

"Ew! Snake meat?"

Dean chuckled, lowering his weapon the rest of the way and relaxing. "Snake meat is tasty! You'll like it, you'll see."

Allistor said, "If you guys want to keep foraging, Helen and I will go see this other group. If they're friendly as well, maybe we can all gather this evening for a meal, and I'll share what I know."

Dean nodded. "Be careful. Where do you want to meet up?"

Allistor considered for a few seconds. He didn't want to invite them to the mall yet. But he didn't want to push himself into their home, either.

"You tell me. Is there a place large enough for us to gather that also has a grill or a working kitchen that we can use? Someplace nearby, to reduce the risk of running into monsters?"

Dean replied "There's a rib joint not far from where we're staying. It has two big wood-burning grills out back. Good place to cook snake meat. Lots of tables and chairs."

"Perfect! We'll go see the other group and bring them there if they seem alright. Let's say... 1:00?" He waited for Dean to nod. The others from his group, two more men and a woman, appeared from their various hiding places. Everyone was introduced, and Dean gave them a location for the meetup. Annie gave Fuzzy's ears a final scratch, and the two groups parted ways.

Back in the truck, Helen navigated while Allistor drove them in the direction of the smoke they'd seen. It didn't take long, even at slow speeds, to reach the warehouses. A quick search as they drove down one side street revealed one structure with three trucks parked near the door, and the broken windows boarded up from the inside. Once again, Allistor gave a quick double-honk of the horn, and they waited for some kind of response.

Two full minutes passed before a voice called down from above. "Who are you? What do you want?"

Allistor stuck his head out the window and looked up, finding three men on the roof with handguns pointed at him. He called back, "Name's Allistor. I'm a survivor like you. I'm looking for others to join with us. We have a safe place nearby, and plenty of food."

"We're safe enough here. But I like your truck. Why don't you just get out and walk away. We promise not to shoot if you do as you're told." The same voice echoed off the surrounding buildings. It was coming from the man on the far left. A small, thin man with spiked hair bleached white as snow. He shifted from one foot to the other constantly as Allistor observed him. Almost as if he needed to take a leak.

"I don't think so… I'm sorry, I didn't catch your name."

"Everybody calls me Twitch. You can call me *Mister* Twitch. This is my block, and visitors passing through have to pay a toll. Now, get out of the truck and walk away. You can take your dog with you." He motioned toward Fuzzy, who was curled up in the back seat.

"Listen, Twitch… there's no need to be hostile. I'm trying to be your friend, here. You don't need this truck, you've got three right there. And there are hundreds more around to choose from. Besides, I like this truck. How 'bout we all relax and talk a bit. We can go together and get you a nice Escalade or something later."

One of the other men laughed out loud. "Twitch in an Escalade? That's like havin' a solid gold litterbox. Looks purty and has nothin' but shit inside."

The two men who were not Twitch laughed briefly, then quieted down quickly when they noticed he didn't join them. Sucking air through his teeth, he said, "Shut the hell up, Vern. Or the next time one of them dog-things latches on to you, I'll just watch it chow down."

Allistor tried again. "Listen, guys. How 'bout you come down and talk to us? We found another group nearby already this morning, and they're willing to meet us for lunch. My treat."

All three men were thin, with sunken cheeks that suggested they weren't eating enough. Allistor hoped the temptation of food would be enough to lure them down. Though at this point he was sure he didn't want them among his people. He waited while they mumbled amongst themselves.

Then Twitched called down. "You have that much food? Then you can spare some! Leave the food in the truck and get walking!" He fired a shot in the air for emphasis.

"Trigger-happy psychos," Helen hissed as she gripped the door hard enough to turn her knuckles white. "Let's get out of here before they shoot one of us!"

Allistor had a similar sentiment in his own mind. But also anger at these idiots who were turning down a better life. "Look, Twitch. There are so few of us left. We need to get stronger to prepare for the aliens, not rob and kill each other!"

"Aliens? What aliens. You're so full of crap, dude. There's no such thing as aliens!" The other two men backed away from Twitch as he was waving his gun around wildly. "Get your ass out of that truck and get off my block!" This time he fired a round into the street near one of the tires.

Allistor had seen enough. He cast *Flame Shot* at Twitch, a fireball flying upward to strike the man's chest.

The moment the spell was away, he gunned the engine and the truck shot forward. He knew from experience that every foot of distance from the shooters made it less likely they'd hit him, Helen or Fuzzy. Or a vital part of the truck.

A few bullets plinked off the roof as the engine roared and the truck sped away. He went straight for a block, then turned sharply down an alley. Stomping the brake pedal, he brought the truck to a halt out of sight of the men on the roof. Grabbing his rifle from his ring, he hopped out of the truck and ran back to the corner.

The firing had stopped as soon as the men on the roof lost sight of the truck. But they were still up there. Allistor couldn't see Twitch, but he must have been laying down on the roof, because the other two men were standing with their backs to Allistor and looking down. One opened a can of beer and poured it on his friend. Allistor and Helen could hear Twitch screaming.

"I'll understand if you don't want to shoot these guys," he said to Helen as he raised his rifle and put an eye to the scope. It wasn't a long shot, only a block, but he wanted to be sure of a kill.

Helen's response was barely a whisper. "No, I don't. But I will. They tried to kill us and would have taken everything we had. We can't leave them to kill us or someone else later. When an animal becomes rabid, you put it down."

She took a knee next to him, raising her rifle with the ease and smooth movements of an expert. Taking aim, she said, "I've got the one on my right. You take the other one."

Allistor put the red dot in his scope dead center of the left guy's head. "Three... two... one." They fired nearly in unison. Allistor's target went down with a spray of red mist as his brains exited the other side of his skull at a high velocity. Helen had gone for a safer target, drilling a hole through her man's chest. Both dropped out of sight as Twitch continued to scream, and experience points flashed across Allistor and Helen's interfaces.

"We need to get up there and finish Twitch." Allistor was conflicted even as he said it. They had no way to know who else was inside the building. And an injured but still living Twitch might be very dangerous to confront.

The two of them left the cover of the corner and jogged toward the warehouse door. Seeing that it opened inward, Allistor didn't wait to see if it was unlocked. He simply lowered his shoulder and smashed into it. The door proved to be no match for his improved strength and momentum. It burst open, swinging inward to slam against the wall behind it and bounce back at Allistor. He ignored it as he swept the room with his eyes, his weapon following shortly behind. The place was mostly empty. There were three mattresses set in different corners of the large room, each with a crate next to it. Empty beer bottles and trash littered the floor. Near the center of the room were three chairs set around a steel drum with a metal grill set on top.

Helen entered a few seconds later, making her own scan of the place. Fuzzy was right behind her, his nose twitching. Both of them quickly wrinkled their noses in disgust. "Quite the bachelor pad," Helen whispered. Her hands were shaking as they held her rifle, and sweat beaded on her forehead. Allistor couldn't tell whether she was frightened, or sick over having killed someone.

373

Without a word, he led the way up the rickety wooden stairs at the back of the warehouse. Both of them winced with every creak and groan of the wood as they climbed. They stopped at a second-floor office, which they quickly checked then ignored as they continued up the next flight to the top landing. Here was the door to the roof.

Knowing this one would be unlocked, Allistor motioned for Helen to stand to one side and open it. He backed up to the top step and crouched down, switching from his rifle to his shotgun. Raising the weapon toward the door, he nodded to Helen. She slowly turned the knob, trying to be quiet. When she felt the bolt disengage, she flung the door open, stepping to the side for cover.

Again the door flew open, then bounced back. Allistor got only a brief look outside before it slammed shut again. Helen's eyes grew wide and despite her fear, she giggled. Slamming her hands over her mouth, she shook her head, apologizing with her eyes. Allistor just shook his own head and stood up.

Not having seen anything in his brief view of the roof, he stepped forward and opened the door. Pushing it more gently, he stepped outside with shotgun at the ready. He made it two steps onto the roof when shots rang out. One struck the door behind him, the other ripped through the meat of his shoulder, tearing the deltoid muscles. He fired the shotgun out of reflex, not aiming or hitting anything as he fell to the ground. The weapon left his hands, and his left hand instinctively clamped on to the wound on his right shoulder.

Twitch screamed, "I'll kill you!" and fired again, the bullet digging into the roof material inches from

Allistor's face. Allistor cast *Restraint* on him, but it only slowed him for a second. The man was a mess. His clothes and skin were charred from the center of his chest upward. His hair was mostly burned away, and one of his eyes was swollen shut.

Allistor cast *Barrier* between himself and Twitch, hoping it would absorb enough of the next shot to keep him alive. Then he cast *Mind Spike*, making the man scream in pain and grip his head for a moment. Saliva dripped from his open mouth as he recovered from the mind spike and glared at Allistor with pure hatred.

Twitch was shakily bringing the gun to bear on Allistor's head when a shot from Helen's rifle rang out. In her rush to raise her weapon, she'd fired early. The shot ripped through Twitch's gut, knocking him on his back. He screamed again in pain, rolling onto his stomach.

Allistor, still on the ground, grunted, "Finish him."

Helen took one horrified look at Twitch, then shook her head and looked down at her feet. "I can't. He's... he's helpless."

Allistor nodded. Forcing himself to his feet, he walked over to Twitch. Unable to use his right arm, he pulled his pistol from its holster with his left. Not used to holding a gun in that hand, he leaned down to put it close to Twitch's head and pulled the trigger.

Feeling sick himself, he took a few deep breaths as he first holstered his weapon, then cast a heal on himself. When the bleeding had stopped and he felt steadier, he bent down and touched Twitch's corpse to loot it. Not even looking at what he received, he motioned for Helen to do the same. When she refused, he took her hand.

"You need to do this. I know it seems creepy. But there may come a time when what you loot from a body is the thing that saves your life." He pointed at the corpse, which was thankfully still face-down. "He asked for this. We came here to offer friendship, and he made it life or death. You've done nothing wrong here. He would have killed me if you hadn't fired."

She nodded, biting her upper lip. Reaching down, she looted Twitch. Then Allistor indicated she should loot the other man she shot as he looted his target. They did so in silence, then headed back downstairs. Fuzzy was waiting outside, not wanting to remain in the smelly warehouse. Allistor cast another heal on himself, then asked Helen to take Fuzzy back to the truck while he quickly searched the main room for guns or other useful items. The three men had only had handguns. In a city where half the residents probably had long guns in their homes, this spoke of the men's laziness. Or that they preferred to steal rather than hunt.

Back in the truck, they spent some time cruising the streets of the city to decompress. Allistor put the windows down and spoke softly to Helen about their upcoming lunch with the other survivors. She was mostly silent in the seat next to him, gripping the door handle tightly with one hand and her rifle with the other. Eventually, her monotone single-syllable answers became short sentences. As his words calmed her down, she even turned to meet his gaze.

"I'm sorry, Allistor. I just… I never in my life thought I'd kill someone. I mean, as a ranger there was

376

always a remote possibility that a drunken camper with a gun might get out of hand. Or a fugitive would take to the woods. But in those situations, we would usually have backup, and be thinking arrest, not kill."

"The fact that it bothers you is a good sign, Helen. Along with the fact that you pulled the trigger when you needed to. So you can take care of business, protect yourself and others, without being a trigger-happy psycho!" He grinned as he spoke.

This actually earned a small smile from her. "Thanks for that."

They spent another couple hours cruising the city. Every once in a while, Allistor honked the horn to see if anyone would respond. They drove back out to the missile base and Helen tried cycling through the radio channels again, to no avail. If there was anyone inside, they weren't responding.

On the way back toward their lunch meeting, Helen suddenly pointed and whispered loudly "There! Something just moved behind that car! I think it was a kid?" Fuzzy growled, his nose in the air.

Allistor followed her pointed finger and slowed to a stop. They watched the car on her side of the street for a few seconds before he suggested, "Call out to them."

"Hey there! My name's Helen. Don't worry, we won't hurt you."

A small head popped up to look through the car windows at them. The glass was too dusty for Allistor to see more than a vague outline. After a few seconds, it disappeared just as quickly.

Helen got out of the truck, leaving her weapon inside. "It's okay. We're here to help you. Are you injured? Hungry? We've got food."

She walked slowly toward the car, hands out in front of her patting the air as if calming a fight. "I'm not going to hurt you, little one," she said as she rounded the back bumper of the vehicle.

Something shot forward and leapt up at her face. Her hands, already in front of her, managed to grab hold of it as she flinched backward. The action saved her as two bony arms reached for her face, tiny claws extended and swiping within inches of her nose.

"Aaargh!" She screamed and spun around, tossing the thing away from her and causing it to slam into a nearby wall. Helen fled back to the truck even as Allistor was getting out. The thing, whatever it was, let out a high-pitched screech as it got up from the sidewalk and shook its head. About three feet tall, it had long bony arms and legs, with a head that looked too big for its body. The mouth was full of sharp, serrated teeth. A moment later it was speeding after Helen.

Allistor ran toward the front of the truck, trying to get an angle across the hood for a clear shot behind Helen as she ran. The thing was gaining ground, though, and he wasn't going to get it. So he cast *Restraint* on the creature just as it was about to leap atop her back.

It managed to begin the leap before the spell took hold. So the creature's stunned body left the ground and traveled about three feet before losing momentum and crashing back down to earth. The delay allowed Helen to make it back to the truck, and it gave Allistor a clear shot.

He fired his shotgun, punching a hole in the creature's chest and blasting off one of its arms.

Urban Creeper
Level 6
Health 0/3,000

The blast pushed the dead creeper's corpse backward as if it had been punted. When it came to rest, two more of the things emerged from nowhere and attacked the body, ripping into it with sharp little teeth and tearing off pieces with sharp claws.

Allistor cast *Flame Shot* at the corpse, the ball of flame engulfing the two others before they could react. The impact knocked all three back against the wall as it engulfed them. As the two still-living writhed in pain on the ground, he stepped forward and drew his sword. A quick chop severed the head of the nearest creeper. His first swing at the other one was off and simply sliced into its head. A quick second swing hit the target, severing its neck. Small amounts of xp flashed across his interface as he put the sword back in its sheath. When he bent to loot the creatures, another dropped onto his back from above. Its teeth sank into his shoulder as all four legs began to shred at his back. He straightened up, shouting in surprise as he attempted to reach over his shoulder with his left hand and pull it off of him.

The creature let loose of his shoulder and grabbed hold of his hand, teeth sinking deeply into his wrist. He yanked his hand forward, slamming the thing into the wall. It didn't seem to notice as it ripped a chunk of his flesh free. Blood sprayed from the wound. His health bar dropped by ten percent, and a bleed debuff icon appeared, blinking at him as if he didn't notice the blood pumping from a savaged vein.

Allistor slammed the thing down onto the sidewalk and stomped on it, holding it down with his foot on its chest. It thrashed and slashed at his boot as he increased the weight. As he clamped down on his bleeding wrist with his free hand, the weight of his body finally cracked the little monster's chest, and it expired.

Helen was right there, wrapping a bandage tightly around his wrist to slow the bleeding even as he cast a heal on himself. "What friggin' hole from hell did these things crawl out of?" she asked as her eyes darted around, looking for more of the nasty little things.

Allistor cast another heal on himself as he too searched the shadows. An ominous clicking reached them, sounding like many clawed feet on concrete. It was coming from just around the corner of the shop they stood in front of.

"Back in the truck! Use the shotgun where you can!" he shouted at Helen as he stepped away from the building and into the street. He placed himself in an open area where Helen would have a clear view of him. She obeyed after a moment of hesitation.

Allistor cast *Flame Shot* again, this time channeling the spell as the ball rotated just above his hand, growing larger by the second. He watched the corner, ready to hurl the spell forward.

The first group of three creepers rounded the corner, moving fast. One lost traction, skidding across the concrete to slam into a mailbox before righting itself. Allistor waited two more seconds, then he hurled the spell at the sidewalk right by the corner of the building.

As the spell flew the maybe thirty yards to its target, close to a dozen more of the creatures appeared. They rounded the corner just in time to be engulfed by the flames. Scattered like bowling pins, the creepers screeched and writhed in pain.

The first three had escaped the flames as the fireball flew over their heads. They continued their dash toward him, two moving together and the mailbox smasher a second or two behind them. Allistor drew his sword and crouched into what he considered a cool-looking ready stance. One his game avatars had adopted a thousand times.

Unfortunately, his skill with a sword didn't match that of his avatars. He took a swing as the first two leapt at him. His timing was good, but he turned the blade mid-swing so that when he connected with the creeper mid-air, instead of slicing through its body, it was knocked backward by the flat of the blade. Luckily, his blunt weapon skill kicked in and did some damage.

The creeper's partner latched onto his sword arm and scampered up toward his face with unbelievable speed, leaving tiny bloody scratches and gouges in his skin as it went. Distracted by the imminent face-eating, he didn't see the third creeper leap at him. That is until a shotgun blast and the subsequent explosion of the tiny menace in midair about two feet from his face caught his attention.

Dropping his sword, he grabbed the creeper on his shoulder by the neck. Pulling it off him, he used his free hand to grab a leg and stretch the creature out. He lifted a knee and with both hands slammed the outstretched and struggling creature down across it. The creeper's spine snapped, and it quit moving.

Another shotgun blast rang out, and Allistor turned to look at Helen. She was firing toward the corner where the burned monsters were starting to regain their feet. The creeper he'd battered with the sword was back in action as well, clawing its way up his leg.

Retrieving his sword, he stabbed the little beast in the face, widening its mouth with his blade. When it let go and fell, he whipped his sword forward, flinging the thing into its comrades as it flew off the blade. The desperate move knocked down two others as the rest moved toward him.

Another blast knocked two of the creatures across the pavement as body parts and blood flew in multiple directions. Allistor backed up, waving his sword to keep them at bay while he tried to think. At least six of the little bastards were still coming at him. Worse, they were spreading out to surround him. A single *Flame Shot* wouldn't even get half of them.

Still, he cast it. Dealing with three was better than six. This time he cast it as a pillar of fire crashing down from above to engulf three of the already-burned creatures. He heard another shot and one of the creatures moving to his right disappeared.

A moment later, a fierce growl behind him caused him to spin around. Fuzzy was there, his bear cub jaws clamping down on the neck and shoulder of one of the creatures. As soon as he had a grip, he shook the little thing violently, its legs and arms whipping about like wet noodles. When he was done, he used a forepaw to pin its legs, then lifted his head and ripped the thing in two.

"Right on, buddy!" Allistor shouted as he turned back to face the remaining monsters. The three that had been burned twice were still alive, but not moving other than the occasional twitch of pain. One of the others was moving toward him, and it leapt up to grab hold of his sword arm. Once again, dozens of tiny teeth and claws sunk into him. They penetrated his shirt with seeming ease, blood welling up from the small wounds.

Fuzzy was there again, standing on his hind legs and snatching the creature's torso between his jaws. Letting his weight drop him back to all fours, he pulled the thing free from his human and crunched on it even as another of them jumped on his furry back.

"I got you!" Rage filled Allistor as he grabbed the creeper that was hurting his pet by the neck. Using all the strength he had, he simply squeezed his fist tight, until a popping sound could be heard. It went limp, and he threw it into the burning pile of its friends.

Seeing that Fuzzy had dispatched his second mob, Allistor spun around, frantically searching for more of the creepers. He heard Helen call out, "I think we're clear."

Casting a heal on Fuzzy first, then himself, he stepped over and sat on the front bumper of the truck. "It's official. I hate those things."

"They looked like little albino Gollums, only meaner," Helen agreed.

The fight finished, the two of them went and looted the bodies. Fuzzy moved to a small patch of yard and began eating grass, presumably to get the taste of creeper out of his mouth. Allistor tossed him a piece of snake meat. "You more than earned that, buddy. Saved my butt!"

When everyone was finished and loaded back into the truck, they found their way to the rib joint where the meeting with Dean's group was set. As they pulled up in front, Annie burst out of a gate to the side of the building. "Where's Fuzzy? I have something for him!"

Allistor opened the back door of the truck, and Fuzzy hopped down, green doll once again gripped in his jaws. Annie crouched down in front of him and threw a leather loop over his head. As she tightened it slightly, Allistor could see several shiny stones and some glitter attached to it. His cub had just been blinged.

For his part, Fuzzy strutted around like he was a supermodel, showing off his new attire. Helen snorted, then when the bear turned toward her looking hurt, said, "You look fabulous, Fuzzster!"

Annie led them all through the gate to an outdoor dining area enclosed with a low picket fence. Smoke was already drifting around the corner from the grill in the back. Allistor excused himself as Annie scratched the bear's belly, to go deliver some snake meat to the grill.

He found Dean back there, wearing a full chef's apron and hat. He was mixing some kind of sauce in a deep stainless bowl with a whisk. "Ah, good! You have that snake meat?"

Allistor removed twenty pieces of the meat from his bag and handed them over to Dean. The man began to spread them out in large flat trays, then pour some of the sauce over the top of each. "Give me a hand, rub this in. Then flip them and do it again." He motioned for Allistor to take a position next to him. He quickly ground some salt and pepper over each piece then nodded for Allistor to work the sauce into the meat. "The secret to a good snakebecue is having the grill at just the right temp. Too hot and the edges char. Not hot enough, and the meat turns rubbery. The sauce helps with that, some.

Allistor's drool reflex kicked in. The sauce smelled wonderful, and he had to resist licking his fingers after each snake meat massaged. The minute he was finished he licked every finger he had, and his thumbs too. Dean laughed. "The base ingredients for that are a little bit of beer and bacon."

"It's damn tasty. Family recipe?"

"Yup. My pop taught me, his pop taught him…"

"I take it you've picked up the *Cooking* skill, then?

"Yup again. On the first day. Been cooking for the group as often as I can to raise the level. Annie told me about levels. Tell you what, stand here a bit, help me place these on the grill and tend to 'em, and you might get the skill yourself since you killed this snake. I figured out a while back that the skill levels faster if you're using meat that you've killed, or ingredients that you've gathered yourself, rather than prepackaged food or bottled spices."

"Awesome. And that's great information. I'll pass that along to Meg and Sam, and the others who craft using gathered resources."

As they finished preparing the pieces of meat, Allistor observed the man next to him. He was in his thirties, dark hair with a full beard. Allistor was about to ask him about his attributes when the man spoke. "I gotta ask. I'm looking at these chunks of meat... just how big was this snake?"

Allistor chuckled. "In all, it was about sixty feet long, I'd guess. We didn't stretch it out and measure it. And the system described it as an *infant*! I don't even want to meet its mom. Baby snake nearly killed us both."

Dean just shook his head as he continued to prepare the meat. A few minutes later it was all on the giant wood-burning grill. The smoke smelled sweet and... well, woodsy. Allistor inhaled deeply, enjoying the aroma. He wasn't thrilled about eating the snake meat, but Dean had sworn he could make it taste delicious. There were fresh vegetables grilling on a smaller side grill, and someone had brought freshly baked bread. Checking on the veggies, Dean cursed softly. "Where's the damn butter. I know we brought butter for these... Woman! Where's the butter?"

The loud call startled Allistor, who was flipping a hunk of snake meat and nearly dropped it through the grill into the flames. He turned as 'Woman' approached. An elfish woman approximately the same age as Dean, she had a lovely face and long dark hair. She wore a black T-shirt sporting a white unicorn with a pink mane and rainbow sparkles.

She placed a hand on Dean's back and reached around in front of him to the little grill's side table. "It's right here, mister grumpy." She lifted a hunk of tin foil, wrapped inside of which were two sticks of butter.

"You've saved the day!" Dean exclaimed as he gathered her in for a kiss. "Woman, this is Allistor."

Allistor shook her hand, a slightly confused look on his face. She laughed when she noticed. "My name is Sarah. Dean likes to pretend he's a caveman, calls me Woman and grumps about, growling at people. But he's really just a big softie." She gave his butt a squeeze and kissed his cheek. "Nice to meet you, Allistor."

"And you." Allistor smiled at her. He instantly liked the pair. "Your caveman is teaching me to cook snake. Something I didn't expect to ever learn."

Sarah looked down, her face falling. "We've all had to learn a lot of new things since the Apocalypse." She paused for a moment, lost in her own memories. Then she raised her head and smiled. "Annie tells me you're going to teach all of us a few new things."

Allistor nodded. "Yeah, things have gotten rough. But I'm hoping by working together and sharing information, we can not only survive this first year but thrive."

"I hope you're right! I'll leave you two man-children to play with the fire and burn our food. See you both in a few."

Dean grumbled under his breath. "Burn the food. As if. I'm an artist!" He grumpily flipped a few of the snake steaks. Allistor grinned to himself and did the same.

When the food was prepared and the two men delivered it all to the tables, there was a quick round of introductions. Helen had apparently already met everyone. Allistor was never good with names, and he promptly forgot them as each new person shook his hand. They shared a nice meal, folks enjoying the food and each other's company. Initially, Dean had posted a couple guards to watch for monsters, but Helen had assured him that Fuzzy's nose was a better sentry than any human, so the two men took seats and ate with everyone else. Still, everyone had a weapon handy, just in case.

When the meal was done, they rearranged the chairs in a circle, and Allistor spoke to them about the System and the game-like mechanics that ruled their world now. He covered the attributes and the list of skills that they'd discovered over the past weeks. A few of the new group chimed in with new skills that they'd learned. One had learned *Engineering,* another got *Carpentry,* and two of them had earned *Edged Weapons.* All of them knew how to fire weapons, but apparently using Earth guns didn't grant a skill within the System.

Then he switched to Strongholds and Outposts. This was where he needed to ask the big question. When he'd explained how territory was claimed and the resources needed for the different sized structures, he paused and took a deep breath.

"Which brings me to the reason I'm here talking to you. I've managed, mostly by accident, to achieve a noble title. I'm a Baron now, with ownership of nearly three million acres of land here in Wyoming and Colorado. With that title comes the ability to establish multiple Outposts, Strongholds, and even Citadels." He got to his feet and began to pace as he collected his thoughts and let them absorb what he'd said.

"Helen and I are exploring the area, with plans to establish our claim over as much territory as possible before our one-year Stabilization period is over. Because when it is, the aliens from all the other worlds in this Collective will descend upon us. So far, they've treated us like less than nothing. Vermin to be exterminated from this world so they can make it their own. If we're weak and without resources when they arrive, my guess is we'll be little more than slaves to them. Or maybe just another food supply like cattle. I can claim half of the US in a year, driving from place to place. But I could never hold it. The only way I see us being strong enough to stand up for ourselves is if we work together."

Again he paused to watch them take that in. When he saw most of the heads nodding along, he continued.

"This morning Helen and I established a Stronghold here in Cheyenne. The entire Frontier Mall is now a walled fortress. There's power, water, and living space for a hundred or more people. I am here today to extend to all of you an invitation to join me. To offer you a safe place to live, protection from the aliens – both the monsters that are here already, and the ones to come when our year is up – and the benefit of whatever knowledge and resources we accumulate as a group. Now, this does require an oath of loyalty to me. In order to remain among us, you'll have to follow our rules and laws, which right now are the same as they've always been here. Don't kill people except in self-defense, don't steal, you know the drill."

He stopped when Dean made a shooting motion at him with one hand. He was being told to talk about Twitch and friends. Allistor had given Dean a brief report when they arrived.

"I have come to trust Dean and Annie in the short time I've known them. And by extension, all of you. You would be welcome additions to our community. But not everyone will be. Earlier today we went to visit another group over in the warehouse district. They turned out to be thieves who tried to kill us when I refused to hand over my truck. Helen and I were forced to kill them. I'm sure all of you heard the gunfire." He looked at them one by one to gauge their reactions.

"I can't have people like that within our community. They are a threat to all of us. If you are willing to contribute to the community, follow the laws, and help make mankind stronger to face the coming challenges, you are welcome. If not, you will be barred from the safety and benefits of our holdings. I know that sounds harsh, but this isn't a game. This is about survival. The System has taken from us most of what made us the apex species on this world. Our numbers, and our technology. We *cannot afford* to be anything other than a united force if we're going to continue to survive. And I don't plan to just survive. I want us to *THRIVE*! I want us to be able to grow our own food, raise our own herds. I want us to become master crafters in every trade imaginable, and create items both useful and valuable. Earth is ours, and I'm not ready to give it up!"

There were cheers from most of the group, fists thrust in the air.

"My thought is that all of you, once you have taken your oaths, would run Cheyenne. Live in the stronghold, and grow crops, raise cattle or sheep or goats or whatever. We have chickens and rabbits at the Warren so far." His sheepish grin as he said this earned him some laughs. "Go

390

out and forage for items you can use or valuable items to sell. Right now Earth is a novelty, and we are the only ones with access to Earth's goods. They're selling for thousands of klax on the open market. Once the aliens arrive, the market will be flooded. So let's take advantage while we can. And most importantly, find more survivors. People are now the most valuable resource on Earth, at least to us. And I will expect every single one of you to learn at least one craft - and get good at it! The land we will have at our disposal has plenty of room for farming, lakes and streams for fishing, mines, and quarries, everything we'll need. But we need bodies to do all that work. And to defend ourselves when needed."

He sat back in his chair to let them think. Helen caught his eye, giving him a smile and a thumbs-up. Dean clapped him on the back, then stood up.

"Alright, folks. Feel free to talk amongst yourselves. We'll take a vote in an hour. For my two cents, Sarah and I will be joining Baron Allistor..." He grinned as Allistor rolled his eyes. "And moving into the Stronghold. I'm tired of worrying about real monsters spawning under my bed. And I can't remember the last time I had a hot shower." Sarah stood and moved next to him, taking his hand in a show of support.

Annie jumped up. "Me too! And I'm going to have a pet bear like Allistor."

One by one, the others all stood. In less than a minute, it was unanimous. Helen spoke an oath, which they all repeated together and the green-blue light enveloped them all. Just like that, they had nine more citizens of Allistor's little Barony.

When they'd all retaken their seats, Allistor said, "Thank you, all of you. And welcome! If you want to take some time to gather your essentials, we can go back to the mall and I'll get you all authorized. Helen and I will stay in town tonight so we can talk some more. In the morning we'll try the missile base one more time, then move on. I'm thinking Laramie or Casper is next."

"What about the missile base?" One of the women asked, raising her hand.

"I'm sorry, please tell me your name again?" Allistor gave a little apologetic shrug. "I'm terrible with meeting new people."

"I'm Andrea. Tech Sgt Andrea Miller. I worked at the base before all this."

Allistor's pulse quickened. "Well, *helloooo,* Tech Sergeant! You are just who we've been looking for. Helen and I have been calling the base on every radio channel, trying to raise somebody inside. I want to claim the base, most especially the silos and underground bunkers, as a Stronghold. And upgrade the mall to a Citadel. But nobody has answered. And we were afraid to approach too closely and get shot."

Andrea looked at him, suspicion written all over her face. "Why do you want the base?"

"For several reasons. First, the bunkers sound like a good place to hunker down if we're facing an enemy set on exterminating us. Second, we need to secure any WMD's that are down there. Keep them out of the hands of any unstable elements that might go nuts and destroy us all. And I'm hoping there's communication equipment down

392

there we can use to find other survivors and coordinate. I don't want us to be the only humans to thrive. If we can help others, and receive help in return…"

He stopped talking when she started nodding.

"I can maybe get you inside. We locked down the secure areas right before the Apocalypse. For much the same reason. There are forty techs, airmen, and guards down there, assuming nothing spawned inside and killed them. I can vouch for every one of them."

Helen asked. "You haven't been in touch with them?"

Andrea shook her head. "Commander's orders. No contact with the outside world until he determines it's safe, or he gets orders. He's down there as well. They have surveillance systems with cameras, microphones, infrared, seismic, all kinds of sensors. And access to whatever is left of the military network. He will have been monitoring things topside. I'm not sure why they haven't opened up yet, things aren't all that bad out here."

Helen followed up. "Well, if they're locked down, how do you plan to get us in?"

"I know the codes to open the doors. Assuming they haven't been changed. And I know a pass-phrase that should get the commander to respond on the radio, at least. Even if both fail, we might be able to gain access through ventilation and maintenance shafts. But that would take some explosives and a week or two of hard work."

"Then let's hope they answer your radio call. Or that your codes still work!" Allistor was back on his feet, excited at the prospect of claiming the base. "Let's get all

393

you guys settled this afternoon, have a nice meal this evening – thank you, Dean, by the way. This was delicious! – and tomorrow we can go see if we can't claim ourselves a missile base!"

It took a bit longer than expected for folks to gather up their things, but two hours later a small convoy of trucks passed through the Stronghold gate. Allistor took some time to add the locals as well as his own people from the Warren to the authorized list as they all gathered outside the door. With Fuzzy at his side, holding the green doll and somehow grinning at everyone at the same time, he called out, "Welcome to your new home!"

The gates behind him opened, and the survivors filed inside. He'd chosen to bring them in the former food court entrance, reserving the big box store they had slept in the night before as his own quarters. He was the only one authorized to enter there.

There were a few laughs and gasps of surprise as the group entered the mall. They had, of course, all been there before, but it looked much different now. A few moved to sit by the fountain, running their fingers through the water. Others explored up and down the main concourse. When they'd all had a good look, Allistor called them back together. With the place so empty, his shout easily reached everyone.

As they all took seats in the dining area, he said, "As you can see, there are living quarters upstairs. Choose the one you want and move on in. There's also the crafting hall, with plenty of space for you guys to practice your skills. And if any of you are motivated to do so, you can claim a shop space down here to market your wares. I will not be instituting any taxes during this first year, as I think you should put whatever resources you earn back into improving your skills." This earned smiles from everyone. No taxes was always good news.

"There's plenty of sunlight in here, so if you want to grow herbs and such, I'm sure we can find or build some planters. We can also construct a greenhouse outside when the Stronghold has earned some more points. Same with other types of buildings, like a garage. And there's plenty of grass area inside the wall, as well as a paved area that you could break up and turn into cropland, fruit groves, whatever. And if we're successful in claiming the base tomorrow, we can eventually upgrade this place to a Citadel. A whole little town inside a wall."

Helen stepped in. "We can talk about future plans this evening. For now, here's what's most important. You're safe in here. Nothing will spawn inside the walls while you sleep. There are large monsters out there, like the void titans and dragons that could still be a threat. But the sensors will warn you they're coming, even if your guards don't see or feel a sixty-foot monster stomping this direction." There were a few chuckles, and several people looked over at one particular man, who blushed.

She continued, "But the single most important thing is this: Do us all a favor and go grab a hot shower! Some of you are a bit... ripe. We'll gather back here to talk more when everyone has settled in."

Allistor decided to follow Helen's advice and grab a shower himself. He headed down the promenade to his own quarters, Fuzzy at his heels. After just a few steps he noticed Helen following.

A brief moment of panic ensued, as the thought of her wanting to join him in the shower crossed his mind. Whether they'd formalized it or not, he felt committed to Amanda. Things might be about to get awkward.

He slowed his pace, allowing Helen to catch up. She said, "A hot shower really does sound good right now," letting out a wistful sigh. "Even at the cabin, the water heater pilot went out half the time. The other night at the cabin I was grateful for even the cold shower. But I'm gonna crank up the heat and scour myself clean right now!"

Allistor resisted contemplating that visual as he responded, "I saw a tub in one of the bathrooms. Might feel better to soak a while."

She clapped her hands and grinned at him. "I'll do both!"

When they reached his quarters the doors opened as he approached, the biometric scanners recognizing him. Once inside, he was relieved to see her split off and head across the main floor area for one of the bathrooms that had previously been a public restroom, rather than his 'master suite'. She grabbed her bag and the clean clothes she had claimed the day before, calling over her shoulder, "See you in an hour!"

Left to himself, Allistor opened his interface and found Fuzzy's *Companion* tab. The first thing he noticed was that his bear cub had a new level now. He was in fact level six already. The fights with the snake, the creepers, and maybe Twitch and his guys had granted him some experience. Out of curiosity, he tried adding Fuzzy to the Stronghold's authorized list. The System let him add his pet's name, much to his delight.

"Okay, buddy, you can let yourself in and out now. No waking me up or sticking your nose into the shower if you need to go out. You just go take care of business."

Clearly understanding his words, the bear cub ambled toward the exit and let himself out. Allistor felt a strange sense of pride at this. "My little guy is growing up so fast!" he muttered to himself. Turning toward his quarters, he went to hit the shower.

Chapter Sixteen

What Happens in the Silo…

The next morning, after the group had a nice breakfast together, Allistor and Helen set off with Andrea and Fuzzy to see about the base. Helen rode in back with the bear cub, scratching his belly as Andrea navigated for Allistor. She brought them through the front gate and across the base, pointing out buildings like the motor pool, commissary, and the med clinic. A few minutes later they were parked before a low mound of concrete and earth, a single metal pedestal mounted out front.

Andrea tried the radio first. She tuned it to a specific channel, then keyed the microphone. "Redwing One, this is Tech Sergeant Miller, do you copy?" After a short pause, she added, "Redwing One, please respond. Hippopotamus can fly, over."

Helen snorted behind her. "Nice one."

A voice came over the radio. "Sarge, is that really you?"

Andrea smiled at the microphone. "Jenkins! Of course it's me! For the ALLIANCE!" she shouted.

"For the Horde!" Jenkins' voice came back. "Damn I'm glad to hear from you." Then his voice grew suspicious. "I see folks in that truck with you. Is there a problem?"

She laughed into the mic. "Everything's good. These are friends. Allistor and Helen. And Fuzzy the bear.

We came to get you out of there. Please let the boss know we're here."

There was a long silence, then Jenkins replied. "The boss is gone, Sarge. These things appeared down here and took out a bunch of us before we got them. Been a little... rough down here."

Andrea bowed her head. "How many have we lost? And who's in charge now?"

Jenkins' voice caught as he spoke. "Besides the captain, we lost twelve others. Mostly the guards, and a couple of techs who were working down in one of the pits when these things appeared. As for who's in charge... well, now that you're here, I guess that's you, boss."

Andrea rolled her eyes. "Alright, Jenkins. Send the lift up. We'll join you in a few."

"Roger that, boss. Welcome back!"

Andrea and the others exited the vehicle, and she led them over to one side of the bunker. A moment later the parking area near their feet split apart, two horizontal slabs separating like a giant maw opening in the earth. Allistor moved to the edge and peered down into a deep tunnel that ran straight down a few hundred feet. "Is this... a missile silo?"

Andrea shook her head. "Nope. That would be much larger. This is an access shaft. Mostly used for moving supplies up and down. Like a freight elevator." As she finished talking, a wide metal platform rose up to ground level and stopped. "All aboard!" she called out, stepping over the small gap onto the lift. The others joined in, Fuzzy a little hesitant as he sniffed at everything. When he finally got aboard, she placed a hand on a sensor pad attached to the metal frame of the lift. A green light came on, and she hit the 'down' button. As the lift began to descend, the roof above them slid closed. The deep clang that echoed down to them as the two doors connected was more than a little ominous.

It took a full two minutes for the lift to descend to the next landing and a set of heavy-looking doors. When it came to rest, Andrea pressed her palm to another sensor, and the doors opened. Inside were four men with automatic rifles and body armor. The rifles were pointed toward the floor, but the men were clearly ready to raise them and fire at need.

"Airman Bjurstrom, Campbell, McCoy, and Goodrich. Good to see you guys in one piece. Jenkins said it was bad down here."

"Welcome back, Sarge," the one with *Bjurstrom* stitched on his chest replied. "And yeah. We lost a good bit of the complex down here. The lower levels aren't safe. We fought a running retreat until we could seal off the bottom four levels at one of the blast doors. Lost some good men. The captain sacrificed himself, stayed to distract them while we got the doors shut."

Allistor spoke up. "Let me guess. Octopoids? The things with the stubby legs and tentacles?"

The airman nodded. "Yes, sir. Those and some nasty lil white goblin-looking things. Like a hundred of them. All sharp teeth and claws. Also, these jello-looking slimy things that burn like acid when you touch them. They kept eating through the lower doors. It's why we had to keep retreating. But they can't seem to get through the blast door. At least, not yet."

Goodrich added, "It's like a damn video game dungeon down here, Sarge. Please tell me it's safer out there?"

Andrea shook her head. "It's a video game out there too, fellas. Nasty monsters, even worse than you've seen down here. But yeah, it's safer, if only because there's room to run away. Baron Allistor here has built a Stronghold over at the mall. Nothing spawns inside the walls. And there are other survivors there as well." All four men grinned and fist-bumped each other.

"That's the good news." Their faces fell at that phrase. Every soldier knew what was coming when an NCO started talking good news/bad news.

Allistor took over. "The bad news isn't so bad. I plan to turn this place into a Stronghold too. So that nothing bad can spawn down here. But in order to do that, we need to clear the place. Remove every living thing other than ourselves."

The four men began shaking their heads. "No can do, sir. Even when there was a dozen of us, we didn't have the firepower to take them all out. We're the last of the guard unit."

Helen grinned at them. "I'm Helen. Park ranger and badass monster killer. You might have heard me on the radio in the last few days?" McCoy nodded. "Well, Allistor here is good at killing monsters. And with a little backup from us, I'm sure he can get it done."

To reinforce her statement, he summoned a fireball in his hand, then let it dissipate. "Part of this new game world is the ability to learn magic. To make yourselves stronger, and faster and smarter…"

All four men were grinning at him now. "We know, sir." Campbell thumped his chest. "Lots of us are gamers. Not much else to do when you're trapped down here for weeks at a time. Especially since we have access to one of the highest speed networks on the planet!" The others all gave thumbs-up and shouted, "For the Horde!"

Andrea snorted. "Bunch of PvP animals. Everybody knows the best way to play is PvE, and for the Alliance!"

Bjurstrom tilted his head, looking behind Allistor. "Uh… you guys know a bear followed you down here?"

Helen grinned. "That's Fuzzy - he's bonded to Allistor." Fuzzy nodded his head, the green goblin doll's arms waggling.

"Is that a frog in its mouth?" Goodrich squinted at the bear cub.

"Nope. Goblin." Allistor laughed when they raised their weapons. "Stuffed Goblin. Any of you guys remember Fibble?"

"Ha! I do," Bjurstrom said. "The bear's got good taste."

Andrea said, "You geeks wouldn't know good taste if it bit you on the ass."

The four men joked around with their sergeant for a bit longer, clearly happy to see her. Then at her command, they led her deeper into the complex. After several turns, they came upon a mess hall, where another half dozen men and women were gathered.

When Andrea walked in, they all shot to their feet, standing at attention. She patted her hands at the air, saying, "At ease, at ease. Those days are over, I'm afraid. Unless you've had contact with our command? Or any command?" She waited for one of them to reply, but there was only the shaking of heads and hopeless looks.

"Right! So then we're on our own." She looked at each of the group one by one. Then she pointed to Allistor. "This is the new boss - Baron Allistor. He's gonna help us all survive for the next year and beyond."

Pointing to an airman near the other door, she said, "Amaye! Get on the intercom. I want everybody still alive down here in this mess hall in ten minutes. NO exceptions."

The young airmen saluted and practically sprinted out the door.

Turning to the others, she said, "Get comfortable. It sounds like the scuttlebutt has informed you all that the world operates like a game system now. When the others arrive, Allistor's gonna spend some time filling you in on the details. In the meantime, who's cooking around here now?"

A voice from the back called out, "That's me, Sarge. I'm still here."

Andrea smiled, grabbing Allistor and pulling him toward the back of the room and the kitchen. "Thorne! Good to see you. Fire up the grill. Allistor here has bits of giant snake monster that you can throw a little salt and pepper on and grill up for lunch. I'm sure you guys are a little tired of MREs?"

"Right on! Any chance you've got any bacon, too?" Thorne asked hopefully.

"I'm afraid not, at least not on me. But once this place is cleared and claimed, I can get you some. And maybe we can capture some pigs to raise for a steady supply." He nearly jumped as a round of applause burst out behind him.

For the next ten minutes, Allistor worked with Thorne and another cook to prepare lunch. They had fresh baked-from-scratch bread, canned vegetables, and snake steak for everyone. Between his short time assisting Dean and his shift at the grill here in the Silo, his cooking skill was now up to level 5.

Allistor spoke to the gathered troops as they consumed their first reasonably fresh food in weeks. The discussion went faster as several of them were gamers who followed along easily. He decided to rely on them to explain the fine details to their comrades. Some of them had assigned attribute points already, others seemed to be waiting for guidance. And a few had developed skills, most around their day-to-day duties. Unlike folks above ground, these men and women had continued doing their day jobs. Security patrols, maintenance, system monitoring. Eventually, he got to the bit about claiming the base complex.

"So we need to clear out all the mobs down there. I'll take the lead, but I could use a few of you as backup. Most of you haven't had much of an opportunity to level up. From what I'm told there are a hundred or more mobs down there. Those who join me will gain a good bit of xp. Of course, you'll also be risking your lives."

An airman named Durham spoke up. "Tell us again why you're the new boss? You're not an officer. Not even military. You're just some gamer kid with a bear following you around."

Andrea snapped at him. "He's the boss because I say so! And the bear is not only cute, but he's also a higher level than you. So sit your ass down and shut your trap, Durham!"

Allistor held up a hand. "It's okay, Sarge." He turned so the others couldn't see and winked at her. "I'd ask the same question if I were him." He turned and addressed the airman. He was tall and thin with beady eyes and a permanent scowl on his face.

"You're right. I was just a college kid and a gamer when all this happened. I didn't ask to be in charge. It just sort of worked out that way. My town was flattened by a sixty-foot giant right off the bat. My family was all killed in the first days. I managed to survive, kill some of these things on my own, and save a few other survivors. Then we grouped up and fought more of them, eventually killing the giant, as well as some other elite monsters. The group I was with just sort of made me the leader because I knew what to do. Then I built a Stronghold, helped liberate another one from murdering asshats, built a couple Outposts, and another Stronghold here at the mall. But mainly, it is because I claimed a large quantity of land very quickly, and earned myself the title of Baron. It's like being named a general – it gives me certain powers and authority to do things you can't do."

Most of the men and women in the room were nodding their heads. But Durham's sneer got a little nastier, and he shouted, "Why should we risk our lives so you can claim this place and play overlord over the rest of us?" His face was turning red.

"I'm not looking to be anyone's overlord. I didn't want this responsibility. But it's mine now, and I'm determined to make all of us stronger. To reclaim as much of Earth as we can for ourselves before our year is up. So that we can have decent lives going forward. I'm not ordering anyone down into the lower levels here. Each of your lives is just as important to me as my own. There are so few of us left, every human life is precious. I'll be leading the way myself. I'd appreciate volunteers to help, but I'll go alone if I need to."

"Screw that noise. I'm not risking my life for you. And none of my brothers and sisters here should either!" Durham was on his feet now. He looked around the room for support but received only cold stares.

Bjurstrom stood up. "You've always been a dick, Durham. Sit down." Turning to Allistor, he saluted. "I'm in, boss. Er... Baron?" The other three who had greeted them at the lift stood as well.

"Neither," Allistor said. "I'm just Allistor. There may come a time in the future where we have to pay attention to bullshit like that, but for now, I'm just Allistor. If I understand correctly, Andrea here is the highest rank among you? So you can call her boss."

More of the airmen stood up to volunteer in ones and twos. Eventually, all but Durham were on their feet. Seeing that he'd lost, he stood as well. "Fine. I'll go too."

"No, you won't," Allistor said. "I just met you, but you seem like a self-centered ass. Am I right?" he looked around the room to see many nodding heads. "That's what I thought. I don't need people like you. We need to be a community. To work to support each other. Risk our lives for each other without having to be shamed into it. I frankly don't trust you at my back with a gun. So until you prove yourself worthy of trust, you can stay back here and do something useful."

As Durham turned an even deeper shade of red, Allistor asked Andrea, "What does he do around here?"

"Communications. He runs the radio network and relays orders received."

"Great! Durham you can hang back here and get on the radio. See who else we can find out there. Military or civilian. As I said, people are the most valuable thing on Earth right now."

Durham just scowled and sat down. An airman next to him kicked his ankle and gave him a dirty look. He flipped her the bird and proceeded to sulk.

Seeing this, Allistor added, "It seems we have a problem child. He'll need a few babysitters. In case he gets any bright ideas about sealing the blast doors behind us." The look he gave Durham was full of contempt.

After a moment of thought, he looked at Helen. "You going down there?" She nodded, and Andrea did as well. Fuzzy just squeezed his Fibble and drooled in an affirmative manner.

"Alright. I think maybe six or eight more of you would be good. We have plenty of guns, and I have a few magic ranged attacks. But those little creeper things are fast and nasty. Who here has some melee weapons experience?"

All four of the guards raised their hands. About a third of the remaining airmen did as well. Allistor looked to Andrea. "Okay, I'll leave it to you to choose, as you know these folks. And let's see what kind of weapons we can come up with. Axes, long knives, whatever we can scrounge."

Campbell spoke up. "Each of the rifles in the armory has a bayonet, and we've got a few fire axes."

"Good. I've got a sword and a spear, plus a few other weapons in my ring that I'll share. Who knows how to mix up chemicals to make some sort of napalm or liquid fire? We can make some grenades that should help take down the slimes and the larger groups."

They went to work, the whole group helping to prepare the volunteers who were going into battle. They were very efficient for the most part, their training kicking in. All except for Durham, who continued to sulk. McCoy escorted him to his communications station where he just sat and stared at the walls.

The most valuable items that the crew came up with in Allistor's opinion were the radios. The security team produced throat mics and earpieces that were tuned to the complexes internal frequency. They were designed for use inside the underground complex and were strong enough to transmit and receive clearly - even through layers of rock and steel. This was like having a party chat and would allow Allistor to stay in contact with those who stayed behind. They also each had a camera strapped to their helmets.

Ninety minutes later they were ready to go. Everyone in the party had been outfitted with body armor, helmets with visors, and weapons. Some carried assault rifles, others shotguns. And among the shotgun loads were both slugs and pellet loads for a wider damage spread. One of the machinists had taken some scrap metal and together with Allistor had improvised some rough machete-like chopping blades. Thorne had created a mixture of bleach, grease from the grill, and other chemicals that combined to burn hotly. They used empty jars to create half a dozen grenades. Both airmen had earned the *Improvisation* skill, and Allistor's own had increased one level.

Allistor sent around party invites, and they were ready to go. Twelve people and a bear cub descended to the blast doors that sealed off the lower levels. Three more would be guarding the door behind them, ready to seal it if necessary. Andrea had detailed two burly airmen to watch over Durham, while most of the others gathered around the security stations to watch the team's progress on closed-circuit cameras. As always happened when a large enough gathering of soldiers came together for an event, the betting had already started.

McCoy and Goodrich unsealed the door and pushed it open. Immediately a creeper flew through the widening opening and latched onto Goodrich. He stumbled back a few steps, the surprise setting him off balance. McCoy reacted instantly, using one of the improvised blades to hack the thing's head off as it clung to his buddy's chest.

Shotguns fired as more of the nasty little things rounded the still opening door and flung themselves at the humans. Pasty white bodies exploded or were thrown back. Allistor quickly cast *Flame Shot* through the opening, surprising his people and burning half a dozen of the mobs.

Andrea began to shout. "Front row! Take a knee! Back row fire!" The military members of the team fell into a formation and began to fill the air with deadly fire. Helen stood to one side, shotgun blasting away as quickly as she could fire. Allistor cast another fireball, this one larger. It burned a few new mobs coming at them and finished off several of the wounded creepers. Experience points poured across his interface.

He heard Bjurstrom shouting, "Hell yeah! Sweet, sweet xp!"

The further the heavy door swung open, the more of the creatures poured in. They'd already killed maybe thirty of the creepers, but scores more were pushing down the hallway toward them. Andrea shouted, "Grenade out!" and hurled one of Thorne's jars about twenty feet down the hall. The jar shattered against a panel box on the wall, spraying the chemical compound across the hall. Allistor's fireball struck half a second later, lighting the liquid afire as it covered a dozen or more of the creepers.

She lobbed a second grenade past the first one, this one smashing on the floor about three feet back. The spreading liquid covered the whole floor and ignited when it reached the burning creepers. Now there was a fire barrier across the entire hallway floor about ten feet deep. The creepers that hadn't reached it yet held back, seeming to be afraid of the fire. Andrea called out, "Kill everything on this side of the flames! We'll deal with the rest after."

Her people changed the focus of their fire, finishing off burnt and blinded creepers with speed and accuracy. More experience points flashed across all of their interfaces. The creepers were on average level 4-6. Higher than most of the humans present. So while Allistor got very little from it, the airmen were leveling up quickly.

They took a breather when all the nearby creepers were dead. The ones out past the fire were biding their time, waiting for the flames to die down. Everyone checked ammo and reloaded, took a sip or two of water, and congratulated each other. Allistor said, "You've got one minute to zone out and assign some attribute points. Remember what we discussed earlier. Focus on who you want to be, and assign the points accordingly. Or just save them for when you have more time to think."

Six of the airmen and Andrea leaned against a wall and unfocused their eyes as they reviewed their stat sheets. Most were done in less than a minute. Allistor sent a large fireball downrange, blasting the first several creepers waiting to get at the humans. He saw Andrea getting another grenade ready and shook his head. "Let's save those for emergencies. These first two cut them down to a manageable level."

She nodded, turning to her people. "Two rows! You know the drill. If you can't hit these things in the face at thirty feet, I'm ashamed to know you!"

The airmen quickly formed into two rows, the front row down on one knee. As soon as they were set, she said, "Keep to your lanes! Fire at will!"

The nearly simultaneous blast from nine humans mowed down the front lines of creepers. Shotgun slugs tore through one, then another behind it, and sometimes a third. Bodies and limbs were knocked backward by the blasts. Both lines reloaded and continued to fire as quickly as they could. Allistor sent another fireball to finish off any wounded that might get back up.

Fifteen seconds later, when there were no more obvious targets, Andrea started shouting "Cease fire! Reload!" The weapon barrels dropped and a few people coughed from the burnt-cordite fog that surrounded them.

McCoy took a deep breath through his nose, then sighed. "Ahhh. I love the smell of cordite in the morning!" Nobody laughed. A few groaned.

The fires had mostly burned out, though there were a few hot spots left. One of the team grabbed a fire extinguisher and doused them. At Andrea's command, they all stepped forward and looted the dead creepers. There were some pleased sounds when they received klax and cool body parts like claws and teeth. Goodrich started cursing when he jammed some in his pocket and poked himself. Bjurstrom laughed, saying "You need to buy yourself one of those bags of holding like they have in the games."

Allistor called out "In this system, they're called *Personal Pocket Dimensions,* or PPD's for short. The cheaper ones, like this ring here that has one hundred slots, cost two hundred klax on the open market." He held up the ring. Just for show, he made his shotgun disappear and pulled his spear from it. Eyes widened all around him.

"I'll tell you what. You guys help me clear this place, I'll make it a Stronghold with a market kiosk. And the first thing I'll do is purchase a ring like this for everyone." He paused for a second and grinned at them all. "Except maybe Durham. Screw him." This got him cheers and laughs from the group.

Talk of the market got him thinking about selling the nukes that were down here. And thinking about the nukes gave him a sudden sense of alarm.

"Uhh... guys? Before we go much farther. It's my understanding that there are very big explodey-things down here. And we've been sending a lot of lead and fire flying every which way. Are we in any danger of hitting a warhead and killing everyone? Cuz that would be bad."

A wave of chuckles ran through the group. Andrea patted his shoulder. "Silly bossman. We'll warn you when you have to tiptoe past the explodey-things. Don't worry."

"Right on!" He gave her a thumbs up, grinning widely. "Then let's go kill stuff!"

The group moved on past the piles of dead creepers, those in front kicking the bodies to one side or another to make a path. Fuzzy sniffed at them and raised his snout in disgust.

At the end of the corridor was a T-intersection. To the left was another short corridor with four doors. To the right was a stairwell door.

Allistor looked to Fuzzy, who stood next to him seeming unconcerned. "Fuzzy doesn't smell any bad guys, but let's clear those rooms to be sure. Me and the ferocious bear will guard this door."

Helen stayed with him as Andrea and her team moved down the corridor. They broke into two teams and each hit one door at a time. They found nothing inside, and Allistor had them close the doors behind them as they left. Back at the stairwell, he put his ear to the door for half a minute before opening it.

As soon as he pulled it open and found the landing clear on the other side, he stepped inside the stairwell. From this level, the stairs only went down. A thought struck him, and he motioned for the others to wait while he closed the door. The back side was clean, no scratch marks or blood. Opening the door again, he said, "Nothing tried to get in from this side. Looks like we're clear down to the next level."

Campbell chimed in, "Makes sense. Most dungeons you get a safe zone as you move from one level to the next. The stairs and sometimes a small room at the bottom."

Allistor led the way, his spear still in his hand. With all the firepower behind him, he figured it wouldn't hurt to get some blunt and sharp weapon experience. They reached the next level without incident. Once again he put his ear to the stairwell door. He heard faint noises he couldn't identify.

"Something in there. Moving quietly," he whispered into his throat mic. The others all nodded.

Standing in front of the door with spear at the ready, he motioned for Helen to pull it open. She yanked it hard, allowing Allistor to leap through before anything on the other side could react.

Unfortunately for him, what was on the other side were several dozen small slimes. They had apparently run up against the door and stayed there, their passage blocked. Allistor's first few steps were fine, but his third step landed upon a slime. His right foot sank into the thing, and two seconds later his skin began to burn.

Acid Slime Scavenger
Level 8
Health 3,000/3,000

"They're acid!" he shouted, blasting everything around him with a column of *Flame Shot* fire. The others all backed up as the slimes oozed through the door, the pressure of those behind them pushing them through. Allistor slipped as the slime underneath him moved, losing his balance and falling onto his back, landing on several more slimes. His head struck the concrete floor, and his vision went fuzzy.

The others frantically fired around him as he writhed in pain and tried to get back to his feet. He couldn't get any purchase or leverage, as everywhere he touched with hand or foot was covered by slimes. And he was quickly becoming trapped inside the jello-ish monsters.

Bjurstrom began to shout. "Cease fire! Bullets will just pass through them. We need anti-acid. Or more fire."

Helen stepped forward and tried to reach for Allistor, intending to help him up. He shouted, "No! Don't touch them. Or me. I'm covered in the stuff." Seeing that his health had ticked down to forty percent, he cast a heal on himself, then another immediately. Focusing through the pain, he created a fireball in his hand, burning away the slime on his palm. Using his spear as a crutch, he rolled over and levered himself to his knees. The rough rebar spear gave him enough of a grip to push himself to his feet. He quickly cast *Flame Shot* again, burning the slimes at his feet.

As he stepped back onto the landing, the airman with the fire extinguisher blasted him without warning. The bits of slime still attached to him seemed to crystallize, and several of the airmen wearing gloves helped brush the bits off of him. "Thanks for that, guys. And good thinking!" he said to the fire-extinguisher bearer. None of them would look him in the eye.

"What?" he asked Helen, half delirious from pain.

She grimaced. "Your face, your hands… that's got to hurt."

Not having a mirror, he asked, "How bad is it?" He raised a hand to see that his skin was discolored a nasty yellow shade, with blisters covering most of it. A quick check of his interface showed a poison debuff.

"Shit." He cast another heal on himself. His health bar improved, moving back up to eighty percent. But the skin didn't heal that he could see. "I guess I'll have to wait out the debuff." Even as he spoke, he saw a piece of skin fall from his forehead past his nose. One of the airmen lost her lunch.

"Dude. You make Deadpool look sexy," McCoy said to him.

There was no more time for discussion as another wave of slimes were pushing over the top of their dead cousins. Bjurstrom shouted, "Salt! Anybody got salt? That might work."

Nobody had salt.

The fire extinguisher blasted again, and the oncoming slimes paused, seeming to harden up a bit. Campbell fired his shotgun, and the two nearest the door shattered into pieces. "Right on! Hit 'em again!" he called out. The airman sent another long blast of potassium bicarbonate through the doorway. This time three others fired their shotguns, and chunks of slime mobs flew everywhere. Allistor shot more fire in to scorch the hardened pieces.

They alternated this way, a blast of cold from the extinguisher followed by shattering shotgun blasts, then fire. Two minutes later the hall was cleared of slimes.

Allistor croaked. "When you loot them, there should be cores. That's what gives them life. The cores should have some value, so let's get them all." His throat was raw, some of the slime apparently having gotten in his mouth. Every inch of him screamed in pain, so that he couldn't feel one particular ache over another. He cast another heal on himself as he waited out the debuff. The icon on his interface showed three more minutes and was counting down.

Fuzzy stuck his nose close and sniffed at him, then snorted and backed away. "I don't blame you, buddy."

417

He sat and watched the others carefully loot the slime corpses, afraid of suffering the same kind of burns they saw on his skin. When they were done, there was a pile of thirty-eight cores on the floor in front of him. He touched the pile with his ring and they disappeared.

"Thanks, guys. We'll figure out the value and divide up the proceeds evenly. Just need to rest here a few minutes. The debuff wears off in two min, and I should be able to heal my skin fully. Get nice and pretty for you again."

One of the female airmen coughed. "You weren't that pretty." And just like that, the mood lightened. They all took a seat, leaning against walls or stair rails. Allistor produced some jerky and nibbled at it, hoping it would help his skin regenerate faster. He drank some water to wash down the salty jerky.

Bjurstrom looked at Andrea. "Permission to speak freely, Sarge?" When she nodded he looked at Allistor. "Look, boss. I know you said you'd lead the way. And we all appreciate you lookin' out for us. But I can't sit back and watch you take all this abuse instead of us. It's not right."

Allistor grunted, his throat still raw. "I'm the closest thing to a tank down here. I'm level ten. My health points are two or three times what any of you have. If one of you had nose-dived into those slimes like I just did, you'd have died instead of just looking stupid and ugly."

The others looked around, not liking this answer, but not having a good argument. Allistor smiled slightly. "Don't worry. Pain fades. Healing is much faster in this new world. I can take it. One of the perks of being the boss, right?"

Five minutes and two pieces of jerky later, and his skin was nearly back to normal. Unfortunately, his hair was taking much longer to grow back. He looked like a B-movie mutant with random patches of scorched hair sprouting from his bare skull. His helmet strap had been eaten away, and it lay on the floor in the hall. He had no desire to pick it back up.

"I hope the guys upstairs are seeing this. Even Durham can't complain that you're not sacrificing for the team," Andrea whispered to him.

Back on his feet, he led the way into the corridor. They cleared room after room, finding nothing. Eventually, Bjurstrom observed. "It's like they were all chasing something toward the stairwell, and just piled up against the door and stayed there."

With that floor cleared, they continued downward. There were still more levels to go.

The next level was where most of the humans had perished. According to the airmen, the mobs had spawned on the lowest level, killing two techs before they had time to call for help. Then they'd moved upward and caught the others on this level unawares. This was pieced together from video footage from the security cameras.

As soon as they opened the stairwell door, they found a scattered set of bones on the floor. They had been pulled apart, picked clean, then broken and the marrow sucked out.

"Shit," An airman with "Weiss" on her name patch whispered. "I think this is the captain. *Was* the captain. He held this door while the others retreated up." The others were silent for a moment, bowing their heads in respect.

"He was a good man and a great commander. He will be remembered," Andrea spoke quietly. The others all repeated. "He will be remembered."

Moving on, they were maybe a third of the way down the hallway when an octopoid emerged from a doorway ahead of them.

Octopoid Reaver
Level 9
Health 4,100/4,100

This one was bigger than any Allistor had faced previously. It had clearly killed and eaten several beings – human or monster – and grown strong. Its tentacles waved in their direction as it slowly turned on its stumpy legs and advanced on them.

"Shoot it in the face!" Andrea shouted. An instant later the mob's bulbous head caved in from multiple shotgun blasts. Just to be sure, Allistor hurled his spear, the weapon puncturing its face and driving through the back of its head. It was dead before it even hit the floor.

"Overkill, much?" Helen asked as she bent to loot the corpse. Fuzzy stepped forward and sniffed, then took a bite of one tentacle. Seeming pleased with the taste, he took another.

"The bear likes sushi!" one of the team joked.

"You guys help yourselves. Won't catch me eating that thing." Andrea shuddered.

Nobody stepped forward to harvest any tentacle meat, and after a few more bites, Fuzzy stepped away and picked Fibble back up off the floor.

Moving on, they encountered three more octopoids of a similar size and level in different rooms along the corridor. When they reached the end, a ground-shaking thud made them all freeze.

In front of them was a metal hatch. When Allistor looked to Andrea with eyebrows raised, she whispered back through her throat mic, "Storage. Big room, maybe a hundred feet square."

Allistor nodded and was reaching toward the wheel that would open the hatch when something smashed against it from the other side. He jerked his hand back quickly, then tried to look casual when he saw the others smiling. Fuzzy poked his nose at the door, putting it right up against the hatch's seal. After a series of sniffs, he backed up slowly and sat down behind the rest of the group, shaking his head. A quiet chuff was the only sound he made.

"Whatever's in there, Fuzzy's not looking to play with it," Helen translated for the bear.

"Sounds pretty big for a mini-boss," Goodrich ventured.

"Only one way to find out!" Bjurstrom shouldered his shotgun and took hold of the wheel. "Ready when you are, Allistor."

Taking a deep breath and gripping his spear tightly, Allistor nodded his head. Bjurstrom spun the wheel until the lock disengaged. The moment he heard the click, Bjurstrom leapt back out of the way, in case the door flew open. It would be embarrassing to be killed by a door. Despite the tension of the moment, Allistor smiled to himself, remembering a character named Dave in a book called War Aeternus that was tragically killed by a trapped tavern door.

The smile disappeared when the creature inside the room struck the door again. It flew open, striking the wall with a clang and revealing what awaited the group.

Behind Allistor, he heard Helen gasp. "Is that… Godzilla?"

Agamid Rex
Level 10
Health: 7,000/7,000

The creature filled a good portion of the room. Smashed boxes and shattered crates were pushed up against the walls, and the center of the room was clear except for the lizard-thing. Allistor's first impression was that it looked like a cross between a Komodo dragon and a T-Rex. It stood upright on its hind legs, with a long sinuous body and tail. Its body and front legs were longer than a T-Rex, and as Allistor observed it the thing dropped to all fours and charged toward the door. Its head very much resembled the king of dinosaurs, with beady eyes and massive jaws filled with teeth a foot long.

Fortunately, its head was larger than the hatch. Allistor and several others fell backward as the giant lizard slammed its jaws through the opening. The entire chamber shook under their feet at the impact, and the squeal of bending metal could be heard.

Its jaws pinned shut in the tight opening, it snorted at its prey, showering several of them in grey-green snot. Airman Weiss began making gagging noises as she wiped a blob of it from her face.

Allistor, regaining his composure, leapt forward and jammed his spear point up into one of the beast's nostrils. The weapon sank deep, and he lost his grip as the monster yanked its head back. The moment it cleared the doorway, its jaws opened and it roared in pain. The sounded echoed through the corridor, deafening every member of the group.

Allistor withdrew his shotgun as he watched the creature rear up on its hind legs and thrash its head back and forth trying to dislodge the painful spear. It tried to reach its snout with its forelegs, but they weren't quite long enough.

Allistor pumped a round into the chamber and took aim. He fired at the lizard's exposed belly and watched as the slug embedded itself. There was a small amount of blood, but it didn't look like the wound was very deep.

"Switch to rifles! This thing has a tough hide. Even in the soft spots," he called out, matching action to words. He raised his rifle and took aim. The head was still thrashing too violently to hit with any accuracy. So he aimed at the unarmored spot exposed under the monster's foreleg as it continued to try and reach its snout.

This time when he fired, the round went deep. Blood sprayed, and the agamid roared in pain. Behind him, several other shots rang out, and trickles of blood appeared in various spots on its belly.

The creature spun with surprising agility, slamming its tail against the doorway and blocking their view. When the tail moved away, so had the monster. Sounds of crashing crates off to the right told them where it was.

McCoy whispered, "That damn mob just LoS'd us!" A few of the others chuckled nervously, adrenaline pumping through their bodies making them jittery.

Allistor let out the breath he'd been holding. When that thing charged, he'd very nearly pissed himself at the sight of those massive jaws closing on him. He was still shocked to be alive. After a couple more breaths, he said, "Looks like we're going to have to go in after it."

There were groans from nearly everyone in the group. He held up a hand. "I'll run in and distract it. You guys wait a few seconds, then get in there and fire. Stay close to the door so you can retreat if necessary."

He stepped close to the door and paused. Behind him, Helen said, "The thing seems smarter than the average bear. No offense, Fuzzy." She looked at the bear with a smile. "If I had to guess, it's waiting to nail you the moment you step through that door."

Allistor nodded. "I was just thinking the same thing." He looked at the door again and shook his head. "If this thing gets me, you guys promise to sing songs of my bravery?"

"We'll sing songs alright," Bjurstrom said. "Anybody know what rhymes with 'stupid'?"

Allistor rolled his eyes and took a few steps back. Then, with a wink at Helen, he said, "Fuzzy, you stay here, buddy," and dashed toward the opening. He used his last step to propel himself forward as he dove headfirst through the door and into a forward roll.

The group in the hall cried out as the massive jaws shot down from above and clamped together just inside the door, where Allistor had been half a second earlier. A few of them had the presence of mind to fire, one hitting the creature's eye before it raised its head again. As soon as the massive skull wasn't blocking their view, they saw Allistor running full speed away from the monster. A ragged cheer went up when they saw he was still alive.

Allistor made for the nearest wall and the pile of damaged crates. He slid behind them even as the monster turned in his direction. Peeking through a hole in the debris, he saw the others begin to charge through the door behind it. On a whim, he tried casting *Restraint.* The massive thing instantly froze in mid-step. Unable to plant its foot, or move its tail for balance, the lizard's momentum sent it tipping forward. It crashed like a meat statue in the center of the room, still unmoving.

Allistor and everyone else raised their weapons and poured on the damage. He fired directly into its open mouth, shattering teeth and turning them into shrapnel that shredded its gums and throat. Andrea was shouting something about focus at her team, but Allistor only half heard it. He managed three shots in the ten seconds the giant mob remained stunned.

"Not so smart after all, are ya, big boy?!" he shouted. T-Rex's were known to have tiny brains, and despite its clever actions, it seemed this big look-alike wasn't much more intelligent, based on the duration of the stun.

The moment the stun wore off, the creature loosed another deafening roar. A few of the airmen dropped their weapons to cover their ears. The mini-boss was back on all four feet in an instant and turned to swipe its tail at Allistor. The massive thing had to weigh a ton or two all on its own, and a wave of debris was pushed along like a bow wave in front of it as Allistor scrambled to get out of the way.

He didn't make it.

The end of the tail smashed into his back as he ran, lifting him off his feet and sending him flying into a deformed metal shelving unit and a pile of cardboard boxes. His health bar dropped by thirty percent.

The impact knocked the breath out of him, and when he tried to recover it, nothing happened. He wheezed, panicking as the air failed to fill his lungs. Gravity rolled him over onto his back as he descended the pile to the floor, and when he hit the concrete, his lungs opened up and he inhaled deeply. Immediately he felt a stabbing pain in his chest, the result of broken ribs poking at his muscle and lungs. A slight groan of pain was all he could manage.

Rapid and sustained gunfire rang out from the direction of the door. Allistor couldn't see the monster, or manage to adjust himself so he had a better view. He lay there wheezing as he cast a heal spell on himself. After a few seconds, he shifted his body enough that he could tilt his head and see the creature.

It had its back to him, tail thrashing wildly as it recoiled from the combined damage the others were inflicting. Allistor watched it advance on them as he cast another heal on himself. His breathing eased a bit, and he was able to get back on his feet. Out of malice, he cast *Restraint* on the mini-boss as it charged toward the other humans. Once again, it fell on its face. The others fired away, blasting big chunks out of the thing's face. Both eyes were gone now, and a pool of blood was forming on the floor under its head.

Agamid Rex
Level 10
Health: 2,100/7,000

As its head was near the door, and his friends, he shouted, "Get back out the door! Fire from there!"

Andrea began shouting, and the group walked backward, firing as they went. Allistor was proud of them. They kept their cool and acted like professionals, even when up against a creature from a child's nightmares.

Allistor limped over to a different pile of crates about fifty feet away. He barely made it by the time the stun wore off. Hunkering down with only a wince at the pain in his chest, he watched the monster get back to its feet. The action was much slower this time, and its legs wobbled slightly as it rose.

Still behind the creature, he cast *Flame Shot* in the form of a pillar of fire descending from the high ceiling. It splashed down upon the lizard's head, burning into the damaged eye sockets and cooking exposed flesh. The giant actually screamed in pain, thrashing blindly, frantically trying to locate its tormentors.

One of the airmen, whose name Allistor couldn't recall, charged forward. He had an improvised machete in one hand and a .45 in the other. Dashing up to the thing's right rear leg, he began to hack at it with the blade. Two others joined him, laughing wildly as they charged. The rest continued to provide cover fire, aiming for its face. Allistor looked around him, choosing a mostly intact crate and casting *Levitate,* he flung the five-foot-square box at the monster's head.

The blinded creature didn't see it coming, and the impact knocked it off balance again. The severely damaged leg that his companions had been savaging with their blades buckled under its weight, and the creature fell again. The airmen dashed to one side, as any good gamer would. But one of them was too slow, and he disappeared beneath the creature's bulk.

The others moved forward now, concentrated fire pouring into the monster's eyes from just a dozen feet away. Eventually one or more of the rounds reached its tiny brain, and it stopped moving.

There was no celebrating over the kill or the fact that they'd leveled up. Every single team member dashed toward the spot where the airman had fallen. Shoulders were wedged against the thing's body, and they managed to roll it onto its back far enough for someone to grab a boot and pull the airman free.

"Medic!" Andrea yelled, before realizing they didn't have one. Allistor cast a heal on the man, shocked he was still alive. A quick check of his health bar showed it was rising from about five percent. Allistor cast two more heals on him before he opened his eyes and groaned.

"Don't move!" Andrea ordered, pushing at his chest to keep him immobilized. "You're busted up pretty bad, Jenkins. Just hold still."

"That thing smells like baked ass," he complained, closing his eyes and relaxing on the floor.

"You wouldn't have had to smell the ass up close if you'd moved your own a little faster," Airman Weiss teased him. She'd been right next to him, as evidenced by the bloodied blade still in her hand.

Allistor handed Andrea a healing potion, which she poured down Jenkins' throat. A minute or so later he was feeling well enough to sit up with his back against the dead boss. Allistor reached out a hand and looted the corpse, receiving three hundred klax, the creature's heart, ten sharp fangs, two stacks of agamid meat, one stack of agamid leather, and one foreclaw.

He pulled the claw from his ring to examine it while the others looted the corpse. It was longer than his forearm and curved. The wickedly sharp point gleamed an ebony-blue in the fluorescent light, and the inner curve was honed to an edge both jagged and sharp. Already in his mind, he was working out a way to affix a handle and make a wicked scythe weapon out of it.

Before they left, Helen recruited half the team to help skin some of the tough hide from the creature. When she mentioned that it could be used to craft armor, she had no shortage of volunteers. As they exposed some of the flesh, Fuzzy went to investigate. A quick sniff followed by an experimental lick, and the bear decided raw lizard was tasty enough. He took a few enthusiastic bites as Fibble and the airmen watched with equally blank expressions.

429

Allistor and Jenkins rested and recuperated as the others went about their work. Allistor gave Jenkins some jerky to chew on. When he was fully recovered, he went to reclaim his spear. When he pulled the snot-covered weapon free of the nostril, he almost abandoned it. The foul-smelling slime coated the lower half of the weapon completely. Instead, he set it on the floor and used *Flame Shot* to burn away the slime. Then he used the butt end of the spear to break off several of the massive teeth, and put those in his ring along with the spear.

Ten minutes later everyone was good to go. They hit the stairwell and descended to the fourth and final level without incident, as expected.

Beyond the door, they found a mostly empty corridor. The walls and ceiling were blackened with soot, and some small debris was scattered here and there on the floor. Wires hung down, along with scorched ceiling insulation. There was a strong odor of burnt… something in the air that Allistor couldn't place.

Jenkins, at the back of the group and still moving slowly because his mind told him he should still be hurt despite being fully healed, said, "I've seen this before. When a ruptured gas line ignited. It created a flash burn like this here. Really hot, but over pretty quick. A few folks died, but it was the lack of oxygen that killed them. Their bodies were barely burnt."

They proceeded carefully down the corridor, Allistor in the lead once again. Each room they checked was the same. Either the door had been closed during the fire, and the room was untouched, or the door had been open and the room was just as black as the hallway.

430

Jenkins piped up again. "This doesn't seem right. The rooms shouldn't be as burnt. At least not on all the walls and the entire ceiling. The blast should have funneled down the hall..." He trailed off as his eyes got wider. Everyone turned to look at what he saw.

Rounding the corner at the end of the hall was a dragon. A tiny, flying dragon. No more than three feet tall, not counting its tail, the little thing resembled a mature dragon in every way except its size. Tiny horns protruded from its head and the joints of its wings. Sharp talons adorned all four clawed feet. A ridge of spines ran down its back to the tip of its tail, which was itself a hardened leaf-shaped spike.

The moment it saw the group of humans, it belched a gout of flame that extended maybe six feet from its snout. Then it let out a squawking cry that was quickly answered by several others.

"Oh, hell no!" Andrea said. "Friggin' dragons? Really?"

Bjurstrom said, "Relax, they're just babies. Check them out."

Allistor and the others all *Examined* the one they could see.

Infant Fire Drake
Level 6
Health: 3,200/3,200

The baby dragon hovered as if trying to decide whether to attack. As the humans and dragon stared at each other, Weiss murmured, "So much for your gas explosion. I'm guessing these little guys have just been practicing their flaming skill on everything in sight."

Jenkins nodded. "Yeah. Short bursts, probably really hot. This is going to suck."

Allistor thought they could probably take down this one infant drake before it got close enough to burn anyone. But if there were several... "Hey, guys, let's retreat into one of these rooms and close the door. We need to figure out a strategy before the others arrive."

Without hesitation, the others picked one of the undamaged rooms, entered, and secured the door. They'd chosen a bunk room, which made the quarters feel a little close with so many bodies. Several of the airmen took to the bunks, making more room for those still standing. They stayed silent for a minute or more, waiting for some kind of attack on the door. But they heard nothing at all, no scratching or flapping.

"Maybe it forgot about us?" McCoy ventured, his voice barely above a whisper.

Helen nodded. "If it has a tiny or undeveloped brain, it might have the attention span of a newborn. Out of sight, out of mind."

"Okay, so maybe if we keep it from making noise, it won't call for backup." McCoy gave a single nod as if sure the statement was fact.

Helen added, "Allistor can stun them, maybe keep them from flaming while we shoot them down."

Bjurstrom asked, "How quickly and often can you cast that? Does it have a cooldown like in the games?"

"It takes me a second to cast. And no cooldown that I'm aware of, but it's not guaranteed to work. There's some formula with levels, intelligence level, maybe a dice roll from the RNG in there somewhere." He shrugged. "Also sometimes the stun is only for a second or two. Or like with the big lizard, as much as ten seconds. And I can cast it maybe twenty times before I'm out of juice."

They all paused as a flapping sound outside the door was quickly followed up by a questioning squawk. A moment later flames licked under the door, causing those closest to it to press back against the others. They all remained silent as the flapping sound continued, then faded away.

Whispering now, Allistor asked, "So do we try and fight them in the corridor? Seems like a tight space. I think it might be better if we could spread out, maybe kite them around a big room? Is there something like that down here?"

Andrea grinned. "The pool! The pool is on this level."

Helen blinked a couple times. "You guys have a pool down here?"

Andrea nodded her head. "I mean, it's not meant for recreational activity. When you dig this deep underground sometimes you run across natural springs. Can't have damp, drippy halls and rooms, so the engineers redirected them into a great big natural cavern cistern down here. It's deep enough to hold a lot of water, and we use it as a supply for both drinking water and fire suppression."

433

"And it's a great place to go swummin' if ya don't mind the cold water," Goodrich added.

Helen nodded. "So we could fight them in there. Hop in and dip under the water if they get too flamey?"

"Yeah, but how do we get there? The pool is at the end of Corridor E. That's about a hundred yards from here. If more of those things are between us and that door…"

Jenkins, who had been only half listening as he munched on some more jerky, suddenly looked up. "The pool? Shit… I got this!"

He pulled one of the blankets from the foot of the bunk nearest him and wrapped it around himself, covering his head. Then he grabbed a fire extinguisher from the wall. "Wait five seconds, then follow me!"

Before anybody could stop him, he yanked open the door and dashed through. There was a squawk in the hallway, followed quickly by a blast from the extinguisher and some wild laughter.

"Jeeenkins!" Andrea yelled after him, but he was already gone. "Shit! Let's go!" She followed him out into the corridor in time to see him rounding the corner ahead with a white-coated and angry dragonling flapping after him. The entire group rushed out to follow, Allistor moving to the front in hopes of stunning the little dragon chasing the airman.

They heard two more blasts of the extinguisher before Allistor reached the corner and was able to see Jenkins again. The man was far down the corridor, still laughing as he ran. Behind him were three of the baby dragons, all flapping after him. Allistor watched as Jenkins hit the ground in a baseball slide and blasted two more of them as he passed underneath. In a flash, he was back on his feet and sprinting away. The first three dragonlings crashed into the two who'd just been blinded, slowing all of them down as the insane airman turned another corner.

Allistor held the group back until all the dragonlings had disappeared after Jenkins. There were a few hissed protests, but he used his radio and said with a whisper, "That lunatic is either dead, or he's actually accomplishing his mission and leading them to the pool. We can't aggro any of them here, or they might turn back. Let's follow at a safe distance."

He matched word to deed and started down the corridor at a brisk pace. The others followed right behind, weapons ready. Two more airmen ducked into rooms to grab fire extinguishers. When they reached the next corridor, Allistor peered around quickly and whispered, "All clear," into his throat mic.

Andrea whispered, "The end of this corridor, turn right and the door to the pool is right there, about twenty feet down. They must all be inside now."

Allistor took off at a run. The others picked up their pace as well. Reaching the end, he didn't bother to slow. The dragons had to be in the room ahead. He could hear angry squawking. Rounding the corner, he found the door wide open, and about twenty dragonlings flapping about in the large chamber on the other side. Below them was a large pool that stretched off toward the back of a natural cavern.

There was no sign of Jenkins.

Allistor was about to enter the room and search for the crazy man when his head popped up out of the water. He shouted, "Little help, guys!" before taking a deep breath and plunging back below the surface as several of the dragonlings shot flames in his direction.

Allistor cast *Restraint* on the one closest to Jenkins, causing its wings to freeze before it plunged into the water right above Jenkins. There was a thrashing below the surface, and he assumed Jenkins was trying to kill the mob.

Andrea took charge, saying, "Focus on the closest ones in your lanes. Headshots if you can. You guys with shotguns, shred their wings. Be ready with the extinguishers if they look like they're going to flame."

The group advanced into the room, guns up and ready in a rough half-circle. Each of them chose a target in their firing lane. When Andrea gave the command, they fired. Six of the dragonlings went down bleeding, two more were injured but remained airborne. All of the rest focused on the humans and attacked.

Allistor stunned as many as he could as quickly as he could. A few more got dumped into the water, but most fell on the stone floor between the pool and his group. Helen and the airmen picked those off with easy headshots at close range. Some of the ones who'd been downed but not killed by the initial volley were hopping or crawling their way closer. A gout of flames scorched two airmen on the right side of their arc before one of the extinguishers could stop it. The two men fell screaming, rolling around trying to put out the flames.

Allistor cast heals on both of them, but the damage was too severe. The dragon fire wasn't going out as they rolled, and the extinguisher blast didn't put it out either. The screaming stopped as both airmen died.

"Sons of bitches!" Bjurstrom shouted, switching his rifle to automatic. He took aim at a group of the grounded dragonlings and cut loose. Dragon flesh exploded as thirty rounds pounded into them in just a few seconds.

Allistor went back to focusing on those still in the air. There were only four of them left, and they had been distracted by Jenkins, who'd burst from the water for another breath and blasted them with his extinguisher. Allistor hit each one with *Restraint*, dropping them into the water. Just as the last one hit, Jenkins resurfaced.

Allistor shouted "Run to us!" but he needn't have bothered. Jenkins was already running as fast as he could in the waist-deep water, pumping his legs and shouting "Mama!" for some reason. A few of the airmen chuckled at his antics even as they finished off the dragonlings that were on solid ground.

Their laughter stopped abruptly when the water behind Jenkins erupted, spraying nearly to the cavern ceiling. When the water succumbed to gravity again, it revealed a much larger dragon.

Fire Drake Matron
Level 12
Health: 9,000/9,000

"Jenkins, move your ass!" Andrea was screaming at him.

The terrified man was reaching knee-deep water and plowing forward as quickly as he could. He let the wet blanket drop off his shoulders and dropped his nearly-empty fire extinguisher to lighten his load. He was screaming one long word as he ran, pausing for breaths then continuing. "Shiiiiii…iiiiiii…iiiiit!!

Behind him, the drake took a moment to survey the cavern. Upon spotting her offspring lying dead or dying, she raised her head and let out a roar that caused rocks to shake loose and fall from the ceiling. Turning toward the humans, she began to stride through the deep water.

She was massive, larger than the forest drake that had snatched Candy from the wall of the Warren. Though half her body was still submerged, her neck extended a good twenty feet from shoulders to head. About twenty yards back from her shoulders, a spiked tail emerged from the water and slapped back down. Her scales were a deep crimson, shining wetly as her body undulated. Spines on her forehead looked long enough to impale a buffalo, and her eyes glowed a bright flaming orange. A bow wave formed in front of her as she pushed her way into the shallower depths in pursuit of Jenkins and the murdering invaders.

Jenkins cleared the water amid much shouting and arm-waving encouragement. Andrea screamed, "Back through the door!" and her people immediately complied. Allistor hesitated a few seconds, trying *Restraint* on the monster. The spell had little effect, only causing her to pause for a second and stumble in the water, angering her even more.

Allistor fled like the rest. Campbell was waiting by the door, slamming it shut the moment Allistor was clear. He cranked the wheel that locked the hatch shut even as the drake's roar was followed by a sound that could only be flames beating against the door. Campbell pulled his hands away, saying "The door's gettin' warm already."

A moment later, a heavy weight slammed against the door and wall. Metal complained as it bent slightly.

"How the hell do we fight something like that?" Jenkins gasped, hands on his knees and breathing heavily. "Also, I might have shit myself."

Nobody took time to laugh or tease the soaking wet airman, though a few took a couple steps back from him. Everyone was staring at the door, which was beginning to ping from the metal being heated.

"That door won't last long," Andrea observed. "Any ideas?"

"We could open the door and get it to stick its head in. Then chop at it?" Helen offered.

"That head comes with some nasty teeth, spikes, and fire," McCoy countered.

Allistor liked the idea though, and a plan was forming in his head. He thought it out loud for the others. "If just a couple of us stood on either side of the door, the rest of you could be around the corner. You could pop out and fire between flaming breaths while we damage it from the sides. I'll try to stun it before each breath, to maybe give you more time to hit it. I tried once, and it only worked for half a second, but that might be enough."

Bjurstrom nodded, reloading his weapon. "If every shot is a head shot, and we can get some crits while it's stunned... might work? Are crits a thing here?"

439

Allistor nodded. "Yeah, the usual. Sneak attacks, hits from behind, incapacitated opponent, and just the RNG granting you a lucky shot." He looked around. "I'll be by the door. I won't ask anyone to stand there with me. It'll be dangerous, maybe suicidal."

Airman Weiss held up her blade. "I just put two points into *Strength*. I'll hack pieces off mama dragon with you."

Campbell held up his hand to volunteer, but Andrea stopped him. "No. You're a marksman. We need you out here shooting." The other three security officers who'd been about to volunteer lowered hands that had been on the way up.

Another airman named Corvin volunteered. Someone handed him one of the blades, and he took a couple test swings. "I've got a four in strength, and I'm good with blades." was all he said.

Allistor said, "We won't have room for any more, I don't think. If we're too crowded together we lose the ability to dodge." He looked at the two of them. "Each of you grab an extra blade, in case you break yours. And a fire extinguisher. They won't do any good all the way back here. Might work as an interrupt once or twice."

The two airmen did as he asked, and the rest of the group retreated down the hall around the corner.

Allistor and Weiss took up position on the right side of the hatch, while Corvin stood back on the left. When the door opened, it would open to his side. Then he could step forward and attack. Each of the airmen set a fire extinguisher on the floor next to the wall. They each gripped a blade, and kept a spare stuck in their belts. Weiss's spare was the fire axe.

Allistor pulled a pair of leather gloves from his ring and put them on. Taking hold of the wheel, he began to turn it. The heated and possibly bent mechanism was difficult to turn and required a significant bit of his strength. After just a few seconds, the gloves began to get hot, then started to smoke. Allistor was forced to let go and pour some water on them.

His second attempt went better, and the door finally unlocked. Allistor didn't open it, diving back to his position on the right, instead. There was no doubt the drake would hit the door again, and he didn't want to be standing in front of it when that happened. Or open it himself and get roasted.

They waited, the tension increasing as the seconds ticked by. Corvin adjusted the grip on his machete, his knuckles whitening. Weiss, who was behind Allistor, shuffled her feet and coughed once. Allistor gripped his trusty rebar spear and clenched his jaw tightly shut.

Without warning the door burst open as a withering wave of heat blasted through the opening. Some of the backlash from the door angled toward Allistor, scorching his armor and searing his exposed skin. He cast a heal on himself and felt the pain ease slightly as the flame subsided and shots rang out from down the hall.

The monster roared, the sound coming from just inside the door. A moment later its scaled and horned head jammed through the door, jaws open and another gout of flame was sent down the corridor.

Allistor didn't take time to see if his people got out of the way. He lunged forward, jamming the point of the rebar spear into the side of the dragon's neck just behind what looked like ear holes. The spear point penetrated a spot between two scales, and Allistor put all his strength into driving it home. Even then, it only sank about two feet deep in the creature's flesh. He was about to twist the weapon and yank it out for some tearing damage when a thrash of the drake's head knocked him back. He struck the wall hard, bruising if not breaking some ribs.

Weiss and Corvin both stepped forward, hitting the neck with downward two-handed chops. Their first blows were turned aside, but neither let that deter them. They struck, again and again, trying to weaken the scales and get some penetration. The crew down the hall began firing again, and Allistor could hear the slugs and bullets striking the creature's head. One struck a bony protrusion above its eyes and ricocheted into the wall not far from Weiss.

Allistor and the airmen were taking a huge risk of being hit by friendly fire in addition to the damage this beast could dish out.

Getting back in the fight, he stepped forward and took hold of the spear's shaft with both hands. Grunting from the effort, he twisted and pulled on the rebar, yanking it free in a spray of hot, tangy blood. Without even blinking, he cast *Restraint* on the beast and instantly jammed the weapon back into the same hole when it froze. This time the point went much deeper, nearly all the way through the monster's neck.

Fire Drake Matron
Level 12

Health: 5,300/9,000

The drake screamed as blood began to flow freely and pool beneath the wound. It attempted to withdraw its head from the doorway, but the spear caught on the door frame. Sheer force bent the shaft about forty-five degrees, while at the same time causing the tip to slice and tear through flesh and muscle inside the neck.

Allistor left the spear where it was, effectively trapping the drake's head on their side of the door. Pulling out his sword, he began to stab at the beast alongside Weiss. The monster ceased trying to withdraw, learning that it caused pain. Instead, it belched fire down the hallway again. The gunshots paused as the group hid behind the corner. Allistor cast *Mind Spike*, and the flames ceased as the pain seared through its brain.

A jerk of the drake's head sent one of its spikes into Weiss's shoulder, pinning her to the wall briefly. She screamed and dropped her blade, both hands grabbing the spike that impaled her. The drake's head moved again, and her unconscious body flopped like a ragdoll in the air, still hanging from the spike.

Corvin shouted in rage and stepped to the side, narrowly missing being stuck with a spike himself. He drove his blade deep into the drake's eye, then fell backward, leaving the weapon stuck inside the orb. Now on the ground, he rolled backward until he came up against the wall, where he huddled to avoid the spikes thrashing about above him.

The reaction from the drake shook Weiss free, sending her flying into a wall. Allistor hit it with *Restraint* again, and this time it froze. Its head was tilted almost

443

ninety degrees to one side, the spikes pointed just above Corvin's head, and its throat exposed to Allistor. He lunged forward and drove the sword up under its chin. He felt the blade pass through the soft tissue of its skin and tongue, then there was a moment of resistance as the point pressed against the harder roof of its mouth. A half second later, it pushed through with a sort of pop and penetrated further.

The stun wore off and the dragon, disregarding the lesson it learned just seconds earlier, yanked its head back through the doorway. The rebar spear bent further as it was pulled through the opening, and did more damage inside the monster's neck as it was forced through. When it opened its mouth, the tip of the sword blade withdrew from the roof of its mouth, and thick blood poured forth.

Allistor dove to the side as the drake once again spewed fire through the opening. The heat, even off to the side out of the flame's path, was intense. He cast a heal on Weiss, taking a moment to make sure the flow of blood from her shoulder slowed, and her health bar stopped dropping. Since she was unconscious and couldn't drink the health potion he produced, he uncorked it and poured some of it directly into her wound. Putting the cork back in, he placed the potion in her lap.

The trail of blood on the floor leading back into the cavern was thick. If a human had lost that much blood, they would have expired. But the drake was the size of a few dozen humans, and Allistor had no illusions that it would bleed out soon. He'd already lost two airmen in this fight, and the longer it went on, the greater the risk of losing more. Having lost both his spear and sword, Allistor searched his inventory for a weapon that would be effective against this beast. When he found a particular item, he smiled and withdrew it, gripping it tightly.

Unable to see the drake's head, as it was currently well above the door opening, he targeted its body and cast *Mind Spike* again. The answering roar and rain of blood from above the doorway told him the spell had struck its target. With a shout of "Cease fire!" for his comrades down the hall, he dove through the door, the still-dripping blood soaking him as he passed through. He ignored the burning sensation as he drove forward with his legs, pushing back to his feet.

He managed to reach the drake's chest without being hit by the thrashing head. Turning to put his back to its chest, he waited until the head bent low to the ground, and cast *Restraint* again, freezing the head in place. Knowing he only had a second, he lunged for the neck, bringing his new weapon to bear. Just as the drake started to move again, he slammed the envenomed fang he'd taken from the giant snake into the monster's neck right where the rebar spear had opened a wide wound. The fang sank deeply, and the drake howled in pain, raising its head.

Still holding the fang with one hand, Allistor gripped the spear with the other and held on tightly as the boss monster lifted him off his feet and swung him around. When its neck made a sort of whiplash motion, even his improved strength couldn't help him. He was thrown loose and sent flying twenty feet through the air before impacting the stone wall.

The impact knocked the breath from him and sent his vision fuzzy. He lay on the ground at the base of the wall, struggling to take a breath. His vision faded even more as he heard gunfire and the roar of the beast. Trying to focus on the big red blob in front of him, he cast *Mind Spike* once more and passed out.

Chapter Seventeen

Victory And Death!

Allistor woke to the sensation of a bear cub tongue licking his face. And the stench of whatever Fuzzy had been snacking on.

"Gah! What the hell, Fuzzy?" He was trying to push the bear away from his face when he remembered the drake. Adrenaline rushed through his system and he sprang to his feet, frantically searching for the boss monster. His head pounded, and he lost his balance, leaning against the wall for support.

What he saw was most of his group standing around smiling at him, some laughing. "Way to fall asleep on the job there, hero." Helen winked at him. Notifications flooded across his interface, but he swiped them away.

"What happened?" He looked behind them at the inert form of the fire drake. "Did we win?"

Bjurstrom smirked at him. "Nope. We wiped. We're all dead. This is hell."

His wits still slightly scattered from the blow to the head, Allistor didn't get the joke right away. He opened his mouth, then closed it again a few times, unable to form a coherent thought. Helen stepped forward and grabbed his head in both hands, staring into his eyes.

"You got slammed pretty hard. We weren't sure you were going to wake up. You gotta teach some of us that healing spell. It sucked, just sitting here watching you drool. And Weiss isn't doing all that much better."

"Heals. Yeah." He cast a heal on himself, immediately feeling a little better. "Where's Weiss?"

Helen took his arm and supported him as she led him back out to the corridor, where Weiss sat with her back against the wall. The empty health potion vial sat on the floor next to her. She looked up, obviously still in pain. "It's getting better. But if you could speed things up?" she spoke with her jaw clenched.

He cast another heal on her, feeling a bit woozy still, and she sighed with relief. Hoping for some of the same, he cast another heal on himself.

"What happened?" he asked, taking a seat next to Weiss. His health bar was up to eighty percent, but his equilibrium was still off.

"You tell us." Andrea squatted down in front of him so that they were face to face. "You shouted at us to stop firing, then dove in there like you were friggin' Jenkins." Several of the group chuckled and poked at Jenkins. "We saw you charge the thing, then stab it. Then you went flying up out of sight, and we heard a thud that I'm guessing was you hitting the wall. Hard. We started firing at the thing's belly, cuz that's all we could see. A few seconds later it fell over twitching, then died."

Helen added, "We ran in and found you all crumpled up against the wall. I thought you were dead." There was a hint of tears forming in her eyes. The others behind her nodded, agreeing that he'd looked quite dead.

"I... I used poison," he said as he explored his memory of the fight. "The big fang from the snake we killed. I... think that dragon broke my spear."

448

Jenkins grinned at him, holding up the badly bent length of rebar. "Bent the hell out of it! It looks like some weird piece of art now. We're gonna mount this thing on a wall somewhere to commemorate this battle!"

Campbell extended a hand holding Allistor's sword. "Pulled this out of its jaw. Thought you might want it back."

Allistor reached for the offered hilt but missed. He dropped his hand back to his lap and said, "Maybe hold onto it for a few?" Campbell nodded in understanding.

"Really got your bell rung, there. Just take it easy. We've cleared the rest of this level, so I think the whole place is ours again, boss. Err, Baron, dude." Goodrich looked sheepish.

Allistor rubbed his head gently, saying "Need to claim this place... before more spawns. Hang on, guys."

He closed his eyes to remove the background visual input that was making him dizzy as he looked at his interface. As quickly as he could, he pulled up the Stronghold tab and mentally clicked the green button to claim the complex as a Stronghold. He didn't mess with any of the options like sensors or walls yet, as trying to focus too long on the text was making him nauseous.

Even with his eyes closed, he could see the golden light that surrounded them, and he heard the surprised exclamations from the others. When it faded, he opened his eyes again. The others were all spinning around, taking in their modified surroundings.

Fuzzy sniffed at him a few times, then grunted and plopped down next to him. The Fibble doll in his mouth stared up at Allistor as if pleading for help. He chuckled and reached out to scratch Fuzzy's ears.

When the group quieted down, the radio crackled in Allistor's ear. A voice came across. "That was *awesome, guys!* We got that whole dragon fight recorded. Congrats!" Allistor thought it was Thorne speaking.

Andrea saved him the hassle of answering. Keying her throat mic she replied, "Thanks. We'll be heading back up shortly. There better be a decent meal and some adult beverages waiting for us when we get there!"

The airmen around her cheered, fist-bumping and back-slapping each other. Allistor tried to focus on their faces, then remembered the two who'd been killed. "What about the two inside? We need to bury them."

The group went silent, and Helen put a hand on his shoulder. "There… wasn't much left of them. Looks like the dragon ate them while we had it trapped inside."

"Shit." Allistor bowed his head, the motion slow and gentle so as not to make himself dizzy again. "I'm sorry, guys. I should have found a better way."

"Bullshit!" McCoy's voice was husky. "Those were friends of mine. They knew what they were getting into when they stepped forward. They didn't need you or anyone else to protect them. They died as friggin' heroes!"

Andrea nodded once. "You had a good plan, Allistor. And you fought like a madman. If it weren't for you, we'd have all died down here." Every head in the corridor nodded at him.

"Thanks, guys." Allistor didn't feel any better about the deaths on his watch, but he wasn't going to whine about it in front of his troops. "If one of you can give me a hand up, we'll go loot the boss." He gave them his best possible grin and watched as their eyes lit up. Everybody loved to loot the boss.

Helen supported him again as they assisted both him and Weiss back into the cavern. The dragon's corpse wasn't far from the door, and Allistor leaned against it as he placed his hand on its head to loot. The others all did the same.

He received five hundred klax, one Fire Drake Heart, five stacks of tainted drake meat, two dragon claws, and two stacks of Crimson Drake Hide, the description of which was in bold purple letters. Allistor assumed that made it some kind of rare crafting item.

He sat back down as Helen directed the whole crew in skinning the thick scaly leather from the drake's corpse. They each took their standard issue Ka-Bar knives and went to work. Bjurstrom was actually giggling at the thought of having crimson dragonscale armor.

Allistor took a minute to review all the notifications he'd waved away upon waking up. The first one wasn't a surprise after clearing a dungeon's worth of mobs and a dragon boss.

Level Up! You are now Level 11. You have earned two attribute points.

The next few made him smile.

Attribute Increase: Constitution +1

For repeatedly enduring and surviving physical abuse at the hands of your enemies, your Constitution Attribute has increased by +1

Skill Level Up! *Your* Improvisation **Skill has increased by one point.**

Skill Level Up! *Your* Improvisation **Skill has increased by one point.**

Your proficiency with the Mind Spike **spell has increased to level two.**

Your proficiency with the Nature's Boon **spell has increased to level three.**

Your proficiency with the Flame Shot **spell has increased to level three.**

Congratulations! You have created and secured your third Stronghold!
You have chosen to name this Stronghold 'The Silo'. Please see your Stronghold tab for more information and options.

There were other less important notifications, like increases in his sword and spear skills, the fact that Fuzzy had leveled up twice, etc. He passed over them quickly.

He was about to dump all the tainted meat from his ring when he reconsidered. The meat could be used as bait to kill off canids or other monsters around the two strongholds. When he called Helen over to mention the idea, she frowned. "I don't like it. Too many other critters might decide to take some free meat. Local wolves, cats, foxes, even rabbits. Don't want to kill off everything around here."

"Rabbits? Since when do rabbits eat meat?" Allistor was pretty sure she was screwing with him.

"Since always? They mostly eat plants, but I've seen them go cannibal and eat their own young. It's... not something I like to remember." She made a disgusted face.

"I would think not!" He chuckled, noticing the pain in his head seemed a bit less. "Friggin' carnivore bunnies? That's nightmare fuel."

He dumped the meat tainted by the ophidian poison, assuming that it would fade away. The others all did the same after Helen made a brief announcement. A few of the airmen started sorting through the mostly broken and burnt storage crates in the cavern, emptying a few of the intact ones to fill with the harvested drake hide. Allistor pulled several stacks of it into his ring to lighten the load they'd be carrying upstairs. He also collected several dozen teeth that Helen had them break free from the thing's jaws, and six of its claws. None of the others had rings yet, and the packs they carried on their backs would only hold so much.

As they were finishing up, Allistor noticed that Fuzzy wasn't in sight. "Hey, Fuzzy? Time to go bud, where are you?"

A high-pitched growl answered from somewhere toward the back of the cavern, around the edge of the pool. He called again. "C'mon, Fuzzy! Time to go!" This time there was no answer.

Seeing that he was still unsteady on his feet, Helen offered, "I'll go get him. Wait here." She jogged off in the direction of the growl, Campbell falling in behind her, just in case. A few seconds after they faded into a dark corner, she called out. "Uhhh, I think you are gonna wanna see this!"

Andrea helped Allistor walk the distance to where Helen and Campbell stood looking down at the floor. Following their gaze, he found Fuzzy licking at what he initially thought was a stone. But even with his addled brain, the oblong shape and the fact that it was clustered with several nearly identical twins quickly registered in his mind.

"It's a nest. Eggs. It's a friggin dragon nest full of eggs."

"Thank you, captain obvious." Helen smirked at him as Fuzzy continued to lick one of the eggs like it was made by Cadbury.

Goodrich raised his shotgun. "I got this."

He pumped a round into the chamber and was about to fire when Andrea said, "Wait!" As he lowered the weapon and looked at her questioningly, she asked, "Do you guys not pay attention at all?" Looking around at blank faces, she pointed at Fuzzy. "Who's this?"

Allistor, as confused as the rest, answered. "That's Fuzzy. I introduced you to him-"

She cut him off with the raised 'talk-to-the-hand' gesture. "Okay fine, not who...but *what* is Fuzzy?" She glared at him as if he were the slow kid in class and she was trying to drill simple addition into his brain.

"He's my... oh, shit!" Allistor was suddenly excited. "He's my bonded pet!"

As soon as he said those words, the gamers in the group went crazy. Airmen bent to hug the eggs carefully, whispering sweet nothings to them. Bjurstrom started giggling again. "We're all gonna have dragon pets!"

Allistor cautioned them. "Not so fast, guys. We don't know if taming dragons is possible. But damn, if it is, that would be awesome!" he couldn't help himself. He looked around. There were at least twenty of the eggs that he could see.

Andrea, with visions of her very own dragonling, said, "I want a guard down here watching over these 24/7. Do we need to do something? Keep them warm or something?"

"Probably wouldn't be a bad idea to get a couple space heaters down here. For now, maybe take some broken crate bits and start a fire somewhere near the middle?" Helen added. Her park ranger status gave her words some added weight. The airmen immediately left off their coddling of the eggs and began to gather wood. When it was piled in the rough center of the clusters, he used *Flame Shot* to light the fire.

"When we get upstairs, I'll add a market kiosk. Then we can do some shopping. I'll get rings for everyone, and see if I can find a scroll or book about the *Taming* skill." Allistor promised. Fuzzy continued to lick at his favorite egg.

*****

With the threat of monsters eliminated, they were able to use the freight elevator to haul their loot crates back up to the main level. Helen had insisted they bring the egg that Fuzzy had adopted up with them, packed in a crate with spare clothes wrapped around it. She wanted to study it further. Allistor thought it might be a good idea to have Amanda examine it with her special skill as well.

There was indeed a party waiting for them in the mess hall. Thorne had outdone himself with steaks and potatoes, and German chocolate cake for dessert that even had the coconut mixed into the frosting. Fuzzy was given a plate along with everyone else, and the whole group laughed as he daintily licked all the frosting off the cake before biting into it.

True to his word, Allistor modified the Stronghold after the meal was complete. He added the walls outside, the proximity sensors, and the market kiosk. He didn't need to add electricity or water options, because the complex was already built with geothermal power and had the underground springs feeding it water. He also added the greenhouse outside, believing that every stronghold should be able to raise its own food in the event of a siege.

As soon as the kiosk appeared, he used it to purchase thirty of the PPD rings for storage. He also purchased himself a second ring with a two hundred slot capacity.

He began to pass out the rings, starting with Andrea. As she accepted it, she swore an oath of loyalty to Allistor. The green and blue lights swirled around her, and she became Oathbound. One by one, each of the others did the same. Except for Durham, who flat out refused.

"Don't you guys get it? The world ended! There's no more government. Nobody is in charge. We don't have to follow anybody's rules anymore. The oath I swore when I enlisted is null and void, and I'm sure as hell not going to swear one to this asshole."

The others began to converge on him, some trying to reason with him, others intending violence. Allistor held up his hands to forestall them all and called for quiet.

"Durham... I said before you don't have to swear an oath to me. But if you choose not to, you can't stay here. So, despite the general consensus that you're a whiny, obnoxious, self-centered shit, I'll give you one last opportunity to take the same oath as the others and remain here with us. We'll find a way to live and work together."

"Screw you, college boy!" Durham's face was turning red again.

"Fine. You are hereby banished from any and all lands held by myself and my allies from this day forward. Leave, and don't come back." A red light swirled around him, and his eyes unfocused for a minute.

"No! This is my home! You have no right to force me out!"

Bjurstrom stepped forward, hand on his sidearm. "Allistor came here and put his life on the line more than once to clear those lower levels and make this place safe for us. He has a rightful claim to this place. All you've ever done here is whine about missing the sun and eat more than your share of the food. Walk out of here now, Durham. While you can still walk."

Allistor put a hand on Bjurstrom's shoulder. "It's no small thing to kill another human. Especially now when there are so few of us. Helen and I had to kill three yesterday. We didn't want to, but they attacked us."

Turning to Durham, he said. "Like it or not, this new System has given me the right to claim this place, and I have done so. This is no longer your home, by your own choosing. Now, I'm done talking to you. Leave on your own, or I will have you escorted out and dropped in the woods ten miles from town where you can't bother anyone."

Durham's face was now a splotchy scarlet shade. He clearly wasn't used to being told 'no'. Looking around the room, he saw only hostile faces looking back.

"Screw each and every one of you!" he shouted. He shouldered his way past Bjurstrom, headed for the door. Just as he was passing Allistor and Andrea began detailing an escort for him, Durham spun and drove a steak knife into Allistor's back. Leaving the knife, he turned to dash for the door.

Fuzzy beat him to it, the small bear rearing up on his hind legs in the doorway and giving his best roar, teeth bared and claws extended. Durham plowed right into him, unable to break his momentum. The two tumbled to the floor as Fuzzy latched hold of the man's throat with his jaws and dug into his back with both sets of foreclaws.

Durham screamed, but it was cut off when Fuzzy jerked his head and ripped out a significant portion of the man's throat.

Allistor, now on his knees and trying to remove the knife from his back, cast a *Mind Spike* on Durham, partly to protect his cub, and partly because he wanted the man to die in as much pain as possible.

Bjurstrom dropped to a knee next to Allistor as several of the others jumped on Durham, pulling him off the bear cub. Blood sprayed from his savaged throat, and it was only seconds before the light left his eyes.

Allistor gritted his teeth and nodded to Bjurstrom, who yanked the blade from his back. Allistor grunted in pain, going down on all fours for a moment and breathing raggedly. The knife had penetrated one of his lungs. He cast a heal on himself, and the pain lessened as his breathing became a bit easier. A moment later he cast another heal. Several hands reached out to help him up to his feet.

"Damn. That hurt." He grinned and rubbed his back near where the wound was healing over. A few people chuckled nervously. Andrea began to apologize, but he stopped her. "This was not anybody's fault but his. And he paid the price." He looked around at everyone gathered there. "Let this be a lesson to all of you. Breaking your oath, or breaking the laws by murdering, stealing, and so forth will have harsh consequences." He let that sink in, watching people nod to him, then smiled at them.

"I probably won't feed you to my bear… but the punishment will be severe." This time people actually laughed. Just a few at first, then more as Fuzzy walked over and sat at Allistor's feet, licking blood off his cute little face. Though Fuzzy had leveled up several times and gotten larger, he didn't appear to have aged any. He was like one of those giant teddy bears you get from winning carnival games. Just as fuzzy and cute as the day Allistor discovered him.

Allistor's next order of business was to check in with the Warren and his people there. With Durham deceased, one of the others volunteered to take over communications. It seemed there was a lot of cross-training among the airmen in the complex. Airman Redd was a gentle-seeming woman with a winning smile. She fiddled with the gear for about two minutes, then handed Allistor a headset for privacy.

The first voice he heard was Sam's. "Allistor? You there, boy?"

"I'm here, Sam. Good to hear from you. How are things at the Warren? Has Nancy created any mutant bunnies?"

"Ha! She heard that. And she's giving you the finger," Sam replied. "Things are going smooth enough here. We've been going out and foraging every day. Brought back a few interesting things to sell. Made a trip to your gun shop outpost and loaded up some more weapons. We can talk about that when you get back."

They spoke for a few more minutes, Allistor feeling reassured by how calm things seemed to be at the Warren. He updated them on the two new Strongholds, and the people he'd recruited. His plans for a Citadel had everyone excited. "We're really doing this." Meg's voice was quiet. "We're really going to survive this thing." She sniffed, and Allistor knew there were tears in her eyes.

"I'll be back soon, Meg. I'm going to get things settled here and then stop back home before continuing on to Casper. So I'll see you tomorrow or the next day."

They exchanged a few pleasantries and signed off. Airman Redd accompanied him back to the mess hall, where everyone was still gathered.

"Have you guys got some vehicles? Enough to move everybody here? Except for a few who will stay to guard this place? I want to introduce you to the others at the mall."

Andrea quickly organized three people to stay, temporarily, to guard the Stronghold and watch over the dragonlings. She sent two airmen to grab vehicles and tasked Redd to make sure they had working handheld radios that would reach the mall, and an extra base setup to be installed there permanently. That way the Warren, Mall, and Silo could stay in constant contact.

Of the forty Air Force personnel who inhabited the complex on Apocalypse day, twenty six airmen had survived to meet Allistor, and three of those were now dead. With three more staying behind, an even score accompanied him back to the Mall. He drove his ranger truck with Helen and Fuzzy riding along. Behind him were two dark blue vans with the Air Force logo on the side. He led them out of the Silo's gates, which he set to close remotely, and across Cheyenne to the Mall. He honked his horn as soon as the gates closed behind him, and Dean's survivors emerged to greet them.

He left the introductions to Andrea, who knew everyone in both groups. They all retired inside to the food court, where there was seating for everyone to chat, and plenty of sunlight for the airmen who'd been underground for weeks. They talked about the Apocalypse and their different experiences since. A few of the airmen told the story of clearing the lower levels, and their battle with the drake. The discovery of the dragonling eggs caused quite a stir.

After an hour or so, Allistor pulled Dean, Andrea, and Helen aside, leading them into one of the unused storefronts and shutting the door behind them. Fuzzy sat outside, guarding the door. Which meant he plopped down on his belly and idly chewed gently on the Fibble doll.

"I wanted to speak to you about leadership." Allistor got straight to business. He was anxious to get back to the Warren, but he wanted to make sure things were stable here before he left. "As far as I'm concerned, you three are among my most trusted. Any one of you would make good leaders for our people. So my first question for each of you is: Are you willing to take on that responsibility?"

Dean was first to ask. "What kind of responsibility are we talking about, here?"

"Well, I'm about to turn this place into a Citadel. Which means it'll hopefully have a decent population of survivors, eventually. We can set up a democratic system of government, with some kind of town council or something for each Stronghold or Citadel. They can handle things like planning decisions, whether or not to charge yourselves taxes and how to spend them, assignment of available shops, that kind of thing. But there needs to be one person who has the final word. The person who says whether new survivors found out there are a good fit, and if they get to stay or have to go. Who is the ultimate authority in disputes? And who makes sure everyone is doing their part to grow and strengthen the community."

"So, like a Mayor," Helen suggested.

"Or a Commander," Andrea added with a grin.

"Right. We'll figure out the title if the System doesn't already have one. And down the road, maybe it can be an elected position. For now, the choice will be mine."

"I'm in." Andrea didn't hesitate. "And I suggest the title be Lord Commander. Or Chancellor. Or... Boss!"

Dean chuckled. "I'm up for the challenge. Though I'm no commander. I was a grunt, and that's all I'll ever be."

Helen shook her head. "I'm good with taking a leadership position. I'll help in whatever way I'm asked. But for now, I think I'm best suited to go with you on your little road trips. You need someone to watch your back other than Fuzzy. Maybe when we're done expanding I'll sit my ass down and become a mayor or whatever."

Allistor nodded. "Great! And thank you for being willing to step up. Now, we have two facilities here. And two pretty distinct groups. One being military, trained to accept orders from a superior officer. Which just happens to be Andrea. So what do you guys think of Andrea becoming officially Lady Commander of the Silo? A sort of captain of the city guard with a separate fortress that happens to be filled with nuclear missiles? It would be a subordinate position to you, Dean, as Chancellor of the

Mall Citadel? And both of you would remain subordinate to me, of course."

The two looked at each other, neither wanting to speak first. Finally, Andrea grinned at Dean. "I was already willing to follow Dean. He's been taking good care of us since we gathered together. I have faith in him. Sounds good to me."

Dean nodded, returning her smile. "I'd depend heavily on you to help me make decisions. And I wouldn't want our people to think of themselves as separate groups. Your people should mix and mingle here at the Mall.   And maybe some of my group can go there to train, or help with repairs, do some farming inside the walls, that kind of thing?"

Andrea held out her hand. "Agreed, sir Chancellor!" Dean took the hand and they shook.

"Right! Perfect. Now, I've authorized all three of you for access to almost every door in both places. As well as the two outposts between here and the Warren. I've also authorized you to add others to the list at your discretion. You can control who has access to what areas. The only exceptions are my quarters here in the Mall, and at the gun shop Outpost. And once Andrea explains to me where the big explodey stuff is inside the Silo, that area will be restricted to just the four of us, maybe a few others."

They all made agreeable sounds.

"For now, I think everyone is trustworthy enough to be able to open the outer gates. It might be necessary for their survival if something is chasing them out there. That may not be the case with later recruits. Use your best judgment. And have a plan in place in case there's some kind of mutiny or Trojan horse situation."

"Got it." Andrea gave him a thumbs-up."

"You'll each be in charge of a discretionary fund of klax or system points. We get a specific amount just for creating the bases. I intend to keep selling things through the market to make our communities rich. I'll ask that your foraging teams keep an eye out for rare or valuable items we can sell. This early, Earth items are going to sell for a lot of klax. I've already sold some cool vehicles for hundreds of thousands of klax. Those can be converted into system points that you can use to add onto your structures, or purchase spells and training scrolls for your people. I'll do some of that while I'm here, but I expect you'll continue on while I'm gone."

He looked each one of them in the eye for a moment, his countenance deadly serious. "Getting stronger is the number one priority. And that means everything. Our individual levels and attributes, our crafting and fighting skills, our weapons and armor, and our defenses. We need everyone mentally and physically tough. If one of our people encounters an ass like Twitch or Durham out there, I don't want it to be a fair fight. Our people should be able to crush them. Everybody clear on this?"

"Yes, sir!" Both Dean and Andrea spoke at once, their backs straightening as they unconsciously stood at attention. Helen just nodded her head.

"Good. One last thing… I expect the two of you to be the strongest. People find it easier to look up to strength and wisdom. That means you going out there to forage and fight. Killing whatever monsters you can, both for leveling

465

up and building your combat skills, and to help keep the surrounding area safe. Especially the corridor between the Silo and the Mall. We need that patrolled regularly, if not daily. Clear the roads, secure the buildings along the route. You get the idea. But beyond levels and fighting ability, I want you two to spend a little extra on training scrolls for skills, spell scrolls, etc. I want you to read all you can about the System, and share what you learn with each other and myself. I'll pass it along to the other leaders, and do the same for you. Ramon has been creating duplicate scrolls for the healing spell, among others. I'll have copies sent to you."

Helen, inspired by Allistor's planning and enthusiasm, called out, "Group hug!" and pulled them all together for a moment. Andrea laughed, and Dean blushed for some reason.

They chatted about details for a few more minutes, then rejoined the others in the food court. After checking to confirm whether the population was sufficient, Allistor decided to go ahead and pull the trigger. Several folks had wandered off to explore, so Allistor shouted to be heard by everyone up and down the promenade. "Okay, everybody! Hold onto something. I'm about to upgrade this place!"

Allistor pushed the button to complete the *Citadel* transaction.

A thunderous gong shook the entire building, followed by the expected golden light, and a chorus of trumpets and chimes. The ground shook violently under their feet. On Allistor's interface, golden fireworks were flashing in bursts here and there, and a message in fancy silver lettering appeared.

*World First! Baron Allistor has constructed the
first Citadel on UCP 382!*

*Congratulations, Baron Allistor! May you rule
long and wisely!*

Next was a second message in normal text that
appeared after the first one had faded.

*You are the first on your world to successfully
gather the noble title, land, resources, and people to enable
the creation of a Citadel. The creation of your world's first
Citadel has earned you a unique set of rewards. First, your
title of Baron has been upgraded to Viscount. Your Citadel
will receive complimentary upgrades to its perimeter
defense, communication, and morale bonuses. In addition,
your Citadel will be fitted with a Teleportation Hub, and
licenses for up to six substations free of charge. During the
Stabilization period, the Hub will only connect with others
located on your world. Lastly, you have been granted a
Library. This is a rare and valuable collection of
knowledge that exists nowhere else on your world. Protect
it well.*

When Allistor blinked away the notifications and
looked around, everyone else's eyes were still vacant. He
waited a few moments until Andrea focused on him.

"Oh, shit," was her first reaction.

"I know; that was awesome!" Allistor held out a fist
for bumping.

She obliged, but she corrected him. "Sure,
awesome Citadel, woohoo. But that first thing, it was a
world notice."

Allistor's enthusiasm left him as Helen and Dean listened in. He faintly heard Bjurstrom somewhere behind him echo Andrea's sentiment. "Oh, shit." All the gamers in the room knew what a worldwide announcement of an achievement like this mean. They'd just had a big red target painted on them. It happened in games all the time. A guild would reach the top ranking on a server, and other guilds would immediately begin planning to take them down.

In this particular case, why struggle to create a citadel of your own if you could just take one from the other guys?

As Andrea explained it to Dean and Helen, Allistor's shoulders slumped.

"Well, shit."

Chapter Eighteen

The Citadel

Allistor spent the rest of the evening on housekeeping. The first order of business was the improvements to the Citadel. He told everyone gathered about the information he'd received. They all practically ran outside to see the changes. The first and most noticeable was a second wall outside the first. The original wall was dwarfed by the new one. Forty feet high, with six massive stone towers that extended up another forty feet above the top of the wall. The wall itself was about two hundred yards farther out than the first. Also new, the entire area now sat upon a hill. While the mall had previously sat on level ground, Allistor's best guess was that it was now at an elevation about a hundred feet higher. From where he stood, he could see over both walls and look out over the city. The road leading up from below zigged and zagged through several switchbacks carved into the stone of the hill, making any approach difficult for enemies looking to storm the castle.

And castle it was. The blocky mall building had transformed into a multi-story stone and steel keep with a tower at one corner where his quarters had been located, and another on the opposite side. A steeply pitched roof still held extensive skylights, with the addition of a battlement around the perimeter.

Goodrich made everyone jump when he shouted, "Yeeeeehaw! We got us a castle!"

To one side of the inner gates was a wide metal pad with symbols etched into it. Atop the pad was an arch that rose twenty feet at the top. A pedestal stood to one side. "That must be our teleporter." Dean stared at it with awe. "Is that really a real actual thing now?"

Allistor grinned at him. "Really real. Who brings you all the coolest toys?!"

Helen snorted and said, "Doesn't do you much good unless you have a place to teleport to."

Allistor smacked his head. "You're right. We need to get them at the other strongholds. If our people can teleport between them, that eliminates the risk of traveling the roads. Hold on a second."

He pulled up his Stronghold interface and found the *Install Teleportation Substation* option. There was a little counter next to it showing six units available at no cost. Or rather, the licenses to install them were available. The actual installation of the structure cost two thousand klax. Allistor wasn't about to argue. When he selected the Warren, a three-dimensional map appeared on his display with a movable round icon that he could place in the location he wanted. He thought about it for a moment, then asked his three advisors.

"Hey, guys. I know this is just a wild guess kind of situation. But if we have a teleporter, do you think it could be used to invade this place? Like, could aliens use it to attack the Citadel once our year is up? Cuz if so, I'm thinking hard about where we place these."

Dean nodded, thinking. "I see your point. But, I mean... they have to have some kind of safeguard, right?

An authorization code or something? Otherwise who would ever use them?"

Helen snorted. "Maybe they're some kind of cosmic joke? Like... 'look at the foolish humans installing teleports everywhere so we don't even have to fly over to kill them in their sleep.' or something?"

Andrea sided with Dean. "I mean, I think they have to be securable somehow. But for today, and the rest of this year, the aliens can't come here, right? So all we have to worry about is other humans. And my guess is it will be a while before anyone else earns the ability, or the funds necessary, to buy them. I say we take advantage while we can."

"Good enough for me." Allistor placed the pad for the Warren next to the garage as a sort of compromise. Inside the wall, but outside the securable underground levels. Then he did the same for the Silo. He decided not to place them at the outposts.

Calling everyone together, he told them that a teleport system had been set up between the Strongholds. There was a brief pause of shock while everyone absorbed the news, then a loud cheering began. Goodrich did some kind of weird cowboy dance that fascinated Fuzzy. The bear seemed to think the man was afflicted somehow, and he walked over to sniff at him. Then very kindly set the Fibble at his feet as some kind of 'get well' or sympathy offering. Much to the delight of the crowd.

"So... who wants to be our lab monkey? I mean, this thing might be a hoax. Some cruel joke by the system, or an attempt to wipe us out like lemmings," Allistor asked, sobering the mood quite a bit. But Goodrich couldn't be deterred.

"I'm your huckleberry," he replied in a bad southern accent. He practically skipped over to stand on the pad. Allistor moved to the pedestal next to it, reaching out to touch it. The moment his hand got close, a holo-display appeared. There was a message asking for biometric confirmation of his identity, which he gave permission for. Then he had to choose authorized users. He chose himself, his three advisors there at the Citadel, Fuzzy, Sam, Meg, Luther, George, and Amanda. And he authorized each of them to add more people to the list.

Once that was complete, a menu popped up. It showed one sentient being on the platform and a choice of destinations. Turning to Andrea, he said, "Hey, maybe call the Silo and warn them we're transporting a man over? Ask them to tell us if Goodrich shows up in one piece? Or, you know… a pile of quivering meat, or something." He grinned at his guinea pig, who suddenly looked less enthusiastic. Andrea laughed and used her handheld to call the Silo.

While they waited for a response, Allistor mumbled to himself, "The alert message said something about improved communications too. I need to figure out what that was about. Maybe we won't need the radios?"

"That is correct, Lord Allistor." A voice echoed out of nowhere. It had a monotone voice with no accent and scared the bejeezus out of everyone within earshot. Fuzzy growled and picked Fibble back up, looking around suspiciously.

"Uhm, and who are you?" Allistor asked, suspecting he knew, but still looking around with his hand on his sidearm.

"I am sorry if I alarmed you, Lord Allistor. I am your Citadel's interface. Your link to the operations of this facility. I can also answer basic questions about the System's operations. You should find details about me in your Citadel Operations information."

"Typical. He hasn't bothered to read the directions for this place yet!" Helen smirked at him as the others tried not to smile. Allistor grinned back.

"Alright, thank you... uhm, do you have a name?"

"I am called Interface or Link by most users within the System. However, you may assign a different moniker at your discretion, Lord Allistor. Though, if I may, I would prefer you not assign me 'Sweetie'. This has been a recent trend among noble ladies after a popular Queen chose that moniker, and I find it... off-putting."

This time Allistor did laugh. "I promise not to call you sweetie. We'll figure out a name later. For now, what can you tell me about communications?"

Goodrich, realizing he wasn't about to get teleported, took a seat on the platform and acted casual.

"Communication between facilities owned by a Lord such as yourself is one of my simplest functions. I can facilitate private conversations between individuals or facility-wide broadcasts, or anything in between. At the moment, only audio communications are possible. But with some upgrades, I can provide visual and even three-dimensional holographic connections.

473

Andrea's radio crackled, and airman Redd worriedly reported she had a visual on the teleport pad, but there was no Goodrich. Andrea answered that he hadn't been sent yet. Allistor decided to test the link. "Please give me an audio link to airman Redd at the Silo. Broadcast it so that everyone at both ends can hear."

"Connection established, Lord."

"Hey, Redd!" Allistor unconsciously shouted.

He placed a hand over his mouth when he heard her startled response. "What the hell!? Allistor, is that you?"

"Yup. Sorry about the shouting. Not used to the new speakerphone system. Pretty cool, huh?"

"I'm gonna go with creepy," she replied. "Can you see me, too?"

"Nope, at least not yet. That's an upgrade. Anyway, there's an AI of some kind that lets us communicate between our bases. Whatever you do, don't call him sweetie." He paused while the others chuckled. "Okay, sending Goodrich over in a few seconds. I gotta figure out which button to push. One is green and says *Initiate Transfer*. There's another one that's red, and it says *Deresolution*."

"The green button! The green one!" Goodrich was back on his feet and looking like he was about to leap from the pad. "Never hit the red button!"

Allistor couldn't help but laugh. "Relax, my friend. There isn't really a red button." As he said it, he touched the green button, and a cursing Goodrich blinked out of existence.

"Damn," Bjurstrom said. "That was quick. I expected it to be all sparkly-wavy particles like in Star Trek."

A moment later, Goodrich's cursing could be heard over the loudspeaker. Then Redd's louder voice said, "He's here, boss. Fell on his ass as soon as he appeared. He looks a little disoriented but in one piece."

There were hoots and applause, and several more volunteers to try the thing out. Andrea held up a hand and silenced everyone. "Let's bring Goodrich back, if he's willing, and check him out. Make sure he doesn't … de-res like Allistor suggested. If he's still good in the morning, we can let everyone have a turn."

There was some disappointed grumbling, but the crowd quieted after watching Goodrich return. This time he stayed on his feet, saying, "Takes a bit of getting used to." Then a thought occurred to him. "Hey! I'm the first human ever teleported! I'm like… famous!" He stuck out his chest and marched off the platform, only to be pummeled good-naturedly by his buddies.

While Allistor had everyone gathered, he passed out rings to the rest of his citizens. This quickly brightened the mood among Dean's people. He also turned over two stacks of the snake meat to Dean, who grabbed Thorne and a few of the others and headed toward the kitchen.

Allistor, Helen, and Fuzzy moved inside and went to explore the tower. It was a wide structure with an elevator in its core and a stairway that wound upward along the outer wall. Stepping into the elevator, he didn't see any buttons. So he said, "Top level, please."

"Certainly, Lord Allistor." The doors closed and the lift rose silently, with no machine noise or vibration that Allistor could detect. A moment later the doors opened onto a wide covered balcony. There was a half-wall that encircled the entire area, leaving a four-foot glass window that provided a breathtaking view of the city all the way around the tower.

Fuzzy immediately put his paws up on the wall to look out the window, then just as quickly shrank back and cowered against the wall. He gave a little bear whimper and put his paws over his nose.

"Don't like heights, buddy?" Allistor reached down and scratched his ears. "I don't blame you. We're pretty high up here."

Between the newly risen hill and the height of the tower, Allistor estimated they stood something like twenty stories above the city's ground level. The view was amazing, with the forest and the mountains in the distance. They could easily see the walls of the Silo not so far away. Allistor thought this would be the perfect place for a lookout. They could place telescopes up here, and observe any activity for miles around. He walked around the outer edge, taking in his surroundings. Most of which was now under his control. On the back side of the elevator shaft, he found a step ladder leading to a hatch in the ceiling. Climbing up, he stuck his head through long enough to observe a platform with a railing around it. "Perfect place to mount that .50 cal," he whispered.

Also on this back side was an open trap door to a staircase leading downward. He called to Helen and Fuzzy, who was more than happy to leave the high, open space.

They walked down one level to find a large open room with rounded walls and windows facing each of the cardinal directions. It was completely empty, just the stairs leading up, and another leading down on the opposite side of the room. To one side was a small enclosed bathroom. Helen whistled, and the sound echoed off the walls. "This place is huge. This room must be… what? Forty feet across? So thirteen hundred square feet?"

"Yeah, I'm thinking we could make this a guard station. Put a few beds up here, a desk, dining table and chairs, store some weapons and ammo. The upper level is a perfect lookout."

They descended the stairs to the next level, which was more sectioned off. The stairs stopped at a short landing, then continued straight down rather than being across the room. This was because a wall blocked off the remainder of the space, with a thick metal door standing open at the landing.

Directly inside was the elevator, and the rest of the level was taken up by a residential suite that encircled it. There was a sitting room with a wet bar, a study, and another door that led to a bedroom and luxurious bathroom with separate tub and shower. The bed was the largest Allistor had ever seen. Off the sitting room was a small bedroom with its own basic bath. Each of the rooms had a window. "Looks like we found the Lord's quarters." Helen poked Allistor in the ribs.

"Actually, these are designated as guest quarters for visiting nobles. This level and the one below are identical. The Lord's quarters are the level below that and encompass the entire top level of the main structure in

477

addition to the tower level. Excluding, of course, the atrium area in the center."

Allistor laughed out loud, seeing the look on Helen's face. "This I have to see!" They descended two more levels and found a wider landing with a massive set of double doors made of what looked like mahogany. The doors stood open, and the group stepped through. Directly ahead of them was, of course, the elevator. Surrounding it was a series of sitting rooms and small bedrooms. Behind the elevator was another set of double doors, this set made of some kind of metal core with thick wood on either side, that led to the library.

Both stood with mouths agape. The library was two stories high, and the walls were floor to ceiling bookshelves of dark polished wood. There was a spiral staircase that led to a narrow catwalk around the upper level, giving access to the shelves there. The place smelled of rich Corinthian leather. To one side of the room sat a massive desk with a plush leather chair. In front of the desk, there were two similar chairs facing it. The other side of the library sported a fireplace and sitting area with three sofas, and two long reading tables with six chairs each such as one might find in a public library. The doors on the opposite side of the room were at least a hundred paces away.

"That alert message said we'd been given a library. This place is… it's wonderful!" Allistor moved to the desk and touched the leather chair gently. Fuzzy began to sniff at the books curiously.

Helen moved to the nearest shelf and began looking at the books. "This one says it's about agriculture methods. And this one is called "Alchemy for Beginners.""

478

Allistor sat down at the desk as Helen read off more titles. His insides fluttered and his legs felt weak as he realized what this library must be. Everything his people needed to know might be in these books. There were thousands of them. Maybe tens of thousands. If the books weren't one-time use like the scrolls, he could educate all his people. And he could get Ramon making copies even if they were one-time use.

"Ramon!" he muttered to himself. Looking around, he said, "Um, Interface? Can you hear me?"

"I can hear you anywhere within any structure you own, Lord Allistor. How can I assist you?"

Please open a channel to the Warren. Put it on loudspeaker like you did with the Silo." He grinned, picturing all if his friends about to freak out.

"Connection established, Lord Allistor."

"Hey, guys! It's Allistor!" he called out, probably louder than he needed to. On purpose this time.

A chorus of surprised voices echoed at him from out of thin air. Some cursing, some questioning. He held up a hand, then put it back down when he realized they couldn't see him. "Quiet down, please. I can't understand you when you all talk at once. How 'bout all of you head to the dining area, and I'll talk while you walk. Maybe I can answer all of your questions."

He waited for the murmurs to die down, then proceeded. "So first, I'm speaking to you through our new communication network. It was one of the perks of becoming the first to build a Citadel. Along with a castle that you guys have GOT to come see. In fact, you should all come. Lock down the Warren, leave a couple folks as guards, and the rest of you can come here via the new *teeeeeleporter* you'll find out by the garage!" He drew out the word for emphasis.

Again he waited as people reacted to that news. "Yup! We have our very own teleporter. And Ramon, I'm sitting in a library full of books about… well about everything. So bring your scribey stuff. We'll buy you more when you get here if you need it. We actually got six teleporters, so we can establish more Strongholds!" He tried to curb his enthusiasm as his voice went up in pitch like a teen going through puberty. He heard Sam laughing. "Luther, that means could reopen your Stronghold with a teleporter, and you could travel back and forth instantly."

"That would be wonderful, Allistor. Thank you." Luther's voice sounded pleased.

"If everybody is gathered together, pick somebody to talk first, and I'll answer questions."

Sam's voice replied. "Most of us are here. Nancy and Ramon were out in the greenhouse, but they'll be here in a minute. We saw the notice about you establishing the Citadel. Michael says that's a mixed blessing. Something about people targeting us now?"

"Yeah, that is unfortunate. But I think it will be a good long while before anyone is strong enough to challenge us. A few like Evan might try, but our defenses are strong. And I intend to make sure our people are strong, too."

"We're with ya there, boy. I mean…Lord." Sam's teasing was good-natured. "We've been out foraging and found a few good things for auction. We also found a couple other survivors. They're here with us now. Nathan and Nick. Michael just brought them in about an hour ago. Say hi, fellas."

Two male voices spoke over each other, then one said, "Hello, Lord Allistor."

The other said, "Hiya, Lord."

"Please, despite Sam's teasing, I'm just Allistor. Welcome to our little community. Sam will bring you along to the Citadel, and we can meet face to face shortly."

They chatted for a few more minutes, then agreed that the group, minus two or three who would remain to guard the Warren, would teleport over in the morning. Allistor signed off feeling pleased and quite hopeful for their future.

Helen and Allistor spent the next few hours in the library. Allistor began by reading all of the Citadel information available on his interface, then doing the same for Strongholds. He spent a little time asking questions of the interface but soon grew tired of calling it by that name. He pulled up the tab for it and found that he could make several adjustments. He started by getting rid of the generic monotone voice. Then he gave it a name. After a few other adjustments, he spoke to it out loud.

"Interface, I've decided your name will be Nigel. I hope you like that better than Sweetie."

"I do indeed, Lord Allistor. Thank you."

Helen looked up from a book about xenobiology to see Allistor grinning upon hearing the response. Nigel now spoke with a cultured accent she thought vaguely resembled an Australian, or maybe a New Zealander. "Nice!"

"You are most welcome, Nigel. Now, I have more questions. How far from the outer wall do your sensors extend?"

"An approximate radius of two miles around the citadel's footprint, Lord Allistor. In every direction, including above and below."

"And can you monitor the sensors of the Strongholds and Outposts as well?"

"I can monitor any facility you have claimed and attached to this Citadel. This includes the defensive measures, as well as other vital systems and statistics."

"Great! Please notify me of any intrusions at any of the facilities. Also, what types of other systems?"

"For example, I can monitor the plant growth in the greenhouses, and adjust the sprinklers based on their need, or activate them on a given schedule. I can open and close doors at your command, construct or deconstruct buildings, monitor population, even track the skills and abilities of your citizens for you."

"Okay that last bit's a little creepy," Helen interjected, having abandoned her book to listen in. "Nigel, what do you know about me?"

"Designation: Ranger Helen Rogers. Friend and advisor to Lord Allistor. Level 8. Current skills: Ranged weapon: Rifle – Level 5; Tracking – Level 3; Improvisation – Level 1; Animal Husbandry; Level 2; Horseback riding –

Level 2; Title: Dragonslayer; Last remaining representative of organization known as U.S. National Park Service. Authorized access to all areas of the Citadel, both Strongholds, and both Outposts, excepting personal quarters of Lord Allistor. "

Allistor grinned at her. "That's not creepy. It's not like Nigel told me what color undies you're wearing or who you have a crush on. Just useful information any Viscount should know about his people."

Helen stared at him for a minute, her face completely blank. When Allistor began to wonder what he'd said wrong, she asked, "Who says I'm wearing undies?"

"Ha!" He leaned back in his chair. "Seriously, do you have a problem with Nigel having that information? Are other people going to take issue with it?"

"Nah, I don't think so. A few might be embarrassed by certain skills or lack of them. But I agree that you need to know this information to properly manage a community the size of the one you're trying to build."

The two of them returned to their research until Nigel informed them that dinner was ready. They took the elevator down to the ground level and walked over to join everyone for the meal. The whole group was abuzz with excited conversation. Some spoke about gains in crafting skills. Others planned foraging expeditions, recommending likely places to find useable loot. Campbell was instructing a small group of non-gamers on simple game mechanics and character builds.

Allistor left them to it, making only a brief announcement that the folks from the Warren would be teleporting in to meet them in the morning. When the meal was done, he spent some time checking the market. The first thing he did was research the cost of a teleportation hub license. He quickly discovered that it wasn't an 'auction' item, but was sold directly by the System itself at a set cost of fifty million klax. Each of the substation licenses cost five million.

When Allistor whistled in amazement, Andrea asked, "What's up, boss?"

He looked at his three advisors, who were all sitting nearby. "I just checked. Building the first Citadel got us some SERIOUSLY epic bonuses. The teleporters we got? The hub and six substations? Together they cost *eighty million* klax." He watched as their eyes widened, and they did some quick math in their heads.

"Yeah. So, I think you guys were right - it'll be a while before anyone else on Earth has one. Even with a fleet of RVs to sell and a constant stream of cool antique guns and stuff, it would take me the whole year to earn even the fifty million for the hub."

Andrea nodded her head. "Yeah, so now we know that being the first to do things earns sweet rewards from the System. We need to figure out a few more achieves like that." She tapped her fingers on the table for a few seconds. "I don't suppose there's a wiki that we can consult for some cheats? Like a list of achievements that'll get us legendary loot?"

Allistor laughed. He'd had the same thought. "Not that I'm aware of. But we have a whole library upstairs if you guys want to join me for some reading?"

The four of them and Fuzzy said good evening to those who remained in the dining area, and Allistor led them back up to the library. After a short exploration of the rest of the Lord's quarters and a good bit of teasing, they all sat down and spent the rest of their evening reading.

None of them found a wiki, but they did learn a few useful things that they shared with each other before retiring to their chambers. Helen, not having chosen quarters at the mall previously, just selected one of the guest rooms in Allistor's quarters and crashed.

Fuzzy followed Allistor to his ridiculously luxurious sleeping chamber. It was almost uncomfortably large, with a massive bed placed on one wall facing a window on the opposite wall fifty feet away. There was a sitting area, two large closets, a fully stocked bar, and in the master bath, there was a tub set into the floor that was large enough for three people.

Trying to ignore the opulence, Allistor stripped to his boxers and crawled into the bed. Fuzzy circled the floor a few times and plopped down right next to the bed, his snout resting atop the goblin doll. Allistor was still staring at the ceiling making plans when Fuzzy began to snore. He reached down and scratched the big teddy bear's ears for a while, eventually falling asleep himself.

*****

Sam's voice woke Allistor from a deep sleep, yelling. "Allistor! Are you there? We're under attack!"

Instantly awake, Allistor shouted back. "Sam! What's happening?"

"It's not monsters. It's people! The two guys Michael brought in. They killed one of Luther's people on guard outside. Tried to open the gates. The alarms went off, and we have them pinned. There are more outside the gate trying to get in!"

"I'll be right there!" Allistor was already up and throwing on his clothes.

"Nigel! Do not let anyone open the outer gates of the Warren. And please put me on loudspeaker here at the Citadel."

"Go ahead, Lord Allistor."

"Attention Citadel residents! The Warren is under attack, human infiltrators inside the walls and more outside. I need a few volunteers to teleport there with me to help defend the place. Anyone willing, meet me at the pad in five."

Helen met him in the sitting room as he dashed for the elevator with Fuzzy right behind him. When they hit the ground floor, they sprinted through the promenade and out to the pad. Citizens were running ahead and behind them, gathering quickly at the teleport. He looked around to find that nearly every one of his people was there, or on their way.

His heart full, he was about to thank them all for volunteering when Nigel's voice cut through the early morning darkness. *"Lord Allistor! I regret to inform you that an intruder approaches the citadel. A drake, flying in from the south."*

486

"Shit!" Allistor tried not to panic. He needed to get to the Warren, but he didn't want to leave the Citadel to fend off a dragon without him.

Andrea spun him around. "We got this. We'll take care of this place. You go help your people at the Warren. You don't need us for a few assholish humans." She grinned at him.

He pulled the .50 caliber rifle out of his ring, along with a box of ammo. "Who knows how to shoot this thing?"

Dean whistled at him. "That'd be me, boss. I'll take this bad boy up on the tower. That dragon won't know what hit it!"

Allistor handed over the weapon, then looked at Andrea. "You sure you guys got this?"

"If we can't kill it, we'll hide inside somewhere safe and wait for you and the others to rescue us." She grinned at him, making it clear she was in no way going to hide. Allistor snorted and stepped up onto the pad. Fuzzy and Helen followed.

"Nigel! Please send us to the Warren." He pulled an assault rifle with a night scope from his ring as he spoke. There was a brief flash, and he found himself standing in the dark next to the garage at the Warren. Sporadic gunfire rang out, and he heard shouting.

"Nigel, show me where the intruders are," he whispered. He crouched down on one knee and motioned for Helen to do the same.

A map popped up on his interface. A series of green dots scattered around inside the cavern and up on the surface near the inner doors indicated his people. Two red dots near the outer gates must be the two saboteurs. Outside the gate were ten more red dots, mostly gathered right in front of the doors.

"Nigel, can you share this map with the rest of my people? And link them in so they can hear me, but the intruders can't?"

"Of course, Lord Allistor. It is done."

"Hey, guys, it's Allistor. In case you didn't see the flash from the teleporter, I'm here. I've got Helen and Fuzzy with me. You should all be able to see the map with the bad guys as red dots."

"Glad to have you back, kid!" Sam replied. "We can see them. What do you want to do?"

"They won't get the gates open. So let's take out the two inside, then get up on the wall and blast the others."

"Roger that! I'm in range. Get them to stick their heads out, and I'll make them pay."

Allistor didn't hesitate. He needed to get this situation dealt with and return to help fight the dragon. Turning to Helen, he said, "Stay here, find some cover and a line of sight on these guys. You see one of them, put one in their head." She nodded, and he took off running.

He dashed straight toward the front gates, whispering, "Nigel, loudspeaker please."

He waited a moment, then shouted, "You assholes are dead! You come into my house and eat my food, then try to kill all my people? I'm gonna eat your hearts!"

As he had hoped, the surprise voice distracted them long enough for him to get close to the wall. Based on their red dots, they were actually inside the gatehouse. Probably above the gates trying to get ropes down to their comrades. He switched from the rifle to his shotgun, the one loaded with slugs. Running up the stairs as silently as he could, he cursed as the gatehouse door opened above him. A shadow moved slightly in the moonlight, and a gun fired.

Allistor ducked as stone exploded just above his head. Immediately, shots from his allies rang out, and the shadow ducked back inside. Allistor finished his climb and ran for the door. Just before he reached it, he cast *Barrier* in front of himself.

He kicked the door in, nearly knocking it from its hinges and sent a *Flame Shot* into the room as he stepped to one side to take cover. There was a grunt of pain, and two more shots rang out. Allistor stuck his head out long enough to see two figures, one of them with his clothes afire. The flames gave him enough light to hit the other man with *Mind Spike*.

That man fell writhing onto the floor, screaming and holding his head. Allistor stepped in and fired point blank into the face of the man whose clothes were on fire. His head exploded even as his weapon fired. Allistor felt something tear at his side but ignored it. He pumped another round into the shotgun, then slammed the stock into the other man's nose just as he was sitting up. The intruder fell onto his back, still screaming until Allistor jammed his shotgun barrel into the man's mouth. He felt several teeth break.

"Tell me who sent you here." He growled. Fuzzy, who had followed him into the room, put his snout inches from the man's eye and growled as well.

The man wet himself. He tried to speak around the shotgun, but couldn't. Allistor pulled the barrel back a few inches. "Speak."

"Justin! It was Justin. He's outside with the others. He made us pretend to be lost, so we could get in here and open the gates for him. He wants your head."

"Why does he want my head?" Allistor asked. Then he immediately said, "Wait one."

Pressing the shotgun back down against the man's forehead, he said, "Sam! These two inside are down. Get our people up on the wall as quietly as possible. I want to surprise our guests."

Looking back to the man on the floor, he said, "Okay, why?"

"You killed his cousin, Evan. Says you murdered him in cold blood when he wasn't even armed."

"That's a lie, but it doesn't matter now." Allistor looked at Fuzzy. "Eat his face." He cast *Mind Spike* again.

The man screamed as Fuzzy opened his jaws and roared. The scream became a gurgle a second later. Allistor had already turned toward the door and was on his way out, leaving Fuzzy to do what bears do.

Out on the wall, he found Sam, Michael, Ramon, and one of Luther's guys climbing the stairs, with George crossing the open area a ways behind them, puffing hard. Allistor cast *Levitate* on the old man then pulled him up onto the wall. He gasped out a thank you and put his hands on his knees.

When Sam and the others reached him, Allistor mentioned for them to spread out. He whispered, "Anybody got one of Meg's grenades?"

Every single one of them held up one of the crystal balls. Allistor grinned. "Count of three, you guys soak them with that stuff. I'll light them up. Shoot anything that moves down there." Heads nodded, and they all approached the front edge of the wall. The red dots showed all but one of the enemy clustered near the doors below, still waiting for their friends to let them in.

"Three… two… one!" Five men lobbed napalm grenades down to splash on the humans below. Allistor sent down a column of fire with *Flame Strike*, igniting the flammable mixture of chemicals. The people started screaming and running about or rolling on the ground trying to put out the flames. Sam and the others began firing into the crowd.

Allistor focused instead on the one red dot that stood separately. He was a shadow about fifty yards out, standing alone in the dark. Allistor cast *Night Vision* on himself, and the shadow became a man.

A man who was pointing a rifle up at the wall.

Allistor saw the muzzle flash and heard a grunt to his left. Michael was falling backward, a hole in his chest.

Allistor cast a heal on him and shouted for Ramon to look after him.

Turning back to the fight, he canceled his night vision and cast a light globe so that it hovered right in front of Justin's face. The surprised man ducked down and blinked several times, temporarily blinded by the light. Allistor switched out his shotgun for a hunting rifle and raised it to his shoulder. It took him two seconds to sight in on Justin as the man's eyes adjusted to the light. He was just raising his own rifle again when Allistor pulled the trigger.

Blood bloomed on the man's chest as he fell backward. Allistor chambered another round and waited for him to stop moving, then put a hole in Justin's head. Experience flashed across his screen.

The gunfire had ceased, and Allistor leaned over to look below. All of the attackers were dead or dying. Only 3 of the red dots were still showing on the map, and even as he watched one of them blinked out.

He turned to check on Michael, finding him sitting up with his back against the parapet. Ramon cast another heal on him, and he was looking healthy enough.

When the last red dot disappeared, there was a ringing of chimes, and everyone in the Warren got experience for a successful defense of the Stronghold. Several of them leveled up.

Michael looked at Allistor. "I'm sorry, Allistor. They seemed like good guys. I-"

Allistor cut him off. "Don't sweat it. We knew something like this would happen eventually. It's not your fault. But we gotta talk about this later. I need to get back to the Citadel!" Allistor told Sam and George, who were standing next to him watching Michael get healed. "A dragon attacked the place just as I was leaving to come help you here."

Sam nodded, "Go! I'd offer to go with you, but there might be more of those fellas out there. Just be sure you come back in the morning for the funeral."

"Funeral?" Allistor's gut clenched. "Whose funeral."

Sam lowered his head. "Shit. We didn't have time to tell you."

George put a hand on his shoulder. "Luther's dead. Shot, along with Matt, before any of us knew what was happening. Never even had a chance to defend himself."

Allistor put an arm around the old man. "I'm sorry, George. I liked Luther a lot. He was a good man." George nodded his head but didn't say anything. Tears rolled down his face as he bore the pain in silence.

Sam murmured, "Go, boy. We'll deal with this. Old men get good at burying our dead."

Allistor nodded and leapt down off the wall. Hitting the ground running, he met up with Helen halfway to the teleport pad. She stopped him long enough to let Fuzzy catch up, then all three stepped onto the pad. "Nigel, send us back to the Citadel, please."

A flash of light and they were back in the citadel. The roof of the keep was afire, though it was mostly stone and steel. Allistor could see that some of the skylights had melted. He heard the distinctive crack of the .50 cal firing, and the roar of the drake a second later.

There was a scream that grew louder for a few seconds before a body slammed into the ground not far from Allistor. It was burnt and damaged from the fall, and Allistor couldn't tell who it was.

Casting *Night Vision* on himself and Helen, he searched the sky above. The massive drake wasn't hard to spot. It glided by overhead, one wing tilted down as it banked around the tower. Allistor could see it taking a deep breath.

> **Fire Drake**
> **Level 13**
> **Health: 4,900/11,000**

He cast *Mind Spike* on the beast. This one was larger than the matron they'd fought in the Silo. And a slightly higher level. Still, the spell caused the monster to falter, its wing catching on the tower and sending it into a spin as it roared in pain.

Unable to recover, the monster slammed into the inner wall, one of its wings snapping on impact. It fell to the ground at the base of the wall, then promptly gained its feet. Turning toward the tower, it roared in defiance.

The .50 cal cracked again, and the drake's head recoiled as blood sprayed from the wound. Allistor raised his own gun and fired directly into the thing's face. More of his people joined in, running up next to Allistor or firing down from atop the wall. The monster writhed in pain as round after round stung it. Allistor cast *Restraint* and the beast froze.

When the .50 cal fired once more, the round penetrated its brain, and the monster went limp. A cheer went up from the crowd as they too got defense experience and leveled up. Allistor shouted, "Andrea! Report!"

She came jogging up. "Six wounded, mostly burns, except one with multiple broken bones. They'll all live, if you'll do some quick healing." She pointed to a row of wounded that could be seen through the food court doors. Allistor sprinted over to them, casting heals as he ran. He couldn't tell from there which were the most badly burned, so he just healed each of them in turn, starting again with the first after he'd healed the sixth.

Helen handed out health potions to each one of them as he started a third round of heals. When he was satisfied that all had recovered fully, he joined the others in looting and harvesting the dragon. Nigel contacted Allistor with an inquiry.

"Lord Allistor, would you like me to begin repairs of the damaged sections of this facility?"

Allistor paused. "You can do that? That's great! What will it cost?"

"Based on my damage assessment, repairs can be accomplished in less than twelve hours for a total cost of six thousand system points."

Allistor grinned. The defense of the citadel against the dragon had awarded much more than that. "Yes, please begin the repairs, Nigel. And thank you."

An hour later, he stumbled back into bed, exhausted.

Chapter Nineteen

Endings and Beginnings

Four hours later Allistor was awake again, and half-stumbling onto the teleport pad with Fuzzy, Helen, Dean, and Andrea. They had asked to join him at the Warren for the funeral. When the group stepped off the pad on the other side, folks were already moving around inside the compound.

Allistor saw the gates were open, and the bodies had been cleared. A wooden pyre was being erected outside, and the bodies of Luther and the other man were laying nearby, covered with white sheets. Amanda stood guard over them, shotgun in hand.

"Excuse me for a minute, please." Allistor left the others and walked over to her. He gathered her into a hug that lasted for a long time. "I missed you."

"Yeah? So much ya couldn't call, couldn't write?" She gave him a stern look, but he could tell she wasn't serious.

"The dog ate my postman." He shrugged, suppressing his own grin.

"Oh, that's bad! Too soon, Allistor, too soon." She kissed him lightly, darting a glance at Helen as she did so. The woman smiled and gave a small wave.

"So that's the hottie you've been romping around the countryside with?" she whispered, though the group was too far away to hear her normal voice.

Allistor chuckled. "Yup. That's Helen. And the only romping we've been doing is fighting monsters and bad people. She's the one who accidentally made me a Lord. Saved my ass a couple times, too. Come meet her."

Amanda looked around. "I don't want to leave these two alone. We've had a lot of canids sniffing around lately. They already took the bodies from last night. The ones outside, I mean. We dumped the two you killed in here over the wall." She looked down at Fuzzy, who was smiling up at her despite holding the goblin in his mouth. "Your cub did a real number on that guy's face."

"Oh! You two haven't met!" Allistor made a flourishing motion with his hand. "Fuzzy bear, meet Amanda. Amanda... Fuzzy." Amanda extended a hand for the cub to sniff, much like one would do with a new dog. As Fuzzy checked her out, she whispered, "Is that a frog in his mouth?"

"Nope! Goblin!" He waited for the expected wide eyes, then said, "It's a stuffed Fibble doll he found at the ranger station. He's... adopted it." Just then Fuzzy set down the doll and licked Amanda's hand, giving her a friendly chuff, then lowering his head and bringing it up underneath her hand to demand a scratch.

Laughing, she scratched his ears, earning a pleased rumbling in the bear cub's chest. "I guess we're going to be good friends, Fuzzy bear." She squatted down to hug him, and he licked her face. "Ew! What have you been feeding him?"

"That guy's face." Allistor grinned.

She quickly stood back up, patting Fuzzy's head. "Oh, right." The look on her face was priceless as she used a sleeve to wipe the slobber from it.

Allistor shrugged, saying, "He killed our people. As far as I'm concerned, he didn't die slowly enough. I told Fuzzy to eat his face but my kind, sensitive bear cub killed him first. He watched as Fuzzy nodded, then lifted Fibble and ambled off toward the woods to take care of bear business. "Fuzzy's nose says there are no monsters close by. It's safe for you to come meet the group."

He waved to his friends to approach, and he brought Amanda to meet them halfway. "Amanda, this is badass ranger Helen, Chancellor Dean, and Lady Commander Andrea. Guys, this is Amanda, our resident doctor.

They all shook hands and made small talk for a few minutes until Sam and the others emerged en masse. Allistor left the rest of the introductions for after the service. They lifted the bodies and placed them atop the pyre, then Allistor lit the fire. They watched in silence as the bodies burned down to ash, then returned to the Stronghold, shutting the gates behind them.

Inside, they all gathered in the dining area. Allistor made the rest of the introductions, and let everyone spend a little time getting to know one another. Chloe took charge of leading the newcomers on a tour of the cavern, bragging about how well she and the other children took care of the chickens and bunnies. Allistor winked at Nancy and mouthed the words "No mutants?" for which she shot him the finger.

Allistor was surprised at how small and simple the Warren seemed compared to the Mall. He wondered if his people would even want to stay at the Warren after seeing the Citadel. If they didn't, he decided it was no big deal. The Warren wasn't exactly in a strategic position. He could probably downgrade it to an Outpost without losing anything. Casper wasn't so far away, and he planned to establish a Stronghold there. And the teleporter would make it easy to move everyone, including the soon-to-be mutant bunnies.

Back at the dining area, they all sat down to a breakfast of real eggs, sausage, and grilled onions. Meg and Sam got many compliments on the delicious meal. They got caught up on the night's events, George giving a tearful account of his son's death. Lilly wrapped her arms around the man and let him cry.

When Dean was through telling about the battle with the drake at the citadel, and Sam was through asking him questions about how sweet it was to fire the Barrett, Allistor invited everyone to the Citadel.

"We can leave the place unguarded for a little while," he told them. "Nigel will warn us if the sensors are triggered, and we can be back here in minutes."

"Nigel?" Meg asked, looking around.

"Nigel, say hello to the people of the Warren. And can you tell me how many people can be teleported at once?"

"Hello, good people of the Warren. I am Nigel, your interface at all of Lord Allistor's facilities. And it is recommended to limit groups to no more than twenty persons per teleport.

Meg organized them into two roughly equal groups. There were a total of twenty-four men, women, and children living at the Warren now. Along with Allistor, Fuzzy, Helen, Andrea, and Dean, that made twenty-nine.

Allistor accompanied the first group, ushering them quickly off the pad when they arrived to make room for the second group. Immediately there were gasps of surprise as they looked around the Citadel. More of the same could be heard with the second group's arrival. Allistor gave them some time to look around, then he led them all inside.

Most of the Citadel's citizens were awaiting them in the food court. People mixed and introduced themselves, and several tours were conducted. About midday, Allistor asked Andrea to switch out the three people remaining at the Silo, so the others could join and meet the groups. A moment later, Nigel announced that the repairs to the citadel were complete.

They spent the entire day just mingling and eating, discussing foraging and crafting, telling stories and forming new friendships. A few trade deals were struck, crafters agreeing to share materials or work together in creating something.

Allistor, having been abandoned by Fuzzy who went to romp around with the children, spent most of the day with Amanda. She spent some time checking on citizens who asked for it, and he gave her a personal tour of the Citadel. Then he took her to the Silo and showed her the dragon eggs. She used her *Internal Analysis* ability and scanned one of them.

"It's a baby dragon alright. High concentration of those magic atomic critters swirling around in there. I'd

say the baby is about eighty percent formed. But I don't know how long it'll be till they hatch."

"We've got books in the library that might tell us. Let's head back and have dinner with everyone, then we can hit the books. I think Ramon's already been up there all day." He grinned. Ramon had been ecstatic when Allistor had escorted him into the library. He'd hurried from shelf to shelf calling out titles and laughing like a kid in a candy store.

As they were taking the lift back up to ground level, Amanda asked. "You're going back out, aren't you? To find more people and claim more Strongholds."

Allistor nodded. "I was thinking tomorrow. That's why I wanted a little quality time with you. I... really did miss you."

She bumped him with her hip. "Missed you too, goofball. I mean, there are better-looking men at the Warren. But none of them has a face-eating pet bear. I mean, that's what I've always dreamed of in a man."

"And I thought you were only into me for my big... muscles."

"Those too. I figure that's what Helen sees in you, too." She made a pouty face.

"It's not like that with us. She's a good friend. We work and fight well together. But I made it clear I'm interested in being with you." He held out a hand, and she entwined her fingers with his. He winked at her, adding, "If you play your cards right, you could end up being Lady Amanda!"

"Oh! What an honor!" She rolled her eyes at him. They reached the surface and walked back to the teleport pad. Two minutes later they were joining the others in the food court.

Dinner was still cooking, so they went to the kiosk for some shopping. Allistor divided up the labor, telling Amanda what he was looking for, and authorizing her to spend some of the Citadel's klax. She purchased some training scrolls for the various professions they thought citizens might be pursuing. If they didn't need them, they could always resell them later. Allistor bought some spells. He found an upgraded healing spell called *Restore* that…oddly enough, restored a thousand health points on a target, and purchased six at two thousand klax each. One each for himself, Helen, Amanda, Dean and Andrea, and one for Ramon to learn and copy for the others. Ramon had already distributed *Nature's Boon* to half a dozen of the Citadel's people so that they had heals for the next battle.

He also purchased six copies of an offensive spell called *Vortex* that created a tight spiral of air. It was a channeled spell that could be directed at a target, and it would become stronger the more power was pushed into it. He kept one for himself, would offer one to Helen if her stats leaned toward magic use, and would give the others to Andrea and Sam for distribution to appropriate people.

At their low levels, there were very few spells available to the humans. The only other one he found before the dinner bell rang was one called *Erupt* that would cause a spike of stone to burst forth from the ground and impale a target. He only purchased two copies, one for himself and one for Ramon. Nobody else had the level and intel requirements to use it yet.

That accomplished, he and Amanda returned to the food court where the others were gathering. Sam and Meg had teamed up with Thorne and Dean to create a celebratory meal of dragon steaks, potatoes and vegetables from the Warren's greenhouse, and canned fruit for dessert. After dinner, they broke out beer and booze and Allistor proposed a toast.

"To you, and you, and all of us! I'm proud to know each of you, and I look forward to all of us sharing long lives together. To the survivors!" He raised his glass.

"TO THE SURVIVORS!" the crowd shouted. In the background, someone shouted, "Gnomes Rule!" getting a laugh from the gamers in the room.

*****

Baldur growled his displeasure at his brother and niece. The mist around him curled and swirled, reflecting his agitation.

"A second drake, Hel? You know as well as I that they are solitary creatures and do not invade each other's territory unless it is mating season, or there is a dire shortage of food!"

Hel burbled deep within her amphibian chest, a sort of chuckle for her species. "Do not look to me, Uncle. I like this boy. Since we began observing him, he has killed many of his own kind! I expect great things from him."

Loki raised his tentacles in a sign of peace. "It was not I, Brother. I suspect the drake just sensed the death of the Matron and moved in to claim her territory. Or her

504

eggs. I too am curious to see what this young human does. Already a Viscount, with a Citadel and teleport stations. The only beings I've seen rise to power so quickly after an Assimilation were those who were already in power when it occurred. They simply reinforced their rule and claimed their own holdings or those they could quickly steal. This human has started from nothing. I am impressed. In fact… shall we make a wager on his future?" Loki's voice was smooth and soothing, and Baldur found it difficult to remain angry.

Until he realized his brother was using persuasive powers on him.

Drawing his sword in one tentacled hand, he pointed it in Loki's direction. "I see through your tricks, Brother. And no, I will not wager. That would simply give you incentive to ensure the young human's failure! I know how you think, Brother. And I warn you again. Do not interfere with this human or any other. We have tolerated your twisted sense of humor for too long. That ends today."

"Of course, Brother, of course. The humans are perfectly safe from me. I shall take no *additional* action to encourage their demise." Loki waved his arms in a gesture of innocence. "But forgive me if I hope for the humans inhabiting the island of Oahu to perish utterly. I find it quite beautiful, and I would claim it for myself when the time comes."

Hel nodded in agreement. "Volcanoes."

Baldur let out a sigh. "I did not miss your phrasing there, little brother. What have you done? Tell me now!"

"I simply made a small adjustment to the System notifications. To honor your human, you see? When he constructed his Citadel, I made sure that all of UCP 382 was informed of his impressive achievement. So that nearby humans would know his power. So that those who sought power would stay away out of fear, and those who sought protection would seek him out."

Baldur focused three of his eyes on his brother, glaring at him with contempt. "You mean so that those seeking an easy way to seize power of their own would know where to find him." He shook his head, his weapon still pointed at Loki. "I should gut you, Brother. But I have no proof of your intent - other than my knowledge of what's in your soul. Be very careful. I will be watching."

End Book One